SOMETHING
WICKED
THIS WAY COMES

SOMETHING WICKED
THIS WAY COMES

THE WITCHES OF SALIX POINTE
BOOK 2

NOELLE VELLA

Something Wicked This Way Comes
The Witches of Salix Pointe, Book 2

ISBN: 978-1-955916-12-7
ISBN paperback: 978-1-955916-13-4

Formatted by: Alt 19 Creative

Published by:
Singleton's Press Publishing, LLC

NOT EVERYTHING THAT'S GOOD IS GOOD
AND NOT EVERYTHING THAT'S EVIL IS EVIL...
THERE ARE ALWAYS SHADES OF GRAY...

THE WITCHES OF SALIX POINTE
BOOK 2

CHAPTER 1

TASMIN

NOVEMBER – 2 WEEKS
BEFORE THANKSGIVING

THE LAST TWO people I expected to see walk through Aunt Noreen's door were standing in front of me. I had no idea why they were here, nor had I known they were even coming to Salix Pointe. Based on the worried looks on their faces, and the vibes I was picking up from them, the only thing I was certain of was that whatever they had to tell me must have been extremely important for them to need an actual face-to-face.

"We've been driving all night," my mom said, taking a seat on the couch in the living room. "There's so much we need to tell you."

"Sorry for dropping in on you like this, but what we have to share with you needed to be said in person," my dad added, sitting next to Mommy.

I took a seat in a recliner across from them. "Okay, what was so urgent that you couldn't just call me or video chat?" I inquired, looking from one to the other.

Daddy was the first to speak. "Tazzy, remember when I told you that I had a lead about the fire that destroyed your clinic?"

My clinic, the practice that I had poured my blood, sweat, and tears into had burned to the ground. The police had determined it was arson but couldn't identify the substance used to start the fire. They also couldn't explain why the only building destroyed was the one that housed my clinic, while the buildings on either side remained unscathed.

"Yes, but that was weeks ago, and since I hadn't heard anything further, I had assumed that the lead didn't pan out."

"Understandable. I did learn something, something big," he said, rising from the couch to stand in front of me. "The thing is I had to use…unconventional means to find out if what I assumed was, in fact, the cause of the fire."

"Unconventional means?" I questioned, raising an eyebrow. "What exactly are you talking about, Daddy?"

"This is difficult to explain, so please bear with me," he quickly replied. "When I say unconventional, it means that I had to use techniques other than standard police methods to discover the source of the blaze."

I was becoming impatient, mainly because my dad's nervous feelings were hitting me hard, like a punch to the gut. I could tell he was hiding something, and I couldn't understand why he wasn't just coming out with what he knew.

"What are you not telling me?"

He began to walk back and forth, stopping in front of me periodically, appearing as if he was about to speak, but then changing his mind. It wasn't like him at all to be so flustered. Daddy was usually the epitome of calm.

Finally, my mom spoke up. "Silas, have a seat," she said, motioning for him to sit next to her. "Tasmin, what your father is trying to say is that there are circumstances surrounding the fire that are difficult to explain. The fire wasn't natural, and neither was the method your father used to discover the cause. Sweetheart, what I'm about to tell you, I'm asking you to keep an open mind. You might find this hard to believe, but the fire was caused by something…otherworldly. Your father discovered that it was started by something called brimstone, which is an old school name for sulfur."

"So, Octavian and Dafari were right."

I didn't realize I had spoken aloud until I heard my dad ask, "Who are Octavian and Dafari? And how do they know about brimstone?"

I knew my dad well. Judging by the look on his face and the emotions he was giving off, I could tell he was in investigator mode. I had been on the receiving end of his questioning a few times growing up, and was well aware of how he operated, which was why I felt the need to go on the defensive. The fact that he knew about brimstone, a substance that, according to Dafari, could be concentrated to destroy a target only in the hands of a demon, led me to wonder even more what brought my parents to Salix Pointe.

"They're…friends," I began. "What I'm curious about is how *you* know about brimstone, Daddy. Clearly, there's a lot more you're both not telling me," I said, crossing my arms in front of me.

My parents looked at each other. This time, I picked up on the anxiety coming from both of them. I had a feeling I knew where this conversation was going, I just didn't want to believe it. If I was right, that would mean that my parents had been hiding some huge secrets from me.

My dad sighed before speaking. "Tasmin, you may not believe this, but there are forces out there that…hell, I can show you better than I can tell you."

I watched as he stood, taking a stance in the middle of the room. He closed his eyes taking a few deep breaths before saying, "Ancestors far and wide, I humbly request your inter-session from the great divide. I solicit your aid to bring forth the spirit of one recently departed, one who was respected, revered, and highly regarded. A woman of uncompromising honor, strength, and incomparable wit, I request to speak with our beloved Noreen Chadwick. I ask that her celestial self be visible to us all for this face-to-face, so we may revel in her wisdom, knowledge, and, grace."

I wasn't sure which shocked me more; my father reciting a spell, and effortlessly at that, or him calling on the spirit of Aunt Noreen. I hadn't had a chance to truly absorb what was going on before I saw a brilliant light so bright that I had to shield my eyes. When it finally dimmed and I could see once more, I glimpsed a fuzzy image in front of me. Daddy appeared to be concentrating hard, focusing on the distorted figure. As he did, the form began to solidify, albeit not completely. Its features became more discernable until I witnessed Aunt Noreen standing in front of us. Although her body was somewhat transparent, it was clearly her.

She stood just slightly taller than me, standing at five feet four. Like many Black women, she was a bit thick in the hips, with age adding a bit more to that thickness. Her skin was the color of brown sugar, her eyes hazel. Her thick, curly salt and pepper-colored hair rested on her shoulders. She wore a long, flowing white dress, which, in my mind, was typical ghost garb. Auntie made a beautiful spirit.

"Aunt Noreen?" I heard Mom whisper, her voice shaky.

Auntie had a smile on her face. I missed that smile. I missed her. "Jewel," she said, turning in my mom's direction, her voice calm and soothing. "You look good. You might want to put some teabags under your eyes for those dark circles, though," she teased, not one to mince words.

"Driving for twelve hours straight will do that to you," Mom playfully retorted. Although she had tears in her eyes, she still was able to appreciate my aunt's comical nature.

Turning to look at my dad, Auntie said, "I was wondering how long it would take for you to contact me. 'Bout time."

"I was trying to let you rest in peace."

"While I appreciate your concern for my afterlife, this situation is way too important for me to rest peacefully. I could say I'll rest when I'm dead, but no need to state the obvious." Aunt Noreen always had a quirky sense of humor. "As for you, my favorite grandniece," she said, looking at me. "Tasmin, I'm so proud of you. You've had so much thrown at you in a short amount of time, but you've handled yourself well."

"Tazzy, what's Aunt Noreen talking about? What's going on with you?" Daddy queried, concern in his tone.

"We'll get to that, Silas," Aunt Noreen stated. "But I think the person who most deserves to have some questions answered first is Tasmin."

My dad again sat next to my mom on the couch. Both were looking at me quizzically. I was giving them the same look.

"I know the three of you have many questions that need answers," Aunt Noreen said, immediately taking on her familiar role as family mediator. "I'll cut to the chase. Tasmin, I know you're aware that I was a witch. I'm sorry I never told you when I was alive, but I had my reasons, one of which being you never wanted to be in Salix Pointe, so I never pushed you to become involved in what I like to call the family business, save for learning the basics. Now I wish I had, because it would have better prepared you for everything you've encountered so far. The way your powers manifested—"

"Powers?" Mom asked incredulously. "I mean, Silas and I knew she had potential, but since she never showed any overt signs of having powers, we thought it might have skipped over her."

"Trust me, it didn't," Aunt Noreen declared matter-of-factly. "In fact, she's quite the powerhouse. She's a healer and an empath like you, Jewel. She's also telekinetic and can heal herself. That last power is still a mystery."

My parents' mouths dropped open at the revelation.

"Mommy, you're a witch too?" I asked in disbelief.

"Yes, I am, although not as powerful as Aunt Noreen was."

"You're still a commanding witch in your own right," my dad noted, gently patting her hand.

"And clearly, Daddy, you're one, too."

"Actually," Aunt Noreen interrupted, "Silas is what's called a necromancer. He can interact with the dearly departed in a number of ways, in addition to his being a mean spellcaster," she said with a wink.

I was having trouble wrapping my head around the new information I had just received. The fact that I had been related to not just one but three magickal beings was astonishing. I lived with my parents day in and day out, and not once had either of them ever given me any indication that they had powers. Then again, why should I be surprised by anything that had been revealed? Since arriving in Salix Pointe, my life consisted of one new revelation after another.

"I've been keeping tabs on you and Elisa. I must say, for two untrained witches unceremoniously thrown into the fray, you've both handled yourselves admirably. I see my good friend Dafari and his handsome brother have taken you both under their wings," she said with a smirk.

I couldn't help but giggle at her play on words. "They have. Elisa and I most likely wouldn't have survived without their training."

"Again, I ask who are Octavian and Dafari? And Mama Nall's granddaughter is a witch, too?" my dad questioned.

Auntie turned to face him. "Tasmin will explain in bit. Right now, my time on this plane is limited, and you need to know something important. Soon, you all are going to face some challenges, some of them like nothing you've ever experienced before. This is when you'll have to work together as a family to get through them. Jewel and Silas, you must form a new coven with the Three Merry Widows, Tasmin, and Elisa. Your very lives will depend on it. Tasmin and Elisa have already found the hidden room in The Book Nook, as well as The Book of Magic Enchantment, so you're off to a good start."

"So it's that serious," Daddy replied.

"Serious as a heart attack. In the meantime, the three of you have a lot to discuss, as much has transpired in these past few weeks, so talk amongst yourselves, loved ones. Listen and learn from each other. It will benefit you all." It appeared as if Aunt Noreen was about to leave, but, instead, she turned to me. Leaning down, she whispered in my ear. "I see that fine archangel is sweet on you."

"I thought he was, but I haven't seen him in weeks," I replied in a low tone, hoping my parents couldn't hear me.

"I'm aware of what transpired. He's going through some things. His trauma is his and his alone to deal with. Just be patient, sweetheart. He'll turn up eventually, I promise."

"I hope so." It was in that moment that I truly realized how much I was missing Octavian.

"Ah, first love. It's something, isn't it?"

"What? I never said—"

"Chile, please," she chided cutting me off then letting out a low chuckle. "It's written all over your face. The first step to letting go of denial is being honest with yourself. Try it, you might like it."

It felt as if she placed one hand on my right cheek and had kissed the other. Although she was in spirit form, as she leaned in, I could have sworn I literally felt warmth emanating from her. I found it extremely comforting.

"I love you, Auntie," I replied as I felt a tear involuntarily roll down my cheek.

"I love you, too, Tasmin." She stood then addressed my parents. "I love you all. Be well, and, most of all, be careful. You know where to find me," she said, then faded out of sight.

My parents and I were silent for several moments. I assumed each of us was absorbing what we had learned about one another.

Mommy was the first to break the uncomfortable quietness. "Well, that was…something. Tasmin, why didn't you tell us about anything that happened down here?"

"Probably for the same reasons you two never told me you were a witch and Daddy was a necromancer," I retorted.

"Touché," my dad chimed in. "Tazzy, I want you to know that while we kept what we were from you, we honestly didn't know you would become a witch. Truth be told, your mom and I moved away from Salix Pointe because we wanted to get away from the magick. We knew that if we stayed, we may have to one day pick up the mantle. That life wasn't for us. Since we lived in Brooklyn, we figured that even if you had some latent power, keeping you away from a major conduit for magick would prevent it from manifesting. We actually hoped that was the case.

Addressing my mom, I asked, "So why did you make me spend all those summers in Salix Pointe?"

"We only wanted you to spend time with Aunt Noreen and be in a safe environment during your summer vacations, nothing more. At the time, your father and I worked long hours. Sending you down here was easier than finding someone to watch you during the day. We didn't want you to be a latchkey kid is all."

What she told me did make sense. Back in Brooklyn, I had several friends who had working parents. Sometimes, finding childcare was difficult, especially if the local schools weren't offering summer programs, some would end up being latchkey kids, while others were shipped off to a relative for the summer.

Daddy asked, "Tazzy, what's really going on in this town? We need to know, and don't leave anything out."

CHAPTER 2
OCTAVIAN

7:30 AM
MARCH 13, 1855...

I GLARED AT MY *wife and our daughter. They had to be out of their God-given minds if they thought I was about to sit idly by and watch them go on a suicide mission.*
"Absolutely not! I forbid it," I yelled.

My wife's eyes narrowed then turned to slits. The glare in them would have scared a lesser man, but I was no mere man. She looked as if she was ready to chew train tracks and spit out nails. The bracelet on her wrist glowed bright, and I swore I saw steam coming from her ears.

"You don't forbid me from doing a flipping thing, Octavian Jerrod. I'll do as I darn well please, and I said I'm helping that family escape from the McCoy Plantation tonight!"

"Over my dead body," *I snapped. I rolled my shoulders to keep my wings at bay. I felt my body bulking, but I had no way to control the rage I felt.*

"I'll risk it," *she said through gritted teeth.*

My eyes widened as my fists balled at my side. I didn't know why after all the years I'd been married to the woman, that I was still surprised at her tenacity and fiery spirit. I didn't care what she said, they were not going out there.

"Papa, they sold Sarah Moore's twelve-year-old daughter Sophy today to settle part of Master Williams' estate. His son and that evil wife of his will sell the rest of her children tomorrow. They will be separated. We still have time to save them and Sophy if we move now…"

I looked at my daughter. While she was taller than her mother standing at five-nine, she looked just like the woman who birthed her. For years now, my family and I had helped move enslaved people to freedom. However, Minty wasn't scheduled to come back around until a month from now. The Railroad had been quiet the last few weeks as bounty hunters had been patrolling the area heavily. My brother Dafari and his wife Elisa were laying low after almost being caught helping runaways on the Railroad. While I could send Minty a vision to get a message to her, it would still be risky. I was a supernatural being, but my wife and daughter were human, albeit powerful witches. They could still be hanged. They could still be harmed. They…could still be killed.

I let out a frustrated sigh, but I planned to stand my ground. "I understand—"

Attalah rushed over to me with pleading eyes. "Papa…they plan to sell Jessa May to that scoundrel Tomicus Barr. You know how young girls and women fair on his plantation. She's already had her body violated by Master Bret. That's why his wife wants her sold. What about her daughters Simone and Bianca? You know what will happen to them on Barr's plantation, Papa…"

I SHOOK MY head to clear it. My dreams from the night before haunted me. I'd awakened in a pool of sweat with my body ablaze. When Dafari had tried to calm me, I threw him across the room with a power blast. The dreams were getting worse. Every other night they got darker and more intense. The last thing I wanted to do was relive those last few days before my wife and daughter had been murdered. Yet, the dreams—nightmares would better describe them— were assaulting me nightly and had been for weeks now. They got worse after the fight with my parents. I shook away those thoughts as I trekked ahead.

I probably would have stayed locked away at Dafari's were it not for the fact he and I had felt a dark presence descending on the area. It was something powerful, but also something so wicked that it even gave Dafari pause, and he was half-demon. That wasn't the kicker though. There was something else that Elisa and Tasmin had to be made aware of.

The weather turned nasty. The wind whipped up, rain started to fall, and the air had turned colder than it had been just moments before. I was on my way to Tasmin's to try to squash the distance and tension between us. After riding to Dafari's office with him, I decided to walk to Tasmin's as I needed the space and time to clear my head. While things were good between Dafari and me, there was still much we needed to discuss as well. We had spent days trying to decipher what his father, Azazel, could have meant by the cryptic message he had given me to pass on to my brother.

Most people believed in the axiom that there was only good or evil. However, I'd come to the realization that when it came to Demon Daddy—what I called my brother's father— he had always been in the gray. He was neither good nor evil. One never knew what side of the fight he would be on, which had been proven on Halloween.

I'd come to Salix Pointe of the mind that I had to protect Tasmin and Elisa, two women who didn't know they were witches, from my uncle—a Fallen who had escaped his prison in the Valleys of the Earth. I was as sure as the day was long that he had been the one to murder Noreen Chadwick, town matriarch and powerful witch in her own right. However, once all the smoke had cleared, Uncle Azazel had not been the culprit.

It had been my parents who were High-Archs to the Most High. They claimed they had used a witch from Noreen's own coven to help murder her *for the greater good*. In order to keep Elisa and Tasmin from realizing their powers, they'd not only killed Noreen, but also Elisa's parents and her grandmother, another powerful witch whom all had called Mama Nall.

It had been a sobering moment for a son who thought his parents could do no wrong. The results had been my brother and I fighting our mother and my father. Uncle Azazel had come in to save me from my mother's blades and myself. Because I'd thought they were trying to take Tasmin away from me again, in addition to finding out they had been behind all the killings, I was set to murder my father in cold blood, something I would have no doubt been casted into a lake of fire for. I was just that distraught at the thought of losing her yet again, and that they would be so cold as to kill to make sure things stayed to *His* liking.

I came back to the present when a small child ran up to me and grabbed a hold of my hand. My body relaxed and my mind calmed. "I can see your wings," she whispered, her wild fro blowing in the wind and her brown eyes sparkling. "You should put them away before the bad things see them."

I smiled down at the child. I saw her little halo which made me remember that most children were innocents until life and adults did something to scar them mentally and sometimes physically.

"Nazila," I heard someone call and looked up to see a buxom Black woman rushing to get the little girl. "Come back here. You know I told you not to talk to strangers!"

The little girl let go of my hand then ran to her mother. "It's okay, Mom. He's an angel."

"Nazila, do we need to talk about your wild imagination again?" Her mother looked embarrassed as she gazed at me and then said, "I'm so sorry," before she rushed away, taking her child with her.

Nazila's mother would probably be in for the shock of her life if she knew her little girl was a seer. I could feel that the child had been born with a veil over her eyes. The little girl turned to wave at me before skipping off alongside her mother. I took Nazila's advice and pulled my wings back in. While the naked human eye couldn't see them, other beings could, and I wasn't ready to reveal what I was just yet. I suppose grief had made me lax in protecting myself.

Thanksgiving in Salix Pointe had come and gone. The denizens of the quaint, sleepy town were now putting up Christmas decorations. I surmised that while some still talked about the alleged storm that had come through the town on All Hallows Eve, most of the din had died down. I nodded politely to those who called out to speak to me as I made my trek to Tasmin's. It was all by rote as my mind was all over the place and the weather didn't bother me.

I was so lost in thought that by the time I made it to Noreen's house where Tasmin had been staying, I didn't realize that I had knocked on the door to announce my arrival. She and I had needed to talk. However, when she opened the door, and when I opened my mouth, no words would come forth. My anger, resentment, and shame still had a hold on me.

On the flip side of that same coin, her regal beauty had stunned me to silence as well. It was as if I was seeing her again for the first time. Her locs were pulled back into a ponytail, bringing my attention to the natural beauty of her brown face. Her skin glowed, and her eyes, while sad, shone with something I couldn't put my finger on. It made me wonder if there was something that had changed about her. Had her realized powers made her beauty even more appealing? Or had the weeks I'd been away from her made me take for granted the ways in which I had always been enamored with her…in another time…in another place?

I'd thought of her mercilessly since I'd gone back to my brother's home. Sometimes I couldn't sleep without daydreaming of times' past. To think of her being ripped away from me again so soon turned me into a complete nutter. I was set to strike my father down for heaven's sake! She had no idea in which the ways she and I were connected. I'd done many good deeds, had gone above and beyond the call of duty so that I wouldn't have to walk the earth another hundred years before I found her once more. How would I ever tell her of the love that had bonded us together for centuries and the curse that had ripped us apart over and over?

What would she say, or think, knowing that I had yet again kept something from her? However, I knew to open that door meant I would have to open many more, and I wasn't ready for that. For I knew that if I did, Dafari would also be caught in the crosshairs, and he had far more to lose in this lifetime than I did. He too had been blessed with a never-ending love and cursed the same as I had been.

Tasmin gazed up at me, confusion etched across her features. "Octavian," she called. "Are you okay?"

I shook myself out of my stupor then blinked. She had to think I was a bloody simpleton by now. Still, I forged ahead. "Yes, I'm well," I said. "Do you have a moment? I'd like to speak with you about a few pertinent things."

Tasmin glanced over her shoulder then back at me. "Um...I—"

"Are your parents still visiting?" I asked.

She quirked a brow then chuckled—albeit a bit sarcastically— while shaking her head. "I don't know why I'm shocked that you know my parents are here."

"Dafari made mention of it when I got back two weeks ago."

Her eyes widened. "You've been back two weeks and didn't let me know, Octavian? Thanksgiving has come and gone. I've been worried sick about you, and you couldn't even at least send word you were back?" she asked, hurt residing in her voice.

"Tasmin, please understand the mess I was in. Being in that cave and then coming out...it was as if I had to face what I'd done—what I had become all over again. I can't—"

"I get that, and I understand it, but common courtesy wouldn't have hurt you," she said, iciness in her tone.

I saw the hurt in her eyes, and it was like a sucker punch to the gut. "I'll not argue the fact that I was inconsiderate if you do not argue that I needed space to grieve in my own way, on my own time."

She folded her arms over her chest then sighed while rolling her eyes. "I guess...okay."

A barrage of emotions was wafting from her. Her aura glowed an array of colors that would make an empath dizzy.

"Tasmin, baby, are you alright?" I heard from behind her.

I gazed over Tasmin's head to see a woman who looked so much like her, I had to assume it was her mother. She was dressed in jeans, a cream-colored blouse, and high-top sneakers. The jeans and sneakers were often a part of Tasmin's attire, and so were the locs that crowned the tiny woman's head. I couldn't help but call her tiny compared to my warrior's height and build. I was well over six feet and towered over both of them.

Tasmin dropped her arms and tried to feign an upbeat nature for her mother. She smiled and then turned to the side giving her a full view of me. The way the older woman's eyes scanned me told me she was reading me or at least trying to. She regarded me with the air of an elder who had been here before. Perhaps her Ancestors had left her with the gift of sight? Though I'd rather doubt it, seeing as if I could tell that she didn't quite know what to make of me. I stood wide-legged, hands in the pockets of my peacoat; stance reminiscent of the soldier I was trained to be.

"Top of the morning to you, Ma'am," I greeted with a gentlemanly nod of my head.

"Good morning," she said with a warm smile as she moved closer to her daughter. "Quite an accent you have there. I hear a bit of Cockney, Brixton, and dare I say...Oxfordshire?"

I was impressed. "Most people hear Cockney and tend to think all of Brixton speaks with the same South London accent," I said. "However, many British people born, living in, and around Brixton may have a more neutral, middle-class Estuary accent, or even a posh one."

The woman's smile widened as Tasmin looked on wide-eyed. "Ah, yes. Most people also forget that accent and dialect in Britain are a matter of social class as well as geography. And it sounds as if you may have lived in many areas and grew up around the upper crust as well as the working class."

I gave a small smile. I was happy to be talking about anything to get my mind off my troubles. "You could say that, Ma'am. I see you dabble in a bit of dialectology?"

She moved forward. "I have a thing for studying accents, syntaxes, tones, and dialects, as AAVE— Ebonics for a lack of better explanation— is a language unto itself and should be recognized as such. One that I think has several different regions blended into its core formation."

"Ah! So, sociolinguistics then?"

She beamed. "I do love to converse with smart men. You would be absolutely correct. I do dabble in a bit of both, only in my spare time, but I won't bore you with my ramblings just yet. I'm Jewel, Tasmin's mother, and you are?" she asked while holding her hand out to shake mine.

"Professor Octavian Jerrod. It's a pleasure to meet you," I said, taking her hand then kissing the back of it.

The woman blushed and hid a smile. "I haven't had a man be such a gentleman in a while," she said.

"Mommy," Tasmin interjected, "Daddy is a gentleman all the time."

"Yes, but not a distinguished gentleman like your friend here. Is this the Octavian you were telling us about?" she asked Tasmin.

I looked at Tasmin, quirked a brow then gave something of a smirk.

Tasmin took a deep breath and said, "Mommy, please... not now." She looked at me. "Come in."

As I walked in, I felt the gift that Tasmin's mother possessed, and while she wasn't anywhere near as powerful as her daughter, I could tell she was a gifted healer. The small home was toasty, and I could smell the remnants of cooked bacon in the air.

"I'm going to go call your father to see if he found whatever it was he went looking for, love," Mrs. Pettiford said to Tasmin.

When she was gone, Tasmin turned her gaze to me. She stood across the room like she wasn't sure if she wanted to be next me or not.

"Do I smell?" I asked.

"Huh?"

"Do I still smell? I know Dafari said it would take weeks to wash the stench of the cave off me, but I could have sworn I'd done a fairly good job of washing all my nooks and crannies."

She rolled her eyes but chuckled. I walked over to her and pulled her into my embrace. I'd missed Tasmin and wouldn't make any bones about it. A part of me wanted to lift her around my waist and kiss her like I had been starved of her affections, but I kept in mind that her mother was in the kitchen.

"I'm glad you're okay," she said when we pulled away from the hug.

"Thank you for all the food you left and the heartfelt messages," I said as we moved to the sofa to sit.

"You're welcome. I was worried about you after everything that happened. How are you now?" she asked, concern clearly visible in her eyes.

"I'm fine," I lied. My ears rung and palms burned so badly, I had to make fists. I saw Tasmin paying close attention to me as I tilted my head to the side to try to stave off the ringing.

"Are you—"

I held up a hand to stop her. "We can discuss whatever you want to ask me later. This is important, and I hate to be so abrupt and curt, but this has to be said. When I was in the cave, Uncle came to visit me. He told me that there would be other entities and powerful beings that would be coming to Salix Pointe because of the power flux from you and Elisa. Dafari and I feel something coming and it's bad."

"You feel it?" she asked, wide eyed.

"Yes."

"Couldn't you be wrong?"

I frowned. "What do you mean?"

"I mean…is it possible you're wrong?"

I shook my head. "No. Not only do we feel it, we have confirmation from the underworld that something wicked this way comes."

Tasmin dipped her head and gave me an under-eyed look. "You can't be serious with that old-tale line from Macbeth," she said.

"I am serious, Tasmin. And that's not all."

"Okay..."

"Uncle Azazel is here."

"What? Why? What does he want? Should Elisa and I—"

"Yes. You should be afraid...even if he has agreed to help us and is staying at Dafari's place..."

Tasmin shot up from the couch. "Are you kidding me? Now listen, I know he technically saved us and helped us out after the fight, but there is no way in heck I'm going to get in cahoots with a full-blown demon—a Fallen— who can and *will* hurt me and Elisa...and whoever else gets in his way!"

"Good. You realize that Uncle walks the gray and can in no way be fully trusted. That will always keep you on your toes. However, he is the only ally we have right now. Because of what I was about to do to my father...I nor Dafari can call on...heavenly reinforcements. He's all we have currently."

"So, you mean to tell me I have to knowingly team up with a fallen angel whom I can throw further than I can trust?" she asked, incredulously so.

"Yes, Tasmin. That is exactly what I'm telling you."

CHAPTER 3

DAFARI

8:30 AM
NOVEMBER 24, 1932...

S EVERAL MONTHS HAD *passed since I had returned after taking the punishment for my brother who
had suffered much, and while I felt the justice he delivered
definitely befit the atrocities committed, those Above did not. I
knew Octavian wasn't built for seven long years of damnation
and torture in Hell and, instead, I confessed to his crime, taking
his place. However, I sorely misjudged the duration of my stay.
Time in the realm of mortals wasn't the same as time spent in
Hell. Hence, my seven-year hellacious sentence in fact turned
out to be seventy-seven years above ground.*

*The year I wound up in was 1932. By the time I had re-
turned, the United States was well into the Great Depression,
with Black people being hit the hardest. For example, prior to
the Great Depression, thirty percent of Blacks either owned or
managed land. With the economic downturn, that number
dropped down to five percent. Black people were also the first to*

have their hours cut or lose their jobs altogether during this time. By 1932, Black unemployment was at fifty percent.

That year also saw the start of *The Tuskegee Experiment*, where Black men were led to believe they were being treated for syphilis. That was not the case. They instead were used as guinea pigs to observe the natural course of untreated syphilis. Despite the fact slavery ended, Black people were still suffering.

I wondered if my release from hellish incarceration was even worth it. I had lost everything and was trying to pick up the pieces of my life, such as it was, wandering the planet in an attempt to find some peace. For some reason, I found myself back in New Orleans. Today was Thanksgiving, and yet, I had nothing to be thankful for. My beloved wife Elisa had long since passed away, as had my son Zafer and daughter Safiya. While they were all powerful witches, it was obvious that their powers could not prevent the ravages of time and old age.

I wound up at my family's mausoleum. While it had not been the first time I had visited them, this time held more significance. It caused me to reminisce on the many holidays we had shared together over the years. I was not one to celebrate holidays; however, Elisa loved to partake in the festivities. As such, by virtue of keeping her happy, I participated as well. Every event was a family affair, with Octavian, Tasmin, and Attalah joining us. The women would cook, the children would run off and play for hours, and Octavian and I would partake in bottles of well-aged rum. Those were good times. I reflected on the fond memories for several long moments before preparing to leave.

"I miss you all, my dear family," I said, looking at each monument marker in the family crypt, including those of Tasmin and Attalah.

While I missed each and every one of them, I missed my precious Elisa the most. Every time I lost her it was like losing *a part of myself. We were destined to be together, as we were destined to be torn apart, over and over again.*

MY BROTHER'S RETURN had been both a blessing and a curse; a blessing because he appeared, for the most part, to be on the road to recovery, and a curse because his nightmares of the past dredged up my own bad memories.

I shook out of my reverie, preparing for my workday. I only had two animals at the clinic, both waiting to be picked up by their owners. As I was putting food and water in the cages of the Chihuahua and Siamese cat, I noticed they both bristled. The dog then began to bark loudly, while the cat hissed angrily. I didn't need to turn around to know why.

"You couldn't just use the door like normal people?"

"Now is that any way to greet someone who saved your life? I am no mere mortal, Son. Besides, I much prefer traversing the shadows, whenever possible."

I silenced the animals then closed the doors to the cages. As I turned around, my father, Azazel, was standing behind me. He was never one to be seen without being dressed to the nines. He was attired in a blue Kiton slim-fit Prince of Wales checked cashmere suit jacket with matching Prince of Wales pleated cashmere suit trousers. His ensemble was complete with a black formal dress shirt, expensive Italian loafers, and silver-toned cufflinks, undoubtedly made of an expensive metal. His olive skin tone and wavy jet-black hair, save for some streaks of gray at the temples, made him a stand-out amongst the residents of Salix Pointe.

"You will never let me forget that you saved my life, will you?"

"I will not," he replied smugly.

I sighed as I walked back to my office, my father following close behind. "To what do I owe the...pleasure?"

"Now why don't you seem happy to see me, Son?"

"Because whenever you appear either bad things happen, or you're the bearer of bad news. Since nothing untoward has occurred...yet, it must be the latter."

He smiled showing his perfect white teeth. "You know me so well. I bring news from my above-ground sources. What do they call them? Ah yes, snitches."

I looked at him questioningly. "And why, pray tell, would you need snitches up here when you can get information from those underground?"

Once we got to my office, my father walked over to my bookcase where I kept a bottle of aged rum from the 1700s. He poured a finger of the libation for himself then looked in my direction, holding up the bottle, offering to pour some for me. I held up my hand to decline. He picked up his glass then began to pace.

"Weaving in and out of the shadows has become a bit... tenuous," he said then taking a long sip from his glass. My father was always one for dramatic pause.

I spread my hands in frustration. "Because?"

"Because by helping you, my beleaguered lovelorn nephew, and the witches, I singlehandedly shifted the balance of power."

I raised an eyebrow. "Singlehandedly?"

"Well, I did contribute in large part to the effort. As such, The Powers That Be are intent on holding me accountable. There are those who would sell me out in a heartbeat, if they actually had one, in order to move up in status. I am a wanted demon, and I don't mean in a way I would like. Never mind that I was framed to make it appear as if I had killed Noreen Chadwick, which I'm sure was also part of '*the greater good*'," he said scoffing, making air quotes. "My association with the scapegoat is so very fitting right now."

"Point taken," I replied, sitting behind my desk.

While my father was no innocent in any sense of the word, there were some crimes that he was absolved of. It took Octavian finding a piece of blue kyanite and smelling burnt cinnamon at Elisa's home for us to eventually figure out that my mother and stepfather were, in fact, responsible for not only Noreen's death, but that of Elisa's grandmother and parents as well. While my mother and stepfather were intent on killing Elisa and Tasmin for *the greater good*, Father's interference undoubtedly led to their defeat, which, I'm sure, raised the hackles of the Most High.

"What did your informants have to say?"

"From what they've gathered, there's a dark power rising right here, already in Salix Pointe. One of its residents, Mayor Lovett, is hell-bent on acquiring the epicenter of magick."

"While I appreciate you sharing, your information is outdated. We already knew that. He showed up at Tasmin's bookstore weeks ago trying to persuade her to sell it."

"Were you also aware that the much-despised mayor had a link to a very dark, very notorious figure in New Orleans history?"

"I was not," I replied, anxiously waiting to hear what my father had to say.

"Apparently, Mayor Ephraim Lovett is a direct descendant of Madame Marie Delphine LaLaurie."

I sat up, my interest piqued. "*The* Madame Marie Delphine LaLaurie, the woman who was dubbed a serial killer of slaves?"

"The one in the same. As you know, after her cook purposely started a fire inside her mansion back on April 10, 1834, Madame Marie refused to hand over the keys to would-be rescuers, preventing entry into the slave quarters. They ended up breaking the door down. What they found was a horrendous sight; all of the slaves were naked and horribly mutilated. They were wearing iron collars and were either chained to tables or the wall, or suspended from the ceiling by the neck. Bones were broken purposely so as to heal improperly."

I shuddered at his description of the condition of those slaves. It disgusted me that we were unable to save those lost souls during our time working with The Railroad. It revolted me even more that the monster who committed the atrocities escaped unscathed.

"Yes, I was in New Orleans at the time. There were several theories that were circulating after the fire; she had either died in the blaze, was hiding out in town, or had escaped to Paris. None of them were proven."

"It was also alleged that she died December 7, 1942. I've learned that the most likely scenario is that Madame Marie returned to New Orleans years later, masquerading as a commoner. That was until she made a deal with Mephistopheles himself, who approached her at the behest of his master. In a Faustian bargain, she sold her soul for immortality, vowing to serve Mephistopheles's master; but again, this is just conjecture. While Madame Marie has not been seen in some time, my sources tell me that Mayor Lovett is most likely conspiring with her. He is a Cajun warlock after all and has designs on the bookstore. Since his ancestor is in eternal servitude to a demon, their goal may be to acquire the epicenter of magick for that demon, or maybe even for her alone."

Everything my father was saying made sense, and it was frightening. Not only did Octavian and I have to worry about The Most High sending others to eliminate Elisa and Tasmin, now we had the potential threat of the mayor and his notorious ancestor aiming to procure a limitless source of magick for nefarious means.

"You're welcome," Father remarked, a self-satisfied look on his face.

"Thank you," I replied skeptically. "You don't usually provide information so…freely. What gives?"

"What gives indeed," he said with a chuckle.

And there it was. My father was back to being his riddle-spewing self.

I was about to question him some more when Elisa walked into the room. I had forgotten that she had planned to stop by for a brief visit when she had a break at the café.

"Oh, hell no. What is *he* doing here?" she questioned, pointing at my father.

He turned and stood. "Well good morning to you, my favorite barista."

Elisa stopped dead in her tracks. "Did Hell freeze over? Dafari, why is he here?" she asked, her gaze steely.

"You may address me directly. You're the second person today who doesn't seem happy to see me. I did, after all, help save your lives," my father replied, unfazed.

"You also attacked me and Tasmin, and almost killed Octavian," Elisa shot back. "And you saw me naked." She visibly shuttered.

"Yes, well, some of my actions were for *the greater good*," he remarked, sarcasm in his tone as he said 'greater good'. The way he ogled Elisa as he said those words made me want to pummel him like I did the night of the mayor's jubilee on All Hallow's Eve.

"And your other actions?" I queried. "As Elisa pointed out, you almost killed my brother. What good did that serve?"

"It brought out the healer's gift, did it not?" The smug look on his face annoyed me to no end. "Aside from grappling with his…demons," he said, laughing at his own irony, "he's fine. Just remember, I was the one who went to Octavian when he was wallowing in that cave of self-pity, bringing him out of his funk, figuratively and literally," he said, turning up his nose as if smelling bad meat. "On that note, I'll take my leave, but before I do, I wasn't the only one who shifted the balance of power. Please tell my dear nephew to sleep with one eye open." Before I could ask him anything else, he was gone.

"What was that about?" an unnerved Elisa asked.

I rubbed my palms down my face. "My father brought news of a potential new enemy."

I motioned for Elisa to have a seat then quickly filled her in on the information given to me by my father.

"Do you trust him, because I surely don't."

"While many of my father's actions have been suspect, to say the least, this time, my gut tells me that he is being truthful. Fact remains that Mayor Lovett has approached Tasmin looking to purchase the bookstore. We assumed it was to get to the epicenter of magick. It appears we were correct. However, Father revealing this information in such a straight-forward manner gives me pause. When I questioned him about it, he just replied with another one of his many cryptic responses. Knowing him, he has an ulterior motive. Regardless, we must remain vigilant."

"I agree, but the mayor has another thing coming if he thinks Tasmin and I are going to allow him to get a hold of Salix Pointe's main source of magick. We'll be ready for him."

"I appreciate your moxie, Elisa; however, now that we have confirmed that Mayor Lovett is a warlock, and is in league with an evil immortal relative, we can't get too cocky. We need to plan. The first thing we need to do is find Octavian and Tasmin to advise them of the current state of affairs. When I last saw him, he was on his way to Tasmin's. Perhaps he's still there."

As I said those words, Elisa was pulling her phone out of her bag. She dialed Tasmin, putting her phone on speaker mode.

"Hello?" I heard Tasmin say.

"Hey, Tasmin. Is Octavian still with you?"

"Yes, but how did—"

"Not important. You and Octavian need to get to Darfari's office as soon as possible. Don't ask why. He'll explain everything once you get here."

"Sounds ominous, but okay. We're on our way." Tasmin disconnected the call.

I waited for Elisa to put her phone away before I spoke. While we were still a couple, the dynamics of our relationship had changed since she had moved back to her home. I didn't see her nearly as much as I had when she was living with me. We still trained together, and she spent some nights with me, but it wasn't the same. Truth be told, I missed her constant presence. The threat of this newly revealed danger may have given me just the excuse I needed to get her to move back to my home, *our* home.

"Now that my father has made us aware of the mayor's plot and his alliance with Madame Marie, you may want to reconsider staying with me. I can better protect you if you're at the house."

"I appreciate your offer, Dafari, but I'll be fine. I already have wards up at my place to keep evil out, and I've learned plenty of protection spells since coming into my powers. And don't forget that Tasmin and her parents are just a stone's throw away. With all that magick around, I'm completely safe."

I stood, walking to stand next to her. She wasn't going to make this easy. She was determined to avoid leaving her home, despite the danger. I needed to know why.

"Elisa, what is your aversion to moving back in with me? I had grown accustomed to you being there, waking up with you in my bed."

"So had I and that was the problem." She sighed. "You initially brought me and Tasmin there to keep us safe. Our cohabitation occurred as a result of your father's machinations, and if I recall correctly, it wasn't even your idea, it was Octavian's." She stood, looking up at me, her eyes questioning. "Our relationship only blossomed because of our living arrangement. If none of that had happened, could you honestly tell me you would have given me the time of day? You hadn't looked at me twice until all the madness started."

I couldn't very well tell her that I would have in due course romanced her properly, and if all had gone as planned, would have eventually made her my wife, as I had done in the past. I couldn't tell her how deep my feelings ran for her, and that we had a love that transcended time, only to have it taken away from us again and again. No, it definitely was not time for that discussion. I decided that a partial truth was better than the whole truth.

"I had every intention of approaching you, it just so happened that fate accelerated my timetable. Either way, you would have been mine," I said smiling down at her. I closed the gap between us, placed my arms around her waist, and pulled her close to me, my hands naturally gravitating to her thick, round hips.

Over the past few weeks, Elisa had let her hair grow out even more. Her large curly afro was pulled back and bound together with a thick headband. I breathed in the sweet aroma of jasmine and lavender from her hair. I was glad she pulled it back today. It allowed her beautiful dark brown skin to shine.

She reached up, her arms wrapping around my neck. "You're awfully sure of yourself, aren't you?"

"I don't think you'd be with me if I wasn't."

Just as I was leaning in for a kiss from her lush, full lips, Octavian walked in with Tasmin, and asked, "What is this news you have for us, Brother?"

As always, my brother had impeccable timing.

CHAPTER 4
ELISA

9:30 AM

"THIS ALL FITS," Tasmin said as she stood by the window in Dafari's office.

She and Octavian had just been told what Azazel had relayed to Dafari. For some reason, Tasmin kept looking out the window. She and I had been talking a lot since the fiasco at the mayor's manor, trying to cram all we could from the Book of Magic Enchantment, as well as come to terms with all that had happened.

After she had introduced me to her parents, I'd felt a strange connection to her father. Strange because I'd just met the man, yet he seemed oddly familiar to me. I wanted to tell Tasmin but wasn't sure how she'd react to me telling her that her father made electricity shoot up and down my spine. While I knew for certain it wasn't anything sexual, the way it would sound gave me pause. Telling a woman who had become a good friend to me that her father, who was married to her mother, made me feel things as such didn't even sound good to my own ears.

Tasmin's mother, Ms. Jewel, was a sweet woman. The last thing I needed was for her to look at me sideways because she sensed I had some strange affinity for her husband. She was an empath and could already feel I was a nervous wreck the night I met them, I was sure.

Furthermore, I got huge power surges around the man. I couldn't stand to be in the same room with him for more than a few minutes, as it felt as if I was going to pass out. I had no idea what that was about and had no clue how to broach the subject with Tasmin without sounding like a hifalutin harlot. I chalked it up to him being a powerful spellcaster and necromancer.

I came back to the present to deal with the matter at hand. "What do you mean?" I asked Tasmin.

"Remember when I told you and Dafari about what Octavian and I had found in the mayor's office at the manor? He has his own Book of Shadows and there was also a spell to trap a disembodied spirit right on the first page. It was, and still is, my thinking that there is someone's spirit trapped inside that cat."

Octavian grunted as he paced, hands clasped behind his back. "Never mind the fact the mayor is a lecherous manky prat, but he is also dabbling in what you lot like to call dark magick. Thinking back to when I initially met him here, when they came to pick up that animal, I couldn't read him. It was as if he had intentionally taken steps to use magick to hide his energy trail."

I watched Octavian as he talked. Before, when we'd first met him, there had been a jovial nature about him. Now there wasn't. He seemed more serious, more like Dafari, than he had been before. He normally had a ready smirk or a smile to go with most anything he said. Now his face was stern and his eyes a bit lifeless. I suppose he had reason to be sullen after all that had happened. I had to admit though, I missed jovial Octavian. His cheery disposition was needed to balance out Dafari's moody one.

"This will take careful planning. Like I told Elisa, while I know she and Tasmin will take this on with little fear, the demon Mayor Lovett's ancestor has aligned herself with means that this woman is no easy fight," Dafari said. "And considering her sordid past, it would be best if we find out who our allies are and aren't."

"I know you guys want us to play nice with Demon Daddy and all," Tasmin said, "but I don't trust that...supernatural being."

I had to laugh at her trying not to cuss. "Imagine my surprise to walk in and see him sitting casually in Dafari's office," I said. "I don't trust him either."

"None of us do," Octavian said as he walked to stand near Tasmin. I was sure he looked out the window because she kept doing so. "However, I trust him more than I'd trust anyone else at the moment outside of this group. At least with him, we know what we're getting. It wouldn't surprise us if did something treacherous. I think when my brother mentions allies, he's talking about more than Uncle. The Merry Widows...you and Elisa will have to have a parley with them soon. It's imperative."

Tasmin stopped looking out the window to scowl at him. She tsked then shook her head. "I don't know about that..."

He looked at her. "Put your feelings to the side and think about what's at stake, Tasmin," he said. "Your coven must be seven at all times. Sure, the old bitty had a hand in Noreen dying, but it was my father who actually did the deed. She deserves a bit of extended grace."

Tasmin rolled her eyes. "If you say so," was all she said, and I knew Octavian would have to do more persuading than that.

Octavian studied her with keen interest, and I could have sworn he smirked. He didn't say anything else though as he turned his attention back to the window. Then his eyes narrowed. "I've never seen that bloke before," he said.

Tasmin said, "Me either," as she moved the blinds back again. "But he keeps checking the door at the bookstore. It's clear it's not open for business, but he won't stop."

Octavian grunted. "Either he's a buffoon or he has a real hankering to read something specific in your store."

I got up and followed Dafari to the other side of the window. He stood behind me as I discreetly pulled the right side of the blinds back. At the front door of the Book Nook was a young male whose race was ambiguous. He was tall and lanky but looked to be in good shape. His hair was cut in a close crop of silky curls atop his head, and he appeared to be studying the window on the second floor. I followed his gaze and my eyes widened when I saw the same woman—well ghost—from before. She looked to be…frightened. Her brows were furrowed, and tears were rolling down her cheeks.

I looked at Tasmin who had been watching me. "She's there again," I said as I rushed from the window and headed toward the front door.

"Who's there?" Dafari asked, voice booming behind me.

"The ghost from before?" Tasmin asked, rushing to follow me.

I heard Octavian parrot, "Ghost?"

"Yes," I said. "And she's crying. I'm not sure if it's because of the man or what." I snatched the front door to Dafari's office open, only to have it slammed closed again.

I looked up to see Dafari's hand on the door and him glaring down at me. "What in hell are you doing?"

I blinked slowly, a bit annoyed at his rudeness. "Going to the bookstore if you don't mind."

"No, you're not. I just told you my father said there are dark forces at play, there is a stranger trying to get into the bookstore, and you're about to run off because you *claim* to see a ghost?" he asked.

I took offense to the way he said the word claim. I inhaled and exhaled slowly. "I don't *claim* to see anything. I *saw* a ghost, Dafari, and I've seen her more than once."

"Sure, you have," Octavian said. "But what if it's just a projection? What if you're seeing what someone or something wants you to see? You and Tasmin can't just go running off at a time like this."

I turned to look at the man who reminded me of a big brother I never had. "Excuse the hell out of me, but I don't appreciate the tone you've taken as if to insinuate I don't know my own mind."

"And who said we were running off?" Tasmin snapped. "We're going to the bookstore."

"There is a *stranger* trying to get into your store, Tasmin. What part of we have to be careful did you two not get?" Dafari asked slowly, as if Tasmin and I were daft.

"And before you two think we're trying to control you and go all fourth-wave feminist on us, please bear in mind all we've just been through. We've not even fully dealt with the aftermath of my parents' murderous spree on your families, let alone what the fallout will be because of the actions we've all taken to protect you. So pardon my brother and me if we want to pause before we let you two skedaddle off just because Elisa *alleges* she sees ghosts in a window of your dead aunt's bookstore," Octavian all but growled out.

I would have been set to go off, as I was sure Tasmin was about to do, but we remained silent for the simple fact he had bulked in size and his eyes had started to glow a color of red I'd never seen on him before. His breathing was ragged, and he looked as if he was about to change into something horrid. The bracelet on my arm radiated with power as it glowed bright, matching the light from Tasmin's. The palms of my hands itched and burned as it had done times in the past when my fight or flight instinct kicked in. I felt fireballs itching to be released. I clenched my fists to keep them at bay.

"Octavian," I heard Dafari say. "She's right there. Right in front of you, Brother. Calm yourself."

Octavian turned his red glare to his brother then slowly inhaled and exhaled before closing his eyes. Once he opened them, they had gone back to their natural oil black color, and he was slowly coming down to size.

"My apologies, ladies," he said. "I'm...just going through some things at the moment. If you would excuse me," he said then turned to head back to Dafari's office.

Tasmin went to follow him, but Dafari cut her off and went after his brother instead.

When Dafari closed his office door, I looked at Tasmin. "What do you think all that was about?" I asked.

Tasmin sighed. "I'm not sure, but I would guess it has to do with what I told you he said about me not being taken away from him ever again on the night of the fight with his parents. I don't know what he meant by that as we've yet to discuss it. It is frustrating to the nth degree."

I looked toward Dafari's closed office door. I heard their murmurs. I was annoyed that they had closed us out after everything we'd just been through.

"Wish I knew what they were saying," Tasmin grumbled.

I barely heard her utter the words, but I did make them out. My ears rang and it felt as if I was in a tunnel underwater. I stumbled then felt dizzy. The world tilted and as if I had been yanked out of my body, I crumbled to the floor. When I opened my eyes, through a fuzzy haze, I saw a black door.

"I think it's best we tell them, Octavian…"

"We can't. Now isn't the time…

"There is none like the present…"

"They're not ready! We can't keep piling things on top of what they have to prepare for…"

"We also can't keep putting it off, Brother. How do you think this will play out if we wait any longer?"

"Are you sure you're even ready to open that door?"

"Ready or not, Octavian, I have to tell her…"

Their voices faded in and out. I saw flashes of them standing in Dafari's office as they talked. I reached for the doorknob to try to open it. It didn't budge. I yanked and pulled at it, and still, nothing.

"No," I heard Dafari yell.

The aggressive nature of it startled me so badly, I stumbled backward. The power surge I felt made me feel as if I was drunk or high on some kind of exotic drug. A gust of powerful wind knocked me back hard enough to break bones midair. When I landed, it was with a loud thud.

"Elisa! Elisa! Are you okay?"

I opened my eyes to find Tasmin gawking down at me with worry marring her features. I sat up then reached for her hand when she held it out to me. "I-I- it was like I was inside of Dafari's mind…I'm not sure, but I heard him and Octavian talking in bits and pieces. There was a black door, but when I went to open it, Dafari yelled and the next thing I knew, I was being shoved back—"

I stopped talking when Dafari snatched open his office door with such vigor it slammed into the wall. The force of the move caused the ends of his white lab coat to fly back. His eyes glowing golden as he glared at me. "Don't you ever do that again, Elisa," he snapped as he stormed toward me. "You do not have permission to enter my mind uninvited! It is an invasion of privacy—"

"I didn't know I was doing it. It happened so fast—"

"Mind your thoughts! Especially around that one," he snapped then jerked his head toward Tasmin.

"Um…this may not have been her fault," Tasmin said. "I kind of…made a wish in her presence and I'm sure you can figure out what that wish was…It wasn't her fault, Dafari." She sighed. "Blame me for that one."

"Seems as if we're all a bit off kilter," Octavian said, coming down the hall. "Let's all get together at Dafari's place later for dinner. That way we can strategize and think clearer."

Tasmin nodded. "I'm fine with that."

"Okay. As soon as I leave the coffee shop, I'll head to Dafari's."

I turned my gaze back to Dafari. While he still had a scowl on his face, judging by the calm nature of his breathing, it was safe to assume the storm had passed.

"Fine," was all he said. "Now please leave. I have appointments soon."

By the time Tasmin and I made it outside, the man in front of her store was gone, and so was the ghost. That annoyed me. I felt as if the ghost had been trying to tell me something, tell us something. Sure, she had technically shown me where our Book was, but I felt there was more. Tasmin and I went our separate ways, but only after Octavian had searched my shop from top to bottom and had done his own version of a protective spell. I could only assume he would do the same at the Book Nook.

"Ah! Good moning, Elsie," Rufus said as he briskly walked in then locked the door behind him.

Good morning from Rufus sounded more like good moaning, but that was neither here nor there.

I looked up from the pastry glass then smiled. "Good morning, Rufus!"

He grinned wide and there was a bounce in his step as he made his way behind the counter. "I got down yonder to the farmer's market like you been askin'," he said. "They didn't have that 'Gascar 'nilla like you wanted, but hear me out, okay?"

I knew he was talking about the Madagascar vanilla extract I asked him to pick up for me. I stood up straight and then put my hands on my hips. "O...kay," I said cautiously.

Rufus pulled what looked to be a clear open pontil bottle with a cork in it from his apron pocket. Inside was a golden-brown liquid.

"What is that?" I asked.

"This heah?" he asked with a smile as he held it up. "It's better than any extract you can buy. Think of it as...fairy dust but in liquid form. It's...um..." he cleared his throat then sheepishly looked away before looking back at me. "It's ah...maple syrup that's been heated with cinnamon, nutmeg, a dash of allspice...and my Yom-Ziza's secret ingredient."

"Your Yom-Ziza?" I asked.

He nodded. "Yeah. My grandmaw. She give me this recipe before she transpetitioned on."

I quirked a brow. "Did you mean *transitioned* on, Rufus?"

"Yeah, that's what I said; transpetitioned. Anyhoo, this is just as good if not better than that 'Gascar 'nilla."

I'd been using Mama Nall's recipes for almost every pastry, cake, and pie on my menu. I wasn't so sure about switching it up now, especially since I'd started grieving her all over again.

"Listen, Rufus, I don't know about this," I said, taking the bottle as he passed it to me. "These are my grandmother's recipes and—"

"Your grandmaw's sweet tater pies use my grandmaw's here flavoring. I knows because I done tasted plenty of'em," he said with a wide grin. "You just think she made her own 'nilla extract. She didn't. She use this right heah. Pop that top and smell it."

I did as he said and took a sniff. Sure enough, it smelled like Mama Nall's extract she'd always used. She did always have those kind of pontil bottles in her pantry.

"Well, I guess I can try it," I said, still a bit skeptical, but since I was out of Madagascar vanilla extract, I didn't have a whole lot of options.

"This stuff can also be used for protecting ya home and place of bidness. You just put some on ya door seal and anything or anybody meant to cause ya harm gonna not step one foot in the door. I know it's old superstickchuns stuff, but ya can't never be too careful." Rufus smiled then took the vial. "I'll get started on the rest of baking then. You 'bout wanna deal with other stuff anyhow. I can't thank you enough for trusting me with this, Elsie. Can't thank you enough," he said, with an extra spring in his step.

I shook my head at the spry older man then got to prepping for the store to open in an hour. After Rufus had gotten the croissants and cookies into the ovens, I watched as he took some of his grandmother's extract and wiped down the door seal with it. As he did so, he sang a little song that sounded a hell of a lot like a chant. Once he saw me watching, he smiled, stopped singing and then started humming.

Just as we opened for business, we saw Sheriff Donovan Benson speed down Main Street like a bat out of Hell. A few seconds later, his deputy, Henrietta Ross, was right behind him. I wondered what that was about. It was so rare that anything criminal happened in Salix Pointe that it was easy to forget we even had a sheriff's office. Just as the thought crossed my mind, like clockwork, Dafari walked in.

"No need to even order, Dayfari," Rufus said, coming from the back. "Already know what'cha want and got it coming right on up. Elsie there done told me you always get the same thing: a white chocolate mocha, almond filled croissimin, and two chocolate chip cookies."

Since Rufus had started, I'd still been the one to handle Dafari's orders. I fought to hide the laugh threatening to erupt when Dafari stopped and quirked a brow at seeing Rufus behind the counter. His stoic face reminded me that he rarely smiled, but he had smiled at me this morning. It had been alarming and disarming at the same time. It had also caused heat to settle between my thighs. Perhaps after dinner later, I'd stay the night at his place? I missed sleeping with him.

"And good morning to you, too, Rufus. Thank you. I appreciate the prompt service," Dafari said then glanced at me with annoyance.

Since getting to know him better, I'd come to realize he hated abrupt change. He was so used to seeing only me behind the counter that having Rufus fix his morning delicacies probably frustrated him.

He had been angry with me when I'd left his office. He didn't seem to be in a better mood since then. He walked up to the counter to pay for his order. Rufus cheerfully rang him up.

"How's your brother Octovian?" Rufus asked, handing Dafari his order.

"Octavian…is fine," he said, putting his change in his pocket.

"I'm glad to hear it. That freak the mayor done said Octovian offended his wife, and he got some words for him. It's been the rumors all over town. People be talkin', and I said, I told'em, that Octovian don't look like the type to do no such thang. Now you may offend some folk, Good Doc. We all know you's as ornery as a wet cock, but not that Octovian. I told that old, hen-pecked Cajun, he'd bet not go startin' no trouble with ya brother."

By the time Rufus was done talking, it was so hard for me not to laugh that I was about to burst at the seams. Even Dafari looked amused.

"You told him that, did you?" he asked Rufus.

Rufus, with his chest poked out and pride written all over him, said, "I shole did. He done threatened me, too. Tell me to mind my own business if I knew what was good for me. And I told him that if he knew what was good for him, he'd not threaten me again. These people 'round heah think I'm some pushover, Dayfari, but I tell ya, I knows a few thangs. Yes, good ole Rufus knows some thangs," he said then hummed his way to the back of the café again.

Dafari quirked a brow and when he stared at the place Rufus had been standing, I knew he was reading his energy trail and thinking the same thing I was. Did Rufus have some magick about him? Dafari glanced at me and was about to say something until his phone rang.

He pushed a button on the device in his ear then answered. "Doctor Battle…"

I finished wiping down the last table then made my way behind the counter. I hollered to the back and asked Rufus to run another errand for me. He was more than happy to and rushed off before I could thank him. Really, I needed some privacy. I'd hoped to be able to test the waters and see if Dafari was actually still mad at me. I knew I had a lot more work to do when it came to honing all my gifts, and I understood why Dafari was mad at me dropping into his head uninvited. However, I still wanted to know what that black door meant.

"Say that again," I heard Dafari said then his brows furrowed. "Drained of blood and brain matter?"

My ears perked up and I stopped wiping down the checkout counter to eavesdrop more.

"I'll be right there," he said then looked at me.

"What is it?" I asked.

"That was Sheriff Benson. He's over at the Cummings farm, and according to him, seven of the cows have been slaughtered and one of their field hands…The cows and the man look to have been drained of blood and their brains are gone."

Shock jolted through me. "What?" I all but yelled.

Dafari nodded. "Yes. I have to get over there. He wants me to take a look and see if a human or another animal has done it."

"Doctor Benu can't tell him that about the man?" I asked

Dafari shook his head. "Apparently Doctor Benu isn't answering his phone. Deputy Ross has gone to check to make sure he's okay."

"Oh no…that's not like him to not answer."

"I know, but I'll speak with you later," he said then gave me a quick kiss to the lips.

I wondered who or what would slaughter seven cows and a man as such. That made no sense to me. This town was big on farming. I couldn't imagine one of our own actually doing something so heinous. And where was Doctor Benu?

My bracelet vibrated then glowed bright. That gave me pause. It only did that when danger was near, or when I was in fight or flight mode. A chill settled over my whole body like a soiled blanket. I looked at my front window to see that young man who had been at the Book Nook earlier standing just outside the door, watching me. Hands in his pockets, gaze steely and cold. His eyes narrowed, glowed green, and then I felt a flash of pain right between my eyes.

I hissed and grabbed at my head. Dafari's voice was in my mind telling me to guard my thoughts. I remembered his lessons well. However, the pain was so intense that I found guarding my thoughts was the least of my problems. I gritted my teeth then tried to think...but my mind went blank.

"You will release your hold and not cause disaster. I bind your works and send you back to your master. Let you not return to this place lest you reveal your true face. And upon the revelation, let your true form cease creation."

The man roared back and exposed his teeth. Four jagged fangs on each side of his mouth dripped with rancid saliva and he snarled at something or someone I couldn't see.

"Let your intentions unfold so your master will be exposed. Let me make my intentions clear, adze, you are not welcomed here!"

I heard that chant in my head, saw a bright flash of light, heard something squeal and screech so loudly that my ears rang. The man who chanted had a voice that was strong, clear, and precise. The power he wielded emanated from him like electricity.

Then... I felt the pain subside second by second. When I finally opened my eyes and looked outside, Tasmin's father was standing where the young man had once been.

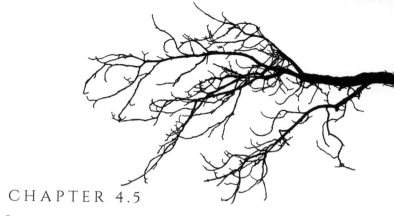

CHAPTER 4.5

MADAME MARIE DELPHINE LALAURIE

10:15 AM

SITTING IN THE middle of the solid mahogany bed, Madame Marie fell into a trance-like state, her mind connecting with her impundulu. As always, she allowed him to roam free at night, permitting him to feed on whomever or whatever he wanted at his whim, lest he feed on, and possibly kill, his mistress instead. Afterwards, he would return to her, fulfilling her every demand. This morning, what she wanted more than anything was to rid herself of Salix Pointe's newest witches, as they were preventing her from acquiring what she wanted most, the epicenter of magick.

"That's it, my troeteldier," she said, which translated to pet in Afrikaans. "The young witch is alone and oh so vulnerable. It's a shame they split up, but no matter; the other one will fall into our clutches in due time. Do my bidding. Strike now!"

Madame Marie watched through the impundulu's eyes as Elisa grabbed her head in pain, a brain fog overcoming her.

"Yes, that's it, lover. Slay her, and make it quick, then drain her body."

Madam Marie gleefully observed how Elisa was trapped in the thrall of her dutiful servant. She licked her thin lips in anticipation, the thrill of the kill imminent. She had watched him slaughter many over the decades at her command, but this one was different; it was special. The very thought of possessing Salix Pointe's source of magick aroused her.

"Serve me well, Lefu, and I will service you well upon your return," she said then smiled. She chuckled at the appropriateness of his name, which literally meant death.

She watched as Elisa's life force had begun to ebb, her lethal assassin focused on his task. Then she felt it; an abrupt power shift, the words of a protection spell being projected loud and clear. Lefu howled in pain, his true vampiric form exposed. His mistress screamed as she felt the full force of the opponent's assault, the attack on her familiar incapacitating them both. He turned in the direction of his assailant, a Black man who appeared to have enormous power. Who was he, and why was he protecting the witch?

"Damn it!" Madame Marie cursed angrily, her impundulu's obvious agony also her agony. "Lefu, return to me immediately!"

As Lefu fled, abandoning his mission, the intense pain subsided, and they both began to recover. Once she had regained her wits about her, Madame Marie realized that she needed to discover who this new, and clearly formidable, enemy was, lest he prevent her from gaining the power she felt she so richly deserved.

CHAPTER 5

TASMIN

10:20 AM

"PUT ONE OF each crystal in every corner of the basement now," I heard my father say, as I walked through the door to the café. He handed Elisa several small, labelled Ziploc bags, each containing black stones.

I had rushed over from the Book Nook after Elisa's frantic call telling me she had been attacked by the same man who was loitering in front of the bookstore earlier. She said that her bracelet, the identical match to mine, went off in warning, then she saw him standing at the café's front window. She realized how much danger she was in when his eyes turned an 'eerie glowing green', as she put it, then he used some sort of mind attack to incapacitate her. She had also told me that if my dad hadn't shown up when he did, reciting some incantation, she might not have made it. I had so many questions, like how did my dad know that Elisa was in trouble in the first place?

"Okay, I'll be back," she replied. "I sent Rufus on a few errands. That should take several hours, and that 'Closed for inventory' sign will keep the customers away. That will give us the time we need for this meeting," she said, as she quickly walked off.

My dad simply nodded, locked the front door then turned to me, handing me bags of the same crystals he had given Elisa. "Tazzy, put one of these in every corner of this room. I'll take care of the back of the shop. Oh, your mom is on her way, so unlock the door for her when she gets here."

"Got it, Daddy." I quickly looked at the labels on each bag. Black tourmaline, staurolite, black obsidian, Apache tears, black jade, jet stone, and black kyanite; the same stones I used for Aunt Noreen's letting go ceremony, and all protection crystals. I opened the bags, placing one of each in the four corners of the room.

My mind was churning. I kept thinking about the man who was standing in front of the bookstore. Who was he, and why did he attack Elisa? Why did that ghost appear again, and why was she afraid and crying? Why was her spirit tethered to the bookstore? Better question, who was she? I put my thoughts to the side when I heard a knock at the door. I thought it was my mom, but I turned around to see Octavian standing there. He entered quickly as I opened the door then locked it back.

"What are you doing here?" I asked. I was still unnerved by his transformation at Dafari's clinic and wasn't sure how to speak to him. His recent behavior left me on edge and, in a way, I felt a bit uncomfortable being around him.

"Dafari called me," he said stepping further into the dining area. "He's still at the Cummings' farm assessing the seven dead cows and deceased farm hand, and—"

"Wait, what? When did that happen? And how come Doc Benu didn't go to see about the farm hand? He is the medical examiner after all."

"From what Dafari told me, the cows and the farm hand had been butchered. Their brains were missing and their blood exsanguinated. As far as the town doctor is concerned, it appears the sheriff was unable to reach him. A deputy was sent to check on his whereabouts. Dafari asked me to come here in his stead to check on Elisa, and to stay with her until he got back from the farm."

"Wow. What is going on in this town? Exsanguinated cows and a farm hand, and Doc Benu is M.I.A.? I've known him since I was a child, and he is not one to shirk his duties. He has an impeccable work ethic. Something must be seriously wrong."

"While I haven't been in town long, from what I have perceived, I tend to agree."

"I hope he's alright."

"As do I," Octavian replied.

He was staring down at me, a look in his eyes that I couldn't discern. Then again, ever since he emerged from his self-imposed exile, there was a lot about him that I couldn't figure out.

"Tasmin, I need to apologize to you for what happened earlier."

"You mean for mansplaining why Elisa and I couldn't 'skedaddle off' as you put it," I started making air quotes, "then going postal on us?"

"Going postal?" he asked quizzically.

Sometimes I forgot that Octavian came from a different time. "You became uncontrollably angry."

"Ah yes, well, that. I apologize for all of it. What I won't apologize for is caring for you deeply."

This time the look in his black eyes was very familiar. I had seen it several times before, including the first time we trained together and when we were in the mayor's office the night of the jubilee.

"I-I don't know what to say, Octavian. A lot has happened over the past few weeks. I honestly didn't know when you'd be back, or *if* you'd be back. You say you care about me, but you didn't even let me know when you returned to the land of the living until two weeks after the fact."

"Poppet, I wasn't in the right frame of mind. I didn't want you to see me like that. Bad enough my...uncle had to snap me out of my funk, and my brother had to endure the smell of my funk after I emerged from the cave," he said half-smiling.

He actually made another joke, the first being when he came to Aunt Noreen's house. His frequent comical utterances had been few and far between, and it was the first time since he got back that I had seen anything close to a smile on his handsome face. Lastly, he called me Poppet, his term of endearment for me. I had actually missed that.

"I just needed time to gather myself, get my bearings, before I saw you. Please tell me you understand," he said, closing the gap between us, taking my hands in his. "While we may have been physically apart, you were never far from my heart."

He was making it extremely difficult for me to be mad at him, my uneasiness melting away. "Well, when you put it that way, I guess—"

Octavian didn't give me a chance to finish my sentence. Before I knew it, he leaned down, his soft, warm lips locking with mine. The last time we kissed was at the jubilee, and just like then, his kiss sent my heart racing and my head spinning. He wrapped his arms around my waist, his body becoming flush with mine. I flung my arms around his neck, savoring the moment. I couldn't deny it any longer; I did have feelings for Octavian, more than I cared to admit. While I was an empath, I didn't need powers to sense Octavian's emotions; his feelings for me were coming through loud and clear. We were so lost in each other neither of us noticed that we were no longer alone.

"Eh-hum."

The distinctive sound of my father pretending to clear his throat stalled the kiss between me and Octavian, as I turned to see him standing near the pastry counter. Octavian and I getting caught took me back to a time when I was fifteen years old when my dad had caught me and my first boyfriend Jason kissing on the stoop. I was so embarrassed. Needless to say, I got chewed out by both my parents, and although I didn't see the big deal, they forbade me from seeing him again. After that, Jason avoided me like I had the plague, relegating me to the friend zone. Come to think of it, back then, boys in general avoided me like I had cooties or something. I thought it was because they knew my dad worked in law enforcement, but now, after finding out about my parents and what they could do, I had to wonder.

"Daddy," I said, disengaging from Octavian. "This is Professor Octavian Jerrod."

My dad walked up to us, coming to stand in front of Octavian. While he was a couple of inches shorter, my dad was still an imposing figure.

"Pleasure to finally make your acquaintance, Mr. Pettiford," Octavian said, his hand outstretched in greeting.

"So you're Octavian," Daddy said, taking his hand to shake it, a distrustful look on his face.

I had seen that look many times, particularly when he was discussing cases with my mom and something felt off to him. He stepped a bit closer to Octavian, his grip on his hand firm. "The same Octavian whose parents almost killed my only child and Elisa and succeeded in taking the lives of Elisa's relatives and our family matriarch," he finished, looking Octavian directly in the eyes.

Their first meeting wasn't going well at all.

"Sir," Octavian started, breaking their handhold, taking a few steps back, "you have my sincerest of apologies for my parent's actions. I know it by no means makes up for what they have done, nor atones for all the pain they've caused your family. You have no reason to trust me considering; however, please be assured that my brother Dafari and I were prepared to lay down our lives for Tasmin and Elisa," he answered, looking at me.

"And my son and nephew may well have given their lives had I not been there to intervene."

We turned suddenly when we heard the deep bass, honey-coated voice of Azazel, who was standing next to Elisa.

"And you won't let us forget that, will you? What do you want?" I asked, suspicion in my tone.

"I found him lurking out back. He said he has some new information to share," Elisa replied, moving away from him.

Although she was accompanied by the demon bane of our existence, I was grateful for Elisa's timely interruption. Things were quite uncomfortable between my dad and Octavian.

"You couldn't just knock on the front door, Uncle?" The annoyance in Octavian's voice was evident.

"And interrupt the tender moment between you and the good doctor? I would never interfere with the course of true love."

As I felt my cheeks become flushed, I was loathing his presence with each passing second. Luckily, just as I was about to make a snarky remark, the Universe intervened, and my mom knocked on the door. My dad opened it, ushering her inside.

"Sorry I took so long," she said. "I wanted to make sure the house was fully protected before I left."

"I don't believe we've been introduced," Demon Daddy said, walking over to my mom, taking her hand and kissing the back of it, eyeing her longingly. "I'm Azazel, uncle of Octavian. And you are?"

"My wife," Daddy replied, taking back her hand. He then did something that made me want laugh, but I refrained. He grabbed a napkin from one of the tables, wiping the area on the back her hand that Azazel had kissed.

"I see gallantry runs in the family. I'm Jewel, mother of Tasmin, and this is my husband, Silas."

"Jewel, your name suits you. A beautiful name for a beautiful woman. I see where Tasmin gets her stellar looks."

"Excuse me, but can you stop hitting on my wife?"

"Forgive me. You're a good-looking man, Silas. I wouldn't want you to feel left out."

Octavian sighed. "Uncle, if you can't act with any sense of decorum, you can go."

"Fine," he replied, taking a seat at one of the tables. "I'll share my information then make my leave. But first, my favorite barista, would it be too much to ask for a beverage? I'm quite parched." He gently ran his hand down the front of his throat for dramatic effect.

After Elisa stared at him for few seconds then rolled her eyes, she replied, "Let me get him something to drink so we can get him out of here as soon as possible."

She quickly returned with a full pitcher of sweet tea, and some plastic tumblers. After filling each glass, she passed them around.

"Octavian, I forgot to ask why you're here." She took a seat next to my mom.

"Dafari called me. He sensed you were in danger and knew I could get to you posthaste."

"Why couldn't he be here?" my dad asked.

Elisa reiterated the reason for Dafari's absence to my parents and Demon Daddy.

"I would bet anything the creature that killed those cows and the farm hand is the same one that attacked Elisa," Daddy said. "I'm sure it was one of the African vampire species, an adze, in particular."

"Mr. Pettiford," Octavian began, "if I may interject, while I agree with your assessment that a vampire is committing these horrendous crimes, I don't believe that it's an adze."

"And why do you say that?" my mom asked.

"The modus operandi doesn't fit. An adze would generally take on the form of a firefly. If captured, it could take on a human-like form, having jet-black skin, a hunchback, and sharp talons. When in this extremely dangerous form, this type of vampire was known to kill its prey, drink its blood, and eat the heart and liver. Also, this type of vampire was known to target children for food. I believe the creature you're referring to is an impundulu."

"What's the difference between the two?" I asked.

I knew absolutely nothing about vampires. Heck, I didn't even think they existed until this conversation. I thought they were nothing more than made up stories based on some blown-out-of-proportion historical fact. Then again, up until a few weeks ago, I didn't believe in witches, magick, angels, or demons.

"Three distinct differences, Tasmin," Octavian began, pacing back and forth and talking with his hands. "First of all, an impundulu not only feeds on humans, but on cattle as well. This would explain the drained cows and farm hand at the Cummings' farm. Second, this vampire does not appear as a monster, but instead takes on the form of an attractive young man. While I don't fancy men, it's a reasonable presumption that the chap who Tasmin, Elisa, Dafari, and I saw lollygagging in front of the bookstore, and later assailed Elisa, was reasonably good looking. Ladies, wouldn't you agree?"

"I guess, if you like that type," Elisa replied with a shrug.

"He was a'ight," I added nonchalantly.

Octavian had an amused look on his face then continued on. "Lastly, an impundulu can both be considered a witch's servant and her familiar. According to the writings, the vampire serves the witch until she passes it on to her daughter—"

"And here's where my information comes in handy," Demon Daddy chimed in, looking at Octavian for permission to continue despite interrupting him in the first place. "I have it on good authority that Madame Marie Delphine LaLaurie did not arrive in Salix Pointe alone."

"Wait a minute, did you say Madame Marie Delphine LaLaurie, as in the notorious 19th century slave serial killer?" my mom asked. She loved to study many topics, including obscure history.

"I see where the good doctor not only gets her beauty, but also her intelligence," Azazel said, smiling appreciatively at my mom.

"What did I say, demon?"

I could tell my dad's patience with Octavian's uncle was running thin. While I had explained to my parents who, and what, Azazel was, a Fallen *and* an incubus, that still wouldn't stop my dad from checking an immortal being who he felt was disrespecting him or someone close to him.

"I was merely complementing the ladies; however, in order to keep this…fragile peace, my apologies, Silas," Demon Daddy replied then chuckled lightly. Knowing him, he didn't really mean it. "But I digress," he continued. "To answer Jewel's question, I am referring to *that* Madame Marie. Rumors of her death were purely unsubstantiated, and have been proven false altogether. So as not to have to repeat myself, when you see Dafari, he can reiterate the circumstances surrounding her deal to obtain immortality. What I will tell you is that she arrived in town with, let's just say, a companion in tow, and she is residing with that Cajun warlock descendent of hers, the mayor."

We all sat in silence for several seconds, taking it all in.

"What Uncle says makes sense," Octavian uttered, breaking the silence. "As I was saying before his interruption, a witch who controls an impundulu usually passes it on to her daughter. However, with immortality, there would be no need to transfer power, and she could use the beast in perpetuity to do her bidding."

"From what I've ascertained, oftentimes, a witch would take on the vampire as her lover. What better way to have a being in servitude, and then be able to send him away at her whim?" Demon Daddy interjected, appearing to be very entertained by that tidbit. "That said Madame Marie must release the creature to feed nightly, lest it turn on her and kill her. But don't take my word for it. I'll gladly defer to my learned nephew, the professor of all things mystical and paranormal."

With Demon Daddy it was hard to tell if he was being sincere or condescending, although, much as I think he would hate to admit it, I believe he had some semblance of respect for Octavian.

"Correct, Uncle. Herein lies the rub, which is twofold; there is no known method of killing an impundulu. Also, Madame Marie is immortal, and even if we found a way to kill her, doing so would result in the impundulu becoming an ishologu, an uncontrollable creature without a master. This is a conundrum indeed."

"So as far as this ancient evil and her minion are concerned, we're basically up a creek, is that what you're telling us?" my dad asked.

"I wouldn't necessarily say that, Mr. Pettiford. I will say that we will have to buckle down and diligently research the matter. Luckily, I know our group is more that up to the task."

"I agree," Demon Daddy added. "I too have some additional sources that I need to confer with. It may take a bit of time since they are not...local."

I was curious to know what additional sources he was referring to. Knowing him, they were none too savory. I didn't get a chance to inquire because there was a gentle knock on the front door. We all turned to see who it was.

"Oh look, it's the Three Merry Widows," Demon Daddy uttered. "Except...they don't look so merry. On that note, I think I'll take my leave. Jewel, it was my ultimate pleasure," he said, bowing to her.

"Demon, be gone," my dad said, waving his hand as if to shoo away an annoying insect.

Azazel looked at my dad, smiled, and disappeared into a shadow.

"Is he always so...extra?" my mom asked.

"Always!" Elisa, Octavian, and I said in unison.

"He has no chill, no filter," I added.

Elisa let out a hefty sigh before standing up. "I guess we better see why they're here." She opened the door slowly. "Martha Lee, Mary Ann, Cara Lee," she said, greeting each sister individually.

"Hello, Elisa," Martha, the eldest sister replied. "May we come in? We won't take up too much of your time."

Elisa turned to look at me and my parents. We, in turn, looked from one to the other. As much as Demon Daddy worked my last good nerve, I'm ashamed to say that I would have much rather dealt with him than Martha. My mom, the consummate peacemaker, simply nodded on behalf of the three of us. As each one filtered through the door, the room became deafeningly silent.

Martha was the first to speak. "I realize that it still may be too soon for any of you to accept my heartfelt apology, but time is of the essence. I wanted to explain the details of my involvement regarding Noreen and Amabelle's…deaths—"

"Don't you mean murders?" I quickly interjected, crossing my arms in front of my chest.

My mom placed a hand on my shoulder. "Let her finish, sweetheart. The sooner, the better."

Martha hung her head, but then raised it high. "While I don't have time at the moment to explain the circumstances of my collusion with Archangel Michael regarding what transpired, as I had once promised Elisa, I will say that I am beyond remorseful for what I've done. Nothing I can say or do will ever make up for my complicity, but please know that I am genuinely sorry for my participation. I am aware that no matter how many times I say that, only each one of you can decide, when, or if, you'll grant me the forgiveness I seek. However, I…we," she said, looking at her sisters, Cara Lee standing to her right, and Mary Ann to her left, "Come bringing a message."

Cara Lee stepped forward. "Noreen came to us."

"We were performing our weekly chanting when she appeared with this message; 'The coven must be restored'," Mary Ann added.

"She basically said the same thing to the three of us when Silas invoked her spirit at her house recently," my mom said. "Martha, while I understand the urgency of re-forming the coven, I hope *you* understand that we have every right to feel trepidation regarding working closely with the woman responsible for the murder of Aunt Noreen."

"Understood," she responded. "I do have much to atone for. All I ask for, when there is more time, is the opportunity to share my side of the story and to make amends to each one of you."

"Our sister is genuinely contrite," Mary Ann said.

"And the three of us can promise you that, should you all decide to join us, no action involving the coven will be taken without the full consensus of the entire collective," Cara Lee finished.

"I want to hear that from Martha, since she was the one who acted on her own," my dad replied.

We all looked at her, waiting for her response.

"You have my word that I will not act without group consent." Then she turned to me and Elisa. "I would still like to speak with the two of you. There are things I must relay that are for your ears only. I will make myself available whenever you're ready to talk."

Elisa spoke first. "I can't speak for Tasmin, but I need a day or two. We've had a lot dropped on us in just the past few hours, and we need time to absorb it all. I can't make any promises as to how I'll feel after our conversation, but I'll hear you out."

"That's all I ask. And you, Tasmin?"

I stood up, got face-to-face with the woman responsible for my aunt's death. While Martha was taller than me, I faced her and stood tall as if we were the same height. "I know you gave us your word, such as it is, and it appears that we have to form this…unholy alliance, but just know that I don't trust you as far I as I can throw you, regardless of whatever explanation you give. I'm doing this for Aunt Noreen and to protect the people of Salix Pointe. And as far as forgiving you anytime soon…don't hold your breath."

I didn't wait for a response. Without another word, I stormed out of the café back toward the Book Nook. In that moment, I realized how much anger I still had inside of me. I was angry at the woman who allowed herself to become a willing participant in taking her dear friend, my Aunt Noreen's, life; angry at the archangels who tried to kill me and Elisa and succeeded in killing members of our families; and angry at The Powers That Be who orchestrated everything, simply because we were witches. After what just happened, I realized I just wasn't ready to forgive any of it, and I may never be.

CHAPTER 6

OCTAVIAN

6:00 PM

TASMIN WAS STUBBORN, that was for certain. My intentions had been to apologize for my outburst and leave it there for the time being. However, I should have known she wouldn't let well enough alone. It had been a bone of contention in our marriage many lives ago, and it didn't seem as if she had changed in this lifetime either. To have to, basically, repeat myself as to why I didn't tell her I was back, after explaining it to her earlier that morning, showed me that she was more of her old self than I'd realized. That worried me. It was what had gotten her, and our daughter, killed in another life.

Still, the way she looked up at me with worry, something akin to fear, and adoration all at the same time made me want to wrap her in my wings and take her away from all danger. That was why I'd kissed her. I knew it would only be a temporary fix, but I wanted to protect her and keep her next to me by any means necessary. I couldn't lose my family again; that included Dafari and Elisa as well. What happened all those lives ago ripped our family so far apart, we were never the same.

On another note, I worried that my uncle was allowing Mr. Pettiford to refer to him as *demon* for a darker cause. Uncle was big on respect. He believed in giving it when it was given to him. He also believed in skinning men alive for lesser offenses. It would do Mr. Pettiford some good to remember that one of the offenses Uncle had been casted down for was refusing to bow to man.

However, even I found that Mr. Pettiford referring to Uncle Azazel as *demon* when he very well knew his name a bit distasteful, albeit warranted since he was openly ogling the man's wife. Still, Uncle never allowed mere men, powerful spellcaster and necromancer or not, to disrespect him as such. Something was up. I'd have to keep a butchers on that to be sure Tasmin's father didn't get in over his head.

"What's got you sitting on my porch looking as if someone has let the wind out of your sail?"

I looked up to see my brother pulling off his soiled lab coat and removing his muddied boots. He did it rather cack-handedly as if he didn't want any more of it to touch his skin. A couple of hours had passed since the café incident. I assumed he would have wanted to see Elisa first. I told him as much.

"She'll be here for dinner as planned. A lot has happened in one day. I don't want to overwhelm her. With the mood I'm in, I'd want to take her, and she wouldn't understand that currently," he said, his gaze flashing red then back to gold.

I grunted. "I, too, have a hard time understanding that side of your nature, but it is not meant for me to. Though... why would you want to take your woman after being at a death site all day, Brother?"

Dafari cast a deadpan glance in my direction. "You wouldn't understand, *Celestial*."

I chuckled at his jibe. "Fair enough. It would do you some good to know that after the day we've all had, I agree with your earlier assessment. We should tell the ladies the whole truth. A good old chinwag with the women is in order."

After Dafari had fully disrobed down to his knickers, he took the water hose attached to the spigot on the side of his house then washed away the grime on his body, face, and hair. My brother had always been a bit of a neat freak.

"And what brought this on?" he asked once he was done.

"Tasmin's father is hiding something. In his quest to try to size me up earlier, he let his guard slip for just a second, but it was all I needed to pick up on the familial line between him and Elisa."

Dafari whipped around to look at me. "They're related?" he asked, confusion in his tone.

I nodded. "He's her uncle." My brother's eyes widened. I nodded. "Neither she nor Tasmin has any idea. And that's not the showstopper, dear brother."

"Go on…"

I told him about what had happened at the café down to Tasmin storming off after snapping on Martha, then I said, "Tasmin has a spiritual chastity belt attached to her aura—"

"That explains the smell." I cut my eyes to the right to see my uncle slowly emerging from the shadows of the trees.

He brushed bloodied entrails and gook from his expensive suit and looked annoyed while doing so. His brows were furrowed, and mouth set in a scowl. I felt my hackles rise as I knew exactly what smell he was referring to. I hadn't paid attention to it at first. I was so busy trying to protect her and Elisa that taking the time to thoroughly read her aura had slipped my mind completely.

"I didn't want to believe it, but now it all makes sense," Dafari said, staring his father down. "Have you been in a fight, Father?" he asked him.

"What all makes sense now?" I asked Dafari.

"I knew she had a distinct smell. As I'm sure you did, too," he said, still not taking his eyes off Uncle.

Uncle shrugged nonchalantly. "You say fight, I say negotiations," he replied then turned red eyes on me. "I prefer my women be a bit more experienced, Nephew. Calm yourself. Virgins are not my cup of tea. They're no fun and require too much instruction. I like my women to know how to swallow my cock and take every inch without being afraid of it or running away from it." He said that then smiled wide with a mouth full of jagged fangs.

"You've been to Hell," Dafari growled. "The smell of sulfur and flesh-rot is loud on you."

"I may have stopped on levels one and two for a brief moment. Trying to help your witches is becoming a bit dangerous for me. I had to physically defang two hellhounds after negotiating with their handlers. As they say in my favorite neck of the woods, the block is hot."

With that, Uncle disappeared without revealing what he'd found out. Minutes later, Dafari and I saw his guestroom light come on. No doubt Uncle was washing away the evidence of his trip. I still couldn't get over the fact my brother was allowing his demon daddy to rest in his home. My, my, how things had changed in a matter of weeks.

"I plan to visit the Widows," I said to my brother.

"Does Tasmin know?" he asked.

I sighed then stood. "No, but I need to know how my father convinced Martha to aid him. I need closure just as much as Tasmin does."

My brother studied me for a moment before he nodded once. "Give me a few to shower and change. I'll accompany you."

THIRTY MINUTES LATER, I stood on the Merry Widows' front lawn with my brother and uncle. I hadn't invited him, but he wouldn't be denied front row seats to a good show, as he'd sardonically put it. As the Widows met us on the lawn, I noticed that they stood in a triangle formation same as my uncle, my brother, and me with Martha and my uncle holding point.

While Uncle stood dressed in all black, legs shoulder width apart with hands in his pockets, Martha stood with her staff in her hand dressed in a long, flowing golden dress. Her fro flew wild as the wind whipped it back and forth. Her eyes were trained on my uncle. The cold look in them suggested she was offended he had even stepped foot on her property. Mary Ann and Cara Lee stood in yellow and amber dresses. In their left hands were also their staffs, each of the three carved with Adinkra symbols. A peacock strutted across the yard while a vulture flew overhead.

Uncle chuckled as he eyed the peacock then the vulture. "Interesting," he growled low in his throat. He blinked once, when his eyes opened, they glowed golden.

"Interesting indeed," Martha said. She closed her eyes then opened them. They were a coral color I had never seen before. "Try it at your own risk…Azazel, Prince of Hell," she said.

Uncle grunted but didn't say a word. However, I felt his power spike. I looked to see Martha's sisters' eyes shone whiter than fresh snow. She had also called my uncle by his whole moniker which meant she knew the full extent of his powers. The fact that she and her sisters had invoked a powerful Orisha made note of that.

"One must always call a thing a thing," Martha said then eyed me.

I'd intentionally left my mind open to them as an olive branch. It was to show I had no hidden agenda.

"We come in peace," I said before things could go any further.

"You did. We're not so sure about those two," she said nodding toward Dafari and then Uncle.

"You've known me for years, Martha," Dafari said. "I've never caused you harm nor have I brought any to your door."

"Yes, but we didn't know *that one* was your father."

My brother took a deep breath. "I'm the same being I've always been. You know me."

She watched my brother for a moment then turned to me. "What do you want?"

I decided to cut to the chase. "How did my father get you to go along with his plan?"

"Does Tasmin know you're here?" she asked.

"This isn't about her. I, as Michael's true son, deserve to know how he got you to betray Noreen."

Her sisters turned white eyes to her then back to Dafari and Uncle.

"I don't give the Fallen or his son permission to enter my mind," she said then tapped her staff to the ground seven times. Once she let it go, it hovered just above the ground. Martha moved her hands in tutting moves, and I watched in awe as a glowing, white arc formed over her third eye.

Before I could register that she had made protective Adinkra symbols around she and I, my head slammed back.

I saw Martha talking to Noreen. I couldn't hear them just yet but judging by the aggressive hand gestures as they spoke, I could tell the argument was heated. Both women were noticeably younger, but the wisdom in their eyes belied their true ages. Then their voices faded in…

"Duma-Nolan, Akasha, Silas, and Jewel all agree with me. This is for the best. Elisa is already communicating with Duma-Nolan telepathically. She can hear him speak to her internally

and then respond in her own way. He said her messages to him in his head sound like Morse code. Little Tasmin moves things just by looking at them. They're just babies! Imagine how powerful they will be by seven! We have to clip their powers. In the wrong hands…" Noreen let her words trail off and shook her head as if she couldn't bear the thought.

"I don't think it's a good idea to keep Elisa and Tasmin in the dark, Noreen. Sure, they're babies now, but they will grow up and be clueless as to who and what they are. That could be dangerous and leave them unprotected! What if—"

"There is no what if, Martha," said a voice from the side of the room.

The woman was tall, voluptuous, and dark skinned. A blood red headwrap hid her hair underneath it. Her skin was vibrant, eyes alive with worry, and a radiant power emanated from her that told me she was wholly in touch with her Ancestors. Her nails were long and delicately curved. There were rings on each of her fingers and her feet bare. Her long black skirt brushed the floor as she walked.

"Elisa and Tasmin can in no way know who they are. It would put them in danger," she said.

"They are in more danger if they don't know, Amabelle. The fact that we can't even read their lifelines in their palms attests to that," Martha quipped, slapping the back of one hand in the palm of her other.

"Martha," Noreen snapped. She called the woman's name with a finality that caused Martha to clamp her mouth closed. "It is final. They cannot know! They will never know!"

"That's the end of it, Sister," Amabelle said, her tone, while calm, left no room for doubt. "Their power in the wrong hands is something we can't risk."

The scene faded and seconds later, another one came into view.

"I think we made a mistake," Amabelle said.

She was dressed in an all-white flowing dress, as they all were. Her eyes were sad, and tears threatened to fall. In the background, on top of a mantel, sat a picture of a man and a woman. I saw Elisa in both their features.

Now Noreen paced the floor. "Something's not right. Duma-Nolan should have been able to right his car. He and Akasha are too powerful for a car accident to take them out. They could have traversed that storm."

"Easily," Martha said coming into view.

"What y'all thinking?" Cara Lee asked. She had her staff in her hand and she stood by a window in the small room.

Were they in the basement of the bookstore?

"Martha been told y'all keeping them away from their powers was a mistake," Mary Ann fussed as she waved her hand. "Now look. Perhaps if little Elisa knew of her birthright, she could have used her powers to—"

Mama Nall slammed her hand on the round wooden table. "Don't you dare place the blame of her parents' deaths on her. She's a child! Barely ten years old. What could she have done?"

Mary Ann tempered down her anger. "I'm sorry, Amabelle. That's not what I'm saying. I would never suggest such a thing. I was only saying—"

"She was suggesting that perhaps if little Elisa knew what she was, she could have balanced her parents' powers to help save their lives. That's all," Martha said, defending her sister.

The scene blurred then another came into view.

"What do you mean she has to die?" I saw Martha ask my father.

He wasn't in the flesh, but an aura of white light with only his wings visible. He hadn't come to her in human or true form, but as a bright white celestial light. They were standing at the Gourd near the Ross Farm. Animals sat around them as if they were listening in. Birds of all kinds flew overhead. The grass and leaves on the trees and bushes gently swayed in the wind.

"Just as the One True Son had to sacrifice himself for the greater good, Noreen has to do the same. For if her bloodline gets wind of their true powers, it could mean death and destruction of the world as you know it."

Martha nodded and frowned. "I know—we all suspected this. But…you said no one would be hurt if I just got her to remove her birthright."

"She will not be hurt."

"You said she has to die!"

"Yes, but she will not be hurt."

Martha looked confused and troubled as she paced in front of my father. "I don't want her to die. She has been a great friend and confidante to me and my sisters and the coven. She is like a sister to me. The coven is already fractured with the loss of Amabelle, Duma-Nolan, and my husband. What will we do without Noreen? The town will be vulnerable."

"Do not worry about the town's protection. My wife and I will see to it that no harm comes to Salix Pointe. Noreen Chadwick of the Bloodline Tituba has to die lest she reveal her niece's birthright and true powers. Same as Mama Nall and her son of the Bloodline Leveaux. If those two come into the knowledge of what they are, you know what can and will happen. You have a chance to not only save Salix Pointe, but the world as well."

Martha continued to pace and she wrung her fingers. The woman was conflicted; it was clear by the way her emotions flittered across her face.

"And she won't be in any pain?"

"She will fall asleep and nothing more. Her time here on earth will be no more."

"I'm skeptical of this, Archangel Michael. We've already lost so much…"

"Then let me carry this burden for you, Martha…"

Martha sighed. She slapped away the tears on her cheek then handed my father a small bag. "She'll only drop her guard if you show her this…"

The scene faded before I could see what was in the small bag. I came to just as my uncle threw his jacket off and rolled his shoulders. Dafari's eyes had gone red, and his face enlarged, fangs battle length. His hair grew down his back and his body bulked to inhumane proportions. The wind whipped violently, and the smell of sulfur was so strong it was suffocating.

"Incoming," Mary Ann yelled as she raised her staff above her head with both hands.

Cara Lee stood back-to-back with her sister, her staff angled at a forty-five-degree angle. Martha snatched her staff from its hovering position then held it as if it were a sword.

I rolled my shoulders then ripped my shirt off as my wings wanted release.

"Do not," Uncle shouted. "Do not release your wings!"

As he said that, the earth trembled, and a loud screeching rent the air.

"What in bloody hell is that?" I asked.

"Bats," Uncle snarled. "Bats out of Hell. Do not release your wings no matter how much you feel the need to. They will shred them until they are no more. Full-blooded angels with injured wings from a Hell entity never fully recover."

The screeching got louder as the colony of bats flew toward us. They eclipsed the moon, bringing with them dark shadows like never before. Beady glowing red eyes made a beeline for us. They weren't like any bloody bats I'd ever seen. Their teeth with like canines. The nails on their feet like razor-sharpened talons, and they were as big as Steller's sea eagles.

The first set attacked Uncle. He threw a meaty fist at one, knocking it from the air. He snatched another, then ripped the wings off its body. Dafari fought next to his father, knocking bats out of the air, tearing their wings, then tossing their battered bodies to the ground. I noticed that for some reason, it looked as if they were afraid to fly directly at Uncle but were being forced to. They did attack Dafari like ravenous, mindless zombies though. One dropped down on his back, talons digging into his skin. He reached over his shoulder, ripped the creature from his back then spit in its face. As it fell to the ground, the bat's wings covered it's burning, melting face while it wailed in pain. My brother gave a low chuckle that caused hives to rise on my skin. Fighting next to his father seemed to reinforce his already formidable powers.

Bats flew at me as if my blood called to them. They aimed for my eyes and neck. I knew they were anxious to draw blood which made me regret ripping my shirt off. As I stopped a cloud of bats from my front, another flock attacked my back, causing a burning pain that made me grit my teeth.

"They out for blood, Nephew. Yours specifically," Uncle yelled then chuckled as he snatched a bad midflight.

Did he just put a bat's head in his mouth?

I yelled out when a bat's claws dragged down my back. It took everything in me not to release my wings, take flight and fight them midair.

"I wouldn't do that, Octavian. I know you don't readily trust me, but do trust me on this," Uncle spat.

I had never battled bats out of Hell before, but I surely understood the saying 'running like a bat of Hell', Americans often used. The bats were lightning fast and moved in formation as if they were being controlled by someone or something. As they came at me like rockets, I moved and pivoted in ways that protected my back and front. I clapped my hands twice, formed a white arch then shoved it forward. I watched bats catch fire midflight and fall from the air.

I found myself back-to-back with Martha who used her staff like a sword and a bat. She moved with a swiftness that belied her age, staying in stride with me as we moved left then right, up the middle of the yard then backwards again.

Martha yelled out when a bat's talon raked her cheek. "Son a bitch," she snarled. She tossed her staff in the air then yelled, "Vultures, as given permission by the Orisha Oshun, take flight in our defense!" Electricity crackled around her fingertips as she used the energy to spin her staff and take out bats in our immediate vicinity.

Loud squawking mixed with the screeching of the bats as vultures the size of large monkeys flew toward the cloud of bats. The winged creatures fought midair. Feathers, talons, and bits of flesh falling from the sky.

Cara Lee and Mary Ann worked in tandem, running, leaping, and jumping as bats swarmed them. Like skilled ninjas, they kicked bats away from them with screams of war on their lips. Using tut moves they swatted and slapped bats out of the air as their staffs spun next to them. If I hadn't known these women were in their old age, judging by the way the fought, I would have never guessed it. They mirrored the other's moves in sync as if it were a battle dance.

The more we fought, the more winged hellbeasts seemed to materialize.

"Someone is controlling them," Dafari yelled.

"I tire of this," Uncle growled. Blood dripped down his fangs and lips, showing he had indeed bitten the heads off several bats. He stopped fighting. His body bulked until he was almost his full demon form. Leathery black wings with a seven-foot wingspan sprouted from his back. With a voice booming like thunder, he spat, "Go to Hell."

The ground quaked and the skies thundered. I grabbed Martha back as the earth split beneath our feet. The bats squealed and screeched as they tried to fly away. As if they were fighting some kind of magnetic force, they were pulled down into the fire burning just beneath the cracks of the ground below us.

Before they could all be sucked down, Uncle snatched one out the sky. The bat cried out in a horrible high-pitched scream then covered its face as if it was cowering in front of my uncle. "Show me who sent you."

When he let the creature go, it flew around disoriented before making a beeline in the direction of the mayor's manor.

CHAPTER 7

DAFARI

7:30 PM

"IT HAS TO be that bitch LaLaurie," Father spat. I couldn't be sure if he was spitting in disgust at Madame Marie or to remove bat parts from his mouth. Either way, I found it uncouth and repugnant.

"Yes, I agree," Octavian said. "We must go to the mayor's immediately. This inexcusable attack cannot go unpunished! If she targeted me, she will, unquestionably, go after Tasmin and Elisa!"

The anger on my brother's face was incontrovertible, his eyes turning red as his body began to bulk considerably in size.

My father and I shared knowing glances as we ran over to Octavian, each one of us grabbing him by an arm. Considering the current state he was in, my brother clearly was not in his right mind, and was about to do something he would most assuredly regret.

"I concur, Nephew. However, we cannot allow you to go off half-cocked! You will get yourself killed, and will undoubtedly tip our hand," he shouted as Octavian struggled to release himself from our grasps.

I couldn't believe the words that were about to come out of my mouth, but they needed to be said. "Octavian, Father's right. We need to plan, strategize against this new threat, one that we virtually know nothing about. More to the point, we only know about Madame Marie, the mayor, and this impundulu you mentioned earlier. Who knows what other threats lay in wait for us at the mayor's mansion? This blind quest of yours is sheer folly, and in the end, will leave Elisa and Tasmin without our protection. Is that what you want?"

Evidently, that last bit reached him, as Octavian stopped thrashing about, his size returning to normal. He hunched over, breathing hard, then fell to his knees.

I placed my hand on his shoulder. "I promise you, Brother, we will handle this threat, but only when we are better prepared. Besides, don't you still want the closure you were seeking?"

Octavian's breathing slowly returned to normal, as did his jet-black eyes. Those same eyes showed the palpable fear I knew he was enduring at the thought of losing his beloved Tasmin once again. I understood that pain all too well.

"Thank you, Brother," he said, standing slowly. "Your reasoning is valid, as is yours, Uncle. I just need to compose myself."

The Widows were staring at us, particularly Octavian; the surfacing of his latent demon side was a shock to them. Thanks to my father, my brother had become a loose cannon. He needed to find a way to control himself, lest he become a liability to us all.

"We had no idea you possessed demon blood," Martha said, taking a defensive stance, her sisters following suit.

"Its emergence was…a recent occurrence," my father stated, a sense of pride in his voice and a smug grin on his face.

"This meeting is over," Martha affirmed, the Widows slowly backing away from us.

"No, wait, please!" Octavian pleaded. "I need to know what was in the bag you gave my father, what subterfuge he used in order to get Noreen to lower her guard. Show me that and I promise you, we will trouble you no more."

Other than the sounds of nature, stillness rent the air for several minutes, as it appeared the Widows were in silent contemplation.

"Sister, perhaps you should allow him this last bit of information," Mary Ann said breaking the silence, her steady gaze still on Father, Octavian, and me.

"Yes, I believe he will keep his word," Cara Lee chimed in.

Martha's stance softened a bit. "Fine, but once I provide you with what you've asked, you must leave. You've already brought enough peril to our doorstep. The longer you stay the chances of more danger arriving increases."

My father stepped forward. "Might I remind you that although Tasmin and Elisa are powerful witches, the fact remains they are novices, while you three are powerful old witches, emphasis on *old*. Chances are those bats were not only sent after my nephew, but also the three of you."

"Well, isn't that the pot calling the kettle old, demon prince?" Martha sneered.

"Yes, but at least I look good for my age," Father snapped back, never one to back down from a verbal sparring match.

"Please, you two, we don't have time for the sniping. With all due respect," I said, addressing the Widows, "although rudely spoken, what Father said makes sense. If Madame Marie is aiming to possess the epicenter of magick, she will also look to eradicate all those who guard it."

Martha exhaled, her demeanor relaxing a bit. "You are definitely more eloquent and tactful than that thing that spawned you, Dafari."

"Thank you, I think."

"Sticks and stones, you crone, sticks and stones," Father retorted.

"Your presence is an annoyance, hellspawn, like hemorrhoids. That said we need to wrap this up. As the attack occurred out in the open, Octavian, I propose that we take this into the house. Your brother and the demon prince will have to remain out here."

I stepped forward. "I cannot allow that. You are asking me to trust you with my brother, yet you refuse to extend that trust to me, someone you've known for years. While I understand your need for safety, *I* need to protect my brother. That is non-negotiable. After all, I am my brother's keeper."

"He has been nothing but respectful to us, Martha," Cara Lee noted.

"And Noreen was always fond of him. She was always a good judge of character," Mary Ann added.

Martha studied me hard before saying, "We will allow you into our home, but we will keep this brief."

Wordlessly, Octavian and I followed the Widows inside. The cozy foyer led to a stairwell immediately off to the right and a sitting room to the left. We all followed Martha into the sitting area that looked as if it hadn't been updated since the 1970's. An old olive-colored couch and matching loveseat with plastic furniture covers, as well as an outdated recliner of the same color sat in the room. A cherry mahogany coffee table sat in front of the couch, with a pair of matching end tables on either side. A burnished brass table lamp sat atop each end table.

"Please have a seat, Dafari," Martha said, nodding in the direction of the recliner then taking a position in the center of the room. I sat down, making note of how lumpy the chair was.

Cara Lee and Mary Ann took point on either side of me. *So much for trust.* Martha then motioned for Octavian to stand in front of her. As she did outside, she performed the same ritual with her staff, then she and Octavian appeared to be in trance-like states. After what seemed to be an eternity, they both emerged from wherever she had taken them.

"Thank you, Martha. You've given me everything I need. Dafari, we must go," Octavian said, hurriedly heading toward the front door.

ON THE DRIVE home, Octavian remained silent. I asked him what he had discovered, but all he would say was that he wanted to wait until Elisa and Tasmin were in attendance. For once, Father knew to leave well enough alone. I called Elisa to tell her that due to circumstances, dinner would be pushed back a couple of hours. Although, after the news Octavian and I would share, I doubted either of the ladies would be hungry. She, in turn, let me know that Tasmin would be joining us later, as she and her parents were having a family meeting. I passed the message on to Octavian.

Once we arrived home, I asked Octavian to afford me some time alone with Elisa so I could explain our situation to her in private. He understood. We both needed to explain our separate, yet very intertwined, circumstances individually and then collectively.

While I was anxious to see Elisa, my battle wounds were slowing me down. Although they were healing, Octavian and I still had deep lacerations from our battle with the hellbats, his, by nature of being an angel, taking longer to heal than mine. I showered and dressed gingerly as even water hitting the gashes was quite painful.

Just as I was coming downstairs, I heard the front door open. Although Elisa was no longer residing with me, I allowed her to keep the set of keys that I gave her. I wanted her to know that she was welcomed at any time. When she walked in, I realized at that moment how much I needed her presence. Her thick curly mane was pulled back with a coral headband, highlighting her beautiful facial features. Holding her black leather jacket, I noticed how her coral long-sleeved, quarter zipped shirt hugged her ample bosom. She had it zipped low enough to show just the right amount of cleavage to entice me. Her black fitted jeans accentuated her curvaceous hips, her combat boots that she loved to wear rounding out her attire. My urge to take Elisa had diminished a bit, but only because of the gravity of what Octavian and I needed to discuss with her and Tasmin. I walked up to her, took her face in my hands and kissed her gently on the lips.

"So you're not mad at me anymore?" she asked.

I wrapped my arms around her, held her tightly. "No. I realize that, although you are becoming quite proficient, you've still only recently come into powers, some of which are more difficult to master than others. However, while I'm no longer angry with you, you might be angry with me after our discussion."

She pulled back a bit, a look of confusion on her face.

"There is something I've wanted…no, *needed* to tell you for quite some time; the right moment never seemed to present itself."

Elisa's brows furrowed and she cast a nervous glance in my direction. "Sounds serious."

I took her by the hand, leading her to the living room. I sat down on the expansive sectional, motioning for Elisa to join me. I looked into her beautiful brown eyes; eyes that I had stared into time and time again over the decades. I never tired of gazing into them.

"When I…snapped at you earlier for entering my mind, there was a reason."

"Dafari, I really didn't mean—"

"I know," I said, stopping her mid-sentence. "I wasn't saying that to chastise you, Elisa. It's because I didn't want you to see what I was hiding." While I didn't want Elisa to 'see' our time together in the past, my gut told me there was something I also didn't want to remember.

Her shoulders stiffened as if she was waiting for the other shoe to drop. "Why not?"

"Because I honestly didn't know how you would take it. It's yet another unexpected occurrence that you could not see coming."

"What…is it?" she asked, hesitancy in her voice.

"It's better that I show you," I said, taking her hands in mine. "I'm allowing you access to my mind."

She tensed up a bit, looking unsure.

"Elisa, it's okay, I'm inviting you in. Just use the lessons I've taught you."

"O-okay, but I passed out back at your office."

"Then make yourself comfortable," I said.

Elisa turned around, placing her head on my lap. She took one of my hands, interlocking her fingers with mine. She then closed her eyes. "I'm ready," she affirmed.

I opened my mind to her, giving her unfettered access to my memories; some of which brought me unimaginable joy, while others, incomprehensible pain. Elisa's grip on my hand tightened as she saw what I saw; our two lifetimes and the events that brought us together, and those that tore us apart. Once the memory flashes ended, Elisa sat up with a start.

"Oh my Loa," Elisa said in barely a whisper. "What was that?"

"What did you see?" I asked.

"I-I saw us, bu-but it couldn't be, because it appeared to be in the past. I mean, it could be you, because you're three-hundred years old, but not me. These…scenes appeared, and they seemed to be from two different movies. One was set in the days of slavery, and the other in the 1940's or 1950's. Tasmin and Octavian were in some of the scenes, and I also saw some children. Dafari, what's going on?"

I sighed deeply. There was so much that needed to be explained to her, and yet, I feared overwhelming Elisa with too much, too soon.

"Yes, it was me, but it was also you, as well as Octavian, Tasmin, and…our children."

"*Our* children? How is that even possible? How is *any* of it possible?"

"There is so much to explain."

"I have so many questions—"

"I know, and it's completely understandable. I will do my best to tell you everything you want to know to the best of my ability. However, I think it would be best if Octavian and Tasmin were here for some of this conversation," I said.

"Okay, but I need to know, how is it me, how is it Tasmin? And how is it that we end up married to you and Octavian in both time periods?"

"To answer your first question, you may not believe this, but you and Tasmin are reincarnated souls. The fact that you end up as the same beings speaks to how special you two are. Your powers are needed, no matter the era. As to why we are always coupled, Octavian and I are still theorizing about that. It could be as simple as we all have lessons to learn, or the reasons could be more complex." I lowered my head, took a moment before continuing. "Regardless, every time I lose you, it is always painful, as I know losing Tasmin is for Octavian. It was especially painful for both of us the first time."

"That's why his vernacular is stuck in the past, right?"

"Yes, and that is why he is so determined to safeguard Tasmin at all costs."

"Dafari, what happened to him? What happened to Tasmin?"

"That, Elisa, is not my story to tell. Octavian can share his tale, but only when he's ready."

"And why was that time so painful for you?" she asked, placing a hand on mine.

"As my emotional wounds are linked to my brother's, I prefer to wait for him, if you don't mind."

"Fair enough, I'll respect that," she replied, her eyes reflecting sympathy. "In that case, our children, tell me about them."

Few things in life gave me pure joy, among them being with Elisa and our children. "We had a son, Zafer, and a daughter, Safiya. They were born two years apart. Zafer was very much like you; strong-willed and passionate, a real fighter. Safiya, she took after me."

"Broody and bossy," she said then chuckled.

It actually made me smile in turn. I had to admit to myself, that was a rare feat for me.

"I prefer reserved and assertive. She was also fiercely protective of those she cared about."

"She definitely sounds very much like her father. She sounded like a wonderful young lady."

"They were both wonderful children."

"Did they have…powers?"

"Yes, they did. Zafer could project realistic illusions, while Safiya could communicate and bond with animals."

"She really was her father's daughter, and Zafer—"

"His mother's son."

We sat quietly for a few minutes. I wanted to provide Elisa with the opportunity to absorb what I had shared with her so far. I was surprised at how well she was taking my news. Perhaps she was in shock and there would be a delayed reaction later on. As I was about to provide her with a bit more information, the doorbell rang.

"I'll get it," Octavian yelled, already walking toward the foyer.

It took some time for Octavian and Tasmin to get to the living room. I assume it was because my brother was greeting her.

"Hey guys," Tasmin said, joining us on the sectional, studying our faces. "You all seem so...intense. The energy coming off you all is almost overwhelming. What did I miss?"

"Let's just say it's been a very trying day, to say the least," I responded.

"Indeed, brother. We have much to discuss with both of you," Octavian added, sitting next to Tasmin.

"Okay, so spill."

"Well for starters, I had planned to visit the Merry Widows in order to find out how my father convinced Martha to help him. I intended on making the trek alone, but Dafari insisted on accompanying me, and Uncle made himself an unwanted observer. However, as much as I hate to admit it, his unwanted presence once again probably saved my life."

"Demon Daddy? How so?" Tasmin asked.

"Hellbats," I broke in. "We were attacked while Octavian was conferring with the Widows."

"Yes, and had it not been for my uncle, I probably would have fared far worse than I did. As it stood, I only suffered some extensive gashes."

"Wait, you got hurt?" a clearly distressed Tasmin asked.

"Yes, but I will heal—"

"Octavian, let me see. What good is my healing ability if I can't use it?"

"How in the world did those two stay together the way they go at it?" Elisa thought to me.

"I had oftentimes wondered that myself. Then again, my brother generally acquiesced to Tasmin's wishes when it came to matters as such. You know the adage; 'happy wife, happy life'."

True to form, Octavian gave in to Tasmin, allowing her to see his wounds, which she promptly healed.

"Dafari was hurt as well," Octavian voiced.

"Stoolpigeon," I replied, scowling at him.

"I didn't want you to feel left out, dear old brother," he shot back.

Elisa stood, placing her hands on her full hips. "Oh, so you want to be all manly and not tell me you were hurt too, Dafari?"

I looked up at her then rubbed my palms down my face. "That was not my intention. I merely felt we had more pressing matters to address."

I already knew where any further discussion would lead; therefore, I allowed Tasmin to also heal me. Truth be told, I did feel better. Once Tasmin had completed her task, Octavian began to share with the women what he saw and heard during his mind meld with Martha.

"Tasmin, Elisa, there are some things that I am about to tell you that you may find difficult to hear, and I share no pleasure in relaying this information; however, we feel it is in your best interest to know."

Octavian recounted in detail all he had learned; the families knowing that Elisa and Tasmin had powers from infancy and how they clipped said powers so they would be none the wiser, as well as the coven's meeting after the murders of

Elisa's parents, save for the part about Elisa possibly being able to balance her parent's powers in order to save their lives. She had carried much trauma surrounding their deaths. The last thing she needed was to add unwarranted guilt. He then filled them in on Martha's collusion with Michael, and how he was able to get so close to Noreen. The looks on Tasmin and Elisa's faces were a combination of shock and outrage.

"So you're telling us that our families knew the entire time and that my own parents lied to my face when they said they didn't know I had powers?" Tasmin appeared as if she was about to have a conniption.

Octavian placed his arm around Tasmin's shoulders in an attempt to comfort her. "I'm sorry, but yes, that appears to be the case."

"And you actually believe Martha, in light of all she's done? How do you even know those memories were real? She did make herself and her sisters look like innocent bystanders where our powers were concerned, after all," Elisa countered, clearly agitated.

"Martha may have been deceptive with regards to Noreen Chadwick's murder, but I sensed no such subterfuge with the information she shared. While your skepticism is completely understandable, perhaps what I tell you next will convince you that she speaks the truth."

Octavian recounted how my uncle told Martha that preventing the ladies' powers from manifesting would save Salix Pointe and possibly the world. He also spoke of the bag Martha gave Michael, the very bag used to make Noreen drop her guard.

"Did the bag have Adinkra symbols on it?" Tasmin inquired.

"Why yes. In fact, it was a purple velvet bag with the Adinkra symbols Akoma Ntoso symbolizing linked hearts,

Me Ware Wo symbolizing commitment and promise—I shall marry you— and Gye Nyame, God's protection, embroidered with pink thread."

"Let me guess, inside the bag were crystals, flower petals, and a small piece of paper."

"How do you know all of that?" I questioned.

Tasmin stood up, walking back and forth in front of us. "I remember that bag well. The crystals were rose quartz, black tourmaline, and selenite. The flowers' petals had significant meanings; forget-me-nots representing true love, primrose symbolizing our love is eternal, and stock meaning you'll always be beautiful to me. On the paper were the words '*No matter how far apart we are, you will always have my heart, my love, my loyalty. Forever yours, Adofo*'. Aunt Noreen always kept that bag close. She said that Doctor Ange-Diable had given it to her on their seventh anniversary. She cherished it. Then one day, just like Doc, it disappeared."

"Question is why would Martha have it, and why would she give it to Michael?" Elisa asked.

"I didn't have time to ascertain that. Perhaps, you can ask Martha those questions when you finally speak to her, Tasmin. Although I am in no way justifying her actions, she appeared to be extremely conflicted regarding her participation in your aunt's murder," Octavian said.

"And yet, she still helped your father. Screw her being conflicted. In my book she's just as guilty as he is," Tasmin spat angrily then turned to face me. "Dafari, I owe you an apology. Before I really knew you, I actually thought you had something to do with Doctor Ange-Diable's disappearance. For that, I'm sorry."

"No apology is necessary. The timing of his disappearance and my arrival in Salix Pointe could be viewed as suspect."

Octavian joined Tasmin, pacing as he oftentimes did when he was deep in thought. "Has anyone noticed the striking parallels between my brother and the missing doctor? They are both veterinarians. Doctor Ange-Diable was involved with a powerful witch, as is Dafari. Also, based on his last name, I suspect that Doctor Ange-Diable was a half angel-half demon, just like Dafari. It's as if the doctor's disappearance and my brother's arrival were pre-ordained."

It appeared that Octavian was on to something. "Suppose you are correct in your assessment of the situation, little brother. Why would someone go to the trouble of eliminating Noreen's paramour, save to make her vulnerable, but lure me to Salix Pointe knowing that I would protect Elisa with my life?"

"It is a conundrum indeed, one that I intend to explore further."

"I still can't believe our families lied to us. Makes me wonder what else they were hiding," Elisa said, getting up and walking toward the bar. She poured herself two fingers of rum, drinking it in one gulp, indicating how distressed she was.

"Do you think it's wise to tell them about their familial relationship at this moment? Elisa is still digesting everything, and you still have yet to speak with Tasmin," I thought to Octavian.

He didn't have the opportunity to respond before we heard, "Oh look, a party, and I wasn't invited."

"Father, please, we are in the middle of something."

"One would think I'd get some gratitude after helping out tonight, but noooo, I'm always the outcast," he said feigning hurt.

Elisa and Tasmin rolled their eyes, and Elisa sucked her teeth.

"Ah, my favorite barista, or should I say bartender? Pour me a drink, would you?"

"Pour it yourself," Elisa shot back.

My father simply smiled at her then chuckled. That laugh was so maniacal it actually sent a chill down my spine. As he watched her intently, I saw Elisa grip the edge of the bar then stumble as if she was going to pass out. I ran over to her, grasping her arm to steady her.

"Uncle, I think it would be best that you leave," Octavian said, walking in his direction.

"Why?" he asked, with a not-so-innocent shrug. "I did nothing wrong. Maybe she had a power flux or something. She is still learning her powers."

"Uncle—"

"Fine, I will take me leave. Good night, tart maker," he said, bowing in Elisa's direction. He then looked at Tasmin saying, "Good night, vestal virgin…for now." He once again chuckled and looked at Octavian.

"What…how…," Tasmin started in disbelief, lunging toward my father, causing Octavian to place himself between the two of them.

"Father, leave. *Now!*" I commanded.

He once again gazed from Elisa to Tasmin before disappearing into a shadow.

Octavian was still trying to quell her fury when I stated, "Tasmin, I apologize for Father's disrespectful behavior. I assure you, he will be…dealt with, but right now, we have more important matters to tackle."

Despite my words to Tasmin, I was keenly aware that I needed to keep a very close watch on my father.

CHAPTER 8
ELISA

9:15 PM

"**T**ASMIN, PLEASE, CALM yourself and sit down. There is more I need to tell you," Octavian said as he ushered Tasmin back to the sofa once Demon Daddy had taken his shadowed leave. "Elisa, you sit, too. I want this all out in the open. I find myself annoyed with all these secrets that need to be exposed."

Octavian removed his shirt once more. I watched in curiosity as he rolled his sculpted golden shoulders then turned his neck from side to side as if what he was about to reveal had been heavy on him.

Tasmin quirked a brow. She glanced from me to Dafari then back to Octavian. "More secrets?"

"Yes, Poppet. With all that is going on, it's best we put everything all out in the open, for if we continue this route, we will waste precious time needed to defeat that old hag and her minions. So, yes, more secrets. I suspect Dafari has already told Elisa and shown her some things. It's my time to do the same with you, and as our lives are interconnected, it's best I do it now."

"Are you sure you want Elisa and me here with you for this part, Brother?" Dafari asked Octavian.

"Yes. We all should get it out in the open." He took Tasmin's hands in his then turned his solemn gaze to hers. "You and I have a history that spans time. We have loved one another centuries over and back again."

Tasmin glance over at me as if to see if I was just as confused as she was, then back at Octavian once more. "You're not making any sense," she said.

"Tasmin, for once, be silent and let me finish explaining," he said.

She flinched like he had all but physically assaulted her. The slow blink she gave afterwards told she was as taken aback as I was stunned. I hadn't heard Octavian take that tone with her since he had been in Salix Pointe, so he must have been in a frame of mind that said he meant business and would pull no punches. His brows were furrowed and his face set in a hard scowl that softened with each breath he took.

I found myself wondering if he would rush through telling Tasmin as Dafari had done with me. I had so many questions and my mind was all over the place. However, I felt Dafari had been holding back. I hadn't been able to aptly express my thoughts in the moment. I'd been so overwhelmed, but there was something missing from his trip down memory lane with me. It had felt hurried, and I didn't like it.

I mean, I enjoyed hearing about our children and seeing the flashes of our times past, but…something was off. Why didn't Dafari go into more detail? Was it not important? Was I not important enough to warrant more of a thorough explanation and journey through time?

"You and I met when you were fairly young. You were all of seventeen summers and I was of the same human years, but being that I was, and am, an immortal, I was far older than you in angel terms. Still…it was around 1833 when I started courting you—"

"Excuse me?" Tasmin blurted out loudly. "What-what are you even saying? 1833? What?" Her face was a shroud of confusion as she looked at Octavian as if he had sprouted heads from his shoulders.

He soldiered on as if her outburst hadn't bothered or deterred him. "Dafari and I met you and Elisa as you were raising hell at an American Anti-Slavery Society meeting that was being held in Louisiana at the time. It was one of the first of its kind. You were feminists long before white women overtook the movement and made it about them. Of course, it wasn't called feminism back then. Still, you and Elisa were highly upset that no women had been invited to sit on the board. The meeting was held in secret. Mr. Garrison didn't want to risk the meeting being overrun by white slavers afraid of another uprising. It had been two years since the Nat Turner Rebellion. Dafari and I still mourned our fallen friend at times, but he had refused to go along with our plan. He had grown tired of the mistreatment of Black people, and in his anger, our good friend Nat signed his own death warrant."

As he spoke, I could tell when he opened his mind to Tasmin. Her eyes widened, her mouth dropped open, and she slapped a hand over it to quell the screech that was about to come out.

"During that time Dafari and I had our marching orders so to speak. We were on a mission, but there I was—there we were—courting two young freedom fighters, who happened to be powerful witches. At the time, New Orleans was your home. You and Elisa were slaves on the Williams Plantation.

It always amazed Dafari and I that you and Elisa were so powerful that you could project your images in places where you were not. Together, you and Elisa were practically unstoppable. But because of how your kind were burned, lynched, and even outright murdered, you were careful not to share or show your powers to many."

Dafari said, "Elisa immediately picked up on what we were back then. During that time, you two were in your prime and it was easy for you to *see* us, if you know what I mean. You two were hellcats in your own right. You caused storms to kill crops. Made overseers go mad. Caused accidents with wagons and horses so children wouldn't be sold away from their mothers. Minty loved you two…"

"Minty as in Harriet Tubman?" I asked.

Dafari and Octavian nodded. However, Octavian never took his eyes off Tasmin. It was then that I noticed they were cocooned in some kind of clear glowing dome. Tasmin looked around in awe as if memories were playing before her. It was then that I understood… he was protecting her…

"By 1835, Tasmin, we were wed, and you were carrying our daughter, Attalah. Dafari and I had intentionally gotten ourselves caught and enslaved as you and Elisa refused to leave your family and friends. You felt to run would leave them unprotected, just as it would the other families on surrounding plantations whom you protected. You and Elisa made life tolerable for a lot of people back then. By 1850, as allies to Minty, you helped even more escape up north. However, some didn't want to be saved. They were too afraid or far too brainwashed. By the time you had given birth, yours and Elisa's powers had set off a beacon and awakened every magickal being around. Some good, some so evil even Hell wouldn't take them."

A tear slid down Tasmin's cheek as she watched with wide eyes. It was then that I knew why Octavian had taken his shirt off. I watched as his wings slowly unfurled. He beamed with an ethereal light that surrounded the room and casted a warm glow.

"By 1852, we had been through a lot, seen more, and survived some things that would have killed most. The Fugitive Slave Act of 1850 almost ripped us apart. You two were caught in a sticky wicket thereabouts. We had been helping Minty so much that you and Elisa were almost caught. You two were weak from a particularly gruesome journey. If it hadn't been for Zafer projecting your images in the sugarcane fields, you two would have been accused of slave stealing. As it was, Elisa's children were powerful and Zafer was a master at illusions even at such a young age. The man who said you two were stealing his slaves was thought to be a nutter, as Master Williams vouched that you two had been under his watchful eye all day long."

Dafari stood with his arms folded across his chest. "Later that night, Octavian and I helped most of that man's slaves escape. We also scared him nearly to death. When he awakened the next morning, he told all who would listen about two nigger males with wings and glowing eyes who came and stole away his slaves. Zafer was able to project his slaves with torn limbs and ripped bodies scattered about his property as Safiya caused all of his dogs to go crazy. Most thought his hounds had gotten loose, attacked, and killed his slaves."

"Attalah foresaw this happening. She was a seer. She was so powerful that she often overloaded on her powers and had to lie down. Her headaches were frequent. She was headstrong, same as you," Octavian told Tasmin. "With her guidance, you and Elisa often led runaways to safe locations. I was at constant war with you and our daughter about your shenanigans. You two were a handful, but you were my handful, and I loved you dearly. Together we made many friends, but we also made enemies. Someone whom we thought was a friend, betrayed us... Attalah had been ill, and we didn't know why. It was as if her third eye had been clouded and she couldn't see. Still, she wanted to help her friend's family. Whomever betrayed us told patty rollers of our plans to help the family escape north. Because of that, you and our only child were captured and lynched in 1855... You were ambushed as you snuck onto the property..."

I saw that Tasmin was witnessing the whole thing as she was outright sobbing by then. Octavian's wings wrapped around her as he pulled her against his bare chest.

"We never found out who it was because of Octavian's grief..."

"What do you mean?" I asked Dafari.

It was Octavian who answered. "I was supposed to meet you at a certain location. I had been anxiously awaiting your arrival as you were about twenty minutes late. I calmed my nerves and figured you two had just gotten sidetracked and had to stop for a bit. It had happened before, and you hadn't reached out to me... but then I heard the dogs. There shouldn't have been any dogs because we thought we had only told those we could trust. That was when I realized that a dark warlock had been in our midst.

He used a sort of blinding spell that I wasn't used to. It was as if it had me trapped in some kind of invisible force. Elisa had been given the wrong directions and a confounding curse had been placed on her, which meant Dafari had also been led astray, as he was with her. I found myself alone and imprisoned in a forcefield that I had no inkling of how to counter. I felt your panic, felt your pain. I felt Attalah's fear and grief. I saw them, through your eyes, rip your dresses from your bodies and fondle both of you as they strung you up... Your pain was so palpable, Tasmin, that it caused me to nearly go blind with rage. It wasn't until you called out to me that whatever spell the warlock had cast on me broke…"

Dafari dropped his arms and looked at me. There was something in his eyes I couldn't read, but it looked as if there was shame. *What did he have to be ashamed of?*

"That was when he flew to where she and Attalah had been captured, but he was too late. When he got there, they had already been murdered. He saw his wife and daughter swinging by their broken necks and he could do nothing, nothing to save them. It drove him mad to know he could have prevented their deaths but hadn't been able to. Right there, I saw my brother lose his God-given mind, only I had no idea that the worst was yet to come. I had to get my wife and children to safety as the bounty hunters and slavers were coming for us— for them— next. I ripped a hole between our worlds and shoved you and our children through it. I thought…I thought I would have time…I didn't think…" He stopped, licked his lips then took a deep breath. "I'm sorry," he said, voice grave.

"Sorry? Sorry for what? What happened?" I asked.

"I went on a murderous rage," Octavian said. "I slaughtered every human in sight…those guilty and…those innocent. I set the entire plantation on fire, and it was holy fire. The fire that mere water cannot douse. It burned everything in its wake…"

"I got as many slaves off the planation as I could, set them on a course for north then ran back to save my brother from himself, but it was too late. No ordinary human is supposed to ever see us in true form unless they are crossing over. He had violated supernatural law. It threw things off balance. Uncle Gabriel almost blew his horn…Chaos ensued."

Octavian turned wet black eyes to me. "I'm sorry, Elisa," he said.

I felt my anger rising and I didn't know why. *Why were they apologizing to me? What had they done?* My fingertips burned and my gut clenched. "For what?" I yelled. "Sorry for what?"

Just then, I heard the wind howl outside the window. My eyes burned as tears wet my cheeks. I grabbed at my stomach as it hollowed out and it felt as if someone was twisting my gut in a tightfisted vice-like grip. *Why on earth was I crying and what was I feeling?* Sweat pooled on my temples and my breathing became erratic.

"I didn't know," Dafari said. "When my brother caused a sort of Hell on earth… he had to be punished and was to be sent into the pits of Hell for his affront. However, my little brother is full angel. There was no way I was going to have him sent to a prison down there. No way. He wouldn't have survived with his pure blood. So, I took the blame. I sent him away, put my supernatural marker all over the carnage and took the fall. I was sentenced to seven years hard labor in a supernatural prison on the 7th Level of Hell."

"We were of the impression that seven years in Hell meant seven years on earth," Octavian said.

"We were wrong," Dafari added.

The same look of shame in Dafari's eyes was in Octavian's. "Seven years in a prison of Hell meant seventy-seven years here on earth…"

As soon as the words left his mouth, a jolt of pain coiled my gut. I clenched forward, fell to my knees and then onto floor until I was in a fetal position…And it all came rushing back to me…

"I thought it was only to be seven years," I cried to Octavian, wringing my hands.

Instinctively, I knew it was 1862. The United States was in the middle of a civil war. I was out west with my children in Indian Territory, as they used to call it. It was where Octavian had taken us after Tasmin and Attalah had been lynched. He had surmised it was the safest place for us to be.

The ground was muddy, and the air smelled of incoming rain. Safiya and I had been doing the wash. Lye burned my hands, but I didn't care. We had taken on the job of laundering clothes in the surrounding territory to make extra coin. When Dafari had been abruptly snatched away, all of his earthly holdings and possessions had been taken as well. I had refused to take anything from Octavian. I'd been just that angry with him.

We had been waiting anxiously for Dafari's release. But when he hadn't been set free close to the end of that year, we knew something was wrong. I feared that maybe he had been killed. Perhaps his time in Hell had caused his death or…something. Octavian had gone through to the other side to see if maybe Dafari had been sent there…only to find that wasn't the case. I had been grieving for years. Grieving the loss of Tasmin and Attalah. Anxious for my husband's release and now this?

"I, too, was under the impression that it was to be seven years, but…I'm told that time down there means eleven times more here…"

I felt the bottom of my stomach hollow out. Did that mean that he was to be gone for seventy-seven years? "No, no," I cried. "No! I don't understand. He took the fall for you! Can't you do something?"

Octavian stood before me, looking just as dumfounded as I was hurt. "I didn't know… I didn't comprehend it to mean my brother would be gone for seventy-seven earthly years because of me…"

I saw myself screaming, yelling, and lashing out at Octavian. I had lost too much. Too much… I couldn't take it. I hit, I swung, I slapped, and I kicked at him until I was fading into another scene…

I was yet again crying, in pain…and I felt as if I was reliving it in real time. It was 1864. Black Union soldiers set a long, *rectangular wooden box down in front of me. Inside was my only son. He had gone off to fight for the North as he couldn't deal with his father being gone and possibly never coming back in his lifetime. My gut had told me Zafer would not be coming back to me alive. No matter how many charms and talisman I gave him. I felt that perhaps I was at fault for his death. I had cursed magick and had refused to use it for some time.*

By then, he had looked identical to his father. Tall, dark, handsome, and sinewy with muscle. His golden eyes had lost their twinkle years before. He had refused to marry or get a woman with child as he was afraid of losing them. To see him lying there in a pine box broke me… and I felt double the pain. I felt as if I had relived losing my husband again…only this time, it was my son.

There Octavian was again, holding me, trying to console me as my daughter knelt beside her brother's casket, rubbing his face, speaking and singing to him as if he would respond, as if he could hear her. I cursed the Most High. Cursed the powers that had been bestowed upon me and my children. I cursed Octavian. I blamed him yet again. If it hadn't been for him, none of this would have happened! What use was it having powers? What was the use of my son having his father's blood when he was still mortal? I was inconsolable. I was lost in pain…

The scene faded… It was seven years later…Now Safiya was missing. I'd known that from the moment the scene came into view. It was as if my subconsciousness had awakened. She had walked into the woods one night with a small wicker basket in the crease of her arm and had never come back. A search had been mounted, led by Octavian for seven days and seven nights. I saw him and other mounted men on horses as they rode up and down the plains, searching. I saw them in the woods with lanterns, yelling and calling for her.

As I sat, broken down, in an old rocker on my porch, I knew she was never coming back. My last child was gone. All that had been left behind was the shawl her father had once given her... She hadn't been the same since her brother had been killed. Neither had I. In the end, I thought that maybe her grief had killed her as it had threatened to do me.

My family was being punished for Octavian's crimes. I banished him from my land, from my life. I wished death upon him that would not come. So I cursed him to live with the pain of knowing he had been the reason his brother's children suffered such horrible fates. My sanity escaped me... My journey from the earthly plain came years later, five years before Dafari was released from his supernatural prison.

I snapped back to the present with a large gulp of air as if I had been drowning. Pain still wracked my body. I heard Dafari calling my name. I felt when he cradled me in his arms. There was panic in his voice as he held me close. I couldn't stop shaking. Where was my daughter? Where had she gone?

"Sa-Safi-Safiya...mi-missing," I said through chattering teeth. "Za-Zafer...de-dead. H-how?"

I shivered as if I was cold, but my body was hot.

"You have to move away from her, Brother," Octavian said.

"No," Dafari growled.

"You must. She is coming into her reawakening. By God, man, did you not take the time to ease her into it and protect her mental while doing so?"

Octavian was standing over me. By rote I turned my head to search out Tasmin. She was lying on the sofa, hands resting one over the other on her stomach. She looked to be in a peaceful sleep. How was it that she wasn't hurting? Pain raced through my body like jolts of sharp electricity. I heard myself scream from somewhere in my head.

"I didn't have time," Dafari yelled, still holding on to me.

"Are you mental? Get away from her," Octavian bellowed. "You're making it worse. You bloody well know this!"

My back arched violently, and my fingers splayed so wide it felt as if tendrils of fire were lacing through each one. As Octavian dragged Dafari away from me, I reached out for him…I needed the pain to stop, and only he knew how to end it.

"Please," I cried as hot tears escaped the corners of my eyes.

Dafari tried to break out of his brother's hold. Octavian had to use his arms and wings to keep Dafari away from me. "No, you bloody fool. You'll kill her. Let her come out of it naturally."

"She's in pain!"

"That is your fault for not handling her with care!"

Just as he said that my vision blurred, my heartbeat stopped, and my body floated from the floor…Blackness overtook my senses.

CHAPTER 9

TASMIN

10:15 PM

"ELISA!" I SAID, jolted from my forced slumber. Octavian had put me into an involuntary sleep; I suppose to give my mind time to acclimate to the emotional roller coaster he had put me on. But Elisa's physical and mental cries for help woke me sooner than expected. I sat up slowly, only to see her body...levitating! *What in the world was happening?*

I struggled to find my voice, but eventually found the words. "Octavian? Dafari? Why is Elisa in the air?"

They both turned around, a look of pure terror in their eyes.

Octavian ran over to me. "Tasmin, you should be resting."

"Do you really expect me to rest at a time like this?" I asked swinging my legs around then placing my feet on the floor. "Elisa needs help. She's in pain, but at the same time, I feel as if she's slipping away. Why are you two doing nothing?"

Dafari's head dropped as if in defeat. "There is nothing Octavian and I can do. If either of us touches her, we can do more harm than good. I should have prepared her better, but there just wasn't enough time."

"So you're just going to leave her there?" I looked from one to the other, completely baffled by their inaction.

"Tasmin, did you not hear my brother?" Octavian barked. "There is nothing we can do. We must wait this out."

Although my legs felt like wet noodles after a long run, I stood up slowly, attempting to walk over Elisa. "Maybe there's nothing either one of you can do, but I'm surely going to try."

Octavian blocked my path.

"Move," I said as calmly as I could muster.

He firmly held his stance. "I will not allow you to put yourself or Elisa in danger."

"You won't *allow* me?" I felt my palms starting to burn then my hands began to glow. "Octavian, I swear, if you don't get out of my way, so help me, I will blast you. I mean it."

"You would really do that, Poppet?" A shocked expression was on his face.

"You're darn right I would, and you know I can do it. The first time I did it was accidental; this time wouldn't be. Now please, Octavian, let me pass."

"Brother, please," Dafari begged, despair in his voice.

Octavian spread his arms, stepping to the side. I walked over to Elisa as fast as my legs would carry me. Luckily, she was hovering low enough for me to grab her shirt with one hand and a pant leg with the other. I pulled her gently to the floor. Assessing her, I quickly ascertained that she wasn't breathing and didn't have a pulse. I placed my hands on her chest, closed my eyes and concentrated in an attempt to heal her. I felt the energy course from my body to hers. It took some time, but I was able to get her heart started again. Yet, something wasn't right. She should have woken up immediately, but she didn't.

"Come on, Elisa. Wake up," I said aloud.

"It's not that simple, Tasmin," Octavian said.

"What do you mean?"

"You've healed her physically, but mentally…emotionally… the damage was far worse," Dafari chimed in. "In my haste to alleviate myself of my guilt for seven years of subterfuge, I failed Elisa, failed to shield her, protect her from the on-slaught of memories that bombarded her. It was too much for her psyche to process all at once. I should have done a better job of guiding her through this process." The tears that refused to fall from his eyes showed me the anguish that Dafari was feeling.

"There is plenty of guilt to go around." Octavian placed a supportive hand on his shoulder.

"There's got to be more I can do," I challenged, shifting my position so that I was closer to her head. I took my palms, placing them on her temples.

"Tasmin, no," I heard Octavian yell.

I had felt intense pain when all my memories came flood-ing back to me, but it was nothing compared to what I was now experiencing. All of Elisa's agony was transferred to me, as were the harsh recollections she endured. I felt her immeasurable suffering when she found out Dafari had taken Octavian's place for what she thought would be a seven-year stint in Hell after Attalah and I were murdered, only for her to go through even greater devastation when it was revealed that he was to be punished for over seven decades. Then to lose both her children; it broke her in every way imaginable. I screamed involuntarily at the misery I experienced on her behalf.

"Octavian, her eyes…" That was the last thing I heard before my entire reality changed.

"Tasmin?"

I blinked a few times, acclimating myself to my surroundings. At first, I saw nothing but blinding white light. Then, as my vision began to come into focus, I saw her running toward me, dressed in a long, flowing white summer dress with flat, strappy white sandals on her feet. Her thick hair was braided into a goddess braid updo. We appeared to be in a garden, replete with flowers of all kinds. It even had the smells of fresh flowers.

"Elisa?" We hugged each other then I asked, "Are you…am I…are we…"

"Dead? No," she replied, alleviating my fears. "You're in my head."

"Like when Demon Daddy attacked you."

"Exactly like that."

She took me by the hand, leading me to a gazebo lined with lavender, lilacs, roses, and baby's-breath. Taking a seat on a black wrought iron bench, she motioned for me to sit next to her. We sat quietly for several minutes, taking in the garden's beauty and serenity. As much as I didn't want to, I finally broke the silence.

"How are you feeling?" I asked.

She looked at me. Although she wasn't doing well in the physical world, in this realm, she looked fit as a fiddle.

"I…honestly don't know. I mean, how am I supposed to react to the fact that I was married to a half angel-half demon twice in an almost two-hundred-year span? Not to mention we had two children. And then there are the circumstances surrounding Dafari's imprisonment. I know Dafari is Octavian's older brother, and he felt the need to protect him, but what about his family? I lost my husband for seventy-seven long, hard years, and our children lost their father. Hell, because of Octavian's actions, I lost my entire family."

I couldn't argue with that. Elisa had lost everything and everyone she loved because of Octavian, and I didn't how she was going to reconcile that. I only felt her pain and it was horrific; she had actually lived that nightmare.

"I don't even know what to say except I am so sorry, Elisa. I can't even begin to imagine what you went through back then."

"What about you?"

"What about me?" I queried.

"Come on, Tasmin. You were blindsided too. How are you feeling?"

I stood up, walking around the gazebo in circles. "I still can't believe that Octavian and I were married and had a daughter. Truth be told, and this may sound ridiculous, I'm angry; angry with Octavian, with whomever sold me and our daughter Attalah down the river, and with those lecherous murdering, racist bastards who molested then killed us. This entire situation makes me angry."

"I don't find it ridiculous at all. I find it normal. I'm angry with Dafari. I have known him for seven years, seven long years, and not once did he lead on about our past together. And then bam! He dropped that bomb on me all at once. Who does that? At least it only took you a few weeks to learn the truth, not that I'm trying to marginalize your plight, mind you."

"I know you're not, and I agree with you; seven years is a very long time, to humans like us anyway." I paused, looking around as if checking to make sure no one could hear us, even though I knew that wasn't the case. "Despite them sharing those memories, there's still so much we don't know about either of them. I couldn't believe that Octavian killed innocents. I understand grief, and he suffered tremendously, but to kill those who were blameless? I guess even angels can have mental breakdowns. That side of him…scares me. And now, with Demon Daddy's blood coursing through his veins…it just makes me wary."

"You don't think Octavian would hurt you, do you?"

"No, no, not at all," I spoke quickly. "But we both saw how he reacted during the battle with his parents, not to mention this morning when we tried to go to the bookstore. Any threat to those he cares about—"

"Especially you," Elisa interjected.

"Yes, especially me, triggers him. And that's what worries me. I don't want to see him go down that dark path again." I sat back down next to Elisa, waiting to hear what she had to say. Instead, she just smirked at me.

"What?"

"And it only took Octavian letting you see your past together for you to admit you have feelings for him."

"I admit nothing," I said then chuckled lightly. "Besides, whatever it is I'm feeling, he already knows, not because of anything I said though. So much was going on earlier I didn't get a chance to tell you what happened this morning when Octavian came to the café."

"What did I miss?" Elisa leaned in as if she was about to hear some juicy gossip. I wouldn't dare disappoint her.

"First, Octavian apologized for his outburst at Dafari's office then he said he wouldn't apologize for caring about me."

"You have to give it to him; he is consistent. He totally wears his heart on his sleeve."

"Yeah, and that kiss he laid on me—"

"Hold up," Elisa cut in. "Where was I when this happened?"

"You were out back dealing with that prowler, Demon Daddy."

Her mouth slowly dropped open. "That's what he meant about interrupting a tender moment between you and Octavian. He saw you two."

I nodded in acknowledgement. "He wasn't the only one. Unlike Demon Daddy, who at least tried to be discreet, that is before he dimed us out to you, my father showed us no such courtesy. Instead of walking out, like he easily could have, he blatantly went out of his way to make his presence known.

"No!" She let out a hearty laugh. Hearing her laughter did my heart good. It meant that, despite her physical condition, her soul was still intact, and that was a good thing.

"Yes. Then he proceeded to do the dad thing and tried to intimidate him. You know, the firm handshake, giving him the hard eye stare. I'm a grown woman, but I felt like a teenager all over again."

"I guess Demon Daddy and my showing up stopped that uncomfortable situation."

"Yes, it did, and don't you mean your father-in-law?" I teased.

Elisa gave me a serious side eye. "Aww, hell," she said in disgust. "In all the confusion, I hadn't had time to even think about that. I can hear that jackass now. He won't call me tart maker or his favorite barista anymore; now it'll be, 'Hello, my favorite daughter-in-law.'

Now it was my turn to laugh. "Your imitation of Demon Daddy was a bit too on point, which means he's around way too much."

"Tell me about it. I wish I knew what his endgame was because I know he's up to something. He caused me to have that spell earlier, I just know it." Elisa replied in an irritated tone.

"I wouldn't doubt it. And I agree with you, he definitely has an agenda, but we'll probably only find out what it is when he's good and ready."

Elisa became pensive for a moment. She opened her mouth as if about to speak but stopped.

"What?" I asked.

"I want to ask you something, but I don't want to pry."

I tilted my head to the side, a puzzled look on my face. "As much as we've already shared, why would you be afraid to ask me anything?"

"I just don't want you to feel embarrassed is all."

"Oh," I said, catching on the moment the words came out of her mouth. "You mean what Demon Daddy called me." I let out a long sigh. "It's true."

"So you and Octavian…"

"We came as close as I've ever come to me being with any man, but no."

"I'm sorry Demon Daddy put your business out there like, Tasmin. I have to say, besides you, I seemed to be the only one who was surprised. It was as if Dafari and Octavian already knew."

"Now that you mention it, you're right. I was so busy trying to get at Demon Daddy so I could slap the taste out his mouth that I didn't notice it at the time. Sounds like yet another secret that I need to talk to Octavian about, but enough about me and my drama. What can I do to get you to wake up?"

She hung her head, sadness in her eyes. "You've already healed me physically, and I appreciate it." She took my hands in hers as tears welled up in her big brown eyes.

"Then let me stay here with you, so can help heal your mind," I said, my tears matching hers.

"I-I know you want help, but this is something only I can do. I need time to rest, piece together all these memories in my head, and figure things out for myself. Tasmin, please tell me you understand."

"Yes, I do. I hate the thought of leaving you here alone, but I do understand."

"Thank you. When I'm ready, I'll call out to you, I promise. Now, it's time for you to head back. I'm sure the guys are wondering what's taking you so long. Tell Dafari not to worry, and that…I love him. Now go."

I was at a loss for words, so I simply hugged her then broke our connection.

"Tasmin, can you hear me?" I heard Octavian ask.

"Yes, I hear you."

I removed my hands from Elisa's head just as Dafari and Octavian ran over to me, helping me up from my kneeling position. They walked me over to the sectional where I sat down, both of them sitting on either side of me.

"Tasmin, did you see her?" Dafari asked, clearly anxious.

"Please, Dafari, give her time to recover her wits about her."

"No, I'm okay," I quickly replied. "I saw Elisa. She looks good. She had a message for you, Dafari. She said to tell you not to worry and that she loves you."

The pained look on Dafari's face showed more than words ever could. "When is she coming back?"

"She didn't say. All she told me was that she needed to rest and figure things out. She needs to heal. I offered to help, but she said there was nothing more I could do."

Dafari stood, walking over to Elisa then kneeling at her side. "I caused this. I failed you...again. For that, my love, I am sorry," he said, leaning down to kiss her forehead. My heart broke for him.

Octavian placed a hand over mine. "What I don't understand is why you were able to reach out to Elisa and returned completely unscathed."

"Brother, perhaps their direct familial bond allowed physical contact to occur without undue harm coming to either of them," Dafari said matter-of-factly.

"Dafari!" Octavian snapped.

Direct familial bond? What was he talking about? I turned, gazing directly at the brothers. "Octavian, what is Dafari talking about? Direct familial bond? Are Elisa and I related?"

Octavian threw his head back, inhaled then exhaled deeply. "I was going to wait before revealing that bit of information; however, because of Dafari's unexpected gaff," he said looking at his brother with annoyance, "has forced my hand. Yes, Tasmin, you and Elisa are related. In fact, you are cousins."

CHAPTER 10
OCTAVIAN

II:OO PM

TASMIN WAS IN a silent fit of rage after I showed her the rest of what Martha had revealed to me. I opened the little black box in my mind and allowed her to see Martha's memories. Tasmin studied me for a long while afterwards. I didn't know if she was trying to assess if I was telling the truth or if she was looking for something else.

"Everything is and was a lie," she spat. "That means they intentionally kept us in the dark."

I nodded. "Yes, my love, it would mean just that."

She was quiet for so long, I wondered if she would say anything else at all. Then she stood and walked to kneel next to Elisa again. As she talked, she ran her right hand over her cousin's supine body. I watched as trickles of static electricity extended from her fingertips and danced across Elisa's body, stopping along her pressure points to linger. "I feel all this power, rushing through my veins. It's like a hit of the most potent drug. Part of me wants to rip my clothes off and run naked under the full moon…Another part of me wants to rage with anger, but I know if I do…I'll never be rational enough to hear what my parents have to say for themselves."

The male in me came roaring to life. Thinking about her running naked anywhere caused my nature to stir behind my zipper. I should have been ashamed of myself, but I wasn't. I'd gone too long without this woman, without her love… without her touch…without her affections…without the feel of her body writhing beneath me.

In the same breath, I was alarmed at her calm demeanor. People accused me of being a hothead, but Tasmin was a bird of a different flock. Normally, her being this calm meant she was about to blow her wig. With all that had been revealed and more secrets lurking around the corner, I prayed Tasmin hadn't gone mad.

Dafari and I waited as Tasmin chanted over Elisa. She used both hands now, drawing dark currents in the air as she did so. It was as if she was siphoning Elisa's pain and angst from within her. Anytime tendrils of dark smoke left Elisa's body, strands of energy from Tasmin attacked it with fervor, until the darkness was no more.

"Dafari, I know you have cloves. Get some for me, please, along with a mortar and pestle," she said.

My brother looked stricken but nodded and headed toward the kitchen to get what she asked for.

A few seconds later, Dafari returned. He handed the items to Tasmin then asked, "Will she be okay after all this?"

"We won't know until she either wakes up or gives us some kind of sign. Please give me space to work," Tasmin said.

Dafari moved but not far. I knew he would not leave Elisa's side no matter what anyone said. I moved further away so I could watch Tasmin in her element. In our past lives, it had always been a treat for me to see her share her secret rituals with me. I'd always looked on with pride, elation, and awe. This time was no different.

Tasmin grinded the cloves as her mouth moved in a chant we couldn't hear. Dafari bristled then grit his teeth. The demon side of him had always had an aversion to their spell work. I knew from past experiences that cloves drove away hostile and negative forces. So when Tasmin lit the clove dust and blew the smoke over Elisa's body, I wasn't surprised.

"She's in pain…the kind of pain a mother suffers when she loses her children violently…the kind of pain a wife feels when her husband is snatched away from her without notice." Tasmin stood and slowly circled Elisa's body, using her hand to fan the smoke as she did so. "Her mind has retreated into itself. It's as if she's stuck, trapped inside herself. I have to draw out the negative energy she feels… the hatred and anger she feels toward Octavian and you, Dafari, for leaving her to suffer such a fate." Tasmin stopped above Elisa's head, held up the mortar as brown smoke rose. "The burning powdered cloves will also protect her from a magickal attack while she's comatose. So if that wicked witch from Hell tries to attack while Elisa is down, she'll be in for a rude awakening."

Tasmin closed her eyes and took several deep breaths. When she opened them, it was as if she was in a trance. "Ancestors hear me, take up our fight. I call on you to protect Elisa with all of your might. Danger's afoot, around every corner, even in her darkest time, you must warn her. Her mind is fragile, her nerves are emotionally sterile. Remind Elisa that she has always been a rebel. Show yourselves to her so that she may know, that you have never forsaken her so…The time has come to show us the way… to keep all hurt, harm, and danger at bay…" Tasmin closed her eyes then opened them. "This should keep her guarded and protected until she wakes. I've done all I can for now. The rest is up to her…"

Dafari nodded but remained silent. I could tell he was at a loss.

Tasmin turned to me. "Octavian, I have to go see my parents now."

I didn't answer right away. I did not fancy her traipsing off in the middle of the night alone. However, I didn't want to fight with her, and I knew I would have to if I tried to stop her or go against her wishes.

"I need to get Elisa upstairs to my bed where she can rest properly," Dafari said, breaking my train of thought.

"After you have bathed her, dress her in all white, preferably a gown of delicate fabric. Yes, I know we wear white when grieving; however, in this case, it's just because she was so vibrant and beautiful with it on when I saw her."

My brother nodded once more. Tasmin stepped back as Dafari scooped Elisa into his arms. Elisa's limbs hung limp as my brother disappeared upstairs. Dafari's pain, guilt, and regret cloaked him like shadows. The energy he left behind was palpable.

I turned my attention back to Tasmin to find her watching me. "Is there anything else you need to tell me?"

"Anything else *I* need to tell you? No. Anything else you should know? Yes. However, I think it would be far better to have your parents reveal all else to you for all my secrets have been laid bare," I said.

She moved closer to me, forcing me to look down at her. "I remember things. Flashbacks assail me here and there, but in bits and pieces. Still, my soul recognizes yours. I remember…I remember…"

Her small hands came up to caress my cheeks. Warmth encapsulated me, making me roll my shoulders to keep my wings furled. I felt my eyes glaze over and knew they glowed white as I gazed upon her regal beauty.

"I need to talk to my parents. Alone," she said quickly as if she knew I was about to volunteer to go with her. "Let me do this alone, but once I come back, you and I have a lot of catching up to do."

With all that had happened, all the emotions floating around, all the memories resurfacing, and a mad as a hatter immortal witch out to get Tasmin and Elisa, all I could think about at that very moment was taking this woman to a distant cave, creating the perfect enclave for her, and then loving her until she exploded into the heavens.

While I hoped with everything in me that she and I could pick up where we left off, that was wishful thinking. I knew it wasn't time for that. She was right. There was a lot we needed to discuss.

"I know we do, and when the time is right, we will. For now, you get to your parents and then we reconvene here. I wish you would allow me to at least escort you," I said. "My gut is telling me not to let you walk out of here by yourself."

She said, "This one time, I'm going to ask you to ignore your gut. I promise you, no witch, vamp, imp, or bat from Hell wants to test me right now."

As she said that, I felt her power in the room. At the same time, her eyes shone pure white, and by all that was good and holy, I wanted to take her then and there. It took everything within me not to. I was almost crazy with the need to ravish her.

Still, I was smart enough to back away. I didn't want her to kiss me nor touch me again, for if she did, she wouldn't leave this house anytime soon. The door opened with just a thought from her I suspected. As the wind whipped around outside, Tasmin walked down the stairs and disappear into the night.

CHAPTER 11

TASMIN

THEY LIED TO me. The people I loved and respected more than anyone else in the world *lied* to me, kept an integral part of who I was, who I *am,* from me. My parents and Aunt Noreen knew I had telekinetic powers from infancy. Worse, they kept the fact that Elisa and I were first cousins from me. I could have driven my car, but I wanted to get to Aunt Noreen's house, and to my parents, as quickly as possible. The moment I stepped out of Dafari's home, I performed a teleportation spell, which allowed me to reach the house in no time flat. I attempted to calm myself before entering, to no avail, the memories Octavian shared with me running through my mind over and over again. I opened the front door, intent on closing it gently; instead, I slammed it shut.

"Tasmin, honey, is that you?" I heard my mom ask from the kitchen.

When I walked in, she and my father were sitting at the dining room table. The moment she looked at me, my mother knew something was amiss.

"Sweetheart, what's wrong?"

I tried taking a few deep breaths, hoping to dispel some of the immense anger growing inside me. When I spoke, my words came out harsher than I expected. "Call Aunt Noreen, now," I demanded, looking directly at my father.

He stood up and walked toward me. "Young lady, I suggest you watch your tone."

"Don't tell me what to do. You don't have the right. Call... her...*Now!*"

Never in my life had I snapped at my parents; I had too much respect for them...until today. They needed to know how much I despised what they had done to me and Elisa, and I didn't care how my feelings came out. Before I realized it, a surge of energy coursed through me then items in the kitchen began floating in the air. Mugs, utensils, the toaster, anything that wasn't bolted down.

"Tasmin, please, tell us what's wrong," my mother pleaded. The look on her face told me she was afraid, very afraid. "What did we do to upset you like this?"

"Jewel, stay back. I think I know what's troubling her," my father said, quickly turning to look at her then back to me, giving me a wide berth. Just like my mother, he seemed terrified of me. I planned to use that to my advantage. "Tazzy, I'll call Aunt Noreen, but only if you calm down."

"No deal, Dad. Call her first, then I'll *think* about calming down, but I can't make any promises."

He gave a sigh of resignation then performed the same ritual he used when he first summoned Auntie a few short weeks ago. She materialized before our eyes; her arms crossed in front of her.

"Tasmin Zina Pettiford, I understand that you're ticked off, but I need you to chill out and put those things down. You do that and we can talk. Don't think you flexing your powers scares me, missy."

Although I was thoroughly irate with the three of them, I couldn't help but laugh a little in my head at Aunt Noreen's use of slang. I gently lowered everything back in place, waiting patiently to hear what they had to say.

"How did you find out?" Aunt Noreen asked.

"The how is not important, the fact that I know is," I shot back. "You all covered up my entire existence. You knew I had powers when I was baby, but you blocked them. Not to mention erasing an entire familial line. All the time I spent in Salix Pointe not knowing that Elisa was my cousin, someone my own age whom I could relate to…," I said, my voice trailing off.

My mom placed her hands over her heart. "Oh, my gosh," she said in a low voice.

"Yeah, Mom, I know *everything* you all did. What I don't know is why you did it and why you lied."

"First of all," my father began, "we didn't lie to you, we just never told you."

I looked at him like he had three heads. "Seriously, Dad? That's what you're going with? This coming for the same people who always taught me that a lie by omission is *still* a lie. The three of you stood in this very house and acted brand new, like you didn't know I had powers."

"Child, you have no idea the lengths we went to in order to keep you safe."

I leaned against the kitchen island, placing my hands on my hips. "Please, Aunt Noreen, enlighten me."

Her form floated across the room to stand in front of me. "I'm going to let that snarky little attitude of yours slide because of the situation but be mindful that you get more flies with honey than that vinegar you're throwing at us. Do you think this was easy for any of us? Your parents, Elisa's parents, Amabella Nall, and I all agreed that you and Elisa could have wound up targets for forces that could have attempted to use you two for ill-gotten gains. As your elders, we were obligated to protect you both. It was our duty."

"That's all well and good, and I understand that, but why keep Elisa and me apart?"

"Tasmin, baby, we couldn't run the risk of you two... feeding off each other, so to speak, and triggering each other's powers. Both of you were so young and vulnerable," my mother stated, a pained look on her face. "I'm so sorry that you found out this way," she said.

"Are you really sorry, Mom, or are you sorry the rabbit's finally out of the proverbial top hat? Maybe if you had told me, Elisa and I would have been better prepared for everything that happened, for the things that are happening now. Instead, we were caught off guard, running around like chickens with our heads cut off, trying to learn about our powers. As much as I despise Azazel, had he not scared the daylights out of us, forcing us to use our powers, one or both of us might be dead."

"Yes, and I'm still skeptical as to why that demon would lift a taloned hand to help either of you," my father chimed in.

"While I question everything he does, Dad, he's not the issue right now. I'm still not done with you three. What's so cruel is you sent me down here all those summers, and I could have been bonding with my cousin, but no, you robbed Elisa and me of that. Do you know how lonely I was not having anyone my age to talk to?"

"We never really thought about it, Tasmin. The only thing on our minds was keeping you two safe," my mother responded.

"Okay, well what about telling me the truth when I became an adult? What stopped you then?"

"You had graduated from medical school, then residency, and then you opened your own practice. When you became an adult, your life was so…normal. At that point, we felt it was better to let sleeping dogs lie."

"Well guess what, family, the dogs woke up, and their barking loudly."

The room became silent before Aunt Noreen spoke. "This is exactly what I meant when I said that the family was going to face some challenges. I get that you're upset right now, but I will not apologize for protecting the ones I love by any means necessary, and never will."

"I second that," my father said.

"Honestly," Aunt Noreen continued, "I wish you had never come into your powers, because now you're a target for some evil, immortal bitch. Now you can choose to stay mad at us or, as I told you before, you can work together as a family to deal with this situation. The best thing you can do for yourself is get over it. The choice is yours, Tasmin."

I looked at my mom, my dad, and Aunt Noreen. Intrinsically, I understood what they were all saying, but the lack of remorse from Aunt Noreen and my dad irritated me to no end.

"You know what, Auntie, you're right; I will have to get over it eventually, but it won't be tonight.

I left them in kitchen, heading upstairs to my bedroom to pack a bag. When I walked back downstairs, I grabbed my keys and the set Elisa had given me. After everything that had transpired over the past few weeks, we decided that we should exchange house keys, just in case we ever needed to check on one another.

"Tasmin, where are you going?" my mom asked, now in tears.

"I'm going to Elisa's. I can't even look at you three right now. I need some time, and I'm asking you all to respect that. I'll be back when I'm ready and not a moment before."

CHAPTER 12
OCTAVIAN

SEVEN DAYS LATER...

I JUMPED AWAKE FROM a horrible nightmare that had haunted me for years. I thought that after Tasmin got all her memories back, the nightmares would stop. No such luck. I knew Tasmin would be angry. Why wouldn't she be? Her family had lied to her for years. If I were to be honest, even I was a little upset about that part...for my own selfish reasons of course. Perhaps if they had told Elisa and Tasmin of their true lineage then Dafari and I would have been able to get to them sooner?

The first twenty-four hours away from her had been torture. She had gotten her memories back. I wanted her to be all over me, anxious to get to know me the way we once knew one another. Yes, even with all that threatened us, I wanted my woman to be glad to see me for the first time... again. Even after she had fussed her parents out, as I was sure she had done, I wanted her to come back to me. She hadn't.

I waved my hand and watched the curtains to my room open. Sunlight beamed down on me as I threw my legs over the side of the bed. I hadn't been able to sleep through the night. I tossed and turned, worried about Tasmin. While she sent signals out periodically to let me know all was well, I still had a good mind to go seek her out, chase her down and demand she come back home with me.

When she felt me try to do just that after seventy-two hours of not seeing her, she forbade it. She didn't have telepathy, but she still knew how to get her message across. She sent a bevy of doves to circle my head. It was her way of telling me to respect her request. While doves were spiritual messengers, they also carried the energy of promise. Since one had a small dagger attached to its leg, I knew Tasmin was sending me a threat, a promise to have my head, if you will, if I didn't allow her space. I had to chuckle at that.

While I waited, impatiently I might add, for her to return to me, I put out feelers around the area to see what else had been happening in Salix Pointe. Dead animals were steadily turning up around the town. More cows had been slaughtered, yes, but also dead cats. Doc Benu was still missing. Even when Uncle and I went to his home, we couldn't pick up on a single thread of evidence to show or tell us what had happened to the man. Although at some point during the visit, Uncle behaved rather strangely by standing in the center of the front room and tilting his head as if he heard something I couldn't.

"It's as if he has disappeared into thin air," Uncle Azazel said as we studied the man's front room.

His small cottage-like home was clean enough that one could eat off the floor. There were no signs of distress or struggle. There wasn't even a trace of scent in the air. It was as if his home and all the energy around it had been wiped clean.

It was when we'd left the doctor's humble abode that the fourth day turned sour. Uncle and I had just trekked into town, set to visit the coffee shop to let Rufus know Elisa was still ill and would be taking a few more days off. I was used to people staring at me, as they had been doing it since I'd shown up in Salix Pointe. However, Uncle had a particular aversion to being gawked at.

"The thing I despise about small towns are their ability to make even the most conceited of us hate being the star of the show," he spat with a scowl on his face.

I had to agree to a certain point, but then chuckled when he spotted a voluptuous woman with child-bearing hips smiling at him. His golden eyes twinkled with mischief, and I knew why. The woman all but oozed sex appeal.

"Uncle Azazel, leave the women of this town in peace, please. To take a human woman to your bed would cause chaos. You know this," I said to him telepathically.

With his eyes on the woman and his smile causing her to blush, he responded, "No worries. I've learned from past mistakes, Nephew. Doesn't mean I won't invade her sweet dreams later," he said. "Perhaps I'll give her a beautiful nightmare…"

I grunted but didn't say anything else about it. My mind was on Tasmin as I looked toward the bookstore. I half hoped she would make an appearance to at least open the store. She did not. We stood in front of Elisa's shop, waiting for Rufus to open the door. There was already a line of people, waiting for Elisa's, and now Rufus's, specialties. Uncle's hair flowed down around his shoulders, and he was dressed in a pair of creased black trousers and a collarless blood-red dress shirt that called attention to his chiseled physique. I was dressed similarly and both of us wore long black trench coats to stave off the chill in the air. While the sun was shining bright, it did nothing to warm up the town. The wind chill didn't make it any better.

"Well, if it isn't the uncouth scoundrel who insulted my wife in her own home," I heard snarled behind me.

The crowd lined up at the coffee shop turned and so did I. The mayor, in all his greasy sleaziness stood there, dressed in an olive-green suit with a top hat to match. There was a brown cane with a silver handle in the crease of his right arm. Black shoes adorned his unnaturally long feet. Ilene, in all her imagined beauty, had a handkerchief to her horribly lined eyes as if she were crying. She had on a cream, almost sheer slip of a dress that was far too thin for the weather, and a big fur coat. On her feet were strappy, heeled sandals. Her hair was pulled back into a messy ponytail and judging by the sallow look of her pale skin, she looked ill.

I remembered the mayor's crude words about Tasmin at his jubilee and my eyes narrowed. "Is there something you wish to say to me, mayor?" I asked coolly.

"You need to apologize to my wife, you ill-mannered swine. How dare you threaten her with sexual violence and bodily harm," the mayor yelled as he used his cane to point at me.

The crowd around us murmured and whispered behind hands as they looked on.

I cut my eyes at Ilene. "Not only are you an insipid shell of a woman, you're also a malicious liar," I said to her then turned to the mayor. "Before you go accusing a man of insulting this slag, make sure you yourself are not the infidel you accuse him to be." I stepped closer to the tall, rail-thin man of Cajun ancestry. "I did no more to your wife than she asked of me. She wanted me to take her to my bed. I, instead, showed her what would become of her if she ever approached me in such a manner again. I showed her the hell *she would burn in lest she stay far, far away from me. Now please, remove yourself and this daft minger from my presence."*

I was set to turn my attention back to the bookstore until I heard, "You dare call my wife a liar and insult her further!

I'll show you!" I turned around just in time to see him raise his cane. "You will pay for your insolence, you—"

Before he could finish, I backhanded him across the face. He went flying backward, landing on his hind parts. The momentum caused Ilene to go sprawling down next to him. Women in the crowd gasped. A few men chuckled, and Uncle outright guffawed.

I ignored all of them as I walked over and yanked the man up by the lapels of his suitcoat. I pulled him close so only his ears could hear what I had to say. "I heard what you said about Tasmin at your little jubilee. If you, your wife, or that bitch of a witch you're harboring go anywhere near her or Elisa, in Hell will you lift up your eyes...war-lock," I growled then shoved him back down to the ground.

The mayor stared up at me with shock in his eyes and fear in his heart. I felt it just as sure as he saw my eyes glow white. Ilene, like the damsel in distress she pretended to be, scrambled to her feet while clutching her pearls. She took one look at my face and scampered off running down the street like a mad woman.

"There, there, Octavian," Uncle said, placing a hand on my shoulder. "Let's not draw too much attention to ourselves..." He gently pulled me away from the flabbergasted man and I stormed inside the coffee shop just as Rufus opened the door.

By day five, my patience had worn thin. Tasmin's wishes be damned, I was going to get her...until a canary came flying at me. I tried to bat the worrisome, winged creature out the air, only to have it zoom around me then sit on my head. A canary from her in that sense, meant freedom. She had been caged far too long and she wanted me to know that she was free now and still didn't want me meddling in her affairs. She wanted me to know she could and would handle it herself. I was angry, pissed off even, but I turned and headed back to Dafari's. It reminded me of times past when we were working on the Underground and she had been determined to free as many enslaved people as she could.

It was now day seven and I didn't think I could go one more day without seeing her. I got up and walked to the bathroom. Handled my manly business. Tried to contact my parents again to no avail. I knew what they had tried to do to Tasmin and Elisa, but I needed to know they were okay so I could at least get more answers as to why the Most High had a hit out on the two witches. Sure, their powers could cause the Second Coming if not careful, but there had to be more that I was missing.

Then my mind went back to Elisa. She was still comatose. I'd checked on Dafari throughout the week. My brother looked as if he had died, gone to Hell, fought with Uncle Morningstar, lost and was then tossed back on earth to suffer a fate more horrible than death.

I slid my feet in a pair of expensive loafers after donning a pair of black trousers, and a dapper dress shirt. I headed downstairs with my mind racing a mile a minute. I got to the kitchen, made a pot of coffee. I pulled at the ties that bound Tasmin and I as soulmates. I had to admit, it felt good to be able to do such a thing again after so long. When I felt her return the tug, I knew she was okay, or okay as she could be after all that had happened.

Tasmin had the reaction I expected her to have after learning of her parents' betrayal. Had she not, I'd have thought she'd lost the plot. I had a good mind to go to her; however, with all that was going on, it was best I stay behind and do some reconnaissance work. Since I knew I wouldn't be able to tear Dafari away from Elisa's bedside, that left me with one other option with whom I could partner, and even though he and I had been getting along fairly well, I still didn't readily want to spend as much time with him as I had been.

"Don't be so enthused, angel whelp. I don't particularly like partnering with you either," Uncle said as he rounded the corner.

It wasn't the comment that made me turn around. It was the angst in which my uncle said the words that had me on high alert. I turned to face him, expecting him to be wearing a smug smirk. However, I was surprised, and a bit cautious, of the weariness it his eyes. It actually alarmed me. I'd never seen him look less than nob, and while he was still dressed to the nines in a bespoke gray suit with a blood-red dress shirt, tie and biscuit-toe dress shoes to match, the pain in his eyes told a different story. His skin didn't have the usual glow and his hair was pulled back into a ponytail which was as rare as ever.

"Been to Hell again, have you?" I asked.

He cut his glowing eyes at me then snapped. "No."

"Then might I ask the reason for the sour mood, Uncle?"

"No, you may not."

I quirked a brow as he walked over and poured himself coffee. Uncle didn't drink coffee. He rarely partook in human consumptions. If he did, it was for show to keep them from picking up on what he was. At least that was the way it had been since he'd been back in our lives.

"Will you stop gawking at me and tell me your plans of getting at that mangy witch and her harpies?" he snapped without turning to look at me.

He took a deep, slow breath. I watch his back expand so wide I thought he was battle bulking. *Yes, yes…something was up with him.*

"Are you even fit to go on this mission with me?" I asked.

He whipped around on me so fast, I jumped back and took a defensive stance. His fangs had elongated to throat ripping proportions and the nails on his fingers looked as if they were prepped for a heart snatch. I called my bec-de-corbins to me. They whizzed through the air hard and fast then slapped into my palms with a loud clap.

"Is there a problem, Uncle Azazel?" I asked coolly.

My uncle and I circled one another like the enemies we truly were. No matter how much he helped us, my guard was always up, and he was a trickster after all. Who knew what had goaded him to anger?

Uncle made a dash as if he were about to attack, but like he had run into a brick wall, he stopped, and crumbled to the floor. He yelled and roared out. His back arched so far it looked as if it was bowed. He tore at his shirt until buttons went flying across the room. Slobber pooled from his lips and dripped down his fangs. His body grew in size as his suit jacket and shirt ripped against the strains of his bulking. He sat back on his haunches with his back to me. His arms stretched wide, almost as if in a crucifix on his knees.

Dafari came running down the stairs, his eyes glowing red, body bulked and ready for battle. "What is this madness?" he asked, eyeballing his father who was writhing in pain on his kitchen floor. "What have you done to him?"

"I've done nothing to him. Something or someone else has a hold of him. Look," I said, pointing to the red marks and lashes appearing across his back, sides and stomach.

Uncle's hair had come loose, it grew longer and cascaded down his back. The veins in his arms were thicker and coiled under his skin like steel ropes.

"They're torturing him," Uncle Azazel roared.

"Who?" I asked.

"Who's torturing whom?" Dafari yelled.

Uncle's tormented screech rent the air again. "Please," he whispered on a gasp. "Make it stop…"

I watched as new lashes sliced open the skin on his back. I didn't know what to do or say. I'd never seen uncle in a such a...humanized manner in all my existence.

"They're...torturing...my brother," he cried.

"Your...brother?" Dafari asked as he took cautious steps toward his father.

"Which brother?" I asked.

My uncle looked up at his son with water in his eyes. I couldn't readily tell if they were tears or not. I didn't know if the water was from physical pain or mental anguish. "Get the door," he pleaded through jagged fangs. "Your uncle is nigh."

"My uncle? Michael?" Dafari sneered. "He would dare show up here?"

My heart beat against my rib cage in anger. If my father had the unmitigated gall to show his face here and now, he had a death wish. If Dafari didn't kill him, surely the Merry Widows or Tasmin would try. I'd bet my earthly possessions Elisa would awaken and try, too.

I stalked to the front door, weapons still in hand and at the ready just in case... I felt a familial presence afoot. His energy was scattered about. He, too, was in pain; mental, physical, and emotional. I saw a white light in a tunnel spin in my brother's yard. I saw the outline of a person as he knelt with one knee, one hand on the ground before he stood.

I yanked Dafari's front door open, expecting to see my father, Michael. I got the shock of my life to see... "Uncle Gabriel?"

CHAPTER 13

DAFARI

THE MESSENGER ANGEL stood before us. While his anguish was nowhere near as bad as Father's, Uncle Gabriel was still clearly in distress. He stepped through the door, not even acknowledging Octavian or me. I took note of his mien. Centuries ago, Uncle appeared to humans in his true form, which could be quite frightening, as could all our forms. I chuckled inwardly as I remembered the night Octavian revealed the embodiment of his true self to Tasmin. It earned him the distinction of being blasted across Elisa's living room by Tasmin and landing squarely into a bookcase.

Nowadays, Uncle chose a form more aesthetically appealing to humans. While they were brothers, he bore no resemblance to my father. Standing at roughly six feet four inches tall, Uncle Gabriel had a flawless, caramel-hued complexion; almond-shaped, hazel eyes with flecks of green in them; and full lips surrounded by a neatly trimmed black mustache and goatee with touches of gray. While both Father and Uncle's hair was black with gray at the temples, unlike my father's wavy texture, Uncle Gabriel's head was adorned with locs that hung just below his shoulder blades. Like his brothers, he always dressed to impress. As his signature fabric was linen, today he appeared to us wearing a cream rope-shoulder linen-blend suit jacket with matching high-rise pleat suit trousers. His attire was complete with a crisp white cotton-poplar dress shirt and cognac-colored cordovan derby leather shoes.

"Why...are...you...here?" my father asked between labored breaths, his mysterious wounds leaking black ichor.

Uncle Gabriel stood over Father, who was still in a prone position on the floor. "I'm here because of you, Fallen," he replied, his deep bass tone tinged with a hint of a refined Barbadian accent. He was attempting to mask his own obvious discomfort with little success. "I'm here with a message, and, although it is your fault that our brother Michael is suffering greatly at present, I'm here to...help you."

Octavian and I passed surprised looks at our uncle then at one another. The Most High, for all intent and purposes, had written Father off as a bad seed centuries ago. Why wouldn't they considering the chaos he caused? Why would Uncle Gabriel be here to help him?

"And why would you, one of the four who caused me to be labelled a Fallen in the first place, help me?" my father understandably questioned.

Uncle Gabriel crossed his muscular arms in front of his chiseled chest, his stance authoritative. "Because despite my sheer disdain for you, you are still my brother. Just be gracious for once, Azazel."

Just as father was about to respond with what I suspect was to be a deprecatory remark, I saw a bright flash of green light outside, then heard a loud boom. Octavian again walked to the door. When he opened it, we were shocked to see yet another family member standing there.

Father looked up to see who it was. "How dare you... darken my son's...doorstep, imprisoner," Father spat indignantly despite his obvious agony.

Just as Uncle Gabriel had done, Uncle Raphael walked into my home without so much as a word of greeting to Octavian or me, his attention squarely focused on Father. "While I may have imprisoned you, it was by no means the punishment I was ordered to dole out. Had I done as I was instructed, you would have had your hands and feet bound, I would have opened up a hole in the desert of Dudael, tossed you in, then would have covered you with rocks and dirt, leaving you there in complete darkness until judgement day. Instead, I only bound you to the side of a mountain. You're welcome," he countered in his silky-smooth baritone timbre. "I'm still paying for that transgression. After tonight, I'm sure I'll have even more."

Uncle Raphael, the tallest of all the brothers, standing at seven feet tall, resembled a Black Seminole. His rich hickory-hued skin stood in stark contrast to his low-cut, straight black hair. His round, haunting green eyes, Nubian nose, and bow-shaped lips added even greater distinction to his refined appearance. His tall frame belied his muscularity. He was dressed in a black silk dress shirt, black crepe suit trousers, and black suede tassel loafers. The Angel of Healing never wore a suit jacket, as he always wore a hooded mantle in his signature color of emerald green. Solid gold jewelry in the form of a stud in his left ear, watch on his right wrist, serpentine chain with a caduceus pendant around his neck, and a left pinky ring adorned his person.

"Lucky me," my father snidely remarked. "What did I do to garner help from two of my betrayers, brothers I haven't seen for centuries?"

"Nothing," Uncle Raphael stated. "Truth be told, had it not been for the fact that the five of us are linked, and are all smarting because of Michael's torture, albeit to varying degrees, we would not be here."

"I see. So you're only here to help me because it helps dear brother Michael." He chuckled at the irony. "How does brother Uriel feel about that?"

Uncle Raphael walked to Father, standing over him. "It was his idea. As the Angel of Wisdom, and as the angel who is involved in science and education, he theorized a plan that could potentially ease Michael's pain. Since we cannot directly interfere in his punishment, Uriel came up with a way that it can be done indirectly, by using you as a conduit. Not only would I relieve you of your pain, but because of our...bond, such as it is, our pain as well."

"I feel so used," Father snidely remarked. "Where is Uriel anyway?"

"He stayed behind to keep an eye on Michael, and to send word if Michael's pain has lessened after Raphael completes his task," Uncle Gabriel replied.

"Uncle Raphael," I cut in, "If you are all linked, why not alleviate the pain of Uncle Gabriel or Uncle Uriel, as opposed to taking the time to track down my father?" I asked dubiously. "After all, you said it's a theory."

"Fruit of my loins, I would ask...that you refrain from asking questions...that could prevent me from benefitting from this plan...lest your uncles feel challenged and leave." Father's pain must have been intolerable for him to try to quiet me.

"No, Azazel, Nephew may ask, although *you* may not like the answer." Uncle Raphael turned to face me. "That was the first thing we tried, but Michael's pain only dwindled slightly, as did ours. Then we figured that since Michael's torture was a direct result of your father's meddling in affairs not his own, he must have been experiencing the exact same torment. While he most assuredly deserved it, Michael did not. As such, here we are."

Father keened his gaze on Uncle Gabriel. "So all that talk about…helping me because I'm your brother was a… bunch of bull."

"We are helping you and, unfortunately, you are our brother. Where's the lie?" Uncle Gabriel had a self-satisfied look on his face, and although, in this instance Father was right, Uncle was also correct.

"How is Michael faring?" Father asked.

"As well as can be expected, considering," Uncle Raphael replied.

"Considering he failed? It happens. However, I never imagined the golden boy's punishment would be this severe. And his…wife, how is she managing?"

"Your *ex-wife's* penance is almost just harsh as Michael's."

As angry as I was with Mother at present, hearing that she was being tortured gave me no joy or satisfaction. The worried look on Octavian's face told me he was feeling the same.

"How long will their expiation continue?" I asked.

"That we do not know, Nephew. I assume until The Most High deems they have fulfilled the punishment for their failure."

"It appears that even failure is a sin," Father expressed. Once again, I silently agreed with him. "Well get on with it then," Father demanded. "While I know I look a mess, neither of you are looking daisy fresh either."

Had it not been for the fact that Uncle Gabriel, Uncle Raphael, and Uncle Uriel were sharing Uncle Michael's misery, I'm sure Uncle Raphael would never have done as Father had ordered, at least not without letting him suffer some more first. Uncle lowered himself to his knees, placing his hands on Father's shoulders. He closed his eyes as if concentrating.

I observed a pale green glow surrounding them. As the radiance became brighter with each passing second, Father's wounds began to heal. Seconds turned to minutes until he, along with his brothers, appeared less distressed, Father's wounds completely healed.

"If Father is healed, wouldn't that also heal Uncle Michael's wounds, and wouldn't that alert his punishers that outside intervention is at play?"

"Fair question, Nephew," Uncle Gabriel began. "The answer is no. Michael will continue to have his wounds, which will heal naturally in due course; however, he will have no pain. Uriel has already advised Michael to continue the ruse as if he's hurting. Hopefully, they will be none the wiser."

"It appears you've thought of everything," Octavian chimed in.

Father stood up, his clothes in tatters from when he bulked in size. "Although this was not for my benefit, I thank you, dear brother."

"If you really want to thank me, Azazel, the best thing you could do is return with us and own up to your part in this latest infraction of yours."

"I graciously decline," he uttered, stepping into a shadow. "And best for whom? Michael and his wife will earn back the favor of The Most High in due course. Besides, there is an ancient evil here in Salix Pointe gunning for the witches, and my services are needed. I'm assisting Dafari and Octavian in finding a way to vanquish this vile threat."

"At what cost? What's in it for you, Brother?"

"Knowing that I have protected Dafari and Octavian, and by extension their women, is all the reward I need."

My uncles passed knowing looks at me and Octavian. They knew we no more trusted my father than they did.

"Nephews, be careful. When you let a snake into your home, you're bound to eventually get bitten," Uncle Raphael stated.

"Says the angel who proudly wears a symbol that contains two serpents," Father countered.

"The caduceus represents healing, you clod. You represent no one but yourself. I guarantee that your supposed acts of selflessness toward my nephews harbor ulterior motives."

"I only mean to help my son and my nephew, nothing more."

"The same way you 'helped' the humans?" Uncle Gabriel questioned. "Let us count the many ways your assistance did them more harm than good."

"Let's not and say we did."

"You taught them about the earth's metals and how to create with them," Uncle Gabriel began, ignoring my father.

"Which is why my son has such a nice car."

"Thank you for throwing me under the bus, Father. Let's not forget that you drive a Lamborghini Diablo."

"Touché, my son. Touché."

"You schooled them about jewelry and precious stones," Uncle Gabriel continued.

"Dear brother Raphael, nice trinkets you have on. A bit much for my tastes, but the look works for you."

"You showed them the art of facial beautification."

"Let's be honest, some woman and some men, need to know that skill."

"You coached them on the use of dyes and colors."

"And we all have fancy duds to show for it. Tell me Gabriel, is that a new suit? I love it!"

"Worst of all, you instructed them on how to make swords, knives, shields, and breastplates. You also educated them about the metal antimony, which is used for many things, including making bullets. You indoctrinated them in the ways of warfare, and because of that one singular act, millions have perished, and are still perishing, the world over as a result."

"Is it my fault that humans cannot work out their differences peacefully?" Father retorted.

"This is not a joke, Azazel," Uncle Gabriel yelled. "You revealed heavenly secrets not meant for human ears."

"I was *not* the only one," Father countered, raising his voice. "The other Watchers also taught the humans heavenly secrets. Their leader, Semjaza, taught spell casting and root cutting. Others provided instruction in other topics; Armaros, counter-spells; Baraqijal, astrology; Kokabel, constellations; Ezeqeel, knowledge of the clouds; Araquiel, earth signs; Shamsiel, sun signs; and Sariel, the course of the moon. Not to mention that all one hundred and ninety-nine of them, including Samjaza, took human women as wives and impregnated them, giving rise to the Nephilim. I was the only one who did not partake in that debauchery. Those Nephilim giants decimated humankind, and then began to slay each other."

"The Nephilim learned how to kill because of *you*, Brother," Uncle Gabriel shot back indignantly. "The other Watchers' offenses pale in comparison to yours. Your actions corrupted the entire world; hence you being given the moniker *All Sin*. Well deserved, in my opinion."

"Yes, and the four of you couldn't wait to snitch on us, especially Semjaza and me. I truly understand that human phrase snitches get stitches."

"We had a duty to uphold."

"And you minions did so without question. Let's see, Uriel was tasked with going to Noah and preparing him for the end of the world. It's odd that humans appeared to be absolved of all wrongdoing, as blame was placed squarely on the backs of the Watchers, yet most humans were eradicated. Contradiction much? After that pesky flood, Noah and his flock were supposed to create a world that was to be a utopia with nothing but unicorns and rainbows. How did that work out?"

Neither of my uncle's had a response for him.

"Gabriel, you were supposed to coax the Nephilim into destroying each other. Clearly, that didn't go as planned since the witches have Nephilim blood."

"I'll give you that, Azazel; however, it didn't help that Octavian and Dafari had taken up with said witches in their previous incarnations and continue to do so in this lifetime."

"It appears as if Tasmin and Elisa are being targeted, in part, for what the Watchers did. Their existence is not their fault. Or is there more to this story than you are telling us?" I asked.

"We only know what we know, Nephew," Uncle Raphael replied.

"That was cryptic," Father instigated.

"Bottom line, you both defied the natural order of things for those witches, descendants of the Nephilim," Uncle Gabriel firmly stated.

"And I would do it a million times over to be with the woman I love," Octavian proclaimed.

"As would I, in a heartbeat," I declared. "And anyone who gets in our way be damned."

"Well said, you two," Father interjected. "Now on to Michael, the favorite son; he was to deal with the Watchers, save for me, making sure the Nephilim were slain in front of their fathers. Once that occurred, the Watchers were to be bound under hills for seventy generations, after which they would all be taken to the lower depth of Hell where they would meet fire and would be locked away forever. Oh well, at least he got the second part right. And last, but not least, Raphael, you were my brother, but also my jailer."

"Obviously, you weren't locked up well enough, else you would not be here in Salix Pointe wreaking who knows what kind of havoc," Uncle Raphael quipped.

"Currently, that distinction goes to another. And don't forget, the real reason I can roam Salix Pointe at my leisure is because Michael purposely freed me in order to frame me. Not that it matters to either of you."

"You're right, Azazel, it doesn't matter. You atoning for your misdeeds does matter. Every single Watcher begged for forgiveness eons ago, asking the scribe Enoch to write a petition on their behalf, all except you."

"And that worked out so well for them, didn't it? Besides, I kowtow to no one, human...or otherwise. After that vapid Enoch appeared to me bringing a message from On High, I already knew the writing was on the wall. There would never be peace or mercy granted to me. I will forever be reviled in the annals of heavenly history. *C'est la vie.*"

"Be that as it may, you need to stop being a coward and come out from the shadows," Uncle Gabriel challenged.

"I am no coward. I am also no fool," Father replied, not taking Gabriel on.

"You taint everything and *everyone* you touch. Your interference turned the tide of the battle. Had you not directly inserted yourself into the fray then corrupted our nephew," nodding in Octavian's direction, "we wouldn't be here now."

"For the record, my blood was already coursing through my nephew's veins. My then-wife and I had a *very* active sex life, and I had saturated her womb with my essence many, many times. I only gave Octavian the...push he needed to save his lady love, to save all of them. I should be commended, not ridiculed."

"Again, I wonder to what fiendish ends you are providing your so-called assistance to Dafari and Octavian. There's always a catch with you."

Father did not respond. Instead, he flashed a toothy grin, visible even through the shadows. I found it unnerving. Like my uncles, I wanted to know what his agenda was, why he was providing so much support to Octavian and me. I was aware of what father had done, all the harm he had caused. He was not to be trusted. Unfortunately, he had also proven to be a valuable resource. For now, treading carefully, and playing his game, was the only option available to us.

Suddenly, I heard a voice in my head calling out to me. *"Dafari?"* It was weak, but the voice was clearly Elisa's. She was awake. My love had finally arisen from her seven-day slumber.

"Elisa, I'm so glad to hear your voice. I can't wait to see your beautiful face. Don't move. I'll be up in a minute. Can I bring you anything?"

"You don't have to. I know it's only been a few days, but I feel like I've been cooped up for a lot longer. I need to stretch my legs. I'm coming downstairs."

"I've been giving you intravenous fluids, but you're probably weak from lack of actual food. Let me prepare something for you, get a meal into your stomach before you get out of bed," I replied, doing my best to remain calm.

I needed to prevent Elisa from walking in on this highly dysfunctional family reunion. The last thing she needed to see was two more archangels who only lived to do the bidding of The Most High, part of which was getting rid of her and Tasmin.

"I appreciate that, but I can't stay up here a minute longer. I'll be down shortly."

I would have attempted to dissuade her further, but I knew it would be fruitless. The time had come for our family meeting to end.

"Uncle Gabriel, Uncle Raphael, while it was...interesting seeing you both, I must respectfully ask that you take your leave. I have an urgent medical issue that I must handle immediately. You can see yourselves out." What I said wasn't wholly a lie; I did need to tend to Elisa, as she had not been well for seven days.

Both looked at me suspiciously but made their way toward the door.

"This is not over, Azazel. We shall return. Nephews," replied Uncle Gabriel.

"It was a pleasure, brothers. Let's do it again sometime," Father said then chuckled.

Uncle Gabriel and Uncle Raphael walked outside, closing the door behind them. When I saw two flashes, one white, the other green, I knew they were gone.

"About time," Father said, finally stepping out of the shadows, fully clothed in a deep purple Italian cashmere, silk, and linen suit with a silk ecru-colored dress shirt, and brown leather cap-toe oxford shoes. "I thought they'd never leave."

"You look none the worse for the wear," I remarked.

"Yes, well, archangel healing will do that for you."

As much as I wanted to question Father regarding his intentions, I knew it wasn't the time or the place, as I heard Elisa's footfalls coming in our direction. When she turned the corner and walked into the living room, my heart skipped a beat. Despite her ordeal, she looked as vibrant as ever. She had put on the peach nightgown, matching robe, and slippers that I had set out for her, just in case she woke up and I wasn't by her side. Her thick, coiled locs were set into a large afro puff, allowing her lovely dark brown skin to shine through.

"Elisa," I said, taking her hands in mine. I leaned down, lightly kissing her full lips then asked, "How are you feeling?"

She leaned back, studying my face for a long moment, as if I was a stranger. "Physically I'm fine. Emotionally, mentally..." Her voice trailed off.

"I understand. Much has been thrown at you. You haven't had adequate time to filter though all you've learned, and it was very traumatic for you. That is my fault, but I promise you, I will help you through this. You won't have to deal with this alone."

She didn't respond, but instead looked from me to Octavian.

"Brother, I think I will take my leave," he said, taking note of the uncomfortable air in the room. "Elisa, I'm a chuffed to see you are looking well. I will get word to Tasmin immediately. She has been sick with worry. Dafari, I will see you later. Uncle." Octavian quickly exited through the front door.

Elisa simply nodded then shifted her attention to my father. Her eyes became thin slits. She released my hands, started walking in his direction.

"Daughter-in-law, glad to see you up and about. We were all so worried about you."

"Were you?" she asked. Her calmness was unsettling, considering her obvious contempt for Father. "If you were so worried, why were you in my dreams almost every night?" she questioned, raising her voice. "It felt like you were probing my mind for information, something I had no clue about."

I quickly walked to Elisa's side, my gaze squarely on my father. "Well, Father? What do you have to say for yourself?"

"Son, daughter-in-law—"

"Don't call me that," Elisa angrily spoke.

"Elisa, I would never take advantage of you during your infirmity. While I have...visited you in the past, I assure you, I did no such thing now, especially not while residing under the same roof as you and Dafari. That would have been disrespectful."

His face looked sincere, but my father could twist the truth without breaking a sweat. So much so that even the most pious person who knew his reputation would probably buy what he was selling. I, however, didn't believe him.

Elisa's features softened, and in a low voice she said, "Maybe I was mistaken." She ran her palms down her face. "Maybe they were just nightmares."

"Perhaps they were," Father replied.

I took a stance between Elisa and father. "I need to speak to Elisa, in private."

"As you wish, my son. Daughter...Elisa," he said, making a slight bow. He was about to step into a shadow before I stopped him.

"Before you depart, Father, a word." I led him to my study, shutting the door behind us. "I'll make this brief. When it comes to those I love, be mindful of your actions. You do not want to test me."

"Ah, what the love of a good woman will make one do."

"While she is my main priority, I'm not just taking about Elisa."

"Yes, our favorite angel and his beloved vestal virgin. I understand. But I must ask, am I included in those you love, oh son of mine?"

I looked Father in his eyes, and the only thing I saw was guile. He never did, or said, anything without a reason. While I was curious to know what his denouement was, I had neither the time nor patience to figure it out. I needed to get back to Elisa.

"Good night, Father," I replied, turning my back to him and opening the door. I turned my head briefly to see that he was gone.

CHAPTER 14

ELISA

I T WAS SOME hours later, and I was laid out in what Dafari called his sanctuary, an ice-cold towel to my forehead. It reminded me of a Japanese Zen garden with all the fixings, including rhododendron, hydrangea shrubs, a circular island of moss, bonsai trees, a small bridge, white sand, a stream, stones, and a waterfall. He'd brought me here after a dizzy spell had overtaken me, but I had refused to go back to his bed. I would not be laid up like an invalid again.

I had so much anger and so many emotions running through me that I didn't truly know where to begin to piece together all that had happened. I awakened with the knowledge that Tasmin and I were cousins. First cousins to be exact. She and I were as thick as thieves in our past lives, and with all the memories flooding back, it's a wonder neither of us had gone completely mad.

"Seventy-seven years…" I said.

I couldn't see him, but I knew he was there, lurking in the shadows like he'd always done when he knew I was upset with him.

"I thought it was to be seven," his voice floated around the room.

"Seventy-seven…years, Dafari…"

"I'm sorry…"

"Our children made suicide pacts…"

"I didn't know, Elisa, or else I wouldn't have made that decision."

"I lost you…"

"It was an honest mistake…"

"I lost Zafer…He ran off to fight in a war he knew his heart wasn't in…assisted suicide, death by soldier!"

"My boy…my only son. I felt when he took his last breath…even in my hellish prison."

"Safiya went to be with her brother. She didn't even tell me, but I should have known…she stopped speaking, stopped talking entirely, a year before she took her own life. Octavian never found her body, but I knew… I knew my baby was gone…My last child…"

"I never felt her death…"

"Because she didn't die violently. It is my assumption she poisoned herself."

"I…am…I am so sorry…"

"Your apologies mean nothing, Dafari," I yelled, threw the towel from my forehead then sat up. I glared around the shadowy room, not sure where he was, but wanting him to feel my wrath—the anger I felt toward him and Octavian. "And now… Now! Now, I have to relive it, because yet again, my family has made decisions for my life without me. On top of recalling the most traumatic moments of my past life, it's compounded by the fact that in this life, I, too, have to grieve the death of family because of people making decisions for *me*, without any input from me!"

I sensed him about to break the shadows. I stood and felt

my energy crackle around the room. "I would not come out of those shadows right now if I were you."

"Elisa—"

"No. I mean it. My powers are far too volatile right now. My anger is misguided, and I'm well aware of this…"

"I don't care. I've missed you…in so many ways…"

I took a deep breath to steady my center. Like hot lava, my powers coursed through my veins. I needed to get away, to find serenity. I needed to grieve, just once more, in peace.

"Don't leave, Elisa…"

"Get out of my head, Dafari. I did not give you permission to enter."

"You left it wide open."

"I don't care."

"Well, I do."

Dafari emerged from the darkest shadow in the left corner of the room. His hair was down, flowing around his muscled shoulders. His dark skin, like the richest color of chocolate, called out to me like it had always done. His sculpted chest and abs drew my attention like moths to flames. His power reverberated around the room, those holy and those underworldly. His incubus stared at me from behind his golden eyes as he slowly approached me. With his upper body bare and his bottom half only clothed in linen pants, it was hard for the woman I was to stay focused.

I scoffed. "Are you trying to seduce me as I mourn, Dafari? How very carnally low of you. Even if you are half incubus."

I expected my words to cut him to the bone. Instead, they seem to entice him further as he closed the gap between us. He smelled divine, almost like honeysuckle and sandalwood. It was an intoxicating scent that caused my senses to go haywire. My nipples hardened instantly, breasts swelled in anticipation of what I knew he could do, and would do if allowed, to them. My pressure points heated, and I felt my lotus blossom like the traitorous cunt she was.

"Not trying to do anything. It's in my nature," he crooned, voice dripping slowly down my spine like molten lava.

I knew I had to get out of there. Knew if I allowed him to touch me in the mood he was in…with the way my magick was so unhinged…

"Let me heal you in ways I'm most otherworldly proficient," he said as I gazed up at him.

His golden eyes glowed with sensuality I hadn't experienced…well I had but this was a reawakening for me. I yearned to get to know this man…this being—my husband— the way Eve got to know Adam, but…so much time had passed, but…had it? I mean, he and I were an item even in this life so was it really fair to him for me to act as if we were on some new path? I was so confused.

"You can get to know me that way. In some ways, in this life, you already have," he said. "It's okay to be confused. The only thing holding you back is you…"

He was reading my mind. That was my fault because I hadn't closed it. I didn't want to close it. I wanted him to see me…read me…be all over, under, and through me.

He chuckled…flashing fangs as he did so. It wasn't the kind of chuckle that said he found anything in the moment funny. It was the kind that said he, too, was in so much pain, that he was damn near delirious with grief, but that he still wanted me. And even still…it was the sexist thing, the most erotic sound he could have made.

"I know you're in pain, but I can take all of it… I can take every single burden…every single tear, even the smallest particle of your pain," he said as his hand snaked out to move my hair behind my right ear.

I shivered at that slightest touch. To be awakened in this

body…to have all my memories rush through my psyche, taking the shapes and roots of my past lives? It was an overload.

"No," I said then stepped back when he reached out to pull me into his embrace. "No, and you know you're not playing fair, Dafari."

"I don't care about fairness when I'm trying to heal my woman. I'll heal, defend, and protect you by any means necessary. Let me take it all away…"

"Some of this can't be taken away through sexual healing. This absolute grief and despair I'm feeling at the thought of never seeing you again in that lifetime—"

"It's all in the past. I'm here now. You're here now."

"But our children aren't!"

I slapped a hand over my mouth when I realized I'd yelled so loud, my power spiked, and his electricity flickered on and off. He took a step back then flinched as if I'd struck him. The despondent look that overtook his features knotted my stomach. I'd hurt him and that hadn't been my intention, but I was in unimaginable pain myself and didn't readily know where to put it or what to do with it.

I laid my hand over my heart. "I'm sorry, but I-I need to go…I'm sorry."

I LEFT DAFARI'S in the dead of night, under a full moon. I was careful as I could be with controlling my emotions. As a First Order Elemental— one who wielded the power to control earth, air, fire, water, and spirit— being this unhinged could cause reprehensible damage.

Still, some of my anger couldn't be contained. Branches on the trees reached out to me as I walked. The earth felt as if it moved beneath my feet. The wind whipped up and rain pelted down on me. Salix Pointe was asleep for the most part. Porch lights were on but dimmed. I saw holiday wreaths and sparkling lights. It was strange seeing all the Christmas holiday décor when my mood was dark and eerie. Salix Pointe at Christmas looked as if it belonged on a post card. It made me feel out of place.

I thought about how I had lost my parents at ten then my grandmother years later...For so long I'd thought I was the last of my immediate family. The other family that had run from Salix Pointe and never looked back didn't even seem like family to me. They never reached out to me, and I never did either. I thought I was alone, so I made do with that. I was content to build my lonely existence here in Salix Pointe...

Then Doctor Dafari Battle blew into town and with him came the start of change. There had always been an underlying attraction between us, but I was content with leaving it where it was, until I couldn't. I thought about how all of that got blown out of the window as the winds of changes came upon us. I thought about how it all led to the secrets and all the lies that had kept me and Tasmin apart for so many years.

By the time I looked up, I was standing in front of Ms. Noreen's home, where Tasmin and her parents now resided. Before I could stop myself, I caught a gust of wind and threw it toward the door to knock it off the hinges. I stormed up the front steps, itching for the confrontation I knew was coming.

Tasmin met me at the door. There was no anger on her face. "Where is he?" I asked.

Tasmin took a deep breath, then waved her hand behind her as she moved to the side.

There stood Silas and Jewel Pettiford. Jewel watched me with concern, love, and tears in her eyes. She was adorned in a long white dress that signified she was grieving. Her locs fell down her back and she was barefoot to be one with the earth. Silas stood next to her, and while there were no tears, the weight of his deceit was heavy on his face. Dressed in all black, as was customary for the males of our lot when grieving, my anger was directed toward him he most.

"I just want you to know, whatever she says to you, however she says it, you two no less than deserve it for this affront," Tasmin said.

I stared at Silas for so long that even if I'd wanted to stop glaring, I couldn't. He was my father's brother…and now…I saw it. I saw my father in his features. I didn't see it before because I wasn't looking for it. But by all the Great Spirits and Ancestors, I saw my father. They knew why I was there. I had so much anger that I was shivering. I wanted to rant. I wanted to rage!

I wanted to get it all off my chest, but when I opened my mouth, all that came out was, "Why?" I slapped the tears running down my face. "Why?"

He said, "We all thought…we thought we had done the right thing, but we messed up."

"So much could have been avoided if you'd all just told us the truth. I thought I was alone! Do you understand that? I thought I had no one! You could have done something, said something. You could have sent birds, magick posts, or snail mail. Something. I had to grieve alone and the whole time, the whole time…you sat there and left me here to do it alone! Knew what I was, knew the power I possessed. You guys left me here alone! I was a sitting duck."

"Elisa—"

"I had no idea what I was. I could have been hurt or killed and would have been none the wiser as to why."

"We made mistakes," Jewel said, her voice cracking. "We're so sorry."

"No, you're not! Because even after coming here now, you still kept secrets from us! You're absolutely not sorry," I yelled, and the earth shook.

Jewel stumbled, as did Silas, but he got his footing then righted her. She casted a pleading look my way as she walked forward. I stepped back when she tried to touch me. "Elisa, you have to understand the terror we felt as parents, knowing that if we allowed yours and Tasmin's powers to manifest that it would cause people and things—human and non-human—to come looking for you. We genuinely thought—"

"You thought wrong because things and people are still coming after us! We were almost assassinated by archangels and now some immortal evil witch is after us," I cried. "And more things and people are coming. I was left in the epicenter of magick and neither of you thought to reach out? To tell us who we were?" I looked from her to my... uncle. It was hard to look at him, seeing the resemblance to my father. "He was your brother! You didn't even show up to his homegoing."

"I was here," he said, tone firm. "I was...Mama just made me stay hidden, lest you ask questions. You were a very smart and perceptive child, as was Tasmin."

"And what about Mama Nall's homegoing? Where were you?"

He dropped his head then glanced from me to Tasmin. "Here. I was here. You dressed her in red as is customary for a witch of her standing. Even though you had no idea of your birthright, your instincts led you. Her homegoing was beautiful, the offerings, her altar, the food you prepared, the prayers...You were dressed in white. Your hair flew wild and free..."

"I thought I was crazy when I first met you. Thought something freaky and weird was going on because I felt all these jolts of power around you," I said, barely above a whisper as I looked at him.

I felt Tasmin snap her head in my direction at me, as I hadn't even told her that tidbit.

"I thought—I couldn't even tell Tasmin because I thought such implications would come off untoward. But it's because you're my blood relative, isn't it? It's because of the direct line of blood to Mama Nall and my father, *isn't it?*" He took too long to answer. Silas looked as if shame was threatening to cripple him, even as he stood tall like a fighter. I screamed, *"Isn't it?"*

He nodded once. "Yes...yes, it is."

"You're my uncle...I could have...you could have...All I remember of him is his hand reaching into the backseat with my mother's as they spoke in another language and then there was this bright flash of light...My memories of them are starting to fade...It's been seventeen years and I have desperately tried to hold on to any little thing...and you were a direct link this whole time. It's cruel what you have done to us, and I don't know about Tasmin, but I will never, for as long as I breathe in this life, forgive either of you. Never."

With that, I turned and ran from the house. I sloshed across the brook that separated my land from Ms. Noreen's and headed home.

"I KNOW IT'S a silly question, but...are you okay?" Tasmin asked after she walked into my home.

I'd given her permission early on to use my place as her own if need be. I'd been home for about twenty minutes. I was sitting in the middle of my front room with the Book of Magic Enchantment opened before me. I had gone an entire emotional rollercoaster, and still, in the back of my mind, Marie sat idle.

"I'm... here," I responded then looked up. "Nice to see you again...Cousin." I smiled.

I was genuinely glad we were back as we were.

She grinned down at me before sitting next to me. "Nice to see you again as well, cousin. What are you looking at in the book?"

Cousin had been how we'd always greeted one another back then.

I pointed. "Reading up on the genealogical lines. Says here I am a dream walker, but you are not. Still, you were in my dreams, talking, in real time. How'd you do that?" I asked.

Tasmin shook her head. "Honestly, I don't know. I was working my magick to help bring you comfort, protection and peace then I touched your temples...Next thing I knew, I was walking with you."

"Hmm..."

"Why do you ask?"

"I want to attack LaLaurie where she is least powerful."

"In her dreams..."

I nodded. "Something about the way she isn't throwing her weight around that's bothering me. And we've been so distracted by personal things that I feel we have ignored her far too long. She has been able to sit back, plan, and strategize while we have been in a rut with familial drama and love spats."

"True. It's been on my mind as well, but you were down, and I didn't want to be too far away from you just in case she did attack," Tasmin said.

"I've left my coffee shop in the hands of Rufus for a week now," I said.

"You'll be happy to know it's still up and running, too. Rufus has done a great job in your absence. I know because

I checked. He's been telling everyone you've been under the weather and that the animal doc has been taking care of you."

I rolled my eyes. "I can already hear the rumors that are going to spread."

Tasmin chuckled.

"Any word on Doc Benu?" I asked.

She shook her head. "No. Not a word. The sheriff has been dealing with a deluge of calls concerning dead cats and cows." She leaned over then flipped a few pages in the book. She stopped on page sixty-six. "Look at this," she said, pointing.

"You think the dead cats have something to do with blood magick?" I asked.

"Yes. According to the notes, when a witch has taken to using blood magick, it's because she's summoned a demon that she must continue to feed or the demon will turn on her."

"Isn't that the impundulu thing Octavian told us about?"

Tasmin shook her head. "No. This is different. This is hemomancy. She's using blood manipulation for something. I just don't know what yet."

Hemomancy was the forbidden use of blood manipulation to cast spells, mostly curses. Most who practiced the dark arts for evil intent and purposes often resorted to blood magick when they summoned a demon who required payment in blood.

"We know the impundulu is butchering the cows, but what kind of demon would be satiated with only cats' blood?" I asked.

"That's what we have to find out. This would be far easier to ask if I didn't dislike your father-in-law so much," she quipped. I whipped my head in her direction to see a smirk. "Sorry... I had to," she said.

I rolled my eyes and chuckled. "For all intent and purposes, I could call on him to ask, but I feel we'd regret it immediately."

"You could ask Dafari to ask him."

I stood then sighed. "I'm not speaking to him at the moment."

"I would ask why, but I suspect I already know."

I extended my hand to help her up. Once she stood, I picked up the book, placed it on the lectern in front of the bay window, then waved a hand over it to seal it from prying eyes.

"Grab the Himalayan salt from the kitchen, will you? We'll need it when we traverse the astral plane," I said.

As she rushed to get that, I put the book away. I looked outside my window at the biggest tree in my yard then shook my head. She came back with the Himalayan salt and held up a clear vial of something else.

"You made black salt?" I asked, excited to see such a delicacy.

She nodded. "I used the ashes from a ritual fire I'd set to ward off evil while you were down."

"So…how are you and Octavian getting along after everything?" I asked.

She shrugged. "Don't know. I've been away from him for seven days so that I get my emotions in check."

"Oh…I bet that really has a man such as him down."

"Such as him?"

"Yes, one who loves his woman out loud. I can bet that he is down bad, especially after seven days."

"Well how would you know that, Elisa? You've been asleep for seven days," she said, almost as if she was annoyed by the possibility.

I walked over to my window then pulled the curtain back once more. "Come have a look," I said.

She walked over to stand next to me so she could see what I saw. There, underneath the big weeping willow, sat Professor Octavian Jerrod.

"And look, now he's dressed like a night rider from Sleepy Hollow," I said.

And he was. Dressed in a long black trench coat, combat boots, black jeans, and collarless black shirt, he sat with his back against the tree, reading a book. Even though I was angry with him, the dour look on his face actually made me feel bad for him. He looked up as if he sensed us watching him—he probably did— then got up. The man stood in all his male prowess and looked like danger personified. His startlingly black eyes watching us underneath the moonlight was quite eerie. Even under the cover of darkness it was easy to see Octavian's attractiveness. The man may not have had full-blown incubus in him, but he still oozed sex appeal. The archangel blood had done his body good. It was easy to see why Tasmin was smitten, and always had been.

I had to admit, Octavian had always been like a blood brother to me, and to be upset with him hurt. He was my brother in all sense of the word. He and I could chat about anything, and even when I had no idea what he was getting on about, he always took the time to explain it to me in layman's terms. He never made me feel idiotic. Still, I full-on blamed him for my family being snatched away from me. He didn't think about the consequences of his actions.

"I have never seen him dressed in anything less than fancy attire," Tasmin said.

"Yeah, well now he looks like he's going to fight someone. Will you please go and talk to the man and put him out of his misery?" I asked her, half joking, half serious.

She sighed then looked at me. "Do you know why I've stayed away from him?" she asked as if exhausted.

I shook my head. "No, but I'm sure you have a reason."

"I wouldn't have been able to think straight with him under foot. I wouldn't be a virgin anymore in this lifetime if I'd stayed around him while trying to get my thoughts together. I needed seven days to get my mind right without his influence. He may not be an incubus, but he has that *umph* that is just as lethal. I didn't need to be going off on my parents one minute, him another, and then on my back the next. Me being a virgin in this lifetime makes it easier to say no to him...for now."

I quirked a brow but didn't utter a word.

She continued, "And he's anxious. I can feel it, feel him. He wants to get ahold of me in more ways than one. He wants to pick up where we left off, but for me, I don't think I can do that. My last memories are of me calling out to Octavian and him not being there. I can hear our daughter scream out to her father, see her searching the skies and the woods hoping he would just pop up, and he didn't..."

"Oh, Tasmin...it was because of the spell that had been cast on all of us," I said, reaching out to take her hand.

She squeezed mine. "I know that, and logically, it all makes sense, but still... it's hard to traverse those memories and try to get back to who we once were."

I understood Tasmin more than she knew. Listening to her made me reexamine the way I had handled Dafari. What logical reason did I have for not allowing him to take all the pain and angst away? Why did I want to hold on to it? Why on earth would I want to grieve and suffer all over again? It was something to think about.

"You have to try at least," I said. "He's suffered, too, I know. And yes, I am angry with him, but on the other side of that coin, to see you and Attalah murdered and violated in such ways...it drove him to madness. In those seven years we waited, thinking Dafari would be released, Octavian suffered, too. He was off his rocker with grief."

She turned back to the window and gazed out. Now Octavian stood with his hands in his pockets, not even trying to hide the fact he was now watching us in the window.

"I'll figure it out. In the meantime, tell me about this plan of yours to attack LaLaurie.

CHAPTER 15
TASMIN

ELISA AND I had talked for the better part of an hour as she outlined her plan for us to go up against Madame LaLaurie. Being in a self-induced magickal coma for seven days gave her plenty of time to think and formulate a strategy to defeat the evil witch. While it definitely held an element of danger, properly executed, it could work. The immediate problem was we needed Octavian, Dafari, and even Demon Daddy in order to bring it to fruition. Since Elisa wasn't really speaking to any of them at the moment, we decided we would do some more research before discussing things over with them.

"I think we've done enough for tonight," Elisa said as we got up from the couch in the front room. "It's late, and this evening's been trying, to say the least."

"Agreed. After Octavian sent me a message that you had woken up, I had a feeling you'd be coming to see my parents. That was the only reason I went home, to warn them so they would be prepared to be held accountable for their actions."

"Wait, you haven't been staying with them?"

I lowered my eyes, the memory of my own confrontation with them still fresh. "No, I've been staying here. I hope you don't mind. I couldn't even look at my parents, let alone stay in that house, after my blow up with them and Aunt Noreen."

"First of all, Cousin, you know I gave you free run of the place, so of course I don't mind. Second, your aunt...*our* aunt was there too?"

"Yes, I made my dad summon her. She and your grand-mother...Mama Nall, were the ringleaders in the decision making, and since she and my parents blatantly lied to my face, she needed to be a part of the reckoning. Thing is the only one who seemed to have any remorse for what they did was my mom. The only time my father admitted they were wrong was tonight. That's why I haven't been home."

Elisa had a sympathetic look on her face. "Tasmin, you're welcomed here anytime," she said, placing a hand on my shoulder. "Stay as long as you want. I definitely wouldn't mind the company." She gave me a warm smile.

"Thanks, Elisa," I replied, returning her smile. "I think Dafari might take issue with that. I'm sure he wants his lady home with him."

Elisa sat back down on the couch; I joined her. "Dafari needs to realize he can't always have what he wants when he wants it," she retorted with a scoff. "Do you know he thought he could seduce me into staying with him?"

"What else is new?" I asked then chuckled. "He is an incubus after all. It's in his nature. In his defense, he did take great care of you when you were recuperating."

"It was his fault I had to recuperate in the first place," she countered, her voice raising a few octaves. She let out a hard exhale before speaking again. "I'm sorry. I'm just still reeling from everything. I had to get away from Dafari for the same reasons you distanced yourself from Octavian. If I had allowed him to touch me, hold me, kiss me, I would have lost all logical thought, and I couldn't allow that to happen. The chemistry, the love, between us is, and has always been, electric, literally and figuratively. There are times that even when he's not physically touching me, I can feel him. He has this inexplicable hold over me, and sometimes it freaks me out. I needed to clear my head, and I couldn't very well do that with Dafari so close by."

It was my turn to comfort her. "No need to apologize. I get it. You two have an extremely deep bond, one that's existed for almost two centuries. But if you're feeling like that, did you ever think that maybe Dafari's feeling the exact same thing, just hiding it better?" I asked, patting her hand reassuringly. "On that note, Cousin, I think it's time for me to have a talk with the Black Knight," I said, nodding toward the window. I knew Octavian would still be outside, watching over me and Elisa, and wouldn't be going anywhere anytime soon.

"Don't be too hard on him, Cousin. He means well."

I let out a sigh. "I know. This could take a while. You should get some rest."

"You're right. I want to go back to the café tomorrow, and I need to be at my best. Good night, Tasmin, and good luck," she said, walking toward the stairs.

"Night, Elisa. See you in the morning."

As I put on my jacket then grabbed my keys, I wondered what I would say to Octavian. I hadn't seen or spoken to him in seven days. I had only sent messages to him via birds. When I opened the door, I was immediately bombarded by his longing for me, hitting me like a tidal wave crashing onto land. His emotional assault made it difficult to think, but if we were to move forward, I needed to gather myself, find the words to tell him how I felt.

"Why are you out here dressed like Neo from the Matrix?" I asked, walking to stand in front of him.

"Dressed like who from what?" he inquired.

I chuckled to myself at his continued lack of pop culture knowledge. "Never mind. Octavian, what are you doing here? All I've asked was for you to respect my wishes and give me some time to process everything that's happened, but you couldn't do that, could you?"

"Admittedly, no, Poppet, I could not. I bloody well missed you with every fiber of my being."

I wanted to stay mad at him, but it was difficult when he gazed at me with puppy dog eyes looking as if he lost his best friend. I sat down under the weeping willow tree, gently pulling on his hand, inviting him to join me. I looked up at the night sky, taking in the beauty of the stars and the fullness of the moon. Despite the biting December chill in the air, when Octavian sat next to me, I felt a comforting warmth surround my entire body.

"I've missed you, too, but…"

"But what, my love?" I heard and felt the urgency in his voice.

"Why couldn't you have been honest with me from the beginning?"

"Tasmin Pettiford, can you honestly tell me you would have believed me? You were skeptical from the outset when I told you about magick."

"Because you sounded crazy," I said then giggled.

"Precisely, and you would have definitely thought I was daft had I told you that we were bound to each other over several lifetimes."

"Most likely, but at least I wouldn't have been so caught off guard. Once I realized magick was real and I started trusting you more, you could have at least tried."

"You're right, I should have, and you have no idea how many times I wanted to tell you, but every time it went all to pot. I could use the excuse that something always came up, but when it's all said and done, I made a cock-up not telling you sooner. I'm sorry. Please tell me you forgive me."

"I forgive you, but don't let it happen again," I teased.

"I promise you, from this point onward I will be upfront with anything you want to know."

"In that case, I have one more question for you. When your uncle…divulged my business in front of everyone, neither you nor Dafari seemed surprised. The only one who seemed shocked was Elisa, which tells me you already knew."

"Yes, both I and Dafari were aware that you are unsullied."

I looked at him and shook my head. "Unsullied? Could you sound any more like you're from the Middle Ages?"

"I'm sure I could—"

"Please don't," I said cutting him off. I noticed a smirk on his face and realized he was messing with me. "Seriously, Octavian, how did you know?"

"Both Dafari and I noticed an aromatic scent you give off. I never paid attention to it before because we were so wrapped up in other issues, but just prior to our latest crisis, I became cognizant of it."

"And this…scent told you that I was "unsullied"?" I asked, making air quotes.

"Yes, it did…it does. Now that I've answered your question, might I ask you something?"

"Of course."

"During the jubilee, we came very close to becoming intimate. Had that night not gone completely awry, do you think we would have…" his voice trailed off.

"Made love?" I asked, finishing his question. "Honestly, I don't know. I can tell you that I wanted to."

We sat in silence for a few minutes before Octavian linked the fingers of one hand with mine then kissed the back of my hand, causing my body to react. My nipples hardened and my lady parts throbbed to a rhythm all their own. This was why I didn't want to see him in person; I knew the effect he had on me. It had always been like that with us; a shared undeniable passion. From the moment we met in our first lifetime together, Octavian and I were instantly attracted to each other, and while the attraction was definitely physical, it was more than that. We connected on a deeper, spiritual level. For both of us it was love at first sight, which was why our courtship was so short and we married quickly; Octavian and I wanted to be together, but he wanted to be honorable. Tonight, however, the desire emanating from him clearly spoke to his intentions.

"I came out here so we could talk, not for you to try to seduce me."

"What kind of man would I be if I didn't at least make an attempt?" he asked. Although we only had the dim light of the moon, I could still see the mischief his black eyes held.

"But you're not a man, you're an angel, and I thought angels were supposed to lead people away from temptation, not into the thick of it," I replied.

"My love, you are my one and only temptation."

Octavian dipped his head, his lips finding mine. His kiss was sweet and tender, yet fiery and passionate at the same time, just as I remembered. His hands found my waist then he lifted me up and swung me around to face him while I straddled his lap. I felt his pulsing need for me. I wanted him to make love to me, and do things to me that no angel should, like he had done so many times before in our other lifetimes. We kissed like we hadn't seen each other in days. Then I remembered we hadn't, and the last time we had kissed, my father had blatantly interrupted us. Through his kiss, I felt every bit of affection Octavian had for me, felt his elation at the fact that he had the woman he's loved for eons back in his arms.

"Tasmin, I want to make love to you," he said, sliding my jacket off, placing it to the side.

"Why, Octavian Jerrod, would you have me lose my virtue under this willow tree in the glow of moonlight?" I asked teasingly.

"If that's what you wish, Poppet, absolutely."

I did want it, I wanted him. This time I kissed Octavian, my tongue finding his. My need for him was overwhelming. Octavian lightly kissed my neck while unbuttoning my flannel shirt. I, in turn, unbuttoned his shirt, my hands running down his muscular chest and well-defined abs. He unhooked my front-close bra then gently caressed my B-cup breasts. My breath hitched and my eyes closed when his mouth latched onto one of my already hard nipples, his tongue slowly circling it. He then moved onto the other one. I was more than ready to give myself to Octavian, and was about to, when I noticed the weeping willow tree began to illuminate, first green, then red, and finally white.

"See, even the Ancestors approve," Octavian said as he unbuttoned then unzipped my jeans.

I looked up toward Aunt Noreen's house and saw the light in my parent's bedroom turn on. The window blinds opened. I saw my mom and dad looking directly at the tree. Luckily, Octavian and I were hidden behind the large tree trunk.

"Or maybe the Ancestors were snitching on us," I said in annoyance. "The light show caught my parents' attention. The last thing we need is for them to catch us out here."

"Bloody hell, you're right. Your father was mardy when he walked in on us snogging."

I had a feeling that one or both of my parents would come outside to investigate the tree's light show, so we quickly stood up, fixed our clothes, and positioned ourselves against the tree trunk, obscured from the view of the house. No sooner had we done so the front door opened. The footfalls on the porch sounded heavy; I assumed they belonged to my father. By the time he arrived, the tree lights had finally begun to dim, which was advantageous for me and Octavian. It couldn't have been longer than a minute or two before he went back inside.

"That was close," I said after peeking around the tree trunk to make sure he was gone.

Octavian took my hands in his, a plea in his eyes. "Come home with me, Tasmin. We can pick up where we left off."

"I want nothing more than to be with you tonight, but as much as Dafari made me feel welcomed, that's not my home. Besides, with Demon Daddy living there now, I definitely wouldn't feel comfortable. Considering everything that's happened, that's not my home either," I said, nodding in the direction of Aunt Noreen's house.

Octavian let out something akin to a groan. "And out of respect for Elisa, knowing she is none too fond of me at the moment, I would not darken her doorstep. While it pains me to not have you next to me…under me…on top of me…," he said between kisses, "I fear we will have to put our amorous liaison on hold for the moment. In the meantime, my love, go get some rest. I'll be right here when you wake up on the morrow."

"Octavian, go home," I said. "When Elisa was indisposed, I stayed at her house and made sure it was warded every day from top to bottom. She and I will be fine. Please don't worry."

He looked down at me, firmly stating, "Unless I am physically by your side to protect you, I will *always* be concerned about your safety and well-being, understand?"

I wasn't about to argue with his logic, especially considering I had all my memories back. "Understood."

"I will, however, trade favors in kind."

I raised an eyebrow, looking at him quizzically. "Go on."

"I will go home to Dafari's if, and only if, you go speak to Martha."

I threw my hands up. "Octavian—"

"Hear me out, Tasmin. Notwithstanding your anger and resentment directed toward her, while justified, it's time for you to confront her, if for nothing else your own peace of mind. Not to mention the coven must be revived in order to properly fight, and hopefully defeat, this LaLaurie. Do this for me, I beg of you."

While Octavian and I butted heads often in our past lives, and in this one, I was learning to be less resistant and more willing to take his advice. As such, I reluctantly acquiesced to his request.

"Fine, I will go see her in the morning, okay?"

"Smashing. I will see you tomorrow, but before I go, I'll leave you with this."

Octavian picked me up so that I was eye level with him then laid a kiss on me that had me swooning and speechless. After he put me down, I walked up the stairs to the front porch.

When I turned around, Octavian said, "Sweet dreams, my Tasmin. Now off with you."

THE NEXT MORNING, Elisa left for the café before I had even gotten up. She left a note letting me know there was a plate with pancakes, eggs, and turkey bacon in the microwave. Once I had performed my daily grooming, I quickly heated up and ate my breakfast. As much as I was dreading seeing Martha, I had made a promise to Octavian, and I wasn't about to renege. That said I wanted to see her and get the meeting over with as quickly as possible. It was still early in the morning, and I wanted to catch Martha before she and her sisters headed to the café for their daily fix. When I pulled up to their quaint home, Martha was standing out front.

"Good morning, Tasmin. I was expecting you."

Yeah, that's not creepy. "Martha," I replied, taken aback that she knew I would be visiting her. "Where are Cara Lee and Mary Ann?" I asked looking around.

"I sent them ahead to Elisa's. I wanted to give you the opportunity to speak your mind without interruption or interference from my sisters."

I followed her through the front door of the home. Because Octavian had shared his memories of his encounter with the Widows with me, I already knew what the inside of their home looked like. Martha led us to the sitting room, taking a seat on the couch, motioning for me to follow suit. There was a carafe of something sitting on the coffee table. Martha poured herself a cup of what appeared to be green tea. She then offered to pour me one. I put up my hand to decline.

"First of all, allow me to apologize once again for my part in Noreen's death."

"You mean murder," I quickly interjected.

"Yes, that. While I am aware that no words can ever make up for what I've done, just know that my soul will forever be haunted for my participation. Michael may have coaxed me into helping him, but I do realize that I could have declined assisting him."

"Why didn't you?"

"It's…complicated."

"Then uncomplicate it for me, or this meeting is over," I said, standing up.

"Wait, please," she said. I sat back down, looking at her dubiously. "I want to tell you what you need to know, what you deserve to know, but if you would indulge me, I would like to discuss it when you and Elisa are together, as it affects her as well."

"Fine, I've waited this long. A few more days won't hurt. And for the record, your soul being haunted is the least of what you deserve for your betrayal."

"I know," she answered in a muted voice. She lowered her head, shame and anguish written all over her face.

I sat in silent contemplation. That word, betrayal, had more meaning than I wanted to admit. While Martha had betrayed Aunt Noreen, she along with my parents, had betrayed me. And yet, here I was, still harboring anger toward the person who sold her out. But despite what they had done, I still loved and was loyal to my parents and aunt; I just wasn't ready to forgive them yet.

"I sense something else is bothering you. Do you want to talk about it?"

"Yes. And no. The only thing I will say is thank you for trying to keep our families from clipping our powers and hiding our familial link from me and Elisa. It doesn't make up for what you've done, but I appreciate the effort. Things might have turned out differently had you been successful in convincing them."

"You're welcome. I wish I could have done more back then. You will never know how remorseful my sisters and

I are that you and Elisa grew up never knowing your true birthright. But that's a conversation for another time. Tasmin, I'm aware that it may take some time for you to trust me, even a tiny bit, but know that I am truly sorry for all the pain I've caused you."

"I appreciate your apology, but my trust is in short supply, for obvious reasons. I'm not there yet. Aunt Noreen told my parents that they had to form a new coven with you and your sisters, Elisa, and me, and that our lives depend on it. How can I be a part of that if I don't trust some of the people I have to work closely with?"

"Trust is earned," she replied. "My actions, as well as those of your parents and Noreen, created deep wounds. Only time can heal those wounds. We will have to work together as a cohesive group, but we will only succeed if we have complete trust in each other. I can only speak for myself when I say that I will do my very best to earn your trust. I hope you will give me the opportunity."

"I can try. In the meantime, I will talk to Elisa. I'm sure she'll be anxious to hear what you have to say. I have to get to the bookstore. We'll talk soon."

Martha walked me to the front door. Once we said our goodbyes, I started my drive into town. The only thing I could think about was what she had said about Elisa's and my birthright, our *true* birthright. What else has my family not told me?

CHAPTER 16

OCTAVIAN

I KNEW I WAS taking a huge gamble going to see her, but it had to be done. I'd always been a man who prided himself on the healthy nature of all my interpersonal relationships. She had all right to be upset with me, but I was hoping that she would grant me court with her so that I could apologize once more. She and I had suffered together, and while trauma hadn't initially bonded us, it had been another factor that brought us closer.

I materialized out of thin air, knowing if I had knocked on the door, she would have ignored me. I could tell she knew I was there by the way she was using the stainless-steel cutter to aggressively chop the dough.

"What do you want, Octavian?" she asked.

She had a black apron tied around her waist. Flour was lying about the countertops and floor. Her hair had been pulled back into a tight bun and her feet were bare.

"I've come to speak with you if I can."

She kept cutting the dough, throwing it on a food scale and then tossing it on the Saran Wrap she had laid out on

the counter. I wondered where Rufus was as I didn't see or
feel him around.

"I gave him a few days off since he's been running this
place by himself for days now," she said, but didn't turn
around.

I wanted her to know I'd come in peace so my mind was a
wide open space. Since she'd gotten her powers back, I knew
she understood what it meant. I set the gift I'd brought her
on the counter. I looked at the time and saw she hadn't set
up the café for customers yet. Chairs were still flipped over
atop tables. Coffee stirrers were still in the back. Napkins
hadn't been prepped, etc. I tossed my trench coat on the rack.
I then set out to help Elisa prepare to open. It reminded me
of times in the past, before we realized Dafari wouldn't be
returning, when she was a laundress. I'd help her set up for
the day, even went as far as to get her customers from miles
away. She would launder the clothing with my niece, and
I would return them to her customers when she was done.
Anything I could do to lighten her load, I did as penance.

We went on that way; her preparing her baked goods
and me prepping the café to open. However, I did notice she
had taken the gift from the counter. That was something.
When seven-thirty rolled around, I wasn't surprised to see
my brother was the first to stroll in. I didn't know the state
of his affairs with Elisa, but I did know that the energy inside
of his home was so intense that Uncle opted to sleep outside.

I'd tossed and turned most of the night, trying to figure
out what about me kissing and touching Tasmin had made
that willow glow. I had a feeling but didn't know for sure. My
gut told me that it'd had something to do with that spiritual
chastity belt her parents had locked on her. I couldn't say
anything for fear that Tasmin would think I'd lied to her

again or kept something away from her. Technically, I had, but I was steadfast that this wasn't my secret to tell.

My mind traveled to other things outside of my libido. Although that was hard to do. Thinking about making love to Tasmin again had occupied my thoughts and my dreams all night. As a celestial, I wasn't supposed to have what humans called wet dreams; however, because of my uncle's tainted blood in my DNA, I ravished Tasmin in my dreams last evening. Then I woke up with my manhood standing at attention, and it was rigid enough to split diamonds in Sierra Leone.

I heard something spill in the kitchen. My head snapped up. "Elisa? Is all well?"

"It's fine," she yelled back, a bit of roughness to her tone.

"You should probably close off your thoughts about Tasmin if you insist on leaving your mind open," Dafari drawled. "I have no inclination to hear about your stiff cock. I'm sure my…wife doesn't either." He cut cold eyes at me.

"May God blind me! My apologies," I yelled loud enough for Elisa to hear then looked at Dafari. "You of all people should understand my plight. I haven't even sniffed a woman since trailing Tasmin's aura lines here."

Dafari was dressed in all black similar to me, in black combat boots as well, only he had on his white lab coat as opposed to a trench. He folded his arms across his chest. "And you gave me grief about not being with a woman for seven years?" He quirked a brow.

"Well, yeah, it's different for you. You can't help yourself…" Dafari grunted.

"Allegedly," I added quickly so not to offend him.

He was prickly since Elisa had run away from him. I'd no desire to tangle with him in such a mood.

"I'm off kilter here, dear brother," I said, tossing the dish towel over my shoulder. "Don't you have some remedy to help me?"

He studied me a long time then smirked. "No."

He was lying and I knew he was. I got ready to call him a bloody liar but didn't get the chance. Just then, Elisa walked out with his white chocolate mocha, almond croissant, and chocolate chip cookie. She slammed the items down on the counter then tried to make a hasty retreat to the back. She had no such luck. Dafari turned glowing golden eyes her direction as he caught her arm. His thumb was placed directly on the point of pulse just under her wrist. He rubbed his thumb in a gentle circular motion. I saw and felt the visible sharp intake of breath Elisa released.

"Come home tonight," he said to her.

She swallowed as she made eye contact with him. The energy in the room charged up a few notches.

"I...I can't. Not right now."

"Why would you want to voluntarily hold on to all that pain when I can relieve you of it? Pain and anger often blinds us to things—"

"Stop," she snapped, holding up a hand. "Stop trying to manipulate me into your bed."

I pulled the dish cloth from my shoulder and then held it up to my nose. Elisa might have been protesting, but her body's...um...arousal had lit up the air, and it was potent. She and Dafari caught wind of me trying to stave off the scent by covering my nose. I backed away from them until I was in the furthest corner of the room.

"Ah... I see someone has truly awakened."

His voice grated my nerves. From the only shadow in the room emerged Uncle Demon Daddy. Today he was dressed in a blood-red Italian suit with a white collarless dress shirt and black dress shoes to match. His long, wavy hair hung down his back. His pinky ring stood out as did the expensive watch on his wrist.

"Why are you here, Father?' Dafari snarled.

"Can't a man follow his nose—" Dafari bristled then took a step toward his father. "—to get some bakery and coffee," Uncle finished slowly then chuckled. "You and your brother are testy about your witches."

"Did you want something?" Dafari asked as Elisa shot daggers at Uncle with her eyes.

"Hostile couple, eh?" Uncle taunted. "You lot have been so caught up in your personal affairs that you've let this witch run roughshod over your town. Dead cats, cows and now goats. The cows are the work of her little vamp, but the cats...the cats and the goats are blood magick."

"I talked to Tasmin about this last evening. But I thought it was just cats? Now there are goats?"

"Indeed, sweetness," Uncle said. "The cats were no longer enough which meant goat's blood was the next best thing. Goat's blood is pure as seen by how red it is and by how it's used by humans in medicinal studies...You should be more concerned with what demon she is actually feeding..."

Elisa waved her arms. "Will you quit talking in riddles and actually tell me something useful," she all but yelled... which spiked the air even more.

I watched Dafari wipe his nose with the back of his hand. His eyes were glazed over and his breathing erratic. The longer he stood there, the higher on Elisa's arousal he became. Uncle gave Elisa a slow, intrusive once over. He closed his eyes then slightly tilted his head as if he were savoring a taste of something. It was so intense that Elisa gripped the top of her shirt and pulled it together as if she wore a robe or coat. Once he opened his eyes, they glowed just as golden as his son's had. I refused to move the towel away from my nose and mouth for I knew better.

"Honeysuckle…I see your scent hasn't changed over the years. It's only gotten sweeter…more potent…"

Dafari had all but bulked to battle proportions and he was advancing on his father. I used the currents in the air to disappear then materialize in front of Dafari. It had been a mistake as I'd had to drop the cloth I'd made into a makeshift mask. However, I knew if Dafari attacked his father, it would cause more problems than needed at the moment.

I shoved my brother backwards as he was out of his mind with the scent of his woman in his nose. It wasn't as if he hadn't been privy to Elisa's scent before now but being that she was fully awakened and back to her normal self in all ways, just like Tasmin, Elisa's scent was rife with the portents of her arousal. Uncle chuckled behind me, but he did not flinch in the face of his son threatening to do him bodily harm.

"Get ahold of yourself, Brother. I know your father can be an arse, but we don't need this right now," I said, holding Dafari back as best I could.

Uncle strolled up to the counter then picked up Dafari's chocolate chip cookie. Elisa stepped back until she was against the wall. She wasn't afraid of him, that I knew; however, she knew his power. She knew he wasn't one to be taken lightly no matter how much power she possessed. She had always been a smart woman, and nothing had changed.

Uncle took the cookie out of its brown paper package and then bit into it. He chewed slowly and thoughtfully. "I can see why my son is so enamored with your…cookie," he said without an ounce of couth.

He then laughed at his own play on words before casting red eyes at his son then catching a passing shadow. He disappeared the same as he came.

Dafari rolled his shoulders, trying to calm himself as he paced back and forth like a caged jungle cat. Elisa smartly rushed back to her café's kitchen.

"You need to go," I told Dafari.

He whipped around to face me. He'd dropped fangs, his eyes were red, and his breathing erratic.

"Get out and get out now before you do something irrational. You're beside yourself with lust and the need to feed while lusting. You will surely injure her if you touched her now. Go breathe fresh air and then talk to your animals or something. I haven't a care how you do it, but you need to calm yourself."

His fangs had elongated to battle length. He couldn't even form a rebuttal, but he knew I was right. Seconds later, he too caught a passing shadow then disappeared. I shook my head, grabbed my coat then stepped outside to clear my senses. I looked down Main Street to see the town coming to life. It was hard for me to get in the holiday spirit. While Salix Pointe was into the swing of things, I didn't feel all that…Christmasy.

There was no rain, but it was cloudy overhead. The wind blew occasionally. A few lights still twinkled on storefronts. I glanced at the bookstore, wondering what time Tasmin would open it. While Elisa had Rufus to run her café in her absence, no one had done it for Tasmin. I'd been so caught up in my own grief that I didn't think to have her back in that way as well.

Demon Daddy had been right in his other assessment, too. We hadn't really put much time and effort into getting rid of our witch problem, and I feared that would come back to bite us in the hind parts. The witch had turned to blood magick to further her agenda, but exactly who was the demon in question?

I heard raucous laughter behind me and turned to see two young women looking at me while they laughed.

"Who does he think he is, Neo from The Matrix?" one asked while her friend cackled louder.

"Girl, it's always the fine ones who are bat shit crazy. He's probably on his way to shoot up some store or mall or something."

I frowned as they passed me by. While one thought about how she was going to seduce another woman's husband, the other worried about if her husband was cheating on her. Humans always left their minds wide open. There was no wonder why it was so easy to possess them. That was neither here nor there.

Who was this Neo fellow that Tasmin had first said I was dressed like last evening? And what on earth was… The Matrix? I thought as I walked back into the café.

I startled when I heard Elisa laughing from the kitchen. She cackled so hard and long, it almost sounded as if she was crying. She came from the back with a tray of hot croissants, took one look at me, then howled with laughter again.

"Care to enlighten me on the joke, Sissy?" I asked, a bit annoyed.

Once she had set her pastries inside the glass counter, she took a few moments to catch her breath. "Whew! I'm sorry, but you are indeed dressed like Neo from The Matrix."

She pulled her cell phone from her pocket, typed on it for a few seconds and then walked over to show me what she was looking at. I took the device then studied the pictures that popped up. Once I'd had my fill, I passed her the phone back.

I grunted. "I look way better than that Keanu chap and wear this look far better than he, thank you, Tasmin, and those women very much." I scoffed then took off my trench to hang it back on the coat rack while Elisa continued to laugh at my expense.

"While you're over there, will you prop the door open for a bit so my customers will know I'm in here?" she asked.

I did as she instructed only to have a cat rush inside. "Bloody hell," I snapped.

Elisa looked down and said, "Disemspi?"

"Is that Ilene's cat?" I asked.

Elisa nodded as the cat trotted to the front door then back to Elisa. He did that over and over.

"Is it trying to communicate with you?" I asked.

"I think he is," she said as she walked from behind the counter.

The cat ran to the door again then looked back as if waiting for her to follow. She untied her apron then tossed it on one of the tables. She went to the door and gasped as she looked toward the bookstore.

"It's the ghost," she said.

I went to look in the direction she pointed. "I can't see her," I said.

"How are you an angel and can't see ghost, Octavian?"

"It's above my pay grade thank you none too kindly. I don't have that privilege. You would need my parents or Uncle if you want archangels who can see ghosts."

The cat crawled through and around Elisa's ankles as it mewled. I thought back to the night of the little jubilee the mayor had thrown and remembered that there was a disembodied spirit trapped in that cat. Was it possible that the cat could see the ghost and knew who it was?

I knelt then studied the cat. "Blink twice if you can understand me," I said.

When the cat looked up at Elisa and blinked twice, she smiled. "Do you want me to talk to her?" she asked as she pointed at the top window of the bookstore.

The cat blinked twice.

"Do you know who she is?"

It blinked twice once more.

"Hmph," was all I could say as I stood.

I got ready to tell Elisa she should call Tasmin when the cat hissed and then screeched loudly as it glared behind Elisa. She whipped around and came face-to-face with Marie LaLaurie. I slipped into the veil. Marie was as young as she had been back in the early 1800s. However, the evil that surrounded her turned the air sour. She was so far into dark magick that she smelled of rotting flesh. Next to her was her impundulu. He was in human form, dressed in a tan linen suit that looked more like a cotton sack. It was fitting considering who his master was. I noticed that he had stopped just inches from Elisa's shop door. Silas' wards must still be at work.

"Elisa Hunte formerly Elisa Hunte Battle, slave of Thomas Williams," Marie dragged out in an old southern accent.

"Marie...wanted serial killer, wannabe witch and practitioner of Black magick," Elisa said coolly.

"Snarky as ever. Still the uppity dark negress, are we?" Marie snarled, a look of disgust on her face.

Elisa blinked slowly, her shoulders tensed, but she didn't respond.

"Don't tell me you have nothing to say, gal," Marie goaded. "Why I've come all this way just to meet you."

As Marie antagonized Elisa, I moved in and out of the veil while keeping my eyes on her vamp. The thing was so under Marie's spell that it didn't even notice me as it snarled and hissed at Elisa. Neither did Marie. I found it odd that she couldn't even sense another being was near. It made me question if she was truly immortal. What also made me question her true immortality was her repeated use of blood magick.

I didn't know if Elisa had noticed I was no longer behind her. Moving in and out of the veil often meant I moved at the speed of light. What I did notice was Elisa's hand in her apron pocket.

She smiled coolly at the witch. "Why are you really here?" she asked. "That blood magick you're doing tells me you're at a demon's disposal, so why are you truly here, bitch?"

Marie snarled. "You dare address me as such! Back in my day—"

"Back in your day a mob of your own people demolished your precious mansion because of the torture you inflicted on your slaves. Your own…people…"

Marie took a deep breath, but I could tell Elisa's words had rattled her. "You and your family have been a thorn in my family's side for generations, you Black witch. This time, you'll pay."

Just as she leveled that threat, I grabbed the impundulu and dragged him behind the veil. He screeched and hollered as the pure white and golden light eviscerated him. He transformed into his true self as holy fire raced up his body. Marie shot something like an electric charge at Elisa, only for Elisa to dodge it. It hit a tree just as Elisa threw a vial at Marie's head. The glass cracked and black salt spread in a plume of smoke over Marie's face. The smell of my blood rent the air.

The gift I'd given Elisa had been a vial of my blood. Judging by the smell of tar mixed with the faint hint of vanilla extract, it was my guess that Elisa had mixed a bit of my blood with her black salt. While her vamp lay dead at my feet in a pile of ash, Marie grabbed her face and screamed so loud that it caused a couple of windows to shatter.

"Try again," Elisa snarled.

Her hand jutted forward and caught hold of a tree branch. With her other hand she did a tut move that caused other branches to lash out at LaLaurie. The branches attacked without remorse, whipping and slashing at the witch as if she had offended it somehow. Then the roots of the tree crawled up LaLaurie's legs and then her arms until it had her stretched out like she was on a crucifix. Her head lolled forward as if she had been knocked unconscious.

"Now, Tasmin," Elisa yelled, causing me to stumble out of the veil to see exactly where Tasmin could be.

I heard the sound of metal being dragged. *Chains?* Yes, chains, but I didn't see Tasmin or the chains in question. And where was Tasmin? The skies darkened and the denizens of Salix Pointe moved about as if they didn't see the madness happening before them. Tasmin and Elisa must have used an illusions charm. LaLaurie's body jerked violently as her screams lit up the air...only...in front of me, her head still lolled forward. It was as if she were sleeping.

The chains clanked and rattled. I saw them appear out of thin air then coil around her body like the precious metal was a snake. LaLaurie's shrill cries became louder. It continued that way until the chains sunk into her skin to the point of obliteration. She combusted into fiery dust. It was the damnedest thing I'd ever seen, and I was an archangel.

"You have to hurry," Elisa said, rushing to collect some of the dust. "Go wake Tasmin. Make sure she has iron somewhere near her before you do. Once Marie wakes up and realizes what we've done, she's going to be pissed."

I stared at Elisa with something akin to amazement and bewilderment. "Wake her? What in God's name are you getting on about?"

"Yes, Octavian," she snapped as she scooped up a copious amount of the dust then stood. "Tasmin is dream walking. She's in the basement of the bookstore."

"What?" I all but yelled.

How was she so close to me, and yet I couldn't feel her presence? What had these witches done?

"She's been at the bookstore this whole time?"

"Yes! Go wake her! Right this instant lest Marie realizes what we've just done."

"And what exactly have you and Tasmin done?" I asked, wild-eyed and a bit panicked.

"We've bridged the dream world to the waking world in real time. Do you understand? And if you don't get through the veil and wake Tasmin right this instant, she will be stuck there."

"Stuck where?" I yelled.

"In Marie's dream."

Before the words could leave her mouth, I ran through the veil to the basement of the bookstore. There, in the middle of the room on the floor, Tasmin was sleeping. She surrounded herself with some sort of sigil. I didn't even have time to look at the specs of the ritualistic scribing as Tasmin was thrashing wildly about. In one hand, she held steadfast to a nail so big it looked as if it came from a train track. In the other hand was a horseshoe. I feared I didn't have time to waste on prerequisites. I knelt beside her then placed two fingers against her third eye and watched her jump awake. She took a swing at me with the hand she held the nail in. I moved just in time.

I caught her wrists as her eyes roamed wildly around the room. "Elisa!" She panted and looked at me, eyes wider now. "Elisa. Where's Elisa?"

"Elisa is fine, Poppet," I said.

"Did she do it? Did she get it?"

"Before I can answer that, you have to tell me exactly what's going on."

Tasmin shook her head then stood. I released her wrists then took the nail and horseshoe from her grip.

"During our readings—"

"What kind of readings?"

"Not those kind. The Book of Magic Enchantment—anyway, we think we found a link between us, well our families, and Madame Marie. Her mansion was destroyed 1834, during a time when Black people were seen as chattel. Sure there were laws in place that said a master had to take care of his or her slaves, but do you really think they did?"

"I know the story," I said, trying to hurry her along.

She turned to look at me. "Why would white people, in 1834, rally a mob to demolish the house of a white woman and her white husband in a slave holding southern state, such as Louisiana? Keep in mind, no one accused her of witchcraft or anything of the sort. One of the women found in the LaLaurie's mansion was a Black woman with an iron collar around her neck. Keep that in the back of your mind. Again, why would a mob of white people, mostly southern white men, care about the abuse of slaves…unless…"

I shot straight up like a fire had been lit underneath me. "Unless they had been placed under some sort of spell!"

"Exactly," Tasmin all but yelled. "Based on the readings Elisa and I have done, the Black woman with the iron collar was a witch—"

"From your bloodline," I said slowly.

Tasmin nodded. "You've got it."

"Now that you've blown the top off my lid with that bit of information, what does it have to do with what you and Elisa did today?"

"Oh! Elisa and I just made it so the haggard old bat can no longer dream walk. It's how she's been able to move without detection. Did Elisa get the embers and the dust?"

I nodded.

"Elisa and I hadn't planned on doing it today but when you gifted her with angel's blood…well, today was as good as any."

"Dare I ask what you and Elisa plan to do with your bounty?"

Tasmin smirked. "You can ask, but that doesn't mean I'll tell…"

.

CHAPTER 17

DAFARI

I STOOD IN FRONT of the mirror in my office, still attempting to control myself, the urge to go back to the café and take Elisa home to our bed as strong as it had been when I left. I was failing miserably, so much so that my reflection disturbed even me. Two red eyes stared back at me, fangs yet to retract.

"Having trouble recovering, I see," I heard my father say from a shadow in the corner closest to my office door. "Your woman, what's that phrase, ah yes, truly has your nose wide open. In your current state you could severely injure or even kill our dear, sweet barista, and neither of us wants that."

I turned toward the sound of his voice, ready to eviscerate him once he stepped out of the shadow. I was still smarting from his innuendoes toward Elisa at the café. I was so incensed I wanted to thrash him in the same manner I had the night of the mayor's jubilee.

"Octavian had already banished me for the very same reason; however, I know he genuinely cares for Elisa and her well-being. What's your excuse?"

I heard him sigh. "Always with the supposition, my love-lorn offspring. For the record, I've developed a certain... fondness for the witches." Although he remained hidden, I knew full well that he could see me, which is why I eyed him with the dubiousness he so rightly deserved. He chuckled then said, "No worries, Dafari. I have no designs on our tasty pastry maker or Octavian's virgin firebrand. I just admire their moxie."

As always, I believed my father as much as I believed the moon was made of green cheese. Deep down I suspected he knew that.

"As for you, my languishing son, I suggest you take care of your current state before returning to your lady love, perhaps with some otherworldly comfort?"

"No," I firmly replied. "I will not betray my wife by committing adultery."

"Technically she's not your wife," Father countered. "Not in this lifetime, anyway. Besides, who's to know save for the two of us?"

"*I* will know and guaranteed so will Elisa. I will not disrespect her, legally wed or not, even if it can protect her from me."

"Then you, my son, have a long day ahead of you." I heard him snicker. His amusement at my expense annoyed me even more than it usually did.

"Perhaps not," I said, taking off my lab coat and placing it on a hanger on my office door.

"Oh? Do tell."

"It's nothing I care to share. Father, please take your leave. I have somewhere I need to be."

Without a word, he exited my office. I made a mental note to ask Elisa and Tasmin to ward my office, as Father's uninvited visits were becoming a bit too frequent. I, too, made my way through the shadows until I reached Tasmin's bookstore. I wasn't sure if she was even there, but the hope was that she could help me with my current plight. The inside of the bookstore was dark; lights were turned off and blinds on the front door and windows shut. The only reason I suspected she was there was the fact that the heat was on, and the building was nice and toasty. Tasmin always turned the heat on low prior to closing. Just as I was about to search for her, I heard voices coming from the basement, those voices belonging to Tasmin and Octavian. I raised an eyebrow, curious as to why Octavian was in the witches' sanctorum, their refuge, and the epicenter of Salix Pointe's magick. I wouldn't have to wonder long. I probably should have made my presence known immediately; instead, I remained in a shadow, eavesdropping. I realized that at times I was my father's son.

"Why would you use a sigil that could block me, of all people, from detecting your presence?" Octavian bellowed.

Already I found the conversation intriguing and was anxious to hear more.

"Because I knew that if you got wind of our plan, you would try to stop me," Tasmin calmly replied, walking over to the wall outlets, turning on the four fireplaces, which were spread throughout the bookstore. She then leaned up against one of the rectangular tables, arms crossed over her chest.

"You're damn right I would have!" he replied, coming to stand in front of Tasmin, towering over her. "Woman, your plan could have led to sheer folly. What if it had failed and you ended up trapped in the dream world?"

"Octavian, why focus on what ifs? As you saw for yourself, it didn't fail and I'm fine. Take the win for what it is. What we should be focusing on is getting rid of her for good."

My brother let out a hard breath before speaking, placing his hands on Tasmin's slender shoulders. "While I am elated that you and Elisa have bested that vile hag for the moment, and I was able to slay the impundulu, all I could think about was the thought of losing you again. You wouldn't want me to go off my trolley again, would you?" I felt the pain his question held.

Tasmin's demeanor softened as she placed one hand on Octavian's face, the other on his chest. "No, I wouldn't, but you're not going to lose me, you big softy."

She grabbed him by his shirt, pulling him into a sensual kiss, her arms finding purchase around his neck. For as long as I could remember, Tasmin had a flair for getting her way with Octavian. Even in this lifetime, I observed that she wasn't afraid to use her feminine wiles on him. My brother fell for it every time, clearly aroused by Tasmin's kiss. His hands slowly traveled down her back, resting firmly on her backside before he placed his body flush with hers. They were both giving off powerful pheromones. While Elisa smelled of honeysuckle, Tasmin's scent was lavender. The aroma was so strong, it was overpowering. I imagined this was how Octavian, and even my father, felt earlier in the café. They remained lip locked for several minutes, unaware of anything save each other. While I was pleased that Octavian and Tasmin were able to find a moment of solace, a part of me was envious because Elisa and I had yet to find ours.

After what seemed like an eternity, Octavian gently pulled away from Tasmin. "I'm sorry, my love, but it's not safe for me to be around you like this. That kiss, your mere touch is igniting my passion for you. I fear it will overtake me and I'll carry you back down to the basement and enrapture you."

"Enrapture me?" she replied, laughing. "You are so archaic. While that might actually be fun, I understand. We need to remain on task. I'll let you off the hook…for now."

"Thank you, Poppet. Besides, I want our first time together to be as special as you are," he remarked, kissing her on the forehead.

"How can someone be so corny and so adorable at the same time?" she asked, completely enamored by his sickly-sweet repartee.

"It's a gift."

In my heightened state, their lovefest was too much for me to bear. *Get a room already*, I thought. Unfortunately, I didn't realize that I had left my mind open for a second, but a second was all it took for Octavian to become cognizant of my presence.

"Dafari! Stop lurking in the shadows like your father and come out here this instant!"

I slowly stepped out of the shadow, not wanting to alarm Tasmin. It didn't help, as she gasped when she saw me. "What's wrong with you, Dafari? The emotions emanating from you are suffocating."

"Apparently, my dear old brother is still intoxicated from Elisa's...scent," Octavian answered in my stead. "He showed up to the café all but demanding that Elisa return home, then he and Uncle Azazel almost came to fisticuffs. I had to oust him from the shop before he did something he most likely would have regretted. I thought he would have regained some composure by now, but obviously I was mistaken."

"We can't all be like you, little brother," I snidely remarked.

Tasmin looked from Octavian to me. "Guys, no in-fighting, please. What was Demon Daddy even doing there? You know what, never mind. That's not important at the moment. Helping you right now is. I can't have you seeing Elisa like this, especially after everything that went down earlier."

I knew I was in a bad way, but I found it necessary to know what Tasmin was talking about. "What exactly happened?"

"Long story short, Elisa and I figured out a way to prevent Madame Marie from dream walking. The only way she'll be able to do anything now is to show herself out in the open."

"But how—"

"They used themselves as bait; Tasmin in the dream world, and Elisa on the earthly plane. Luckily for them, their little ruse worked with a little help from me and some of my blood, although I was only there by chance. While they vanquished LaLaurie from the dream world, I was able to dispatch the impundulu for good."

I was quiet for a few seconds, taking in what was revealed to me. Then I snapped. "Are you and Elisa insane? No wonder Octavian was upset with you earlier."

Tasmin looked at me quizzically. "How long have you been here, Dafari?" she asked.

"That's not the issue right now. What *is* of issue is your and Elisa's reckless behavior. Why would you two conceive and execute such a plan without advising me and Octavian? You two could have been hurt or worse. I need to speak with Elisa immediately."

"Like hell you will," Octavian said, blocking me.

"You do realize I can traverse the shadows directly to the café," I voiced, my tone low and menacing.

Unfazed, Octavian replied, "And I can bridge the veil just as swiftly. Would you dare to try me, brother dear?"

"Okay, boys, enough," Tasmin said, cutting in to stand between me and Octavian.

My shoulders slumped in defeat. "My apologies for my outburst, and for attempting to leave. My only intention was to make sure Elisa was unhurt."

"No apologies necessary, Dafari. Elisa's fine, but, clearly, you're not. You can't see her right now; not until you're back to your normal moody broody self." Tasmin smiled. I recognized her method of gentle ribbing, something I had truly missed from the time we all shared in their past lives.

"Duly noted, Sister," I said, returning her smile as best I could, fangs be damned. In the past, Sister was my term of endearment for Tasmin. I was glad I could finally refer to her in that way again. "That was why I came here; to ask for your help."

"Then why not reveal yourself in the first place?" Octavian queried.

"I'll admit my not showing myself sooner was...ill-advised, but I was curious to hear what it was that caused you to blow your stack, little brother. Now that I know the full story, I must say your rage was justified. Once I recover, we all must convene in order to discuss the events of today. But first, Tasmin, can you help me?"

"I believe I can, but I prefer if it was just the two of us. That way I can devote all of my attention to the task at hand. I have to gather a few things first."

She started to walk away before Octavian spoke. "Hold your horses, Tasmin. Do you really think I'm going to leave you here with Dafari while everything is not tickety-boo?"

Turning around to face us, she walked back over to him, placing her hands on his chest. "Of course I do, because you know that Dafari would never hurt me, and you trust me enough to know that I'm quite proficient in my craft. In the meantime, you can check on Elisa. I'm sure that would ease Dafari's mind, wouldn't you agree?"

As he looked deeply into her eyes, I could tell he was going to cave. The woman was indeed a master of manipulation where Octavian was concerned.

"As you wish, Poppet. You go collect what you need while I have a quick chin wag with my brother."

Tasmin's eyes became thin slits. She pointed at Octavian and said, "Be nice," then departed for the basement.

"Before you say anything," I started, holding up my hands as if in surrender, "I assure you the only reason I came here was to ask for Tasmin's help, nothing more. I had no idea what I was walking into. Although," I continued, a smirk on my face, "I'm glad to see that you may finally reach paradise. The last thing I need is for you to leave your mind open again projecting thoughts of Tasmin. That was traumatizing, to say the very least."

"Don't be a crass arse, Dafari. I will admit I do look forward to sharing a home, and other things, with Tasmin again."

"I look forward to the same with Elisa, sooner rather than later."

"I know this may be difficult for you, Brother, but be patient with little sissy. Let her deal with her grief and anger in her own way and in her own time, as opposed trying to force her to let you take it away from her. Your proposed course of action could possibly end in resentment on her part, and I know you don't want that. The anguish she is feeling is hers and hers alone to handle, unless she invites you in to share it, and you must respect that. And to be clear, I know you wouldn't hurt Tasmin."

I was grateful Octavian had ended our conversation on that note, as Tasmin was returning, a tray containing a small tea pot, a mug, and some other items in her hands. She walked over to one of the fireplaces, placing the tray on the table situated between two comfortable chairs, motioning for me to have a seat.

"This won't take long," she said to Octavian. "I'll contact Elisa as soon as I'm done."

"I'll be waiting patiently," he said. He dipped his head, lightly brushing his lips to hers. He then stepped through the veil, on his way to the café, I presumed.

"Okay, Dafari, let's get started. I need you sit back and let me do the work."

I made myself comfortable, placing my back firmly against the chair's soft cushioning. Tasmin stood behind me, her index and middle fingers placed lightly on my temples while her thumbs rested directly in front of my ears.

"Now close your eyes and take some deep breaths. Think of someplace peaceful and serene."

While my thoughts should have taken me to the one place I retreated to when I needed the peace and serenity that Tasmin spoke of, my mind wandered to someplace different; to the place where I had set the perfect romantic evening for Elisa in the dream world several weeks ago; YS Falls in Jamaica. The waterfalls above the Black River and its seven river pools were magnificent, the gardens and jungle foliage full, colorful, and lush. When I created the illusion for Elisa, it was nighttime; however, I thought it...unwise to replicate that scenario, as the intentions I had for Elisa back then were the same intentions I have now, the same intentions that have me in this frenzied state.

Instead, I focused on a morning scene, sunrise to be exact. While I had found it difficult to relax and come back to my normal state on my own, with Tasmin's adept aid, I could actually see the orange-yellow sun rising and feel its rays on my skin; hear and see the crystal-clear water from the falls cascading into the Black River; and smell the myriad of garden flowers in bloom, helping me return to my more rational, logical self. Just as Tasmin was finishing up, a mild purple haze enveloped me, filling me with a calm that I had not felt in quite some time. Although it was for completely selfish reasons, I had never been so grateful that Tasmin had fully awakened.

"Feeling better?" she asked, removing her hands then sitting in the chair on the other side of the table.

"Yes, much better. Thank you, Tasmin."

She began pouring whatever was in the teapot into the mug then placed the teapot on the table. After handing the mug to me she said, "You're welcome. Now drink this."

I sniffed the brew. "Is that peppermint I smell?"

Tasmin smiled. "It is, along with lavender, chamomile, and a touch of honey for sweetness. It's a calming blend."

"I hope I didn't startle you too much earlier," I said after taking a long sip of the hot brew.

She picked up the tray, placing it on her lap. "I was a bit surprised that you were so out of sorts, but not so much that I was afraid of you, if that's what you're getting at," she replied while cutting a piece of elastic cord with a small pair of scissors.

Tasmin continued her task as I drank the savory tea. I watched as she adroitly threaded crystal beads on the cord then fashioned it into a bracelet. I thought back to how creative she was. In her past lives, she would make crystal jewelry for various purposes; protection, healing, love, you name it, she could make it.

"Here, put this on," she said, handing me the bracelet. "It's amethyst, black tourmaline, and clear quartz. It should help keep you grounded and balanced, as well as calm your... urges," she said with a smirk on her face.

I took the bracelet and put it on my wrist. It fit perfectly. "Thank you for this, and everything else, Sister. Perhaps you should make one of these for Octavian," I said then chuckled.

Tasmin looked at me and shook her head. "I can handle him."

"As I so clearly observed. You still have my brother wrapped around your little finger."

"I do not," she said. The blush in her cheeks, as well as her giggles, told the truth.

It was good to hear her laugh. She and Elisa had dealt with so much trauma and drama and deserved to have some levity in their lives.

"If you say so, Sister. Any other time my brother would have stood guard at Elisa's home all night in order to keep you two safe; however, he actually returned home last night."

"Octavian and I came to a…mutual understanding. He's not that bad, Dafari." She saw the look I gave her then replied, "Okay, maybe he is. But in his defense, in some ways I've grown to appreciate his overly protective nature."

"My, how we've learned to become a bit more flexible over the centuries. Elisa told me that at one time you once thought Octavian acted like a caveman."

She chuckled before saying, "I still do! But he's *my* caveman. And speaking of caveman, may I speak freely?"

"If I say no, would that stop you?" I asked.

"You already know," she answered returning the tray to a table. "Brother of mine, I understand that you want Elisa with you, truly I do. But your methods won't get you anywhere."

"So I've seen. Let me guess, you have a suggestion."

"You know me so well," she said standing up in front of me. "Just hear me out. Although Elisa was your wife historically and spiritually, in the eyes of the law, she isn't in this one, although you keep referring to her as such. But perhaps if you made a gesture to correct that instead of trying to coerce her, Elisa may be willing to go back home with you. A little finesse can go a long way."

This time it was my turn to chuckle, something I didn't do often, but in this case, I was amused.

Tasmin looked at me raising an eyebrow. "Was something I said funny?"

"Not at all. It's just that Hell must have frozen over because you and my father actually have something in common; you both felt the need to remind me of Elisa and my marital status, or lack thereof, albeit for very different reasons."

"And I was actually enjoying this conversation," she said, feigning as if she was going to vomit. "Seriously though, at least think about what I said."

I nodded. "Coming from you, I will definitely take it under advisement." I paused before continuing. "I missed these candid talks of ours."

"So did I," Tasmin said, a nostalgic look on her face. She reached in her back pocket, pulling out her cell phone. She appeared to be checking a message then she sent one of her own. "As much as I'd love to continue, we have a situation."

I placed my mug on the table. "What's wrong?"

"Apparently, Ilene's mangy cat has been at the café and won't leave, even though they tried to get rid of it. Elisa said he communicated with her and Octavian, and that it has something to do with the ghost in the attic," she replied walking toward the basement. "We figured that since we have the cat and the spell to release a disembodied spirit, we might as well do it now; otherwise, we might not get another chance. Octavian and Elisa are on their way."

Tasmin and I walked down to the basement, checking all the wards to make sure they were still intact. Elisa and Octavian, who was carrying Disemspi under his arm, joined us in short order. While I desperately longed to speak with Elisa and apologize to her for my earlier behavior, I knew this was neither the time nor the place. This was probably our singular opportunity for the witches to release the soul of whoever was trapped inside Ilene's cat. My personal issues would have to wait.

"This infernal beast will not be quiet," Octavian uttered, clearly annoyed.

With a wave of my hand, the feline became silent. Octavian placed him on the floor, with the cat scurrying underneath a chair.

The four of us cleansed the space with sage, frankincense, and myrrh. On top of the sigil, Tasmin and Elisa then formed a large inner protection circle with black tourmaline, fluorite, jet stone, labradorite, black obsidian, staurolite, black kyanite, Apache tears, and black jade crystals, while Octavian and I created an outer protection circle made of black, white, and blue candles. Lastly, as a final layer of protection, Tasmin created an innermost circle using Himalayan pink salt.

"Dafari, since he responds to you the best, can you please put the cat inside the salt circle," Tasmin asked.

I walked over to Disemspi, picked him up and placed the cat within the circle, being careful not to disturb the salt, crystals, or candles.

Elisa removed the Book of Magic Enchantment from a bookshelf. Placing it on a stand, she turned several pages.

"After Tasmin took pictures of the spells in the mayor's Book of Shadows, we transcribed them into the Book of Magic Enchantment. It made them easier to study. Because a spirit is trapped in Disemspi's body, we created a spell to reverse the effect, as well as prevent his soul from being imprisoned again," she explained. She turned to Tasmin, asking, "Are you ready?"

Tasmin nodded, standing next to Elisa then she clasped her left hand in Elisa's right. Looking down at the book, they recited their spell.

"We call on our Ancestors far and near to respectfully re-quest that you make our way clear. Free the spirit of Afolabi trapped within. Release him from the body of Disemspi, let the transformation begin. We ask that you liberate Afolabi's soul,

never again to be confined. Protect him, guard and keep him safe until the end of time.

As soon as the spell concluded, a bluish-purple glow engulfed the cat. His body stiffened and his back flexed. It appeared as if something was separating from his spinal region, an ethereal mist of sorts. When the dissociation was complete, Disemspi dashed out of the circle. I quickly grabbed him up, transporting him through the shadows, only to leave him on the sidewalk. Someone would eventually find him and return him to Ilene Suzanne. When I returned to the basement, the otherworldly apparition was floating in the middle of the salt circle. Judging by his appearance, he seemed to be in his late thirties, early forties. Dressed in a clean white shirt, tan pants, and black leather shoes, his low-cut auburn hair, moustache and goatee, blended well with his gingerbread brown skin and deep-set hazel eyes. Octavian and I stood off to the side, while Tasmin and Elisa spoke to the disembodied entity.

"Who are you?" Elisa asked.

"I am Afolabi," he began. "A slave originally brought to Salix Pointe from Ghana in 1825. I and my wife Aziza were sold to a family with the surname Ossoff."

Elisa had a confused look on her face. "But from what I understand, the Ossoffs had never owned enslaved people. There was nothing in Salix Pointe's history to indicate that. Our family has been friends with the Ossoffs for generations. I grew up with Hickenlooper Ossoff and he's never been anything but kind and generous."

"You are correct, Elisa. The Ossoffs were not involved in the slave trade."

"Then why did they buy slaves?" Tasmin asked, looking just as confused as Elisa.

"Why would they indeed?" Afolabi replied. "The Ossoffs were, in fact, abolitionists. The family purchased as many enslaved people as they could at any one time. While we would work for them during the day picking blueberries, peaches, pecans, and peanuts, under the cover of night they were recruiting those of us who chose to participate into the South Carolina faction of The Underground Railroad. Some decided to actively take part in the cause, while others chose to attempt the journey up north in search of a better life. Aziza and I resolved to stay with the Ossoffs to help further the undertaking, as she and I possessed special…gifts."

Tasmin and Elisa looked at each other then back to Afolabi.

"You two were witches?" Elisa asked.

"Yes, we were, and together with the Ossoffs, we had many successful excursions, with countless enslaved finding their way to freedom. But like all good things, they eventually come to an end. We were unfortunately betrayed by someone we trusted. Aziza and I were slaughtered, our souls left to wander aimlessly."

"How did you end up in that cat?" Tasmin questioned.

"While the mayor's family hails from New Orleans, they also have deep ties to Salix Pointe. A relative of his ensnared my soul and placed it in a cat. As that feline aged, my soul would be transferred to another, and so it went until you two released me."

"And what about Aziza, what happened to her?"

"The ghost in the attic is my Aziza, and she and I are your kin."

CHAPTER 18

ELISA

"OUR KIN?" TASMIN and I blurted out at the same time.

Afolabi nodded. "Yes, and while I would love nothing more than to tell you how, I'm sure you can understand that I need to see Aziza, my wife…It's been so long…"

There was a plea in his eyes that hit me right in the gut. Having just been reawakened myself, I understood his need to see his wife, even if it was in spirit. Just as the thought crossed my mind, a strong gust of wind blew through the place. We looked up to see the basement door open.

"Aziza," Afolabi called out on a gasp before his ethereal form rushed up the stairs.

I watched in awe as two ghosts embraced and—were they crying?

"How long have you been trapped in this building?" Afolabi asked Aziza.

"For about as long as you've been trapped inside those animals," she said, her voice low and soft. "Something tried to snatch my soul before our Ancestors could. There was a fight and the next thing I knew, I ended up here," she said then waved a hand. "No one has been able to see me after Duma-Nolan perished except her." She pointed at me then asked. "Can they all see me now?"

I shook my head. "I'm not...sure. Can you all see her?" I turned to ask the others.

"No, unfortunately, I cannot," Octavian said, a bit of a frown marring his features.

Tasmin shook her head. "No. It's odd, especially since when my father conjured Aunt Noreen, I saw her just fine."

"I can see him, but not her," Dafari answered.

"When a ghost is conjured, it's easier for humans to see them because of the rituals and magick used to call us from the other side. Silas and Elisa are necromancers, same as I was. The only unique thing about Elisa possessing that power is that for generations, it has only been passed down to the males of our family," Afolabi explained. "It speaks to the power she possesses. The reason all of you are able to see me is because I'm a spirit and not a ghost."

Necromancer? I'm a...necromancer? My father had been one, too?

"There is a difference?" Tasmin asked.

He nodded.

"Ah! Yes, of course," Octavian said. "Why didn't I think of that?"

"What do you mean?" Tasmin asked him.

I wasn't surprised when he started to pace the floor. He did that often when in deep thought or talking about something up his alley.

"A spirit is more like a discarnate entity. They are the souls that survive when a person dies and has no physical body to reside in. They are free to move from one dimension to the other and can come and go as they please. A ghost is tied to the location in which they perished. Their deaths are usually violent and tragic. They often don't even realize they're dead. In a lot of cases, the ghosts stay behind as they have unfinished business, so to speak, and they do not accept the way in which they died." He looked from me to Afolabi. "Would one of you ask her if she knows why she is tied to this location?"

I didn't want to tell him there was no need for us to ask as she could hear him just fine. I didn't have to.

Afolabi took her hands in his then said, "This location is where we hid a lot of enslaved people who had escaped."

"Runaway slaves were stationed here?" I asked, awed by it all.

"In this store?" Tasmin questioned.

Aziza flinched and Afolabi rubbed the back of her hands. "She's always hated the term runaway slaves. She feels it dehumanizes those of us who were enslaved."

"Calling us runaway slaves as opposed to enslaved people who escaped horrible conditions takes the onus off the slavers and puts it on us. We were seen as chattel through no fault of our own. We were enslaved. Those were our circumstances. Slave was how we were identified. Traffickers enslaved us. The language we use matters, Elisa," Aziza said emphatically.

Shame covered me like a cloak. I felt as if I'd just been chastised.

"Yes, you're correct," I said before I told the others what she'd said.

Aziza nodded then smiled at me, her eyes still wet with tears, but something akin to compassion and understanding was there.

Afolabi waved his hand. "There is much we need to discuss, but I fear here and now is not the time. There is a reason I was so adamant about coming here today, and why I am grateful to the both of you for releasing me from that pitiful animal."

His brows furrowed. "Last evening, the demon Marie is feeding demanded a purer blood. She all but tossed the goat blood at Marie's face. I fear infants and children are next."

I gasped.

"Over my dead body," Dafari snarled.

"I beg your pardon," Octavian snapped, incredulity in his voice.

"Holy crap," Tasmin whispered. "That explains why I heard the cries of children in the dream world. I didn't think to mention it because I was so focused on banishing her. Perhaps the wails of children were a warning of some sort." The look on her face told me she was kicking herself for not realizing it sooner. Her brows were knitted together and she, too, was now pacing the floor.

"Do you know who the demon is?" I asked.

Afolabi nodded. "Yes," he said then glanced from me to Dafari as if he didn't want to say the demon's name in his presence. "You do know he's half...demon, yes?"

I nodded. "Please tell me you're not talking about Azazel," I all but screeched.

He shook his head. "No, no. It's just...I don't know that he can be trusted being..."

I felt and saw Dafari bristle. It reminded me of days old when I had to constantly defend his character to those who didn't know him and sometimes to those who did know him. His parentage always made some question his trustworthiness. I held out my hand for him to take as I used to all those years ago. I knew he didn't want to, but he did ease my hand into his.

I never break my promises to you, Elisa, he sent me telepathically.

My heart smiled. All those many years ago, Dafari had a temper filled with a rage fiercer than Octavian's when it came to Tasmin. It scared me so badly I'd asked him to make a blood promise to me that before he lost his cool, he would always call out to me. I was well aware that I could quell his rage as well as ignite it.

"He's my husband," I blurted out before my brain could catch up. "Well...he...was, but listen, he's just as trustworthy as any person or entity in this room!"

"Are you certain?" Aziza asked.

"Yes, are you? Especially since his father knows who the demon is. I heard him speaking with her in the shadows."

"Her?" Tasmin and I parroted one another.

"Yes, her," Afolabi repeated.

Then he revealed who the *her* in question was, and we all stood there, dumbfounded.

"IS HE CERTAIN?" Martha asked, horror etched across her features.

Dafari nodded, clouds behind those golden eyes of his. The energy wafting off him was palpable. His breathing was slow and even, but his bleak aura and rigid stance told of his anger.

"He's pretty sure. He said her name and said that she demanded a purer blood," he told Martha.

As soon as Afolabi revealed who the demon was, Tasmin and I agreed that it would be wise to get the whole coven together no matter how fractured we were. We were up against a big bad worse than LaLaurie if we didn't figure out how to banish her before she got any stronger.

"It just doesn't make sense why a demon of such a caliber would align herself with the likes of a disgraced witch," Jewel said.

"When a demon wants out of the pit, it will use any means necessary," Dafari said. "Even if it has to latch on to something else to do so."

I frowned. "What do you mean?"

He folded his arms across his chest, the muscles in both areas straining the fabric of his shirt. His long black, wavy hair was in a ponytail that put his exotic dark skin on display. "When I served my time all those years ago, from the little bits and pieces I can remember, even low-level demons would try to sneak out of Hell on the backs of malevolent beings."

My heart ached when he spoke of his imprisonment. I wanted to ask so many questions about that time.

Later, he said internally.

His voice was a low monotone, and it traveled to places I shouldn't have been thinking about at the moment. For some odd reason, the way he'd said later sent fire up my spine. It was a simple word that held so much promise.

He turned his eyes my way, gave me a slow gaze from head to toe then back up again. *Later*, he told me internally again. This time his enunciation of the word gave me chills.

"Yes, Father and the uncles often spoke of how their 7th Battalion always had to fight for the souls of those the demon latched on to once on earth," Octavian said.

Tasmin asked, "What is the 7th Battalion?"

"Later, my love," he said then walked to Dafari. "So, you mean to tell me, big brother, that the demon in question was so weak that she had to fetch a ride to this plane?'

"That is the only way to explain her presence and why so much blood magick is needed," Dafari answered.

"To that end, what do we do now?" Cara Lee asked. "We've already spent so much time on personal things."

"Yes, I think it's best we put our difference aside at the

moment and figure out what to do to protect our girls and this town," Mary Ann chimed in.

"I agree," said Silas as he cast a glance at both Tasmin and me. "In the meantime, what do we do about his lecherous father? Clearly he can't be trusted."

"I need to speak with him privately before any of us make a decision on that," Dafari said.

"May I ask what for?" Tasmin asked.

"We know my father walks the gray. Do we not want to hear what he can tell us before we banish him?"

"We don't really care what he has to tell us at this point," Jewel cut in.

"I'm with my wife on this one. What he has to say is irrelevant. It's been duly noted that not one of your parents can be trusted in this fight," Silas spat.

"My, my…aren't we the teapot calling the kettle black," Octavian crooned as he eyed Silas and Jewel, his black eyes dark and accusatory. "I don't like nor do I trust Uncle more than any of you, but it would be hypocritical to point the finger at our parentage, when you lot have done your share of keeping secrets and being manipulative."

Silas cut his eyes at Octavian. He visibly bristled when Tasmin stood next to him then rubbed a hand up and down his shoulder. She stood as a united front with him as she cast a sullen gaze at her parents. Jewel looked my direction. I was sure my eyes said all that I felt as I stood next to Tasmin. Not even seconds later, Dafari was by my side.

"It's us being hunted," I said. "For as much as I hate to say this…we wait for Azazel's side of the story before we make a move to banish him from our homes and places of business."

"I'm going to regret this later, I know it," Tasmin griped then sighed. "But…the demon sticks around until then."

"Then it's settled," Martha said as she stood. "We need to make the pact of the coven while we're all here." She removed her jacket then picked up her staff. "Dafari, Octavian, we have to ask that you leave the room while this takes place. It is a sacred tradition of this coven and always has been."

"I'll wait for you at the clinic," Dafari said then placed a chaste kiss on my lips before kissing the center of my forehead. Warmth and calm washed over me.

I didn't hear what Octavian had said to Tasmin when he cupped her face to kiss her because Martha, her sisters, and Tasmin's parents had been moving the tables in the room to make the space we needed to perform the ceremony.

"Wait...where are they? The ghosts?" Jewel asked as she looked around.

"Afolabi isn't a ghost, Mom," Tasmin said. "He's a spirit. Aziza is a ghost."

Jewel quirked a brow. "There's a difference?"

Tasmin shook her head. "You've been married to Daddy for how long and he hasn't told you the differences between the two?"

"No. Your father is very secretive about that side of his magick and powers," she answered her daughter.

"Not secretive, just cautious. It's best those of us who possess the power not be all willy nilly about who we disclose such practices to. Even if you are family and loved ones," Silas said as he focused on drawing sigils on the right side of the wall. "But yes, where did they go?"

"Aziza is in the attic. Afolabi has crossed over to see what information he can glean on how Marie got such a high-level demon on her side," I said.

"Has he told you two how we're all related?" Silas asked.

"No."

I watched him draw an Akoben which symbolized a call to arms. He then drew something that resembled a heart around that symbol which meant Akoma. It was in the shape of a heart because it asked for patience and endurance. On the other side of the wall Martha drew Ananse Ntoso, which looked like a spider's web, then linked it to the Boa Me Na Me Mmoa Wo; a sign of cooperation and interdependence. Next came the Wawa Aba which meant hardiness, toughness and perseverance.

"Ladies, if you would," Cara Lee said as she and Mary Ann carried bowls of what looked like black ink.

"Stand in the middle of the room, will you?" Mary Ann urged. "Shoes off to be one with the earth. Please remove your shirts as well."

"Once your shirts are off, you will each lie in the middle of the circle, opposite ends," Jewel said as she walked around us, forming a large ring of salt.

Tasmin and I did as instructed. We'd gone through this ritual in the past, but in this life, things still felt new and surreal. The concrete floor was cool beneath my back. I wiggled my toes, feeling a power surge that threatened to knock me out.

My eyelids fluttered when Cara Lee placed a piece of gold over my third eye. Instinctively, I knew she had done the same to Tasmin.

Tasmin's left hand was next to my right one, both our bracelets glowing in the room. Soon after, Mary Ann linked our wrists by intricately threading a long piece of golden chain around them.

"We use gold as tribute to our Ancestors to symbolize the purity of the spiritual aspect of all that is," Cara Lee said.

"Gold…is the master healer," Mary Ann whispered as she laid one hand on my abdomen and the other on Tasmin's.

"As we come before our Ancestors today, we wish to seek a healing for Elisa and Tasmin… We use gold to call on the purification of their physical bodies. Elisa, bloodline Marie Laveau and Tasmin, bloodline Tituba, we seek to lessen the trauma that has been experienced during their reawakening."

If I would have been standing, my head would have lolled forward from the natural high my body experienced. Such as it was, I was laid flat on the floor, my limbs went limp, and my body had a floating sensation. I felt when Martha and Silas joined the other three. Cara Lee knelt next to me while Mary Ann moved to the other side of Tasmin. I flinched when the hot quill-like needle Cara Lee held pierced the skin around my navel. Tasmin hissed and her breath caught in her throat when Mary Ann touched the hot quill to her bare skin over her heart.

"The Sankofa is a reminder to never be afraid to go back and retrieve what you've lost," Martha said.

"With all these things fresh in our minds, we alert our Ancestors that now is the time. We have no objections to the rules we must abide, we release all anger and resistance to make room for our ancestral guides," we all said at once.

Martha picked up the Book of Magic Enchantment before taking her place between her sisters. "As the Elders of this coven, we open the door to Silas, Jewel, Elisa, and Tasmin. We welcome you to join the ranks as your Ancestors have done before you. May you grant us the honor of protecting you, give us the right to honor you, love you and respect you. We ask that you grant us the power to guide you as we grant you the same power to guide us…"

As the Merry Widows chanted the ritual and spoke the words needed to solidify the coven, the gold chain tightened around our wrists. Their voices faded in and out along with Tasmin's parents. I smelled smoke. Sage, sandalwood, pepper, pine, and something else so pure I couldn't name it. I heard the chants of my Ancestors. As my world tilted and spun, I saw the faces of my parents… Mama Nall and Ms. Noreen…Attalah! She had wings, black wings. *Why did Attalah have black wings?*

Flashes of my memories assailed me. I saw Zafer and Safiya…but I couldn't feel them. A gray cloud of mist surrounded my children. Zafer looked so much like Dafari, I had to blink rapidly just to be sure it wasn't Dafari. Tall and regal, broad shoulders and a lean muscled physique told me that if he had lived on, he would have been every bit of the warrior his father was. Safiya, also dressed in black, held her brother's hand as her brown eyes watched me. She, too, looked more like her father, but she had my eyes and was just as curvy as I was. Her magick cloaked them both in a protective shield. *Where were they?* My soul cried for my children. As soon as the thought crossed my mind, Zafer waved his hand and the scene changed.

My eyes shot open, and I sat up abruptly. Tasmin did the same. I looked down at my stomach to see the Sankofa symbol that had been tattooed around my navel glowed. I turned to look at Tasmin, wondering if she had also seen our children. The way she slapped tears away from her cheeks told me she had.

Why does she have black wings? I heard Tasmin's mind whisper as she rubbed the Sankofa tattoo over her heart.

"Guard your thoughts," I whispered to her.

She nodded and slammed the door to her mind shut.

Outside, I heard the wind howling so loudly it made my ears ring. Rain sounded as if was hail with the way it beat on the windows. Tasmin and I had our shirts and shoes back on in a matter of seconds.

"This isn't a regular storm," Silas said as he helped Tasmin and me to stand.

"No, it isn't," Martha said as she and the other widows grabbed their staffs.

"That rogue bitch is trying to unleash something and it's causing a disturbance in the earth's atmosphere," Jewel said, a sneer on her face.

Just then, Afolabi appeared. "It's worse than I thought, None of the other spirits were willing to talk, They are fearful of retaliation, and—"

Before he could complete his thought, the door to the basement flew open. Octavian raced halfway down the stairs. "I hope you were able to do all that needed to be done. Even if you haven't, I suggest we move this to Dafari's humble abode."

Our group raced up the stairs as Tasmin grabbed the keys to the bookstore and her bag.

"Where's Dafari?" I asked Octavian as we all ran to the door.

For some reason, I didn't want to be too far away from him. My nerves had me jittery. The fear of losing him was great, and I couldn't explain why.

"Waiting for us just outside the shop, Sissy," he said.

I quickly turned to Afolabi, saying, "Go get Aziza. Take cover wherever spirits and ghosts hide to avoid danger."

He simply nodded, rushing up the attic stairs to find Aziza.

Once we exited the bookstore, the wind almost blew us off our feet. Lightning ripped across the sky just as thunder rumbled the ground.

"My car is here," I heard Silas yell to the Widows.

"Elisa and Tasmin, this way please," Octavian urged as he pointed toward Dafari's truck.

I heard it before I saw it. It sounded as if a prolonged sharp crack pierced the night air. I looked at Dafari's truck then to the big tree on the other side of the street. It's longest, thickest branch had snapped and was set to crash into Dafari's truck.

He was in there! I couldn't see him as the rain was coming down in sheets, but I saw his golden eyes glowing behind the windshield.

In a hurried motion, I extended my hands toward the branch and gritted my teeth. The thick limb went flying backwards, crashing into the window of the church across the street. I had time to do nothing else as Octavian all but shoved Tasmin and me into the backseat of Dafari's vehicle.

CHAPTER 19

TASMIN

SECONDS AFTER OCTAVIAN hurried Elisa and me into Dafari's truck, we saw it; a combination of lightning strikes, oversized hail, and what appeared to be a small funnel cloud, all aimed at the bookstore, too late for anyone to act.

"Oh, my gosh," I cried out.

The four of us looked on in horror as the forces of nature blitzed the Book Nook, all of us thinking that our coven's magickal refuge was about to be decimated, but then…nothing. From the part of the building that was visible to us, the structure was intact.

"What the…?" Elisa started, climbing into the front passenger seat then fastening her seat belt.

I followed her lead, strapping myself in. "I'm guessing that the wards we placed inside and around the building held up and were probably amplified with the reforming of the coven."

"It makes sense," Octavian chimed in. "Now that the coven has its full complement of witches, it only strengthens the epicenter, as well as all magick within and around the premises. While it appears safe for now, there's no telling how long the wards will hold. Brother, we must go."

Without a word, Dafari peeled off from the bookstore, my father following close behind.

As we drove along Main Street, the wheels of Dafari's truck began hydroplaning.

"Damn it," he yelled, turning into the skid, the truck righting itself on the road. It made me flashback to the night Demon Daddy attacked me, but I kept that to myself.

Elisa put her hand on top of Dafari's. He quickly glanced at her, a look that I recognized as one of love passing between them. She always had a way of calming him like no one else could.

Turning my attention back to the storm, I thought how it reminded me of a scene out of The Wizard of Oz, with gusty winds churning up everything in its path. Whole trees were pried from the ground roots and all; parked cars slid from their parking spots. The rain made it difficult to see even a few inches ahead, despite the high beams being turned on. Hail stones as large as baseballs pelted anything in their path, including our vehicles. Elisa did her best to keep them away from us, but they were too numerous to count.

I pulled out my cellphone, calling my mother to check on everyone. "You guys okay?" I asked once she answered.

"Yes, what about you all?"

"We're okay…for now. Did you see what happened?" I queried.

"If you mean that attack on the bookstore, yes, we all saw it."

"I believe that was a calculated strike, meant to kill us all," I heard Martha say.

"I fear you are correct, Martha," Octavian responded.

"Obliterate the coven and it would be open season on the epicenter."

"More than ever, we need to come up with a solid plan to deal with Marie and the demon she's in league with," my father added.

"That we can do once we get to my home," Dafari said, all the while dodging debris on the road. Without warning he abruptly stopped, the reason apparent. Two cars blocked our path with no way around them.

"That witch is really getting on my last good nerve," I said, using my telekinesis to move one car then the other. "The way those cars were positioned, they were placed there on purpose."

"We need to get off the road as soon as possible," Elisa said. "Right now we're nothing but moving targets."

"It's almost as if she's tracking us," Cara Lee noted.

"I agree, Sister, but how?" questioned Mary Ann.

"We can figure that out later," Dafari said, stepping on the gas, driving as fast as he could in the unceasing storm.

Elisa and I kept our attention on all sides, she moving all elemental obstacles in our path, while I dealt with all other threats. It was a slow process, but we eventually made it back to Dafari's house. He opened two empty garage bays. After Dafari's truck and my dad's car were parked and the bays were closed, we felt it was safe to exit the vehicles. Wards had previously been placed on the home and surrounding property, adding to our feelings of security, which we sorely needed right now. As soon as we piled into the living room and had made ourselves comfortable, I noticed that Martha had the Book of Magic Enchantment, as well as another book. I was glad someone was able to procure our tome prior to our hasty exit from the bookstore.

"I was postulating on the way here and have come up with a theory," Octavian started, sitting on one of the recliners then pulling me down to sit on his lap.

I caught the disapproving look from my father, but I didn't care. I was grown. Dafari sat on one end of the large sectional, with Elisa sidled up next to him. They were joined by my parents, Cara Lee, and Mary Ann. Dafari motioned for Martha to take the other recliner, I assumed as a sign of respect, as she was the eldest human in the room.

Octavian continued. "My conjecture is that, in addition to her other nefarious skills, Madame Marie is a storm raiser. The name is self-explanatory. However, I deduce that since she is in alliance with a strong demon, her powers are amplified considerably."

"I fear you're correct, Octavian," Martha replied. "We," she started, nodding toward her sisters, "are well-versed on storm raisers, and while they can be powerful, I doubt that Madame Marie could have created a superstorm of that intensity without help."

"I can understand her wanting to terminate the coven, but why attempt to destroy the bookstore, the place that contains the one thing she wants?" my mom asked.

"The bookstore could be destroyed, but the epicenter of magick cannot," Octavian replied. "It follows the law of conservation of energy which states that energy can be neither created nor destroyed, only converted from one form of energy to another."

Dafari leaned forward, placing his elbows on his knees, his chin resting on his hands. "That makes sense. That demon working with Marie is extremely powerful. I have no doubt that she can find some way to consolidate and transfer the power of the epicenter to another vessel."

"That worries me," my dad said. "Since we're not at the bookstore, there's nothing to stop them from finding another way to get to the epicenter, even perhaps literally going underground. We need some inside knowledge, an edge, regarding Marie and her partner in crime."

"As much as he annoys me to no end, we need to talk to Azazel. Afolabi did say he heard him speaking to the demon in the shadows," I responded.

Dafari inhaled a long breath. "I suppose there's no time like the present. I will ask everyone to refrain from antagonizing him, as we need as much information as possible in order to properly devise our plan."

"Provided he tells the truth," Cara Lee interjected.

"Which is highly unlikely," Mary Ann chimed in.

"Ladies, I agree. My father frequently talks in riddles, much of the time providing only partial truths. However, collectively, I believe we can use whatever information he provides to our advantage. He did, after all, provide us with the information regarding the relationship between Mayor Lovett and Madame Marie."

"While I appreciate your candor, Dafari, your father is a master of deception and concealment. How do we know he hasn't been here the entire time lurking in the shadows, eavesdropping on our conversation?" Martha questioned.

"That is a legitimate concern. However, the wards placed on my home, while keeping out threats, now keep him out as well. He can only be here if I invite him. That was a… very recent development." He looked at Elisa as he made that statement. Knowing him as I well as I did, I was certain it was because Dafari knew that Demon Daddy's presence was not particularly welcomed by Elisa, and more than anything, he wanted her back home.

"Let's get on with it then," she said, her voice tinged with reluctance.

"Ladies, if you will," Dafari said.

With a mere thought, Elisa and I dropped the wards in the living room ever so slightly, allowing Dafari to reach out to Azazel. Within seconds, he stood in front of us. Elisa and I quickly reconstituted the wards. It never ceased to amaze me how an entity such as him could be so vain. Then again, I shouldn't be surprised since he did bear the nickname 'All Sin', vanity being among the seven deadly sins. As always, he was dressed to the nines, this time in a cobalt blue suit, black collarless dress shirt, and black lace up loafers. Cufflinks and a watch that I could only assume were platinum completed his look. His wavy hair hung down around his shoulders, and his stance commanded authority. If I didn't despise him, I might actually be impressed.

"Hello, Son, love of my son's life, nephew, perpetual virgin—"

"I hate you so much," I replied, rolling my eyes in disgust.

"Ignore him, my love," Octavian said, placing one of his hands on top of mine, gently stroking it.

Azazel smirked and moved on. "The lovely Jewel, handsome Silas...cronies. To what do I owe the pleasure of this summoning?"

While I couldn't help myself from responding to his jab at me, everyone else heeded Dafari's plea to not antagonize him. However, if looks could kill, Demon Daddy would be dust.

"I'll cut to the chase, Father," Dafari replied, standing. "We have very reliable intel as to the identity of the demon collaborating with Madame Marie. Apparently, it is an extremely powerful, ancient being. Also, from what we've gathered, someone you know."

Azazel raised an eyebrow, crossing his arms in front of his muscular chest. "Do tell, my son. Who might that be?"

When Dafari revealed who the demon was Azazel appeared unfazed. Placing his arms behind his back and clasping his hands, he flatly stated, "Yes, she and I are well acquainted."

"Do we even want to know how?" Elisa asked, a look of revulsion on her face.

"Ah, my dear, sweet Elisa, let me ease your mind. It's not in the way you think. In order to survive in Hell, I needed to make alliances. She was one of those alliances. As a more senior demon, she demanded respect, and rightfully so. I fell in line with the rest, to suit my own ends of course, eventually earning her favor. I served her, she offered me protection; a truly synergistic quid pro quo. When I had the opportunity to break free of my situation, I took it. While I escaped my hellacious imprisonment, and she remained in residence, she still had my respect on some level."

"So much so that you'd help her escape?" Dafari questioned.

"I said I respected her, but not that much. And to what end would that benefit me? You know I believe in self-preservation, and I like being a top dog up here. I think the role suits me nicely," he said, looking at his well-manicured nails. The sneer on his face made me cringe.

"Full disclosure, Father; our sources tell us that not only do you know who the demon is, but you have also been heard speaking with her in the shadows."

"Sources, you say? And who might these "sources" be?" Azazel asked, making air quotes.

"Now you know we're not going to tell you that," I chimed in.

He grinned, showing darn near every tooth in his mouth. "You show me yours, and I'll show you…mine." He looked down, his hands now placed in front of the bulge in his pants. When Octavian visibly bristled, it was my turn to calm him down.

"Father, enough," Dafari barked, taking a tone with his father that I'd never heard before. "Did you or did you not know she was the demon working with Madame Marie? And why were you talking to her in the shadows?"

Azazel studied the room for a moment. It could have been my imagination, but as he gazed around the room, I sensed a vibe that I had never felt from him before; an edginess that was very unlike him.

"If you must know, I was conversing with her in the shadows down below prior to, what I presume, was her escape. She asked for my help; I declined and haven't spoken with her since. And no, I did not know that she was the demon working with Madame Marie. Now, if this inquisition is over, may I go?"

Dafari simply nodded. Elisa and I again dropped the wards momentarily and in an instant, Azazel was gone.

After the wards were back up, Elisa spoke. "Is it just me, or does anyone else think he was lying through his polished, white teeth?"

Dafari began to pace, much like his younger brother. "While he may embellish the truth, Father does not lie. However, he was being intentionally evasive, purposely deflecting from the subject. He's hiding something, something big."

"We don't have time to figure out what it is. Since he clearly is not willing to share what he knows, I propose he be kept out of the loop from here on out," my father suggested.

"I'm in agreement with Silas. The less he's involved, the better," Martha expressed. Her sisters and my mother nodded in unity.

"Ladies, your thoughts?" Octavian asked, looking from me to Elisa.

Elisa looked at Dafari, her hand reaching out for his. "You

all know I don't trust him. I would feel more comfortable making our plans without him, especially since we now know his affiliation with the demon."

Dafari took her hand, squeezing it reassuringly. "I understand."

"I feel the same way. We can't run the risk of Demon Daddy letting her know our plans. If it suited his purposes, he'd sell us all out. Well, maybe not Dafari."

"So true, Poppet. I'm sorry, dear brother, but I concur with the coven. Uncle cannot be a part of our plans."

Dafari sat back down, sighing heavily. "So be it. That being said, I suggest we get started on this plan."

As he spoke those words, the book sitting on Martha's lap began to glow a bright silver gray. The light was almost blinding. We all shielded our eyes until the radiance dimmed.

"Martha, what is that book, and why did you bring it?" I asked.

"It's termed the Book of Prognostication. It's been passed down from coven to coven in Salix Pointe for generations. To be completely honest with you, Tasmin, I don't know why I grabbed it from the shelf. It was as if it called to me."

Octavian tilted his head to the side. "Prognostication is synonymous with prophecy. Are you telling us that book portends the future?"

"Yes, it does. It's been predicting future events for the covens as needed since Salix Pointe's inception. It only glows like it did when there is a new prophecy to be revealed, appearing of its own accord."

"Don't keep us waiting, Martha. Tell us what the book says," Elisa uttered, excitement in her voice.

Martha slowly opened the book, as if keeping us in anticipation. Suddenly, the pages began to rapidly turn on their own, finally stopping near the middle of the book.

She read the words on the page, "Descendants of the Sybils, the witches two, both women are courageous, upstanding, principled, and true. One is bound to an angel with pure wings of white, a learned scholar who fights on the side of light. The other is coupled to a half angel/half demon. He protects those he loves with force but also reason. Together, the four will duel an ancient evil, protecting Salix Pointe's young, old, infirmed, and feeble. As in times past, though the battle will be laborious, in the end, they will emerge victorious. They will seek out the truth, leaving no stone unturned, working tirelessly until the ultimate lesson is learned."

Elisa and I passed shocked looks at each other then at Octavian and Dafari. The prophecy was obviously referring to the four of us and our present strife. It even spoke of our past conflicts. My curiosity was piqued at the part about Elisa and I being descendants of the Sybils.

"Who are the Sybils?" I queried.

"I can answer that one," Octavian began. "The Sybils were group of women from the ancient world who were said to possess the powers of divination. It was alleged that a Sybil could predict the future speaking through the deity of the temple where she resided. As told in history, the Sybil would go into a trance-like state prior to speaking on behalf of the deity. The oldest known Sibyls were traced back to Africa, specifically Libya, which was part of a large region known as Maghreb, which also included northwestern Kemet, Algeria, Tunisia, Mauritania, and Morocco. It's been said that these powerful Sibyl matriarchs peacefully ruled Africa for 6,000 years, not only foretelling events, but curing people of ailments such a leprosy, blindness, and epilepsy, as well as casting out demons. Unfortunately, centuries later, with the arrival of Christianity, the Sybils, their temples, and their mystery schools fell out of favor, and were outlawed, with harsh punishments, including death, being doled out for those who performed divination and magick, which were deemed as pagan practices. Their temples and other sacred locations were confiscated and converted into churches."

Martha sucked her teeth. "In many ways, that type of persecution continues to this day. But that's a discussion for another time. Tasmin, Elisa, you two apparently come from a very spiritually powerful lineage."

Martha's words lulled us all into silent contemplation for several long minutes.

"I get that the prophecy is about Tamsin, Elisa, Octavian, and Dafari, and who the Sybils are, but what I don't get is what the prophecy meant by 'As in times past'?

I took a deep breath, knowing that what I was about to say was going to sound unbelievable. However, considering everything else that had occurred over the past couple of weeks, the unbelievable was becoming our new normal.

"Mom, Dad, it's like this; Elisa and I have always been cousins, including in our…past lives."

My dad sat up straight, confusion lacing his face. "Your past what?"

"Past lives. Elisa and I have been here before, first time in the 1800s during slavery, and again in the early 1900s."

"Were we your parents?" my mom asked expectantly.

"No, you weren't," I replied. A look of sheer disappointment covered my parent's faces. "Nor were Duma-Nolan or Akasha Elisa's parents. They have been different each time, and all possessed some sort of magick. The only things that have been consistent are Elisa and my familial relationship and…Octavian and I, as well as Elisa and Dafari, being together."

"When you say together, what exactly do you mean?" my father asked.

I looked into Octavian's black eyes, the love I felt for this man-angel stronger than ever before. I turned back to look at my parents. "In both lifetimes, I was married to Octavian and Elisa was married to Dafari." I dared not go into detail regarding the circumstances surrounding our first marriages, as I was still having trouble coming to grips with the numerous tragedies that befell us.

Again, the room became deadly silent. Just by looking at them, I could tell my parents were grappling with all they had just learned. While the sisters were harder to read, my gut told me they, too, were wrestling with this new-found information.

"Why would the Book of Prognostication reveal that prophecy now? Why not when Madame Marie first arrived in Salix Pointe?" my mom posed.

"If I had to take an educated guess, my thinking is there were two events that led to the prophecy being revealed; the first being Elisa's and my awakening, and second, the ritual the coven performed on us."

"Awakening?" my dad questioned.

Octavian continued from there. "Yes, Mr. Pettiford. Tasmin nor Elisa had an awareness of their past lives or their considerable powers."

"They were witches back then?" my mom asked.

"Indeed, Mrs. Pettiford," Octavian continued. "Dafari and I waited as long as we could, for fear of overwhelming them even more, but with the emergence of this new, extremely dangerous threat, we felt Tasmin and Elisa deserved to know all. Now that they are fully aware of the extent of their gifts, they are both stronger for it, know how to protect themselves, and are better prepared to deal with our opponents."

"You had no right," my dad said between gritted teeth. "Now they're in even more danger because Marie and that demon are gunning for them specifically."

"We had every right to know," Elisa said, almost shouting. "The same way we had a right to know about our familial line and powers in this lifetime." Her lingering anger toward my parents was so palpable it almost overwhelmed me. "And for the record, because we were awakened, Tasmin and I were able to come up with a plan to prevent Marie from dream walking and masking her presence. That inadvertently allowed Octavian to vanquish the impundulu. He deserves your praise, not your chastisement."

My mom looked at Octavian, tears in her big, brown eyes. "While we are thankful to you for helping to keep the girls safe, this is all too much. This is why we didn't want you involved in all this magick stuff, Tasmin. We were just afraid for you, and now Elisa. Please tell me you understand."

I understood all too well. I said almost the exact same words about everything being too much to Elisa, Octavian, and Dafari in the very home I was sitting in back in October. It seemed like a lifetime ago. "Mom, I do understand, but, as much as I hate to admit it, this is our life now. Elisa and I, along with Octavian and Dafari, have been tasked with saving Salix Pointe. What comes after that, who knows? Regardless, we have to see this through. I hope *you* understand."

She nodded, silent tears rolling down her cheeks.

"That said," I started, looking in Octavian's direction then Dafari's, "I have three questions; why were we chosen to be bound together, who's responsible for our pairings, and what ultimate lesson is the prophecy referring to?" I let out a long exhalation. "But we can't focus on any of those now. At the moment, Madame Marie and the demon are our priorities."

Octavian gave me a gentle hug. "You're right, my love. Since that needs to be our center of attention, I suggest that, for the interim, we have a central location of operations. Save for Mr. and Mrs. Pettiford, everyone in this room had previously been attacked, and today those hellions attempted to ambush us all. For the safety of the group, I suggest that everyone get used to the idea of staying here. Dafari has plenty of room."

The look Dafari gave Octavian was akin to the one he gave him when he had offered up his brother's home to me and Elisa when I first arrived in Salix Pointe. Once again, Dafari's residence would be our home-sweet-home for the duration of this latest crisis.

CHAPTER 20

OCTAVIAN

"I 'M NOT STAYING here," Elisa said in a tone that held an edge.

Dafari tilted his head, blinking slowly and watched her coolly.

She held up a hand to stop him from responding and sighed. "Look, I'm not about to hide. I'm sick of running and hiding. Tasmin and I have been doing that since your mother and Octavian's father set plans in motion to kill us. Tasmin and I have been studying and reading and doing everything in our power to become even stronger. Now, we've reawakened. We're two of the most powerful witches in this room. I am not hiding anymore. If that witch wants smoke, I can harness the fire and bring the wood for kindling. If she wants a fight, she can bring it to my front door, but I am not hiding or cowering in Dafari's home as if I am incapable of kicking ass and taking names."

"Sissy, I didn't mean my suggestion to come off as such," I said. "I simply meant that by all of us being in the same place, we'd do better at—"

"Hiding," she snapped. "That's what it is, Octavian. We would be an entire coven, hiding. If she wants me, she can come and get me, but I will not cower. I love you, dear brother, and I know you mean well, but I'm not staying here."

"Not that I don't think your idea is grand, Octavian, but I'm going to side with Elisa here," Tasmin said. "How will we ever get rid of her if we always run and hide? I think Elisa and I have already shown that we are capable of leveling the playing field when it comes to that wench. To hide now, after what just happened, will further incite her. It will make her think she has us on the run."

"Well...if Elisa had allowed my brother to finish before so loudly declaring she doesn't wish to stay under the same roof as I, then maybe you two would have known that was what he was getting at," Dafari snarled in a low monotone.

My brother's feelings had been hurt by Elisa's bold declaration. I knew that. I could tell by the way he fought to keep his eyes from glowing red. They flashed between gold and red as he tried to keep his anger at bay.

I tapped Tasmin's thighs, urging her to stand so I could as well. "Yes, that is what I was getting at," I confirmed. I looked at Elisa, whose tough demeanor had softened as she cast embarrassed glances in my brother's direction. "If she thinks she has all of you on the run, her immense arrogance will cause her to attack, thinking she has the upper hand."

Dafari stood and folded his arms across his chest, looking every bit of Azazel's son when he did so. "She will be exceptionally angered at the moment, being that Octavian killed her impundulu and you two have prevented her from dream walking."

"Oh," Tasmin said quietly.

"Yes...that does sound like a good idea," Elisa said just as quietly.

Dafari took a visibly deep breath then looked at the others in the room. "Not to be rude, but I will take my leave for the evening. Octavian and the ladies know where everything is. Feel free to roam about. Just respect my home," he said coolly and with the first shadow he found, he was gone.

Not even a second later, Elisa was racing up the stairs. I was sure she was going to meet him in his bedroom, assuming that was where he had gone.

"Very volatile, those two," Cara Lee said.

"Yes, like you and Dylan once were," Martha replied as she stood.

Cara Lee blushed. "We weren't that bad."

"If you say so," Mary Ann chided. "Will you point me in the direction of the kitchen?" she then asked me.

I did as she requested then watched the Merry Widows disappear into the kitchen.

LATER THAT NIGHT, we heard it. The curses of my brother...The crying and yelling from Elisa.

"They forgot to put up the shield," I mumbled while holding Tasmin, her back to my chest.

I hadn't been asleep and neither had she. I felt and inhaled her arousal, her need to copulate with me, but she couldn't, and she had no idea why. I was sure she could feel my need pressed against her backside. I mean the chastity belt that had been placed on her had no bearings on me whatsoever. I could cross it at will, but I wanted her to be free of it regardless. Parts of me wanted to tell her, if only for selfish reasons. Other parts of me didn't want to. I knew most men would love to hear that their woman hadn't been touched by any other man. In some ways, I was elated at the thought as well, but mostly, I was put off by it.

It was a catch-22 for me. I hated that there was a such thing as virginity as if to say if a woman was a virgin then she was "pure" and that once it was "taken" she would be dirty. I would love more than anything to lay with Tasmin and have my way with her without the deluded issue of "breaking a hymen." It bothered me that her parents were so worldly and cultured and yet had taken such an archaic patriarchal stance.

I wanted to make love to Tasmin without worrying about hurting her, her first time. I'd been robbed of that. I wasn't one of those beings who needed his woman to be inexperienced to hide the fact I didn't know how to please a woman properly. I couldn't believe I was going to say this, but like Uncle, I did prefer non-virgins. Tasmin should have been able to healthily explore her body and sexuality long before now.

"You don't have to keep telling and showing me that you prefer to be away from me at every chance, Elisa. I get it," Dafari roared.

"And you don't get to dismiss the way I feel simply because it isn't what you want to hear!" Elisa yelled in response.

"They must be really angry," Tasmin whispered as she turned to lay face to face with me.

"My brother misses his wife in all the ways a man who was robbed of his time with his wife can miss her. He wants to be able to love her freely and openly and she be receptive as they once were," I said, gazing into her beautiful brown eyes. One of her locs lay against her cheek. I gently placed it behind her ear. She smelled divine. I wanted to devour her as if I was famished.

Her thumb traced my bottom lip. "How would you know that?"

"Because it's the same thing I want," I admitted, sucking the tip of her thumb into my mouth.

"You're not the only one who lost, Elisa. I lost as well. I lost you and our children, too. I lost seventy-seven damn years, but you won't extend to me to same grace you want extended to you," Dafari's booming voice carried through the place.

I didn't know what had shaken the house, his voice or the thunder.

"No one told you to take the fall for Octavian without thinking about how it would affect me and our children. You always do that when it comes to him. Always. You never think, you just rush in to save him or clean up after him."

I flinched. Hard. It was as if Elisa had socked me in the gut with an iron fist. Tasmin slid closer to me then pressed her lips to mine. Her kiss was slow and intentional. It ameliorated the pain I'd felt behind Elisa's words. Tasmin's kiss held healing in it as her tongue searched out mine.

"She's hurting," Tasmin said to me, her lips brushing against mine. "Whatever you hear is from the pain."

"You ever stop to think that if you and Tasmin would listen to reason sometimes that none of this would have happened?"

Elisa gasped so loud, we heard it. "You're blaming me?"

"I'm blaming the both of you since you love to place blame. Octavian and I begged you two not to go on that mission, but you refused to listen."

"We didn't have a choice!"

"You did," Dafari bellowed. *"You had a choice, and you chose violence. Both of you!"*

Now it was my time to hold Tasmin closer. I saw when her eyes widened, and she blinked back tears. I sat up and tugged my shirt over my head. I allowed my wings to unfurl then scooped her onto my lap. She only had on a tank top and her underwear. When she was seated comfortably, I enclosed her in my wings.

"It's just the pain you hear," I said softly.

She held me tighter. I knew she'd felt guilt behind all that had happened that night. It had been her plan, her idea to rescue that family. Because Elisa was always going to back Tasmin, Dafari and I went along with it as well. What other choice did we have?

"Octavian had no choice! What did you expect him to do when he saw his wife and daughter hanging from their necks, Elisa? Did you expect him to run off crying quietly into the night? Was he not supposed to avenge them then and there?"

"He didn't think..." Elisa cried.

"How in hell was he supposed to think when his wife and only child were stripped naked, their bodies violated? What in God's name was he supposed to think about while looking at their broken necks as they swung from a tree, Elisa? Huh? You tell me!"

My brother's voice held a tinge of fear, regret, and madness that only I could recognize. He was going to go too far...I felt it.

"You left me!"

"I couldn't let Octavian serve time down there. He wouldn't have made it!" There was pleading in his voice. He needed desperately for her to understand his side of things.

"What about me? What about Zafer and Safiya?" Her voice held the pain of a mother and wife whose suffering had been never-ending.

Dafari's voice was softer now. "I knew Octavian would protect you and keep you all safe. Those were my thoughts that night, Elisa. Everything was chaotic. The only thing I regret is not knowing the time difference between there and on earth."

"And now…now you just want me to move in with you and be the husband and wife we used to be——"

"I do not. I want us to be who we are now. We can't get that time back. I'm not asking for it. I just want you."

"You want me to get comfortable loving you again."

"Why shouldn't you?"

"Because what if Octavian loses his mind again?"

There was silence now. Even with the wind and rain assaulting the earth outside. I never knew silence could be so loud. There was only one thing that could make me lose my mind. She was wrapped around my waist, arms around my neck…

"Then again, I will serve his time for him. I will never let him do penance in that place, but I would also better secure you here on earth. For as long as I breathe, I will never again leave you unprotected the way I did then. I was hasty in my decisions. I had no idea you would lose access to all my wealth and privilege. No idea the pain you had to suffer."

"I do not want to live through that again, Dafari."

"You won't have to…"

When Tasmin shivered in my embrace, I knew neither of us could stand to be privy to their argument any longer. I sent my brother a mental note to block out his and Elisa's argument. Almost immediately, the barrier went up. I held Tasmin close to me as her tears trickled down my chest. There was still a lot of pain and grief that the group of us had to work through. It wouldn't be easy— not with most of Hell on our backsides— but it would be worth it.

The next morning, I walked downstairs to find that Elisa and Tasmin were in Dafari's sanctuary. Dafari must have been feeling guilty to allow them free reign in there. I stood beside him in the doorway as we watched them perform healing spells, one on the other and then vice versa. They were dressed in long black dresses that flared around their hips and backsides.

"How much did you hear last night?" he asked.

"Enough," I answered. He looked at me, getting ready to speak but I stopped him. "We understand. Don't apologize, Brother. Getting it all out is good for the soul. It was needed."

He studied me for a moment then nodded.

"You two work it out?" I questioned.

"We did."

As soon as he answered, Elisa spotted me. She rushed over to where I was and hugged me as if she were afraid I'd disappear. "I love you, Octavian," she whispered.

I smiled as I hugged her back. "I know you do, Sissy."

I put healing into that hug. I could not pretend I didn't understand her anger. I lived and experienced those lost years with her. Her suffering had been continuous. To that end, I would never be mad at her for trying to work through it the best way she knew how. She was my little sister, and I would guard and protect her with my life.

"The Widows have cooked breakfast. I'll leave you to cry in peace," Dafari said as he turned away from us.

"Oh…like you did this morning when I hugged you?" Tasmin asked in a teasing voice as she joined him.

He extended his arm for her to take. "I did no such thing… someone was cutting onions nearby," he joked in response.

Tasmin laughed. "Yeah, sure. That's your story and you're going to stick to it, right?'

Dafari smiled down at her. "Absolutely."

Tasmin cast a loving gaze at me then winked as they left Elisa and I to our devices.

After breakfast, the four of us drove to Main Street to find most of the town was shut down. The storm had taken out windows, knocked out electricity, and damaged some of the buildings and homes in the area. Salix Pointe Power Company vans and trucks were all around the area with men and women working to restore power. After checking on the café, bookstore, and Dafari's office, he and Elisa headed to her place to do some reconnaissance work. Tasmin and I headed back to his home. The plan was to make LaLaurie think the girls were running.

It was later that evening that things took an interesting turn. The weather still hadn't calmed. Dafari and Elisa still hadn't come back to his home. The Widows had been trekking the land, trying to see if they could draw Marie, the mayor, or Ilene out. I'd taken Tasmin's hand, set to take her up to my room so she and I could talk in private until there was a knock on the door. Tasmin stiffened and my guard shot up. Silas and Jewel stood. Our new-found cohabitation put us on more familiar terms. As such, her parents insisted we call them by their first names.

"Expecting company?" Jewel asked.

I quirked a brow. "This time of the night? Not hardly."

I trekked to the door, my senses on high alert.

"I think you should traverse the veil to see who it is," Tasmin said. "Would be a lot safer since whomever is on the other side won't see you."

I agreed as it was a good idea. I used the veil, expecting to see... I didn't readily know what I expected to see but it wasn't a child. I'd seen her before.

"Nazila?" I called.

She was the child whom I'd seen weeks earlier. The little girl turned to me, tears cascading down her brown cheeks. Her eyes were wild, and she looked as if she had seen a ghost. She ran to me, wrapping her arms around my waist. "You have to help me please. It attacked my mommy, and she won't wake up."

I pried her arms from my waist and then kneeled before her. "Calm down, darling. What attacked your mother?" I asked as the wind and rain pummeled me and the girl.

"It…it…it was a demon. They tried to take me, but Mommy fought so they attacked her," she cried.

Tasmin pulled the front door opened and looked on with startled eyes.

"Please, please come help my mommy," Nazila wailed.

"You walked all the way here in this weather?" Tasmin asked the child.

Nazila sniffled and nodded. "Can you help my mommy?" she asked Tasmin. "Please?"

Tasmin nodded, but Silas laid a hand on her shoulder. "How do we know this isn't a trap?" he asked, clearly skeptical.

"Yes, how do we know? Some random child shows up and asks for help, you don't find that suspicious?" Jewel asked.

Tasmin looked to me.

I shook my head. "No. I've seen this little girl before. She can see what I am. I believe her when she says something has happened to her mother. You two stay here with the Widows. I'll send a message to my brother and Elisa to meet Tasmin and I where this child lives. I can feel she's telling the truth when she says a demon attacked her mother. I can sense the demonic energy around the child."

I didn't waste any time. Neither did Tasmin. We hopped in my brother's truck and sped off toward Nazila's home with her giving us precise directions. The wind and rain be damned, Tasmin got us there. The woman had driven like she was mad. It made me remember how fond she and Elisa were of children and how angry they got when anything or anyone threatened children in their presence.

I wanted to relax and think happily of such memories, but the child holding on to me as if she was scared I'd leave her or let her go took precedence. We pulled into the rock paved driveway of a small cottage. We knew instantly something was amiss. Trees had been uprooted. An electric pole had fallen atop the woman's car. Her front door hung off the hinges and sparks of electricity shot up from fallen live wires.

I passed the child to Tasmin. "You stay here. I'll go in first."

Tasmin nodded as Nazila wrapped herself around my love's waist. "Be careful."

"I will, Poppet. You keep your wits about you."

"You know it."

I hopped out the truck and jogged up to the porch that looked like it had been overturned by an earthquake. As soon as I stepped foot across the threshold, I heard a shrill scream that made my skin crawl.

"Imps," I heard beside me.

It was Dafari. The anger was palpable coming off him.

"Where's Elisa?" I asked.

"In the truck with Tasmin. She braved the shadows with me to get here hurriedly."

I gawked at him momentarily, wanting to ask if he was a nutter, but knew now wasn't the time. A wooden dining room table had been upended. Dishes had been strewn about the kitchen. The smell of gas and sulfur overtaking my senses. We rounded the kitchen to where the blood led us.

There, in the mudroom, surrounded by small impish demons lay Nazila's mother. Small cuts and scratches riddled her face, neck, arms, and chest. In one hand was what southern Black-American Christians called holy oil; oil that had been blessed by a holy man or woman. Since it was the south, more than likely a man. In the other was a cross. The Holy Bible had been haphazardly tossed across the room. The altar she had set up to honor her Ancestors was toppled over, but one picture stood steadfast. It was of a man and woman in priest robes.

The imps zoned in on us, me specifically, as they studied Dafari. They were unsure of him as all demons were. He was privileged in that area. They screeched and bared their jagged teeth and taloned claws in my direction. Some of them had tiny wings while others stooped over, humpback. Their eyes glowed red and they smelled of rotting fish, dead flesh, and sulfur. I noticed Dafari's right eye twitching as sweat beaded his temples.

"We want the child," they hissed as one. "The Dark One insistssssss."

"Yeah, that's not going to happen," Dafari said, just as I made a move toward the tiny demons. "Let's not waste time. They will just multiply like the hellbats. The more we kill the more will vomit up from the pits of Hell." Taking a deep breath, he called out, "Father."

A few seconds later, "You rang?" could be heard in a low drawl from the shadows behind us.

Dafari stepped to the side as Uncle emerged from the darkest corner in the room.

Uncle's nose turned up in disgust. "You call me to such a house and not bother to dilute the religion infused magick?" Uncle spat at Dafari.

"As you can clearly see, time is of the essence," I said, sarcasm dripping as I pointed at the woman on the floor.

"Why isn't she dead?" Dafari asked his father.

Azazel studied the woman then grunted. "She's a true believer. It's why they can't kill her, why her child was able to escape, and why they can only poison her." Uncle looked around then back at Dafari and me. "Where is the child?"

"In the care of Elisa and Tasmin," Dafari said.

Uncle spit on the floor. As soon as it met the holy oil that had been spilled, it sizzled then burst into flames. The imps, screeching and howling, skittered away.

"Ssssssshe wants the childdddd," they hissed in unison, looking at Uncle.

"Go to Hell," he snarled low, waved a hand, and sent all of the imps flying outside.

We followed, watching as he snatched one of the winged ones from the ground before it could swallow all of them down. The wet earth opened up, same as it did with the hellbats that had attacked us before.

"Tell the bitch children are off limits, especially those protected by religious magick," Uncle said.

The imp closed its glowing red eyes then opened them seconds later. It was as if it had relayed the message in real time. "You'llllll payyyyy for thisssss," it hissed.

"I'm sure she thinks so," Uncle spat before ripping the small thing in half. He tossed it into the gaping hole before it sealed itself shut. He turned to me. "Get your witch to heal the woman. Tell her to use her holy oil for reinforcement." Then to both of us, he said, "I have somewhere I need to be. Do not call me again unless absolutely necessary."

Before we could even question the method to his madness, he disappeared into a passing shadow.

"The child is protected by old time religion magick," Martha said.

It was an hour later. Tasmin had siphoned the poison from Nazila's mother and healed all her wounds rather nicely. She now lay in one of Dafari's spare bedrooms while Nazila lay in bed beside her.

Silas frowned. "Old time religion magick?"

Martha nodded. "Yes. Back before Africa was colonized, what the world calls Christianity now went by a different name. It wasn't until the colonizers got a hold of the original scripts and text that Christianity took on a new shape. It coincides with what we just learned about the Sybils. Anyway, Nazila's mother had to have been raised by true believers, the ones whose Ancestors held steadfast to their belief in God when they were stolen and enslaved. The ones who don't live by the new words and rewritten versions of the Bible, but those whose ancestral lines has a direct link to those who believed before the world was colonized."

As they talked, I watched Elisa and Tasmin while they gazed out the bay window in Dafari's front room. The rain had stopped but the wind was still violently howling as it whipped tree limbs and branches back and forth. Instinctively, I knew the two were up to something even if I couldn't see it.

I felt off for some reason. Felt as if something was amiss or as if I'd missed something. I didn't know why the feeling had overtaken me all of a sudden. What was it that I wasn't getting and why did I suddenly feel as if danger was within reach?

CHAPTER 21

DAFARI

"HELLO," A SMALL voice said from behind me, causing everyone in the room to stop what they were doing and look in her direction.

Her afro puffs were sitting haphazardly on her head, and her eyes were a bit swollen from crying, but she didn't look any worse for wear. Her wet clothes had been discarded and replaced with the dry ones Tasmin had grabbed from the child's home. Her brown skin was flushed, but she did look happier than she had earlier.

"Hello, sweetheart," Jewel said. "Are you okay?"

Nazila nodded. "I am now that Mommy will be okay."

"You did a great job finding us so we could help her," Tasmin said.

Nazila smiled at her and Elisa. "You're witches," she said. All of our gazes flittered around the room then back to Nazila. She pointed at Octavian. "He's an angel." Then to me. "He's...dark and light. A...angel-demon?" she questioned, confused. "You talk to dead people," she said to Silas. To Jewel, "Medicine magick and you three...are also witches, the crones, the wise ones." She smiled at the Widows who didn't seem offended she'd called them crones, which was a stark difference in the way they reacted when Father called them as such. Of course, when he called them that term, he was being insulting.

"How does she know all this?" Cara Lee asked.

"She's a seer," Octavian and I said in unison. Octavian told us how he had met Nazila and how she'd alerted him to the fact that his wings were out.

Martha grabbed her chest. "Oh my word..."

"Bless her heart," Mary Ann said.

"I was born en caul," Nazila said. "My grammy says I was born with a veil. And um...I have a message." She said all of that at one time as if it was all meant to be said together.

"A message from whom?" Elisa asked.

"From the bad lady. She sent a message through one of the little evil elves," she replied matter-of-factly.

Silas raised an eyebrow. "Evil elves?"

"I'm assuming the bad lady is LaLaurie and the messenger was one of the imps that attacked her and her mother," I replied.

"Mmm hmm," she said, nodding in agreement.

"What did the imp say, honey?" Elisa asked.

"I'll tell you, but can I have something to eat first? Mommy and I were about to have dinner when the imps came to our house. I'm so hungry."

Had she been an adult, we may have denied her, especially since any message coming from LaLaurie needed to be addressed with the utmost urgency. However, she was only a child, a child who had experienced quite a traumatic event. As such, we all needed to exercise patience with her.

"Sure, sweetie," Tasmin said, taking her by the hand then lifting her on to a chair at the counter. "What would you like?"

"Do you have any ice cream?"

Everyone in the room lightly chuckled. Despite all she had endured tonight, I found her innocence endearing.

Tasmin smiled at her saying, "We do, but I don't think your mommy would appreciate us feeding you ice cream for dinner. Let's do this; I'll make you a peanut butter and jelly sandwich and give you a big glass of milk with it. How does that sound?"

Nazila gave Tasmin a wide grin before replying. "I like peanut butter and jelly. Can you cut the crusts off the bread?"

"Sure thing," Tasmin said, starting to grab what she needed to feed the child, her motherly instincts kicking in.

It caused me to reflect on how regretful I felt for blaming her and Elisa for previous incidences. It was that same passion of theirs that had saved many a life in the past. I was extremely remorseful for my harsh words and wished with all my heart she hadn't heard them. I'm just grateful that she forgave me this morning.

Octavian tapped me on the shoulder. "I sense this will take some time," he uttered low enough for only me to hear. "May I speak with you in private, dear brother?"

"Excuse us," I said to everyone. I looked directly at Elisa. "Be back shortly."

Octavian followed me to my sanctuary, which supplied us with the privacy we required. He crossed his arms in front of him, giving me a look I recognized all too well.

"What troubles you, little brother?" I suspected I already knew.

"What were you thinking taking Elisa through the shadows? She could have easily been injured or worse," he chastised.

I sighed deeply. "She gave me no choice. We didn't have a vehicle and, with the weather, it was too dangerous for me to fly us there. Not to mention she refused to wait for someone to come get us, especially after she heard a child was involved."

"You should have made her wait, Dafari."

"And that's worked so well for us in the past, has it not, brother?" I questioned jeeringly, raising my voice slightly.

Octavian rubbed his palms down his face then hung his head as if in capitulation. "Admittedly, it has not. Both Tasmin and Elisa are extremely determined, especially when someone, particularly a child, is in danger. I'm afraid they are plotting something that will once again lead them headfirst into the fray."

"I share your misgivings, Brother, truly I do. As much as Elisa fears losing me, truth be told, I am terrified of losing her. She was, dare I say, a bit overconfident prior to her awakening. You observed that for yourself at my office when she saw the ghost in the window of the bookstore."

Octavian began to pace back and forth. "Yes, Tasmin and Elisa were hell-bent on running into danger, which is why it's good that we stopped them considering the impundulu was waiting for them. And with their powers at their peak, I'm hoping they won't do something foolhardy."

"As am I. However, between you and me, Tasmin does seem to be a bit more...willing to listen and hear you out. If you ever tell her I told you that, I will finish you." I smirked at my little brother.

The smile on Octavian's face spoke to his elation. "Noted, big brother. Tasmin will never hear it from me."

"Your discretion is much appreciated. Now that that's out of the way, I have a pressing matter that I must discuss with you before we're summoned."

Octavian looked at me quizzically. "What is it, Dafari?"

"As you know, when I took your place, I unintentionally left Elisa financially unprotected. While you were there to keep her safe, as well as help her to some degree monetarily, you could not provide for her the way that I could have. That was on me, and I cannot...no, I will not allow that to happen again."

"What are you saying, man?" Octavian asked, a look of confusion crossing his face.

I put my hands on his shoulders. "What I am saying is this; I am working on a plan to make sure that in the event something does happen to me, Elisa will want for nothing. I just need to know you will back me up when I bring my plan to fruition."

He tilted his head to the side, studying my face. "Dafari, you're not going to do something that will get you killed, are you?"

I looked Octavian in the eyes. "Perhaps," I teased. "But not in the way you think. Fact is I plan on being here for Elisa for a very long time. My only concern is making sure my lady is secure. Can I count on you to help me with that?"

Octavian then placed his hands on my shoulders. "In that case, dear older brother, you have my complete support."

"I thank you, Brother."

Just then Octavian and I heard a knock on the door. I opened it to see my love standing on the other side.

"We're ready now," she said.

Octavian and I exited my sanctuary then I closed the door behind me. Rubbing the back of my hand along her cheek, I brushed my lips to hers. "Thank you, my sweet. "

Although we had business to attend to, her need for me was emanating loud and clear. I felt the same way. I planned to fulfill both our desires soon.

Once we departed my sanctuary, I observed that everyone had moved to the living room, with Martha again sitting in a recliner, her sisters, the Pettifords, and Tasmin positioned on the sectional, with Nazila sitting on Tasmin's lap. Octavian took his place next to Tasmin, while I sat on the other recliner. Elisa appropriately took her place on my lap.

Once everyone was seated and comfortable, Martha asked, "What was the message from the bad lady, my dear?"

"She said she had a message for the witches," Nazila began, first looking at Tasmin then at Elisa. "She wanted them to know that because she was prevented from taking me she will begin taking other children in Salix Pointe one-by-one… unless the witches surrender to her."

Stunned looks filled the room.

"We can't allow that happen," Tasmin exclaimed.

"We *won't* allow that to happen," Elisa followed suit.

"Ladies," I said, hearing the panic in both their voices, "I know what she said was extremely disturbing; however, let's see if there was anything else to the message."

"Nazila, sweetheart, did the bad lady say anything else?" Jewel queried.

"Nope, that was it. Can I go to bed with my mommy now?" The child acted as if it was any other night, not as if she was almost abducted by imps serving an ancient evil.

"Yes, Nazila, you *may*," Tasmin said, correcting her as only a mother could. "Change into your pajamas and make sure you brush your teeth before you go to bed. We'll see you in the morning." She hugged the child then released her.

Nazila was about to leave but stopped. She walked over to me motioning for me to lower my head. "She'll be a little annoyed at first, but she'll get over it," she whispered in my ear. With that, she scampered off.

Everyone was staring at me, I assumed wanting to know what she said. "It was nothing important," I simply replied. Not important to anyone but me anyway.

Once Nazila was out of earshot, Octavian spoke. "If I may, I had an ill feeling earlier, as if there was peril around us. Perhaps the child's warning was what that feeling pertained to. It clearly sounds like a trap to me."

"To me as well," Silas voiced. "Has anyone besides me thought it strange how Nazila knew how to get here on her own? I know she's a seer and all, but I still find it suspicious."

Everyone in the room nodded in agreement.

"While I also find it suspect, I don't feel as if Nazila was being deceptive," Jewel said.

"Nor do I." While Tasmin's mother was an empath, her powers paled in comparison to that of her daughter. If Tasmin felt the child was not intentionally attempting to deceive us, that was good enough for me.

"Do you think she's being used as a pawn?" Elisa asked.

"I wouldn't put it past that witch to use an unsuspecting child in her ploy, thinking we'd be none the wiser," I replied.

"We were so concerned about the condition of her mother and healing her, that we didn't really consider they may have gotten to Nazila in some other way aside from abduction. I suggest we thoroughly cleanse the child now to be certain, as tomorrow may be too late." Martha added.

"We'll go get her," Elisa announced, nodding to Tasmin. They rushed off up the stairs.

Martha looked at me then said, "The cleansing ritual should be done outside, as we don't want that evil, if any, residing in your home."

"We definitely do not want that. Is there anything Octavian and I can do to help?"

Martha stood. "Yes, you can get some Himalayan Sea salt. Go outside, form a large outer circle roughly nine feet in diameter and one inner circle, about six feet around, both in a clockwise direction. The rest of us need to quickly gather our supplies. We will meet you out there."

The group dispersed, focused on our individual tasks. As I grabbed two containers of Himalayan Sea salt from the cabinet, I passed one to Octavian, thinking about how my home had once again become encampment for magickal beings, except this time every last one of them was more than capable of holding her or his own. It was a stark contrast to several weeks ago when Elisa and Tasmin first came into their powers, before they knew who they truly were. Considering what we were dealing with right now, I was beyond grateful for their awakening. Once outside, I noticed how the wind had dissipated even more since we arrived home with Nazila and her mother. Somehow, I didn't find that comforting.

"I'll create the outer circle while you work on the other," I instructed Octavian once we walked out back.

"Fie on LaLaurie for using a child in this fashion!" Octavian spat angrily.

"Agreed, Brother. Her actions are most assuredly egregious. Then again, this is the same witch who tortured all manner of enslaved persons; women, men, children, the disabled. She cared not for whom she hurt. Hell, she even abused her own daughters."

"She was, and is, a blight indeed," Octavian said.

Just as we were finishing up the circles, the Pettifords and the Widows joined us. They all had their winter coats on, as the night air was quite nippy, which was typical for this time of year.

"Sisters, Jewel, Silas, place the protection candles within the big circles," Martha spoke, pulling candles out of a cross-body bag she wore, passing them out to the others. "Position them in an alternating pattern of black, blue, and white with nine candles inside the large circle and six inside the other."

As the other coven members were laying the candles as Martha directed, she pulled a small velvet bag from her coat pocket. She moved to the middle of the smaller circle then poured the contents of bag in her hand.

"These are protection crystals," she noted. "They need to be placed circumferentially three feet around." As she set down each stone just inside the circle, she told us the name and its significance. "Black obsidian to protect from fixation and sorcery; labradorite for added protection against fixation and to shield against psychic attack; black tourmaline to repel lower, harmful frequencies; staurolite to protect against unwanted spirits and attachments; black jade for protection and harmony; fire agate to transform negative energy into positive energy; black kyanite for protection and healing; amethyst for more protection against psychic attacks; and lastly, fluorite to cloak the energy signature in order to avoid the effects of sorcery and further psychic attacks.

"There appears to be much redundancy with these particular crystals," Octavian noted, sounding like the consummate observant scholar he was.

"Exactly," Martha replied. "That redundancy is purposeful. The more protection, the better, as we are going up against a strong power. Once Nazila is released from whatever it is that has a hold on her, she will also be hidden from it and protected from it latching on to her again." The final things she took out of her bag were three more candles identical to the others, some incense cones, and three burners. "Sage, frankincense, and myrrh," she said, taking three cones apiece then sitting one of each type inside the burners. She formed a triangle with the burners just within the circle, placing a candle next to each. She held out her hand. "Dafari, the salt please." After I gave her the container, Martha made a circle around the crystals, incense, and candles.

The candles inside the two larger circles were being lit just as Tasmin and Elisa were arriving with Nazila. They, along with the child, were also dressed warmly.

"Elisa and I placed a sleep spell on her," Tasmin said of the girl in her arms, her head resting peacefully on Tasmin's shoulder.

"Yes, she's been traumatized enough. If something untoward happens, she doesn't need to remember it," Elisa chimed in.

"Tasmin, Elisa, take the child to the innermost circle being careful not to disturb the salt," directed Martha. Once they were in position, she continued, "Set her down in the middle of the circle, light the incense and the candles then join us."

They did as she requested, lying Nazila down in the center of the circle and lighting the candles and incense. Tasmin and Elisa moved out of the circle surrounding the child and took their respective spots, standing between the two outermost circles. Octavian's attention, as was mine, was completely affixed on the coven.

Martha looked at each participant. "Say these words with me, 'We call on our exalted Ancestors, hear our entreaty, protect this child, dispel the evil'."

They began to chant in unison. The phrase was simple; however, experience had taught me that many times the simple spells were the most effective. As the group spoke those words over and over again, the flames from the outer candles shot upward, while the flames from the candles surrounding Nazila comingled with the smoke from the incense. Out of nowhere, the winds started to kick up again, as if attempting to extinguish the candles, to no avail. It made a howling sound, drowning out the coven.

"Chant louder," Martha shouted. "And whatever you do, don't stop."

The members of coven raised their voices, their call to their Ancestors lifted above the drone of the harsh winds, which wouldn't let up, but neither would they. Suddenly, the ground began to shake beneath us, with the coven having to steady themselves where they stood.

Octavian looked just as alarmed as I was. "Brother, I don't like this."

"Nor do I. You cover this side of the circle; I'll guard the other."

Octavian nodded, removing his shirt then spreading his wings, and summoned his bec-de-corbins to his hands, the swords illuminating the night. I ran to the other side, quickly yanking my shirt off then unfurling my wings, my dark matter sword at the ready.

"Dafari, Octavian, do not be swayed," Martha yelled while the others continued to chant. "The wards around the property are strong. Nothing should be able to penetrate, especially from the ground. However, as we cleanse Nazila, whatever it is inhabiting her will try to escape. I suggest you take to the air and be prepared to intercept it, if necessary."

My brother and I rose up, hovering above the circle where the child lay, set to dispatch any entity that crossed our path.

While Nazila was still sleeping soundly, something began to rise from her small body, attempting to cling to her with all its might, its transparent fingers unable to find purchase. As the being was extracted from her, instead of being carried off in the direction of the harsh wind, the incense smoke eerily settled directly over the child like a warm, protective blanket.

"What in the world…?" Elisa asked.

"It appears to be a lost soul; one whose purpose is to wander aimlessly," Silas responded.

"Tasmin and Elisa, use your powers to hold it in place. Silas perhaps you can find out why it was attached to Nazila," Martha advised.

They aimed at the apparition, sending out cords of energy from their hands that locked onto it, preventing its escape.

"Release me!" it demanded, thrashing about angrily.

"Not until you tell us why you latched on to the child," Silas ordered.

"Even if I wanted to, I cannot. I am forbidden."

"Maybe we can give you some incentive to change your mind," Tasmin said. "Elisa, let's put the squeeze on it."

Pulling their hands in opposite directions, Tasmin and Elisa tightened the cords around the entity.

"Stop it!" it shrieked, clearly in pain.

"Not until you tell us what we want to know, else my daughter and my niece will—"

The specter cowered, afraid of the powers of the two formidable witches. "Okay, okay. My-my mistress wanted me to attach myself to the young one."

"For what purpose?" Elisa asked.

"In order for me to see through her eyes. After those two showed up," it said, head nodding first in my direction then Octavian's, "they summoned the demon for help, which turned the tide. Mistress knew the battle would be lost and she would not have the child. She called on me to bind myself to her, knowing that she would go for…magickal help. That way I could see what she saw."

"The proverbial spy in our midst," Octavian remarked.

"And what would you get out of it?" questioned Silas.

The specter tried to remain closed mouth, until Tasmin and Elisa further tightened their hold on it. "She promised that I could have a body if I completed my task," it replied, its voice strained.

"That's clearly not going to happen," Martha affirmed. "It's late, and we need to wrap this up. Is there anything else we need to know?"

"No-no, that's all. I told you everything. So what do you say? How about a little quid pro quo? Will you release me?" it begged.

"We cannot allow it to return to Marie. The energy emanating from it is pure…evil," Jewel said, a look akin to fear in her eyes.

"Mom's right, I feel it, too. If it regains a body, no good will come from it," Tasmin concurred.

"You heard them, Dafari and Octavian. Do what is necessary," Martha called out to us.

My brother and I acted without a second thought. With one slash of my blade then Octavian's, the entity began to dissipate.

"Noooo!" we heard, but it wasn't the entity's voice. This time the voice was that of LaLaurie. "You will pay for this," she yelled, a pair of flashing red eyes appearing out of nowhere.

"Bring it!" challenged Tasmin.

"Oh, I intend to, young one, but not to you, to the people of this decrepit little town. As was passed on to you by the child seer, either you both surrender to me, or the urchins of this burgh will pay."

"You coward! Why don't you face us like a woman instead of hiding behind children?" Elisa taunted.

"Now what fun would that be? No, no, no, my dear, my terms, my turf," she countered. "See you soon." Maniacal laughter rent the air just as the eyes disappeared.

"That's it; I'm done," Tasmin shouted. "We need to finish this."

"Sooner rather than later," Elisa joined in.

"I can't believe I'm saying this," I began, "but I'm with the ladies; it's time we go on the offensive and take the fight to them."

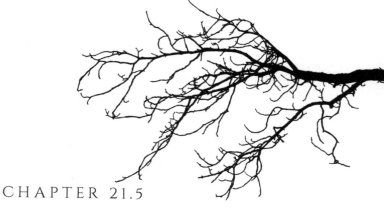

CHAPTER 21.5

MADAME MARIE LALAURIE

SOMEWHERE ON THE other side of town, in a small, dank room that resembled an unfinished basement, Marie LaLaurie scowled at her old body in a cracked mirror that stood on shaky wooden legs. The moonlight casted its glow beautifully on that side of the small space. She saw all her imperfections. Her eyes were sunken, face almost skeletal. Her once plump breasts now sagged. The lush, cream-like color they once had now ashen. She had been doing so well with her projection charm when her impundulu was still alive. Now, without his bite and his blood, she could no longer cast the illusion that she was young and beautiful. It heightend the anger she felt toward the witches.

"You said you would give me more time!" LaLaurie whirled around and hissed at the red eyed demon in the shadows.

She and the demon were conversing after an act of congress. While the demon was female, she possessed a long tail that mushroomed at the end. It resembled an elongated phallus, something the demon didn't mind using on LaLaurie

271

when she'd done a deed that pleased it. That hadn't been the case this evening. Not only had her imps been dispelled, but her spy had been caught and sent back to Hell.

"What I said," the demon spat viciously in a low monotone laced with so much ice that it chilled LaLaurie's bones, "was that with more management of your time, you could have gotten me several children by now, but no...you still want to play ring around the rosy with these witches, and I do *not* have time for this!"

The last part of her sentence came out on a snarl. Her jagged fangs glistened with the poisoned venom she possessed.

"Don't you get it?" LaLaurie questioned as she glared into the shadows with a flare of her arms. "The witches are the key to everything! Why waste time on children when you can have the blood of a virgin and a pure blood angel?"

The demon was quiet a moment, as if contemplating what LaLaurie had said. Could it be true? Could there be blood more potent than a child's? The demon knew that there was once a time when a virgin's blood was considered pure, but that had been in the ages where ignorance and ineptitude also ruled. Still, she was teetering on the desperate side of mental instability. She knew if she didn't inhabit a body soon or get enough pure blood to sustain her, she would not last much longer in this realm.

"Continue," the demon demanded.

LaLaurie stood and walked her naked, pale and saggy skinned body to stand in the sliver of moonlight closer to the shadows where the demon hid. She couldn't wait until she could freely roam the earth as she once did. She missed the days when money, prestige, and being white meant something. While she had been around for centuries, she had not been able to move about as she once had. LaLaurie had to stay hidden lest she finally pay for her crimes against humanity, more specifically her crimes against Black witches and Black people in general.

She smiled a snaggle toothed grin. She hated the way she looked outside of the dreamworld. On the astral plane, she could make herself look as beautiful and as young as possible. On the rare occasions she did trek out, she had to project images she wanted people to see. Alas, she was sure she felt change on the horizon.

"Tasmin and Elisa come from a line of distinguished old witches. Tasmin is still virginal, and the pure blood angel is bat shit crazy about her. I figure if we grab her, he will most assuredly lose his mind and come after her. Then, we will have both of them."

"And what do you propose we use to keep them locked away?" the demon asked.

"Of course iron for the witch. For the celestial, iron from a nail of The One Son's palms."

The energy in the small room changed. One of the demon's taloned feet inched into the sliver of moonlight. LaLaurie backed away. While she was a formidable witch, she had no desire to anger one of the first demons to walk the earth. The Light had archangels. The Dark had archdemons. The one in the shadows is one of the high archdemons of Hell. LaLaurie's heart pounded against her fragile ribs as she inched further away. The demon's leathery face, otherworldly height, bulging red, haunting eyes, thin lips, and snake-like cadence all made for a terrifying experience up close and personal.

LaLaurie tried to stand her ground, but as the demon inched forward, she all but cowered as she stared up in horror at her master. "You dare tell me you are in possession of such a rare piece of—"

"I just got it in my possession after the witches banished me from dream walking," LaLaurie yelled quickly. The demon's venomous fangs were too close to her neck for comfort.

The demon advanced on LaLaurie until her back was against the cool, concrete wall. It's breath hot and reeked of a stench that not even LaLaurie could name. The odor was foul, but the witch could only whimper, hoping her throat remained intact. "Bring them to me or this will be the last night you draw breath above ground."

CHAPTER 22

OCTAVIAN

W E DIDN'T WASTE any time getting our plan together. It was now or never, and we didn't have a moment to spare. We figured out early on that storming the mayor's manor was out of the question. Just like we'd figured out LaLaurie had already more than likely exited the premises, but where had she gone? That was the question. While some of the evil witch's methods were old-fashioned and cliché, she was a smart strategist. She'd managed to dream walk to do all her groundwork and had also hidden herself very well.

Using Dafari's living area as a war room, the coven had drawn diagrams, plots, and written out pros and cons of each plan. Nazila's mother was still bedridden, and the little girl was under all our care. I had to admit it took a bit of adjusting to get used to a child in the house, but it had to be done. Nazila was also a quiet, sweet child. She never got in the way and did as she was told most times.

On the flip side, I was quite cheesed off that Tasmin and Elisa made a trip to town to keep up appearances. I bloody well knew why they'd done it, but I didn't like it. LaLaurie was becoming desperate, more so than she had been before. It wouldn't have surprised me if she outright attacked them in front of the whole town.

Luckily, Rufus had come back to work at the café and had managed, with Tasmin's blessings, to set up a system to run the bookstore as well. There was something magickal about the little man. My gut told me we should explore further exactly what magick it could be that Rufus possessed. He wasn't a normal human. That was neither here nor there.

The Widows had been given instructions to leave and go someplace else. Where that place was, Dafari and I didn't know. My eyes were locked on Tasmin, on her knees in the middle of the room. She was bent over drawing something on the floor, her jean-clad derriere making the perfect heart-shaped distraction. My attention should have been on whatever she and Elisa were plotting, but my primal needs were at the forefront of my mind at the moment. Any sane person wouldn't blame me. It had been a while. I hadn't properly loved on my woman in ages. Still, I had to get my head back in the game. The coven needed me.

"No one here finds it odd that Doc Benu is still missing, and it happened so randomly?" Silas asked out of the blue.

He was standing on the other side of the room, inside a hexagram. At each point he'd drawn symbols that I didn't readily recognize, and Silas wasn't eager to share. He was closed off about his necromancy and the power he possessed. That was a good thing I suppose. Tasmin and Elisa had always said that some of their magick should not be shared with the world. I'd learned to respect that many lives ago.

"People disappear here all the time," Tasmin and Elisa said in unison as they drew quickly. They moved so fast it looked like their hands were being moved by some invisible force. Their voices were in sync, almost as if they were blending.

I casted a glance at Dafari who had been standing against the door frame with his arms folded but hearing them speak as such had caused him to stand straight up. He and I had the same idea as we walked over to examine what they were drawing.

As soon as we got within an inch, we heard in a low growl, "Back. Away."

Again, said in unison, blended as if talking as one. Dafari balked, as did I, but we also knew now would not be the time to test them.

Just as the thought crossed my mind, Silas took a breath so deep and loud it reverberated around the room. His head was back, and his face said he was in pain. "The doctor is dead," he whispered in strained release. "His spirit…gone. He died…violently…" His closed eyes rolled and flickered as if he was watching something only he could see.

And just like nothing had happened, Silas exhaled, coughed and then stood upright. His eyes were red and strained as he glanced at his wife across the room. Jewel was staring into a fire she had made in a large clay pot she'd found in Dafari's storage closet. In one hand was a bottle of my brother's best vodka. In her other hand were pure silver and gold steel medicine balls. She twirled them around in her palm as if she were about to throw them into the fire. Instead, she spit the vodka at the flames. Dafari and I watched as the burning heat went from a golden-orange-reddish glow to a crystal blue flame.

Elisa stood from her position where she had been drawing, walked over to the fire Jewel was tending then leaned forward. She peered into it like she was looking for something. Her hands dropped to her side before she leaned in closer.

"Elisa," Dafari called when her face got dangerously close to the flames.

She didn't even acknowledge she'd heard him. Into the fire, she yelled, "Now!" At the same time, she reached into the fire, grabbed a hold of something unseen on the other side then yanked hard.

Dafari rushed toward Elisa, only to have her snap her other hand outward, stilling him where he stood. My brother's anger took root the instant she used her magick against him. He bulked, yanking his ripped shirt from his upper body. "How dare you use your magick against me," he roared.

Elisa didn't flinch as she continued on with her task.

"Brother, allow them to work in peace. They know what they're doing. A little patience on your end would be nice." I moved—well tried to anyway— only to find I, too, was held in place.

However, I knew Elisa's magick wasn't the culprit. When Elisa used her magick against me, it felt as if barbed wire was crawling over my skin. Tasmin's magick, however, felt as if someone had wrapped me in a straitjacket and sprayed me with a numbing agent.

I felt the moment my power spiked, and my eyes went white. "Bloody hell," I snapped, glaring at Tasmin. "Why are you—"

Before the question could leave my mouth, Tasmin stood abruptly then snarled, "Oh no you don't…" as she made tut moves in the shape of a box.

At the same time, Elisa was yanking some…thing through the fire. "Come here, bitch," she hissed.

She yanked and pulled until a phantasm-like image of Ilene materialized. She was dressed in a frilly green gown with her hair pinned up in a gaudy, messy bun. Gaudy because of the ridiculous number of adornments she had in her hair and messy because of the lack of care used when pulling the bun up. Elisa had the apparition tethered by some kind of blazing, electric-like tendrils.

Ilene looked around as if she expected ghosts to pop up any minute, which was funny considering the state she was in. Just then, my attention returned to Tasmin. There, in the middle of the circle she and Elisa had drawn, stood the mayor, Ephraim Lovett. He was not an apparition, but a full-bodied man. The mayor was shirtless in silk pajama bottoms, and he was barefoot.

"What is the meaning of this?" the mayor croaked, annoyance lacing his tone. "You dare use those three old hags to wrangle me using sorcery?"

"You're going to tell us where the witch is or your wife never wakes up again," Tasmin threatened the man.

My blood boiled at the thought of the coven using sorcery. A witch and a sorcerer were two different things, though the world sometimes used the terms interchangeably. As used by those of us in the philosophical and anthropologist world, a witch was someone who practiced socially prohibited forms of all magick. A sorcerer, on the other hand, was someone who meant to intentionally cause harm by taking on the role of magickal practitioner. I knew that was a bit confusing for some, but I didn't have time to delve further.

I felt a hard tug in my gut, one that told me no good would come of Tasmin and Elisa resorting to such dark practices.

The mayor bellowed. "You dare threaten me, you Black—"

Before the words could fully form, Tasmin jutted her left hand in Elisa's direction. One of the electric tendrils wrapped around her wrist. She then whipped it like a lasso, and I watched it wrap around the mayor's neck then tighten instantly. He dropped to his knees as his skin fizzled. The smell of burning flesh wreaked havoc on my senses.

Tasmin's eyes burned with a rage that bordered madness. "You were saying?" she snarled; rage had gripped her in a fury.

The mayor's eyes bulged as he gasped for air, fingers futilely gripping at the tendrils around his neck. Elisa had Ilene's apparition locked. All it could do was look on in horror as Tasmin threatened to choke the life from Ephraim.

"Where is she?" Elisa yelled at it. "Tell us or one of you won't make it back home."

Ilene's apparition whined and squealed as glass-like tears rolled down her cheeks. "She's on Doc Benu's land. His land holds magick and he was a guardian of the magick. LaLaurie had her little demon vamp thingy attack the doctor and took possession of his property. It was the only way she could bring up the demon. Now, please, release my sweet husband from your wicked hands, you cunt!" She yelled that at Tasmin.

However, none of us were interested in that insult, not yet anyway. We were more taken with the fact that Doc Benu had been guarding magickal land. I could tell by the way all of us in the room casted confused and curious glances at one another.

"What do you mean he was guarding it and when did she kill him?" Elisa asked.

"I refuse to answer another thing until you release Ephraim," Ilene screeched in that southern drawl of hers.

"Not until you tell us what we want to know," Elisa snapped.

Elisa's eyes held a determination I hadn't seen before. She lassoed Ilene's apparition and then yanked down hard. The woman's shrill voice echoed around the room as her eyes widened with fear. It was clear that she and Ephraim had underestimated the two witches. I casted a glance at Dafari to see his attention was focused on Tasmin who had the mayor in some sort of death grip with the tendrils from

Elisa's magick. My brother's eyes shot back to his wife. Mine focused on Tasmin.

Should we intervene? I asked Dafari telepathically.

I'm not sure that would be smart on our end, he shot back. *They're in some kind of united front that I don't think even we can break if we wanted to.*

"Please," Ilene squealed. "She-she said Doc Benu was a Gray-Walker who had turned his back on those like him and that was how he had been granted guardianship of the land."

"What's a Gray-Walker?" Jewel asked, vodka bottle still in her hand, eyes red as if she hadn't slept in days.

"They aren't good beings. They aren't bad beings. They walk the middle," Ilene said on a gasp.

"Kind of like your father?" Silas asked, looking at Dafari.

"I didn't know there was such a thing," Dafari responded.

"We should get to Doc Benu's place to see what we can find," Jewel said quickly.

Silas agreed with a fervent nod. "Maybe the Widows can meet us there."

"You two report back to us with anything you find. We will be right behind you shortly," I said.

They nodded in unison and seconds later, they were gone. The rest of us got back to the matter at hand. Ilene looked as if she was on her last breath. Mayor Lovette harshly gasped for air.

"Madam Marie told us that Gray-Walkers had all but disappeared until recently. His power was a beacon to the magick he guarded or something like that. I don't know," Ilene whined as she casted worried, frightened eyes at the sight of her husband losing the fight to remove the electric lasso Tasmin had placed around his neck. "He wouldn't give her any information on Elisa and Tasmin so she killed him! That's all I know. I swear! Now please, release my husband. You witches are killing him!"

And they were. That alarmed me. I'd never seen the two use their magick in such a way. Still, I had no shame in admitting that seeing Tasmin tap into that side of her power... for a lack of better words...got my juices flowing. I should have been ashamed for thinking such a thing in the middle of a serious situation. However, what couldn't be helped, couldn't be helped.

"Please," I heard the mayor gasp. His face was red as fire and his eyes watered as he gawked up at Tasmin.

Tasmin didn't release her hold though. "Tasmin," I called to her, still unable to move. "You don't bloody well mean to kill the man, do you?"

She didn't speak as tears rolled down her cheeks. "Don't you feel it?" she asked.

"Feel what, love?"

"The same magickal energy from that...night...when Attalah and I were murdered. It's here and it's emanating from this wretched, pathetic shell of a man," she bellowed, her voice bordering shrill.

"Her, too," Elisa added, her voice shaky. "It's the exact. same.energy."

"Are you telling me that these two had something to do with what happened that night?" Dafari barked from where he had been tethered. His fury sprang to life.

"It...wasn't...me," Ephraim let out hoarsely. "Wasn't...me..."

While my heart beat against my ribcage violently, I felt Tasmin's hold on me loosen. I didn't know if that was a good thing, for if I got my hands on the mayor, I was most assuredly going to strangle him myself! How old was this man? Could he be immortal as well? Was it possible that the people who had caused my family so much grief, pain, and heartache had been right in front of me all along?

Tasmin's palms glowed fiery red. Murderous rage pulsed through her veins. I could feel it in my bones. I knew the feeling well. It was the same blind fury that sent me on a killing spree after she and Attalah had been killed. Ilene screamed at the same time I rushed Tasmin. I tackled her to the floor, breaking the circle of salt.

"No, Poppet," I said as I stood and lifted her with me—her back to my chest— thereby releasing Ephraim from his prison.

The man took a big gasp of air before rolling onto his stomach then pushing up from the floor. He swayed as if drunk, took one look at Tasmin and made a clumsy beeline for the front door, muttering curses and insults the whole way.

I held on to my woman as she violently kicked and yelled, "Let me go! It was him. I know it!"

"But you don't know it, Tasmin," I yelled above her fury.

"I felt it. It's the same—"

"Calm yourself, woman! We have to tackle one battle at a time, Tasmin. Just one, my love."

She was shivering, her body quaking with a range of emotions I couldn't pinpoint and wouldn't be able to contain.

"Peace…be still," I whispered in her ear.

Tasmin calmed instantly, but her sobs consumed her. "They killed my baby," she said softly, her voice but a hoarse whisper.

"I know…" It was only then that it had occurred to me that Tasmin hadn't grieved. This whole time, she hadn't grieved the loss of Attalah.

This was the first time I'd physically seen her mourn… Shame on me for not making room for that. Shame on me for being so caught up in trying to get her to my bed that I didn't take the time to counsel her, force her to talk about the pain of that night. We hadn't even taken time to lament our daughter's death as a family unit, as her mother and father.

I felt grief rolling underneath her skin. If I hadn't had a hold of her, I feared she would have gone into a fit. I felt less of a man in that moment.

"I'm so sorry," I told her in the middle of the chaos surrounding us.

How was it possible she had compartmentalized her grief behind losing her only child and still have the will to fight the wickedness chasing her and Elisa?

"Elisa," Dafari roared, causing me to look in her direction.

Raw, unfiltered shock jolted through my body at the sight of red, glowing eyes on my sister-in-law. Before the reality of what was occurring could take root, Dafari broke free of his magickal entanglement and rushed to his woman. He wrapped her in his arms and pulled her free of the magickal imprisonment she'd had on Ilene. As soon as he pulled Elisa away, Ilene's apparition disappeared, and all hell broke loose.

Literally.

CHAPTER 23

TASMIN

"**G**ET OFF ME, Dafari!" Elisa said in an unfamiliar voice.

I was grappling with a myriad of emotions, but I put them to the side as I watched Elisa thrashing wildly about in Dafari's arms, her eyes the color of crimson. The same color as Dafari's when he allowed his anger to overtake him. The same held true for Octavian now that his residual demon blood had been activated. This was bad…very, very bad.

Dafari held on to her, refusing to allow her to wiggle out of his grip. "Octavian, a little help here!"

Octavian turned me around to face him, his grasp still firm. Looking down at me, he called out to Dafari. "Handle her brother! I have my own situation to deal with at the moment."

"No," I said, tears rolling down my cheeks in earnest, "help Elisa, please. Her anger, the rage…" I was feeling every bit of it, on top of everything I was experiencing.

"Tasmin, I —"

"Please," I begged. "I promise I won't run after the mayor." Although everything in me wanted to. I wanted to run from the house as fast I could and chase down that bastard, make him feel every bit of agony Attalah and I experienced before we died. Then after that was done, I wanted to cry, scream, let out every bit of pain, anger, and…guilt I had bottled up inside me. But what I wanted…what I *needed* would have to wait.

My gut said Octavian didn't believe me. The way he eyed me dubiously confirmed that feeling. However, he relented, freeing me from his hold. He started toward Elisa, but then seemed to change his mind, walking back in my direction. "I may require your assistance," he said, taking my hand and leading me in Elisa and Dafari's direction. Deep down, I knew he was just trying to keep an eye on me.

"Release me this instant!" she bellowed in that unrecognizable voice.

Dafari was struggling to keep Elisa at bay. "I can't…hold her…much longer."

Octavian touched her temples, causing Elisa to instantly fall asleep. As her body relaxed, Dafari gently laid her on the floor.

"What's wrong with her?" I queried.

Octavian was the first to respond. "I think I know, but can you give her a quick once-over, Tasmin?"

I nodded then placed my hands over Elisa, scanning her body, so to speak, from head to toes. "She's feeling everything I am, but her emotions, especially the anger, are being heightened by something…dark, something malevolent."

"It's as I feared. Brother, I am of the opinion that some sort of entity latched on to Elisa when you traversed the shadows. While your time there may have been brief, it was just long enough to infiltrate her being. Furthermore, the being is probably one that feeds on anger and rage, hence, Elisa's current state."

"How did I not know?" a distressed Dafari questioned.

"Now that Elisa has fully awakened, her ability to guard her thoughts has grown exponentially, which means she can most likely conceal the thoughts of the entity. However, the use of dark magick, as well as the revelation that the mayor and Ilene may have been involved in," Octavian started but then paused, "Tasmin and Attalah's deaths, may have given the creature the opportunity to overtake her and exert its dominance. You cannot blame yourself, Dafari."

"If that's the case, then we should be able to release Elisa from the hold of whatever it is the same way we detached that lost soul from Nazila, right?" I asked Octavian.

"You are correct in theory, Tasmin. However, the full coven is not in attendance, and even if they were, you'd be down one witch since Elisa is the one afflicted."

"I get that, but we don't have time to waste waiting for everyone to get back. Besides, Elisa and I are linked by blood, and technically, our powers are way older than the coven's. I have to at least try."

"I'm in agreement with Tasmin, time is of the essence. Your calming ability is potent, Octavian, but if Elisa's new-found strength is any indication, the beast that has a hold on her is quite powerful. She won't remain asleep for much longer, and I doubt it will work a second time."

Octavian looked down at Elisa, who was resting peace-fully...for the moment. "Fine, one attempt at freeing her, but if it is unsuccessful, we will need to summon the rest of the coven immediately. I suggest we gather what we need and move Elisa outside without further delay."

Octavian and I rounded up everything we needed; Himalayan Sea salt, candles, crystals, and incense, and met Dafari outside. We worked quickly, configuring everything the way we had previously. Once we were done, Dafari set Elisa in the middle of the inner circle, lit the candles and incense, then took his position on one side, taking flight to hover above Elisa, with Octavian following suit.

"We call on our exalted Ancestors, hear my entreaty, protect my cousin Elisa Hunte, dispel the evil," I said, reciting the chant the coven used to remove the lost soul from Nazila's body.

The ritual was more difficult this time around, as I didn't have the full weight of the coven behind me, but I refused to give up. I repeated the phrase over and over again, watching Elisa for any sign of movement from the maleficent presence. It took some time, but Elisa's back suddenly arched and... something began to rise from her body. This...thing was worse in appearance than the lost soul. I had no idea what it was, but it was hideous. With a skeleton-like face and eyes that resembled black holes, it had unnaturally long, thin, almost spider-like arms and legs attached to a body that made it look like a walking dead.

As if reading my mind, Octavian shouted, "That's a wraith. It must be dispatched immediately before it has a chance to re-bond with Elisa."

"Say no more, Brother."

Dafari's dark matter sword materialized, as did Octavian's bec-de-corbins. This time, it took a bit longer to take out the wraith, being that it was much stronger than the lost soul, but eventually in faded into nothingness. Once it had, I ran as fast as I could to Elisa's side, although I was somewhat drained after expending so much energy. Octavian and Dafari joined me after they landed. I ran my hands over her to make sure she was indeed free of any hostile entities. This time, I still felt her anger concerning the mayor and Ilene, but it was at a much normal level.

"She's clear," I said.

Dafari picked her up and we began to walk back to the

house, while Octavian reached out to me, extending an arm to lend me support. I gratefully accepted.

"Poppet, how are you faring? I imagine the use of all that magick took a lot out of you."

"I am a bit tired, but there's no time for rest now. We still have to meet the others at Doc Benu's place. Octavian, what exactly is a wraith?" I asked.

"It is a creature that is said to be created when spellcasting goes horribly wrong, usually that of a witch or a wizard trying unsuccessfully to extend her or his life or trying to manipulate time. As a result, the wraith becomes immortal, but, as punishment, becomes a soulless creature who can never reach the spirit realm. As such, it seeks to steal the souls of others. They also feed off a person's negative emotions, which is why I surmise the wraith didn't steal Elisa's soul. Who wouldn't want that much power at their disposal?

Anyway, with the way Elisa was feeling, it had a veritable smorgasbord of anger and rage. They are more powerful than demons and ghosts, which explains her unusual strength. Dafari, you are quite fortunate that you are half-angel, as wraiths tend to feed off pure demons and ghosts alike. Had you not held Elisa a bay, she could have actually harmed you. In their true form, wraiths have been known to physically attack people. I dare not imagine what Elisa could have done with the wraith's added power. Had we not rid Elisa of it, that wraith would have remained with her, only to rear its ugly head once she again became angry. While they are typically attracted to children and teens, any available body will do. It can only be killed by a holy presence or weapon, which, in our case, was extremely fortuitous. I, being...mostly angel, am considered a holy presence, and my bec-de-corbins are holy weapons. Dafari, to a lesser extent, is also a holy presence. No offense."

"None taken," he replied, placing Elisa on the sectional in the living room."

"Had we not destroyed it when we did, it may have been able to channel its anger in order to emit energy waves that could have stolen the will to live from all of Salix Pointe's inhabitants."

"And what would have happened then?" I queried.

"The townspeople would have become so depressed that the wraith would have been able to steal their souls."

Elisa began to stir, low moans and groans coming from her.

Dafari quickly knelt at her side. "My love, can you hear me?"

She slowly opened her eyes. "Wha-what happened?" she asked, her voice groggy.

Dafari took her hand in his. "I'll explain all that later, but how are you feeling?"

"Tired, and my body hurts, like I've been in a battle."

"I apologize, Elisa. Some of that was my fault. I had to restrain you—"

"*Restrain me?* Why?" Elisa cut in, attempting to sit up quickly, only to have to lie back down.

We all looked from one to the other, knowing that explaining everything that happened to her was going to take time, something that we didn't have the luxury of at the moment.

"Sissy," Octavian began, "there was a…side effect of your trek through the shadows. But no worries, your astute cousin," he said, looking at me with pride, "with a little help from Dafari and me, took care of the issue."

"Side effect? Was I possessed or something? "You know what, you can tell me all about it in the truck." Elisa attempted to sit up again, this time at a slower pace. "We need to get to Doc Benu's."

"You're in no shape to go anywhere," Dafari said, holding

on to Elisa's arm, giving her support as she tried to stand. "You need to—"

Elisa held up her hand, cutting him off. "What I *need* to do is get to Doc Benu's now, Dafari. We've already wasted too much time—"

"I don't consider saving your soul wasting time, Elisa," Dafari retorted raising his voice, eyes turning golden. "Look at you; you can barely stand without help."

I knew my cousin and Dafari well. This argument was going nowhere fast, and as much as I hated to go against Elisa, Dafari had a point. Elisa wasn't at her best; then again, neither was I. Performing that spell took a lot of out me, left me feeling drained, but like the old adage says, there's no rest for the weary. I needed to douse this potentially explosive situation before it got out of hand.

"Hey, you two just stop. Elisa, neither one of us is in tip-top shape at the moment, and I don't know how much good we'd be to the coven when we join them at Doc Benu's, let alone if the witch is still there."

As I finished what I was saying, Dafari had a self-satisfied look on his face, thinking I had helped him to win his argument. I quickly burst his bubble.

"However," I continued, "it is our duty, *all of our duty*," I said, looking specifically at Octavian and Dafari, "to find LaLaurie and put an end to her madness, and, hopefully, by association, that of the demon." I paused before finishing my thought. "Look guys, I know you're both worried about us, but we know you have our backs and so will the coven. We can rest after this is all over. So can we please just go help the others and see what they've discovered?"

Dafari and Octavian both had concerned, almost fearful, looks on their faces; the emotions I felt coming from them echoing their expressions.

"I don't like this, I don't like this one bit," Octavian pronounced, pacing back and forth. "Regardless, being subjected to your power earlier makes me realize that we don't have much of a choice in the matter. You and Elisa will go running off into the night half-cocked with or without Dafari and me."

"Octavian has a point. For good, or for ill, you both have become increasingly stronger, as my brother and I have experienced. I admit that I would not want to be on the wrong side of either of you. That said, Octavian and I will accompany you to Doc Benu's place. After all is said and done, the four of us need to have a serious discussion regarding everything that transpired here tonight. Are we in agreement?"

We all nodded. Elisa was finally able to get to her feet. "Good, now that that's settled, shouldn't we get going?"

Dafari sighed but extended his hand for Elisa to take. She looked at it reluctantly but took it just the same. I laughed to myself. They hadn't changed a bit over the centuries.

"Shall we, my sweet?" Octavian held out his arm for me. I hooked mine through his as we walked to Dafari's truck.

Once we were all secure in the vehicle, Dafari started our journey to Doc Benu's, which was on the other side of town. We all remained quiet, as our recent discussion was a bit tense. Despite the fact that the silence was deafening, I welcomed it, my thoughts being all over the place. I looked out the window, saw how the wind was blowing through the tree branches, making them sway to-and-fro, projecting eerie shadows on the road. I kept my focus there, trying to keep my emotions at bay. I wasn't doing a very good job, as tears started to roll down my cheeks.

"What's troubling you, Poppet?" Octavian asked, laying his hand over mine. He could always tell when something was off with me, no matter how much I tried to hide it.

"It was all my fault," I said in a low voice, not looking in his direction.

He moved closer to me, wrapping his arm around my shoulders. "What was your fault?"

"I got us killed. Our daughter and I died because of me, all because of the plan I created."

Octavian turned my face to his; gently wiping away my silent tears. "Tasmin, you are not to blame. There were other forces against us. We were betrayed, Attalah's sight was down—"

"Yes, and I knew all this and still went ahead with the plan, *my* plan. I should have known something was wrong when Attalah became ill and I couldn't heal her. I should have known."

Octavian held me tighter, laying my head against his chest. "None of us knew what ailed Attalah, nor did we suspect that anything was amiss. And let's not forget that, despite her illness, our daughter *insisted* that we carry on with the plan. She was just as head-strong as you are. Had you not decided to follow through, I fear she would have regardless. Please, my love, do not carry this burden."

I looked into Octavian's black eyes, saw the pain contained within them. "Be that as it may, because of my actions, so many lives were ruined. You were driven to madness, Dafari was in Hell for seventy-seven years, Elisa was left almost destitute, and Zafer and Safiya…" my voice trailed off.

Dafari and Elisa didn't say a word, both trying their best to respect my privacy in that moment. I felt Elisa's sympathy for me, as well as Darfari's empathy. He could relate due to the circumstances surrounding his taking Octavian's place. He still suffered much guilt and shame over leaving Elisa for more years than he had anticipated, as well as the untimely deaths of their children.

"Just as you claim responsibility for your actions, I do the same with mine," Octavian said, placing his hand against my cheek, the warmth emanating from it comforting me. "I alone am responsible for the crimes I committed. However, none of it would have occurred had we not been betrayed." Octavian's eyes momentarily flashed red. "I know you and Elisa believe that the repugnant mayor and his vapid wife may have been involved based on their energy signatures, and if that is indeed the case, rest assured they will both pay." He placed a light kiss on my forehead, his version of healing balm.

I had all faith in Octavian and knew that if Mayor Lovett and Ilene had anything to do with the tragic events of 1855, they would surely feel his wrath. While that gave me some solace, in my heart, I knew I needed more time to heal, more time to release my pain and anger, to grieve for our only child. But right now, the time that I desired wasn't mine to possess. We had more important matters to deal with.

"What the…?" Elisa began.

Octavian and I looked up to see a bright, swirling, hurricane-like, bluish-purple and white light in the sky, hurling toward us at a rapid speed. Dafari slammed on the brakes, the four of us shielding our eyes from the brilliance. The light slammed into the pavement, causing the truck to shake momentarily. We all climbed out of the vehicle, with Elisa and me standing on the right, Octavian and Dafari on the left. As we rounded the front of the truck, we immediately took defensive stances. Elisa and my bracelets began to glow, as did our hands. Both Octavian and Dafari summoned their weapons. Before us, in a kneeling position, was Octavian's father, Archangel Michael, his blue kyanite sword in one hand, and a large, polished, silver-colored shield in the other. As he stood to his full height, I took note of how much Octavian resembled him. But that was where the similarities stopped.

Dressed in a turtleneck sweater that hugged his muscular chest and abs, jeans, combat boots, and a long leather trench coat, he reminded me of Samuel L. Jackson in *Shaft*, except Michael's attire was all white.

"What do you want...Father?" Octavian asked.

I could tell from the tone of his voice that if he didn't get the right answer, he'd go ballistic.

"Son, step-son, witches, stand down...please. I'm here to help."

"And we're supposed to believe that?" I scoffed. "Just a few weeks ago, you and your wife tried to kill me and Elisa!"

"If you think we're standing down, you've must have lost your ever-lovin' mind," Elisa voiced, her anger matching mine.

"Michael, I suggest you speak your peace as quickly as possible, but know we are *not* standing down." Dafari made all of our intentions clear.

"Very well," Michael relented. "Perhaps a small gesture will ease your minds." His sword and shield disappeared, as if into the ether. "Better?"

"Not even a little bit," I replied.

"Cut to the chase, Father. You said you were here to help. How?"

He took an 'at ease' stance, feet spread a bit more than hip-width apart, hands behind his back. "Son, I'm aware that the demon wants your blood and that of your witch."

"Her name is *Tasmin*, and you will address her as such," Octavian retorted angrily.

"Yes, well, you and...Tasmin cannot acquiesce to her. She cannot be allowed to walk this earth unfettered. It can only lead to utter chaos."

"It's either that or let her capture and drain innocent children, and I, for one, am not about to let that happen," I defiantly stated.

"Nor I." Octavian walked around the truck, coming to stand in front of me. Dafari took the same position in front of Elisa.

"How did you find out in the first place? Better question, Father, how did you escape?"

"As far as me finding out about the demon's demand, I have my sources. Regarding my escape, it's best you not know; plausible deniability and all."

"Then what do you propose they do, Michael? Let innocent children die?" Elisa queried.

"I suggested no such thing. I promised the eldest widow that I would protect Salix Pointe and I meant it."

"In exchange for her assistance in killing my Aunt Noreen," I spat venomously.

"I will not explain myself to you, to *any* of you," he asserted, looking at each of us individually. "My actions were for *the greater good*, the same way I'm sure you and my son feel your actions are for *the greater good*."

"Poppycock!" Octavian retaliated. "Those are two completely divergent situations, Father. Ours doesn't involve taking a life."

"Save, perhaps, your own," Michael countered. "Do you really think the demon will let you go after she gets what she needs from you? I will not allow my son to sacrifice himself, because that is *exactly* what will happen if you give yourself over to her."

"That's a chance I will have to take. Luckily for me, you have no say in the matter. Now, Father, if that's all, we must be going. We're already grossly behind schedule."

CHAPTER 24

ELISA

I DIDN'T TRUST—NOR DID I like—Michael, but I had to admit that I thought along the same lines as he did when it came to Tasmin and Octavian trying to give themselves over to the demon. No, we couldn't allow her to feed on the children of this town, but my gut told me the entity would most assuredly try to take Tasmin and Octavian out once she got what she wanted.

"Very well," Michael said, resignation in his voice. "Go on your suicide mission, but I'm coming along, and there is very little you can do to stop me."

Before any of us could protest, he was gone. It looked as if he has simply stepped behind a curtain and disappeared.

"It's the veil," Dafari growled low. "He can come and go as he pleases which tells me, he didn't...escape."

"Yes," Octavian said, still watching the spot his father had stood in. "He was released. For what reason, I don't know, but I don't bloody well like it."

"Whatever the reason, it can't be good for us...can it?" Tasmin asked, glancing around our group.

"We don't have a lot of time to think about it," Dafari added, his voice grave as he pointed in the direction of Doc Benu's home. In the distance, there was a cacophony of lights flashing. "Forget taking the human route to his home. We need to get there, immediately. Octavian you take the women through the veil. I'll meet you three there."

I didn't want to traverse the shadows again, and I was sure Dafari picked up on that. I didn't want to risk anything else trying to latch on to me nor Tasmin for that matter. Without any pushback, Tasmin and I took Octavian's lead and walked behind the veil. It was by far a more pleasurable journey than the shadows had been. The shadows was a dark and scary place. Every negative emotion I owned was elevated times ten. Walking through the veil was peaceful and serene. I felt weight lifted off my shoulders. I was without fear or a care in the world. I found that I wanted to stay wherever "behind the veil" was, but I knew I couldn't. Just as soon as we had stepped through, we came out on the other side, directly on to Doc Benu's land.

The lights that we'd seen weren't there. The silence was eerie, and there was a strange mist wafting from the damp earth surrounding the place. The stench wreaked of death, something that we hadn't been able to smell before now. I looked around for Dafari but didn't see him, even though I felt him. Octavian had strategically placed himself in front of Tasmin and me, and I figured that was because Michael stood before us, surveying the land.

"The Gray-Walker who lived here has been harmed," Michael stated.

"No kidding, Sherlock," Tasmin said sarcastically, causing Michael and Octavian to look at her. "Surely you know who Sherlock is," she then said to Octavian, playing on the fact he rarely knew pop references when mentioned.

He nodded. "Of course. I just wasn't expecting sarcasm at the moment."

"Yeah, well... we weren't expecting him either, yet here we are," she snapped, still clearly annoyed by Michael's presence.

"She has a mouth like your mother," Michael drawled, cutting a glance at Tasmin then me. "So does that one."

"Tasmin and Elisa," Octavian said coolly. "Address them by their names or don't say a word to them at all...Father."

I quirked a brow at being compared to the woman who tried to kill us. I glanced at Tasmin to see she, too, was put off by it. Her head was cocked to the side, and she looked fit to be tied. In that moment, I realized Michael was an enigma; quiet but spoke his mind. Silent, but deadly. Presents like an open book but is as reserved as a priest or pope. He was a conundrum, and unlike his loquacious brother, Azazel, Michael didn't stand on pomp and circumstance.

Michael stared his son down but didn't respond to Octavian's declaration. "We should proceed with caution. I'm familiar with the archdemon in question. She is...family," he told us.

"Family?" I repeated. "What is it with entities from your bloodlines trying to kill us, and why didn't Dafari and Octavian know she was their kin?"

"I know why *my* son doesn't know. I didn't tell him and forbade others to do so, including his other uncles and mother. However, Dafari spent seven years in one of the pits of Hell; why he doesn't know is baffling indeed."

"Why didn't Azazel at least mention it?" Tasmin asked.

Michael studied Tasmin, then did the same to me, before turning his eyes back to her. "He has his own duplicitous reasons, I'm sure."

Tasmin and I shot curious glances at one another, confused by Michael's ogling—for a lack of better words— of us.

"This has, by far, been some of the worst few weeks of my bloody life. The time for secrets is done. I am at my wit's end—"

Michael cut his son off. "That is something to be discussed at another time," he spat emphatically.

The tone of his voice made Octavian visibly bristle. It was the tone a father used when he wanted his grown son to understand that his age didn't matter and that he, Michael, still had the last word in such matters. I could tell Octavian wanted to say more, but knew his father was right.

Michael continued. "Eve does not want to kill you. She wants your powers. If you're dead, you will be of no use to her."

It was odd how all of our parents and loved ones held many secrets from us. "So what was all that stuff you said earlier about her wanting to kill Tasmin and Octavian?" I asked.

"She does *want* to kill them, but she won't. She *needs* Tasmin's blood for nefarious reasons, sure. She also wants my son's blood, and I will in no way allow that to happen."

"Oh, so now, you're here to protect Octavian?" Tasmin asked, skepticism on her face and sarcasm still in her tone.

Michael turned pitch black eyes to her and said, "Yes, and by rote, you, too. I'm aware of how my son is when it comes to you." His head abruptly turned in my direction. "Elisa, move. Now!"

Even though I couldn't see what he did, I didn't hesitate to do what he said. I'd learned long ago that they could sometimes see spirits and demons when my human eyes couldn't. Octavian whirled around, pushing Tasmin further behind him before grabbing my arm and shoving me in her direction. Because of the momentum, I stumbled and tripped over Tasmin's feet, causing both of us to fall to the ground. I looked up in time to see Dafari, rushing from the darkness.

He was in full transformation and at least two feet taller than a normal bulk. His eyes were a dark, more terrifyingly red. It was as if staring into blazing, blood-red fire. His teeth were all fanged and jagged. Something that I automatically knew was venom, oozed down them. I'd seen him in battle bulk mode before, but this was different.

"Dafari," I yelled!

"Stay back," Michael barked over his shoulder at me.

"What's wrong with him?" I cried.

"He's come face to face with Eve," Michael snarled.

I gasped then felt Tasmin lay a hand on my shoulder. "You don't think she did something to him, do you?" Tasmin asked me.

"I don't know, but he's different," I told her. "I can feel it."

Tasmin stood then helped me to do the same. "I can, too, and I don't like this."

"The…fight…is in the shadows and this world." Dafari's voice was guttural and hoarse. He didn't sound like the man I loved, but like his voice was amplified. It sounded as if a legion of demons was speaking through him. "She ambushed me…in the shadows…She…bit me…"

It was only then that I noticed the reddish-black blood oozing down the left of his neck.

"She force-turned him," Michael said.

"What does that even mean?" I asked.

"Means she bit him to force him to turn as opposed to it happening naturally," Octavian explained, his black eyes trained on his brother, his body bulking before our very eyes.

Michael said, "She bit him to taste your blood, Elisa. Has my nephew ever bitten you in this lifetime?"

"Yes, but—"

"She will use that against him and once she has your scent in her nose—"

"She's coming," Dafari bellowed as the wind whipped up and rain started to fall. "The Widows and Tasmin's parents are steadfast in their fight against LaLaurie, but Eve—"

"Is a force of a nature. She is the blueprint, the creator of the things that go bump in the night." Michael's voice was loud and unpleasant as he spoke over the roar of the wind.

A burst of white light blinded me as Michael and Octavian battle bulked so quickly that Tasmin nor I had time to register what was happening. Octavian and Michael were in their true forms, and that was still just as terrifying as seeing Dafari in his.

I felt the ground shake. Instinctively, my hands jutted forward, calling the earth to me even though I didn't know what was happening. Dirt and roots from grounded trees rose like pillars on either side of me. To my left, Tasmin's hands glowed with power. If it was a fight the other side wanted, a battle it would get.

CHAPTER 25
TASMIN

T HE CONFRONTATION WE were destined to
have was here...whether we were ready for it or
not. Eve, yet another branch on Octavian and
Dafari's very twisted family tree was coming through the
shadows, gunning for us, Octavian and me in particular.
How she was related, as Michael claimed, I'm sure we'd
find out...if we lived through this battle, that is. Dafari,
forced to turn by Eve, was holding a taloned hand to his
neck, trying to lessen the flow of blood from the wound
caused by her bite. He appeared weakened and not in
control of himself.

"Eve is attempting to seek dominance over Dafari's mind,"
Michael's voice boomed as he took flight. "He's fighting it
because of his angel lineage, but the demon side is just as
powerful, if not more so, because of her sway. He may not
be able to resist her much longer."

"If I get close enough, I could try to heal him," I said.

"No," Michael yelled forcefully. "Your healing powers are
strong, but not even you can heal the bite from an original

archdemon. Dafari should eventually heal of his own accord, but it will take time."

"That's something we're completely out of. Can't you do anything to help him?" Elisa shouted to Michael, a plea in her voice.

"I can't make any promises, but I will try to get through to him. Son, you stay with...Tasmin and Elisa."

Michael was an extremely powerful high archangel, as we had all experienced. He had easily bested Dafari in our first confrontation, but now, in Dafari's current condition, I was questioning how much help Michael would be. While he was generally taller than both Dafari and Octavian in their human forms, his vast proportions were even more apparent in his celestial form. His massive size eclipsed both that of his son and step-son, in comparison. However, after Eve's bite, Dafari's size matched Michael's.

"Dafari, Son, get a hold of yourself!" Michael hovered directly in front him, his shield and blue kyanite sword held in defense.

"Don't you think I'm trying?" Dafari growled between gritted fangs, eyes flashing between his normal scarlet red and a deep blood red.

He doubled over, and I could feel his pain as he was trying to rid himself of Eve's poison that was coursing through him. Then he stopped, holding his head up, his eyes appearing one color, blood red. As he floated overhead, I noticed that his wings, which were usually an equal mix of black and white feathers, were now completely black. It sent chills down my spine.

"Run!" we heard Michael say, without looking back at us.

No sooner had Michael said his command had Dafari's dark matter sword appeared in one hand, a single Mabo throwing knife in the other. He let out a roar as he swung for Michael's head with his weapons. Narrowly deflecting the blows with his shield, he flew backwards, allowing more space between himself and Dafari. He briefly looked back to see us still standing there.

"I told you all to run! I'll deal with Dafari. You help the others."

"Is he serious?" I asked. "He's barely handling Dafari, and Eve will be here any second."

"Agreed," Octavian said, watching horror-stricken as his brother and father went blow for blow, their weapons sending out sparks as they connected. "You two go find the Pettifords and the Widows. Hopefully, Father and I can keep Dafari and Eve at bay until you all return."

"Are you out of your mind?" I questioned angrily. "I'm not leaving you with Dafari *and* Eve."

"Neither am I," Elisa affirmed. "If Michael is struggling fighting with Dafari, what makes you think the two of you will fare any better once Eve gets here? We're staying," she finished defiantly.

Octavian looked at us and shook his head. He took flight, taking a position behind Dafari. "Stop this, Brother!" he ordered. "I don't want to hurt you."

Letting out a sinister laugh, Dafari replied, "Oh, but I do want to hurt you. Not kill you, just…hurt you. After all, you and your witch are more valuable to me alive…for now." The voice was a mix of Dafari's and what we could only assume was Eve's. She had complete control of him.

"Dafari, please, this is not you," Elisa yelled. "Fight her hold on you. Do it for me."

Looking in our direction, Dafari immediately stopped fighting Michael and Octavian. It seemed as if Elisa had reached him...or so we thought. Dafari began to lunge in our direction, heading straight for Elisa. She screamed, reflexively uprooting three large trees, hurling them at Dafari, all of them connecting. The force of the objects sent him sprawling backwards, the wind momentarily knocked out of him.

Her emotions hit me like a ton of bricks as tears streamed down her face. "I had no choice."

"I know," I replied, attempting to comfort her.

Bars of raw energy surrounded a staggered Dafari, caging him in on all sides. He knew better than to touch the rods, as holy fire could severely incapacitate, or even kill, him.

"This should hold him, at least for a little while," Michael said as he and Octavian landed to stand near us. "You do know that was not Dafari who attacked you, Elisa. He had no control."

"I-I don't—"

"Now isn't that sweet?" a possessed Dafari spoke. "Is that a bonding moment I see?"

"Shut up, Eve!"

"Now, now, Michael, is that any way to speak to family?" The demon inside Dafari let out a sinister chuckle. "Who am I kidding? You shunned your own brother Azazel, and treated your daughter-in-law and step-daughter-in-law like shit. You tried to kill them for, what was that, oh yes, *the greater good*. Simply because they are witches. How...intolerant of you."

"This coming from an *original* evil. That's rich," Michael spat.

At that moment, I didn't know whom I despised more, Michael or Eve, considering they both wanted Elisa and me dead. Michael's only saving grace was that he knew better than to try again, or else he would have to face Octavian and Dafari's wrath. Eve, on the other hand, was, as Michael phrased it, an original evil.

"I guess what they say is true," Eve spoke. "Misery does indeed acquaint a man with strange bedfellows. Who would have thought that you, old stuffed shirt, boot-licking, lackey Michael would team up with the very witches you were tasked, and failed, to eliminate? The Powers That Be do work in mysterious ways."

"Your blasphemy will not be tolerated, Eve," Michael threatened.

"Oh, kin of mine? What are you going to do, come into the shadows to fight me? Of course not. That would be a fool's errand. Right now, you can't get to me without harming your step-son, and you wouldn't do that...but I would."

It was in that moment we saw the true depravity of Eve. Much to our dismay, Dafari's arm began to move toward one of the holy fire bars. He tried to fight Eve's control, have some semblance of willpower, but her domination over him was too strong. We looked on terrified as his arm touched the bar, searing flesh, leaving a deep laceration. The scream Dafari let out tore at our souls.

"Stop it!" Elisa cried out.

"You want me to stop, witch. Beg me. Beg me to stop hurting your love."

"Do *not* do that, Elisa," Michael interjected. "Eve will not relinquish control of Dafari without a trade-off. If you agree to her terms, you will end up owing her something in return. A Faustian deal of sorts."

"Like the deal Marie made with Eve?" Octavian asked.

Michael nodded. "Exactly like that."

I placed a hand on Elisa's shoulder in an attempt to lend my support. I hated the position Eve put her in. Either she kept allowing the demon to harm Dafari, or she could make an untenable bargain in order to save him. How was she supposed to choose?

Elisa stood tall, shrugging my hand off her shoulder.
"Michael, release Dafari," Elisa said. The tone of her voice
put me on edge.

"Are you daft, woman?"

"My apologies for Father's bluntness, Sissy, but I, too,
have to question the method to your madness. My brother,
albeit possessed, attacked you once. You are tempting fate."

Octavian was right. Dafari was still dangerous and releasing him could give him a second opportunity to hurt her, or
worse. But I could tell Elisa would not be deterred. What I
saw in her eyes, and *felt* in my gut, was the pain of a woman
who was tired of losing her loved ones. In a past life, Elisa
had lost her husband, her children, and her livelihood. In
this one, she lost her parents and her grandmother. She was
determined to not let that happen again. I just hoped that
her thinking with her heart, instead of her head, wouldn't
get her, as well as the rest of us, killed.

"Just do it," she said, taking a defensive posture.

Michael looked at Octavian, who shrugged, but followed
Elisa's lead, standing to her left, his bec-de-corbins appearing
in his hands. I took point on her right.

Letting out a rough exhale, Michael gave Elisa a hard stare,
then said, "Fine, but if this goes sideways, it is completely on
you." He released Dafari, who instantly lunged towards us.

Elisa didn't hesitate before hitting Dafari with a gust of
wind that thrust him back several feet, his balance thrown
off due to his injured limb. "Tasmin, hit him with everything
you've got, and don't stop," she yelled.

I looked at her skeptically, but did as she asked, hitting
him with consecutive energy blasts. Elisa threw everything
at him, save the kitchen sink, and had one been available, she
probably would have thrown that too. I used my telekinetic
powers to hurl the objects she had previously lobbed at Dafari

as additional cover to help keep him occupied. Her rage at Eve was fueling her attack on Dafari, growing stronger the longer the fight went on.

"Do you think a bit of rough weather, a few trees, and some rocks are going to stop me?" Eve asked with a laugh. "You really have become full of yourself, witch."

"Not in the least," Elisa retorted, a look of determination on her face. *"Eve can't concentrate on all of us at once,"* Elisa projected. *"Octavian and Michael, Tasmin and I will keep her distracted. You two head through the veil, circle around to both sides of Dafari, and grab his arms. I'll handle the rest."*

Both angels disappeared into the veil appearing to the left and right of Dafari, grabbing his arms. He struggled fiercely, but they held fast. Suddenly thick roots appeared from beneath him, wrapping tightly around his arms, legs, and torso, pulling him to the ground. The more he fought, the more secure the bindings became. Elisa began to run toward him.

I took hold of one of her arms. "Elisa, what are you doing?"

"I need to free Dafari from Eve's clutches." I could hear the desperation in her voice.

"Okay, but how?"

"Let me go and you'll find out," she said.

I quickly released her, allowing her to stand in front of him. She reached down, touching his temples.

"What is she doing?" Michael asked.

"I assume that since she is a telepath, she's trying to connect with Dafari's mind. The bond they share is strong, and, although it was accidental, she had been able to get in his head before," Octavian explained.

Dafari's head jerked about in an attempt to dislodge Elisa's hands.

"Unloose me, witch!" Eve commanded.

"No, not until you leave Dafari's body," Elisa countered. "Come back to me, my love. I *need* you to come back to me." I saw the resolve on her face as she tried to reach Dafari. "I lost you once, I'll be damned if I let that happen again."

For a few seconds, Dafari's eyes switched from blood red to scarlet.

"Elisa…," a voice said. It was weak, but it was definitely Dafari.

"Dafari?" Elisa fell to her knees, coming face-to-face with the man she loved. "Please, you have to fight her. I won't let you leave me again. Get…out…of… my…husband, you bitch!"

Dafari shut his eyes tightly. When he opened them, they kept flashing from dark red to lighter red, Dafari's internal war playing out in them. He threw back his head, letting out a blood curdling cry. When he finally stopped, his head slumped forward.

"Is he…?" I started.

Michael placed his hand over Dafari's heart. "He is alive… barely. However, he is free from Eve's hold, which does not bode well for us. She will be here any moment. We need to get to the others *now*, ahead of her arrival. Since the fray appears to have moved elsewhere, Octavian, you take Tasmin and Elisa through the veil to the Gray-Walker's residence. More than likely, that's where you will find everyone."

"What about Dafari?" Elisa hurriedly asked.

Michael reached down, picking up Dafari, slinging him over his shoulder in a fireman's carry. "Unfortunately, if we are to have any hope of saving him, I must carry him through the veil. Although he is a half-angel, I cannot guarantee that he will come out completely unscathed; however, I *can* guarantee his safety. As a high-arch, I dare anyone to challenge me." He looked at Elisa, seeing the fear in her eyes. "I promise you, I will do my best to protect him. Tasmin, once we get to the other side, you can heal him. With Eve on our tails, I feel it will be safer once you are reunited with your coven."

I acknowledged him with a nod. After Michael walked through the veil, Octavian opened his own path and walked through, with Elisa and I following close behind. When we arrived on the other side, nothing but sheer devastation greeted us. Seared and decapitated carcasses of what looked to be hellhounds, imps, hellbats, and some others I didn't recognize were strewn out front of the small home. My parents and the Widows were nowhere in sight, but I could feel their disquieting emotions, as well as their fatigue, all around me, which meant they were close by.

"The others," I began. "They're close by, I just can't pinpoint where they are."

Michael, with Dafari in tow, stepped through the veil. Gently laying Dafari on the ground, Michael appraised the area. "Eve unleashed a horde on the coven. After you heal Dafari, we must find them quickly."

I knelt down beside Dafari. His face was ashen, breathing shallow and labored. He also had some superficial burns, I assumed as a result of his time traveling through the veil. Between the physical and mental harm he had endured, it was a wonder he survived at all. I place my hands on his chest then closed my eyes. His mind and his body were damaged, I hoped not irreparably. Life slowly trickled back into his body, as my healing powers began repairing neural pathways, blood vessels, and muscles. Dafari's breathing stabilized and his dark chocolate-hued skin tone returned. He began to stir, opening his eyes.

Elisa was at his side in an instant. "Dafari, can you hear me?"

"Y-yes, my love, I can hear you. I'm sorry." His voice was a bit weak, but he seemed no worse for wear.

"It wasn't your fault," Elisa replied, touching the back of her hand to his cheek.

"I was aware of everything that was happening, but try as I might, I couldn't stop myself."

"Eve is extremely powerful. You were no match for her," Michael countered. "You hold no blame."

Dafari slowly attempted to sit up, leaning on his forearms, only to drop back down. He winced, grabbing the arm on the side opposite to me.

"What's wrong?" I asked.

Elisa removed his hand then gasped, a shocked look on her face. "His arm…"

I couldn't help but echo Elisa's expression when I saw what she was referring to. While most of the damage to Dafari's arm had healed, a large, jagged scar remained.

"It was the holy fire," Michael spoke, standing behind Elisa. "Eve knew what it could do to him. She's responsible for this. However," he continued, remorse on his face, "I'm sorry I had to put you in that position in the first place, Dafari."

With Elisa's and my help, Dafari rose to his feet. "You did no such thing, Michael. Had you not imprisoned me, I would have done something I would have surely regretted. This is all on Eve."

"I can try to heal…"

"No, Sister," Dafari said. The sadness in his eyes made my heart ache. "While I appreciate your effort, the damage will take more time to heal than we have at the moment."

"He is correct, Tasmin. The wounds inflicted by holy fire can heal, but not immediately. He will recover…eventually."

"That-that, *bitch*!" We all turned to look at Elisa. The tears streaming down her face belied the fury emanating from her.

"If she could hurt a family member the way she hurt Dafari, she'll have no qualms about killing Salix Pointe's children, or anyone else for that matter. This has to end."

"What? Eve is...family? How?" Dafari questioned.

"That, Son, shall be explained later. In the meantime, Elisa, you need to channel that rage, because it will serve you well for this battle. I sense Eve is near, as is the coven. We must go."

CHAPTER 26

TASMIN

ICHAEL LED THE way, charging around to the back of the house, where dense woods resided. A swarm of deceased hell entities made a trail, leading further into the dense foliage. He put a finger to his lips, signaling us to remain silent. That was when we heard it, the sounds of battle coming from deep within the woodlands. The Celestials summoned their weapons to them. Elisa and I prepared ourselves, both of our hands glowing in anticipation of the fight to come. Once we traversed the thickets, we came upon a small clearing. On one side of it was the coven, in the midst of the fight of their lives. A few hellbeasts, along with Marie, were attacking my parents and the Widows. Michael, Dafari, and Octavian took flight, strategically positioning themselves in primary battle positions in front of the coven. Michael, always the leader, placed himself front and center, while Dafari placed himself to the right of him, and Octavian to his left.

Martha looked at Elisa and me wide-eyed, a disbelieving expression on her face.

"We'll explain later," I shouted. I didn't want her, or her sisters, tipping off my parents to who Michael was.

She nodded then, being the coven elder, gave us battlefield position orders. "Cara Lee, to my left, Mary Ann, my right. Silas, next to Cara Lee. Jewel, Mary Ann. Tasmin, next to Silas, and Elisa next to Jewel." I knew she was arranging us so as to have a necromancer on one side and a healer on the other, balancing us out.

The battle was all of sudden at a standstill, as if Marie was regrouping; I was certain it was because of the additional five combatants. She looked nothing like the woman Elisa and I fought when she was in the dream world. Instead, she looked like the classic crone that Grimm's fairy tales were made of, death warmed over.

"Oh look, the gang's all here, and with some help." she quipped, her eyes intently locked on Michael. "And who might you be?"

"You may address me as Archangel Michael, Marie Delphine LaLaurie."

When he heard his name, my dad was set to go from zero to sixty, until I stopped him, placing my hand on his arm.

"Daddy, no. This is neither the time nor the place. Besides, he's here to help."

He looked at me then back to Michael. When his eyes finally returned to me, he said in a whisper, "You're right, but when this is over, I have a few choice words for Archangel Michael."

"And I'll be more than happy to hear you out, Silas Pettiford," Michael replied, looking down at him.

Daddy's look of surprise said he wondered how Michael had heard him. "Damn Celestial hearing," he muttered.

"Archangel Michael? Here for lil ole me?" Marie uttered in her Louisiana drawl. "I'm so flattered."

"Don't be," Michael chided. "You're not that important."

I didn't like Michael by any stretch of the imagination, but even I had to stifle a chuckle at his response, unlike Marie. She was none too happy with Michael's insult, which led her to call for her minions to attack. Hellbats appeared above us, imps and hellhounds on the sides and in front.

"Dafari, you handle the bats. Octavian and I will deal with the imps and the dogs. Coven, provide Dafari with additional cover and backup for the creatures that slip past us," Michael ordered as he and Octavian landed.

As much as I hated to admit it, he was an extremely effective strategist. He knew that Dafari could handle fighting hellbats from the air better than he and Octavian could, as any damage to their wings could permanently maim them. While Michael and Octavian were making short work of the hellhounds and imps, Dafari was having a harder time with the hellbats, as there were many, and they appeared to be multiplying.

"We need to get some projectiles in the air," Martha commanded.

Elisa and I hit some of the bats with energy blasts, their tiny bodies falling to earth like meteorites, while the sisters made tut moves with their staffs, creating Adinkra symbols. Martha traced Akoben, which meant war horn, as Mary Ann and Cara Lee both drew Akofena, meaning sword of war. Once the illuminated symbols were formed, the Widows flung them through the air, hitting their marks with precision. My father was able to use his necromancer abilities to resurrect several of the dogs dispatched by Michael and Octavian and bend them to his will, directing them to surround Marie.

"Give it up, Marie!" I said.

"Never!" Marie cried, even as the reincarnated dogs were closing in on her, and so were we.

"Then suffer the consequences," Elisa yelled, flinging a large stone at her. I followed it with a fallen tree stump.

Marie, who was attempting to fight off the dogs with her own magick, screamed and recoiled, arms held up in front of her face. Both objects found their mark, knocking her frail body to the ground. The feeble woman attempted to crawl away, but we surrounded her, ready to do what we had to in order to rid ourselves of this evil once and for all, until, from behind her, appeared a creature of unimaginable terror. I thought Azazel's demon appearance was frightful, but it paled in comparison to that of Eve's. Oversized black ram's horns sat atop a gargantuan head with large, glowing red eyes, lips like slits, and enormous, dripping fangs. That head was attached to a mammoth, although feminine, frame. Long, shiny, onyx nails highlighted her taloned hands and feet. Her tail was long, with barbs along it, except for the end, which was mushroom-shaped. Her frightful appearance was accentuated by her taut, hide-like, amaranth red skin. She towered over Michael, his size appearing child-like next to hers.

She stood over Marie, the reincarnated dogs disappearing with a wave of her hand. She appeared exceedingly calm, which in itself was disturbing. Looking at Dafari, Eve sighed. "I had such high hopes for you, halfling. I hope you know I was only trying to help you live up to your full potential. After all, we are family."

"Octavian, Elisa, Tasmin…and Michael are my family," Dafari countered, landing next to Elisa. "I know nothing of you save for the fact that you tried to force me to kill my own wife."

She huffed then said, "Yes, the little witch that could… get you to come back to her, that is. Ironic how you're the incubus, and yet, it seems *she* has you in *her* thrall. At least you'll have something to remember me by." She chuckled, pointing to her own arm, mirroring the spot where Dafari's scar was. "And *you*, you useless skin sack," she said, pointing a talon at Marie. "Good help is so hard to find. I left you with an entire demonic army to fight on your behalf, and you still failed. It's abundantly clear that if you want something done right, you have to do it yourself."

As Eve was chastising her minion, Octavian connected with me. *"Father is requesting that we all open our minds to him. He wants us to be able to fight as a coordinated unit without Eve knowing what we're planning, and assures me that he will respect everyone's privacy and only unite with everyone for tactical purposes only."*

I looked at Michael for a second then at Octavian. I didn't trust Michael nor did I want him in my head for any reason, but it was a logical plan. We needed to keep Eve off balance as much as possible, and that wouldn't be possible with her hearing every single command that Michael would be shouting to us on the battlefield.

"Fine," I said, *"but I can only speak for myself. I'll ask Elisa to reach out to the others."*

Octavian gave a slight nod of acknowledgement. When I told Elisa what Michael was asking, her response was the same as mine. She also understood the logic of it all, as did the coven once she relayed the message to them. No one was too keen on the idea of Archangel Michael, murderer of Aunt Noreen, Mama Nall, Dum-Nolan, and Akasha, and attempted murderer of Elisa and me, having access to our innermost thoughts, but we had no choice but to take him on his word as an archangel.

Once we were all linked, Michael said, *"As I told my son, first and foremost, I intend to honor your privacy. We need the element of surprise, and this is the most efficient way to achieve that goal. Everyone stand at the ready. I fear Eve is about to strike."*

No sooner had Michael spoken that we were immediately surrounded on all sides. A swarm of hellbats were above us, with imps and hellhounds circling us on the ground, and then there was a new addition to the mix. Beings of pure fire rose up from the earth. The coven instinctively made a circle facing outward, allowing us to see on all sides.

"Those are ifrits," Octavian explained. *"They are spirits of the dead who were most likely inhabiting the doctor's property since his death being that it was deserted."*

Michael promptly started issuing orders. *"Stay as far away from the ifrits as you can. Their touch can be deadly. They are only susceptible to magick. Tasmin and Elisa, handle the ifrits. Dafari, widows, and healer, deal with the other beasts. Necromancer, continue to reanimate the dead creatures. Command them to target Eve. They won't injure her, but they can provide a distraction. Octavian and I will work to keep Eve from creating more minions."*

Without hesitation, the sisters went on the defensive, invoking the power of the Orishas.

"I call on the power of Oshun. Please guide me in strengthening the coven during this battle," thought Martha.

"Orisha Oya, I implore you, intensify our female warriors' spirit," Cara Lee petitioned, followed by Mary Ann.

"Mighty Shango, please hear my entreaty and magnify our will to fight."

The last petition to an Orisha was unexpected, as it came from my mom. I wasn't aware she had any knowledge of the Orishas. Then again, I never knew she was a witch until recently.

"Shaman and healer Ogun, please grant me the shapeshifting ability and ferocity of the Loup Garou in order to overtake our enemies."

The Loup Garou? A werewolf? I wouldn't have believed it until I saw it with my own eyes. My mom, a petite woman, transformed into a massive lupine creature. I stared as she attacked hellhounds with vigor, easily gutting one and slitting the throat of another with her sharp claws. While watching my mom was kind of disconcerting, I was actually fascinated by it. Mom and I would definitely have to have a long talk after this was over.

The Widows made a wedge formation, moving in the shape of a triangle, using their staffs, taking out imps with ease. Dad revived every entity that wasn't tore limb from limb, sending them in Eve's direction. Dafari hovered closer to the ground, slashing at bats with his sword in one hand, and his knife in the other. The bats had followed him low enough allowing my mom to knock several out of the air, shredding them. Michael and Octavian were effectively keeping Eve at bay, for the moment. Their opposing attacks in figure eight formations kept her off-balance, not allowing her room to maneuver. The addition of the reincarnated hounds provided us with enough time to formulate a game plan for the fire demons.

"I have an idea for how to handle the ifrits," Elisa said while tossing rocks and uprooted trees at them. *"I'll tap into the water supply on the property, form a waterspout, have Michael turn it into holy water then I'll douse them."*

I steadily attacked the ifrits with energy blasts. *"That's a great plan,"* I replied. *"And I can gather the discarded trees and rocks then Michael can charge them with holy fire."*

"Let's do it."

The coven and Dafari had successfully eradicated the current wave of imps, bats, and hellhounds. This freed them to cover Elisa and me against the ifrits. She closed her eyes then opened them, their white glow evident that she was tapping into the source of her powers. Her cupped hands, one on top of the other, began to move in a clockwise direction. Within seconds, a small sprig of water rose from the earth, swiftly becoming a towering funnel. While Elisa was creating her waterspout, I used my telekinetic powers to gather a heaping pile of downed trees and assorted rocks. Once we were both done, we quickly relayed our plans to Michael, who promptly switched places with Dafari. As he stood in front of us, his hands began to glow. He reached out, touching the waterspout with one hand, the mound of rocks and trees with the other. The illumination remained after he removed them. He quickly took the battle back to Eve.

Elisa and I took aim, preparing to hit the now-charging ifrits from opposite ends. We mirrored one another, moving in a semi-circle. Elisa doused the beasts with the holy water, each one becoming surrounded by a funnel all its own, only to dissolve into a puff of white smoke; while the ones I hit with holy fire-infused objects were set ablaze, bodies engulfed by flames of pure white, then fizzling out altogether. To our surprise, our actions caught Michael's attention...and praise.

"I must admit, witches, those were impressive displays. I can see, on some level, why my son and step-son are so taken with you two."

"Thanks, I guess," was all I was able to muster.

With the ifrits neutralized, that left the coven free to fight the main source of Salix Pointe's unrest, Eve.

"Everyone, hit her from all sides and don't hold back," Michael conveyed.

He, along with Octavian and Dafari, surrounded her on three sides, forming a triangle, assaulting Eve with sword strikes alternating with holy fire, bec-de-corbins, and Mabo throwing knives, respectively. Elisa stormed ahead, focusing on Eve's right, channeling every elemental power in her arsenal from wind and rain to lightning and earth. I moved on her left, using my telekinetic powers, along with my energy blasts.

The Widows made an opposing trine to that of the Celestials, battering her with the forces of the Orishas. With the last of the reanimated creatures destroyed, Dad also connected with an Orisha, Aganju, manifesting the warrior king's fighting sword, sending off a barrage of divine fire blasts.

My mom, still in the form of the Loup Garou, took the fight directly to Eve, using her claws to gauge into her skin. I thought that with the stronger Celestials being more of a match for Eve, my mom would be nothing but a minor irritation, but I was wrong. Eve locked her gaze on her, raising her tail.

"Mom, look out," I shouted.

It all happened so fast. Octavian flew in my mother's direction in an attempt to block Eve, but he was too late. With a backwards swipe of her appendage, my mom was propelled away from us, her body hitting up against a tree. Eve's tail swung in the other direction, knocking Octavian to the ground. He appeared stunned as he attempted to stand. He fell to his knees.

"Jewel!" Daddy was off in a heartbeat, running toward his fallen wife.

Michael, who observed Eve eyeing my Dad, glided toward him, whisking him into the veil, only to appear next to my mother, her body converted back to that of a human. Dad quickly assessed her.

"She's alive, just unconscious. Nothing appears to be broken," he said.

"Being in the form of the Loup Garou was most likely protective for her. You need to get your wife out of here. The rest of us will stay and continue the fight," Michael said, standing in front of my parents.

I started running in their direction, intent on giving my mom a cursory healing. I was stopped in my tracks when Eve stepped through a shadow, completing blocking them off. She ferociously attacked Michael, her talons hitting his shield, preventing him from becoming airborne, forcing him to his knees. Dafari and the rest of the coven rushed to assist him, while I went to check on Octavian. It was then that I noticed a gash across his chest.

"I'm okay. It's just a scratch," he said. "Go help the others."

"Let me heal you first."

Octavian gently blocked my hands. "Tasmin, there's no time. I need to get back in there, and so do you."

I assessed the current state of the battle. With the full coven and the three Celestials, we were at least holding our own, but now, with my mom down for the count, my dad at her side, and Octavian wounded, we were faltering.

"Agreed, but under one condition. Octavian, we need help. I usually wouldn't say this unless the situation was desperate, but we need Azazel. Call him now, please." I was sure I would live to regret those words.

Octavian looked at me hard, but deep down he knew I was right. *"Uncle,"* he thought, *"we need your assistance."*

Out of nowhere, Azazel appeared. "Didn't I tell you not to call me unless—" He stopped, appraising the situation, seeing Michael under attack, my parents trapped, and the others doing their best to fight Eve. "Oh my," he said, barely above a whisper. "You do need my help. You can thank me later." Darting into a shadow, he reappeared next to Michael, sword and shield in hand. *"Brother, nice to see you looking so...robust."* His shield went up, Eve's talons deflecting off it. *"Were you released or was it a jail break?"*

"What are you doing here, Azazel?" Michael growled.

"I was called here by my nephew. Clearly he was justified. Silas, how's our Jewel doing?"

Any other time, Daddy would have called Azazel out, but

under these circumstances, I get why he let it slide. *"She still unconscious, but stable."*

Azazel, never one to be humble, pronounced, *"You're welcome for the assistance, by the way. You can repay me later."*

Octavian and I had rejoined the fight, but something with him was...off. The more he fought, the weaker he seemed to get. I wasn't the only one who noticed.

"What's wrong, Octavian?" Elisa asked.

"I don't know, Sissy. I all of a sudden felt this all-embracing weakness overtake me."

"He was grazed by one of the barbs on Eve's tail," I added.

"Son, you need to stop fighting. Eve's barbs are poisonous. The more energy you expend, the faster it will run through your system. If you continue, that poison coursing through your veins can potentially kill you. Tasmin can heal your wound, but she cannot eliminate Eve's otherworldly poison. You need to withdraw now," Michael commanded.

"But father, we are barely getting by as it is. I can't just abandon you all."

"Octavian, did you hear what Michael said? The poison can kill you," I chimed in.

"Listen to them, Nephew," added Azazel. *"Besides, we need someone to take Jewel and Silas through the veil while the strongest of us stay here to continue on. Tag, you're it."*

Octavian exhaled hard, but offered no more resistance, which was wise, because he looked to be struggling moving in and out of the veil to get to my parents. He had almost reached them when we heard a blood curdling scream. We looked on, terrified, as Martha had been pinned to the ground by the end of Eve's tail. Her breathing was labored.

"Sister," Cara Lee and Mary Ann yelled, running toward her.

"Uh, uh, uh," Eve taunted. "Come any closer and I will crush this old bag of bones, understood?"

The two widows nodded, backing off, fearful for the safety of their eldest sibling.

"Let her go, Eve!" Michael demanded.

"Ah, my dear Michael, why in the world would I do that? Once I do, you'll only attack me again. No, this old witch is my ticket to what I need," she said, looking first in my direction, then Octavian's. "What's it going be? Your lives or hers?" She lowered her tail a bit more, further crushing Martha, whose gasps for air were becoming less frequent.

We were out of time and options, our choice was clear. It was ironic how I was sacrificing myself for the woman who aided in the murder of her friend, and Michael, who promised to protect her, couldn't deliver. I held up my hands in a sign of surrender. Eve then removed her tail from Martha's body, allowing the others to tend to her. Michael lifted her from the ground, bringing her to rest next to my mother. The looks on everyone's faces spoke volumes. The sisters were grateful for the decision Octavian and I made, while the others... their faces said they understood, but also wished there was another way.

"LaLaurie, for once make yourself useful. Bind the witchlet with the iron chains. And to be on the safe side, have the others chain themselves together."

Marie, who had slunk off to hide during the battle with Eve, reappeared, with iron chains in her hands. She handed one long linked chain to Elisa, watching as everyone, including Michael, cuffed themselves together then she placed a pair on my wrists. "Pay back is a bitch, isn't it?" she said to me, then chuckled.

"Yes, you are," I countered with a smirk.

That's when I felt the sting of her slap to my face, the

taste of blood in my mouth. "Know your place! In my day I would kill your ilk just for the fun of it."

"Strike her again and I will end you, you worthless cow!" Octavian was at my side in an instant.

"I don't think you will," said Eve. "If anything happens to…my minion, your love will die. Either way, I still get her blood." When it came to my well-being, Eve said the one thing that would force Octavian to stand down; a threat to my very existence. "Which reminds me, little angel boy, it's your turn."

Marie pulled out a large spike, intent on skewering Octavian with it. I could only assume it was iron. "This is for my precious Lefu. I hope it hurts as much as it did when you took my impundulu from me."

Just as she took aim, ready to plunge the nail into Octavian's chest, we heard, "No."

"But mistress, I…"

"I said *no*," reiterated Eve. "That honor belongs to another. Azazel."

Not one person looked surprised when Eve called his name. She walked over to him, snapping the chains from his wrists.

"Duplicitous son-of-a-bitch!" Michael spat in outrage. "I knew you were up to something."

"Michael, language," Azazel chided. "Come now, Brother, you know I like to play for the winning team, and, clearly, your side has lost." He walked over to LaLaurie, holding his hand out. "Oh, my, Marie. I thought the Widows hadn't aged well, but they look like supermodels compared to you."

She reluctantly handed over the spike. "Back in my heyday, I would have taken you through your paces. I had three husbands who could attest to that."

"Marie, you never were my cup of tea, even at your best."

Obviously insulted, she huffed, but stepped to the side, allowing Azazel to stand in front of Octavian.

"I hate you."

"Are you sure, Tasmin?" I was thoroughly disgusted when he winked at me. "Nephew, as Marie noted, it will hurt. My apologies in advance."

He then leaned in, whispering something to Octavian that I couldn't hear. Azazel thrusted the pointed metal into his abdomen. Octavian released a guttural howl from deep within. I felt every bit of his pain, which, in turn, caused me to scream. Already weakened from Eve's poison, he fell to his knees, sweating profusely from his brow and breathing hard. I leaned down next to him, intent on providing as much healing as I could.

"Don't even try it. And stop being so dramatic, child. He'll recover on his own…if I allow it," Eve chastised. "If I wanted to kill him, I would have made Azazel stab him in the heart. Instead, I want to break him first…by watching you die. I'm rather looking forward to seeing him go mad again. I heard it was quite the sight the first time around. After viewing your death again, he'll probably beg me to kill him. But I digress. Marie, get the blood from the virgin. Azazel, if you don't mind, your nephew."

Wielding a large knife, Lalaurie made a deep cut across my wrist, a vial held directly underneath to catch the flowing blood. The sneer on her face spoke to her perverse nature. I was glad my blood flowed quickly, because I knew my wound would start to heal at any minute, and I didn't want them to know about that particular power. Azazel bent down, holding an identical vial below Octavian's dripping abdominal wound. I thought he'd be enjoying it more, but he wasn't. Marie took the bottle from Azazel, pouring our blood back and forth between the two. She placed a cork on the one full vial, setting it on the ground.

"The blood has to settle for a few minutes before you drink it, mistress, but soon you will be free to roam this plane in a new vessel."

"In that case, while we wait, Azazel, can you do what you do best?"

"*One* of the things I do best," he said, flashing a grin that I swore showed every single tooth in his mouth. Before we could blink, he had pulled the stake from Octavian's abdomen, and was behind Marie, holding it against the jugular vein in her neck.

"Wha-what is the meaning of this?" a shocked Marie inquired, taken aback by the sudden turn of events.

"Haven't you figured it out by now, or are you just that dense? I have no further use for you. My minion, you have become expendable." Eve spread her taloned hands as if presenting something.

LaLaurie struggled to remove herself from Azazel's grasp. "Bu-but I thought I was to be your vessel."

Eve chuckled loudly, amused by what she had heard. "Why would I choose you with your decrepit, withered husk when I have young, fresh meat to pick from? No, the time for our alliance has ended...happily. Azazel, she's all yours."

"Thank you," he said, gleefully raising the sharp projection.

"Azazel, wait!" I said, interrupting his kill strike.

He looked at me curiously as Marie continued to struggle. "What can I do for you, Tasmin?" he asked, walking toward me with Marie in tow. He stood directly in front of me.

"Nothing. I just wanted to do this."

Raising my bound hands, I pulled back then struck her in the face with one of the iron cuffs. Her head flung to one side, a large red bruise from where my strike landed quickly appearing on her pale, sallow skin. She attempted to right herself, a stunned look on her face. I followed up with a hard blow to her other cheek.

I stared her down. "The first one was for slapping me earlier and telling me to know my place. The second was for trying to stab Octavian." I looked at Azazel. "Now she's all yours." I gave her my back.

"My dear, sweet Tasmin, how deliciously petty of you," I heard him say. "I'm so proud." I bristled at the thought.

"You petulant bitch!" Marie bellowed at me before releasing a scream so shrill it made my ears hurt.

I turned around just in time to see Azazel removing his hand from Marie's chest cavity, a large gaping hole appearing where her heart should have been. He dropped her lifeless body to the ground, black fluid leaking from her chest as her body dwindled into nothingness. With her still-beating heart in his hand, Azazel studied it for a moment, as did I, each beat becoming slower and slower. He appeared to grow weary watching it, so he simply dropped it to the floor, smashing it with his expensive leather shoe. He then wiped the grime from his shoe on Marie's clothing, the only proof that she was even there. Azazel picked up the vial of blood, handing it to Eve.

"I thank you, Azazel." Licking her lips in anticipation, she removed the cork, guzzling down the red substance quickly.

We waited for what seemed like forever, but nothing happened.

"Why isn't it working? Marie assured me that the blood of a virgin and an angel would allow me to inhabit a body and permanently stay on this plane!"

Azazel tilted his head to the side, his arms crossed in front of his broad chest. "Eve, that angel would have to be of pure blood, correct?"

"Yes."

He stood I front of her, smugness lacing his countenance. "Ah, that's where you went wrong. You see, my dear nephew over there is, shall we say…tainted. While he *was* mostly of pure blood, he recently underwent a…transformation of sorts, all thanks to me. Personally, I think he's better for it."

Eve's glowing red eyes reflected her anger. "You knew this and neglected to tell me? Why? Why would you betray me?"

"Why, indeed. Did you really think you could threaten the life of my son," Azazel began, pointing at Dafari, "and I wouldn't seek retaliation? Come on now, Eve. I learn from the best."

Could that be the reason why Azazel was collaborating with Eve; because she was threatening Dafari? While I still didn't trust him as far as I could throw him, it actually made sense. The one person Azazel would overturn Earth, Hell, and probably Heaven for is Dafari.

"I *need* to remain in this world! My plan cannot succeed otherwise. Azazel, I will give you anything you want. Just get me more blood from the virgin and the only pure blood angel here, Michael."

"I don't think so," he retorted. "I've been topside long enough to realize that there's nothing you can give me that I can't acquire on my own, so thank you, but no thank you. And with your tether gone, you don't have long for this plane."

Eve swiped at Azazel in anger, but it was as if she swatted air, her hand going right through him.

"And there it is; your descent back to Hell begins."

"What happened to family loyalty? What about your loyalty to me?"

He laughed heartily. "You know our family isn't big on that concept, save for those two, perhaps." He nodded in Octavian and Dafari's direction.

Eve's massive form continued to fade, becoming translucent with each passing second. "You will pay for this. Mark my words, Azazel, you will pay, my wayward…"

Finally, she disappeared into the ether.

EPILOGUE
ELISA

T HE MOMENTS AFTER battle were surreal. As I glanced around the clearing, I looked at all the injuries we had suffered and felt hot tears sting my cheeks. Chaos was all around me. For the first time in a long while, I wondered if being a witch was worth all this? Was trying to hold on to these powers worth the utter destruction that was coming for Salix Pointe?

Looking at Tasmin as she fussed over Octavian, who looked like he was on his last leg, I contemplated the idea of leaving. Perhaps if I and Tasmin ran away, the other side would be so busy trying to track us down, they'd forget about this sleepy little town. I looked in Jewel's direction, expecting to see Silas, but he had moved over to check on Tamsin.

We can't run away, Elisa, flittered through my mind as Tasmin raised tear-ladened eyes to mine. Had I accidently sent her the message meant to stay inside my black box?

No, love. Your mind is wide open. You're battle weary and because of that, your internal defenses are down, Dafari said telepathically, then aloud, "It's best we get out of here to warded ground."

With the help of Michael and the veil, we were able to get everyone back to Dafari's place. We decided against the shadows for obvious reasons. Once at Dafari's, Tasmin and I went to work, trying to get a triage set up. I couldn't help but think we could have used Jewel's expertise now as well, but she was still unconscious and badly injured.

Martha was put on the sofa so Tasmin could better keep an eye on her breathing. It would have been easy for Tasmin to just heal everyone, but with her being battle weary, it wouldn't have been wise to put that kind of pressure on her. Still, she did what she could.

Dafari, Octavian, Michael, and Azazel had all disappeared to the kitchen. Michael had asked to speak to the three of them privately. I was tempted to try to eavesdrop on whatever they were talking about but knew better. Still, I was curious.

"I'm worried about Martha's breathing," Tasmin told me after checking the old witch's vitals again and listening to her lungs with her stethascope.

Martha did look worse for wear. Her face and neck were littered with scratches and abrasions. Her skin was sallow, lips swollen, and so was one of her eyes. While the elder woman had been valiant in battle, she was still but a mortal. Martha's breathing was labored, and she looked to be in pain anytime she inhaled and exhaled.

"Luckily, she doesn't have a pneumothorax, or else she'd need a chest tube, and we don't have those medical supplies here," Tasmin said.

Cara Lee and Mary Ann didn't look as if they had fared much better, but they hadn't been outright attacked by Eve either. It was safe to assume that because Martha had come into direct contact with the archdemon, it was why her injuries were so severe. The two sisters were on cots right next to the couch as they refused to leave Martha's side.

"I can't stay," Michael said, once he walked from the kitchen. I wasn't sure what the look in his eyes meant, but it was alarming. "I have to get back. My limited time here is up."

And before we could inquire any further, a tunnel of white wind whipped him right out of Dafari's front room.

"Wonder what that was about," I said to Tasmin who shrugged.

"No idea. Something's up though. Did he look panicked or...in a hurry to you?"

"He did. I'll see if Dafari will tell me what that was about."

"Hello," a sweet sing song voice startled me.

I whipped my head around to see Nazila standing there. In the midst of all the chaos, I'd forgotten she and her mother were still in the house.

"Hi, sweetheart," I said.

"Hello, Nazila," came Tasmin's soft greeting to the child.

Nazila innocently asked, "Were you two in a fight? You're so dirty...and what happened to the crones?"

I stood and walked over to block the child's view of all the destruction of bodies in the front room.

"We did have a bit of a fight," I said, urging her back around the corner.

She blinked rapidly as she studied me. "You guys okay?"

"We're...here. How are you? Is your mother still doing well?" I asked the child.

She shook her head. "No, but a fairy man was here. He brought us food and said he would watch the house just in case...um...something...um...happens!"

My senses went on high alert. I yelled for Tasmin, Octavian, and Dafari.

I took both the child's warm hands in mine. "Can you describe the man?"

"What man?" I heard on a low growl from Dafari.

"I don't know. That's what I'm trying to find out. That's why I called all of you in here," I answered quickly.

"Um…he said…wait…" Nazila dug in her pockets and pulled out a handful of what looked to be tiny ashen-black stars. "He gave me this. He said if I ever need him to just throw one of these in water and he will come to help me!"

My heart was beating so hard against my ribcage that I was threatening to tip right over. *A man had been here? What man? How had he gotten in?* We'd warded the land and the house. I looked up at Tasmin with terrified eyes. Her gaze projected the same horror. We'd left this baby and her mama here alone, while fighting for our lives and the town, and they had been exposed to a predator.

After I took the tiny black stars from Nazila, Tasmin knelt beside me then took the child's hand in hers. "Hey, Nazila, did the man hurt you in any way? Did he touch you at all?"

"He didn't hurt me. He helped Mommy. She was coughing and there was blood and the man sprinkled gold dust over Mommy and the blood went away and Mommy stopped coughing and she was okay."

"I thought Tasmin had healed her," came Octavian's sluggish voice.

Dafari said, "I think Eve's energy has the power to have some old and new wounds or ailments reoccur. It's the chaos she brings and the trail she leaves behind. She is an original archdemon."

"We'll go check on her mother. You two keep Nazila down here," Octavian said before he and Dafari took off upstairs.

"Those are crinoid fossils," we heard from behind us as soon as they were out of sight.

Tasmin and I whipped around, having completely forgotten Demon Daddy was still here. Both of us stood then moved the child further away from him. He saw this and smirked.

"What are crinoid fossils?" Tasmin asked coolly before she glanced at me, both of us completely aware that his eyes still glowed red.

He stood feet shoulder width apart, arms behind his back and he moved from the corner of the room to where more of the light shone. He had been in battle with us, but he didn't look any worse for wear. In fact, it seemed that his energy was supercharged. The hairs stood up on the back of my neck.

"The stars the child has…they can be found in…the strangest of places but mostly in rivers in certain parts of the UK where stolen people crossed. When Africans were taken, some of the slavers had no idea of the magickal beings they'd kidnapped, but the other Africans who had betrayed their fellow man knew. Those Africans helped slavers subdue the captive's powers. Those little fossils are fairy coins."

"There are fairies in Salix Pointe?" I asked, completely taken aback.

He smiled, a hint of fang flashing. Dizziness overtook my senses. "There are myriad of beings here in Salix Pointe, my beautiful daughter-in-law."

"Don't call me that," I snapped.

He grinned wider, fangs fully visible. Nazila screamed and almost clawed her way up Tasmin's body.

"You're scaring the child, demon. Put your fangs away," Tasmin snapped as she grabbed up Nazila and held her to her chest.

Azazel's smile faltered. "That will be the last time you or one of your parents refer to me as demon, *witch*," he said coolly.

His voice had dipped to a dangerous octave. The air got cooler, and it was charged with tension.

"We like to call a thing, a thing," I spat.

Azazel grunted low in his throat as he slowly approached me. "*Witch*, don't kill my vibe," he crooned.

Time seemed to stop as the world tilted. His eyes glowed a deep crimson as his hands dropped by his side. Glowing orbs appeared in his palms. My head spun. Something was wrong. Tasmin gripped my arm. Thunderous sounds of running rumbled upstairs. Nazila screamed louder and held on to Tasmin as if her life depended on it.

And Tasmin…she was trying to communicate something telepathically, but my mind was hazy. I couldn't hear or think. Azazel sent the orbs in our direction. Blackness overtook me.

I AWAKENED SOME time later. At least I thought it had been some time. When I opened my eyes to find Dafari kneeling in front of me, it took me a minute to realize where I was.

"What did you do to them, Uncle, and don't you dare fix your mouth to lie," I heard an angry Octavian blurt out.

"Elisa, talk to me. What happened? Are you well?"

"I…don't know. Tasmin and I were talking to Nazila and we were so exhausted, we decided to sit down. Next thing I know, you were waking me up." My brows furrowed.

"What happened before you two sat down?" Octavian asked, eyes still on Azazel.

I glanced at Tasmin who looked around confused for a moment. I turned my attention back to Dafari. "Could some of Eve's energy from her attack still—"

"Elisa, not to sound like a complete horse's arse, but answer my question, Sissy. What happened before you two sat down?"

"Azazel was telling us about the little stars Nazila had. I think…I think we sat down to just…rest."

"I don't know, Elisa," Tasmin cut in, her voice heavy with exhaustion. "I heard screaming."

"Screaming?" Dafari repeated.

"Don't look at me," Azazel said, hands up in surrender as he backed away from his nephew. "I was telling your witches about the little coins the child has. One minute they were listening intently, the next they were asleep."

I grabbed ahold of Dafari's arms and allowed him to help me stand. "His eyes were red—"

"Yes. Leftover adrenaline from the battle and being so close to Eve, archdemon she is and all," Azazel cut in.

Dafari moved to stand face-to-face with his father. His voice was low and came out on a dangerous growl. "Everyone in this room knows you never have the most salubrious of intentions even when you help us. I don't know what you're up to, old demon, but I can promise you, if you hurt one single follicle on Elisa or Tasmin's head, I will call on every celestial and ancient evil to cause you the worst damage. Damage that there will be no coming back from."

Octavian then closed the ranks on his uncle. "And you'd better believe I will not only back his every move, I will personally see to it that the One Son himself makes it so you will never know the light of day again."

"Until the other side needs another scapegoat, right?" Azazel snarled coolly.

The energy in the room intensified. Tasmin cradled Nazila to her chest while I struggled to help her stand. I felt as if I were moving in slow motion. My mind told me to stand but my body wanted to rest.

Azazel chuckled then stepped so close to his son and nephew, it looked as if he was about to headbutt them. "I'm completely over you and my son threatening me. Perhaps it would suit the two of you to remember just who in Hell you're talking to. I am not one of those measly demons you can scare with idle words. I have the power to put the literal fear of God in you and it will reverberate through the next generation of your bloodlines. I suggest you two try Jesus. Try anything but stop…trying…me!"

As soon as the word 'me' left his mouth, Octavian and Dafari flew backwards out of the bay window in Dafari's kitchen. And then, Azazel was gone.

THE NEXT FEW days were some of the most painful. Healing after a battle with an archdemon was far more debilitating than when we'd fought Dafari and Octavian's parents. While Martha and her sisters had gone home three days after the battle, Martha was still severely injured. Jewel was awake but bed ridden. She'd taken a severe beaten and had lived to tell about it. Silas had taken her back to Aunt Noreen's, against Tasmin's wishes, but he insisted he could do a better job of keeping an eye on her there.

Nazila and her mother also went home soon after the Widows. While her mother had seen, with her own eyes, demons attacking her and her daughter, she still had a hard time believing it all. She thanked us for taking care of Nazila and then beat a hasty retreat from Dafari's home. The absolute look of fear in her eyes told us it would be a long time before she forgot what had happened.

We hadn't seen much of Octavian. Tasmin had gone back to Aunt Noreen's so she could be closer to her mother. I didn't know if she was still upset with her parents, but I could safely assume it didn't matter much at the moment. Her mother needed her. I was curious as to how she and Octavian were faring. I wasn't the least bit surprised when he packed a bag and headed out the door behind Tasmin. He had made it clear that he would no longer go a day without her in his arms or his bed—in this case, her bed at Aunt Noreen's. There was something different about my brother-in-law. I could tell that before Azazel had blasted him and Dafari out the kitchen window. We hadn't heard a peep from Azazel since that incident.

Octavian was convinced his uncle had done something to us. Neither we nor Nazila were able to confirm that.

"You should be in bed," came a low rumble from a dark shadow in the room.

"So should you," I retorted as I stood.

"I'm a supernatural being. I heal far faster than you."

"Yes, under normal circumstances. It's been seven days since the battle and only some of your wounds have fully healed."

I glanced at the full moon just outside his bedroom window. It was odd to see it sit so big while a storm raged. I trekked closer to the window to stand just underneath the moonlight as rain beat down on the house. I tensed when I felt him come to stand behind me. The hairs on the back of my neck rose. Only because, instinctively, I knew he was in demon form. He had been fluxing since the battle. One minute he would be in human form and the next he would be his demon self. The first three nights after the battle, he had refused to even sleep in the same bed as me. He left the house to sleep elsewhere so his incubus wouldn't ravish me.

We hadn't been intimate since then either. Between trying to heal and weathering a literal storm, there hadn't been time. Rufus was still running the coffee shop and the bookstore but the whole town had been shut down for days now. Hurricane-like weather during this time of the year was unheard of.

"Hurricane-like winds, flooding in some areas…" I sighed. "I guess it helps us in a sense. It covers up the damage the fight with Eve left behind."

As he moved my hair to the side, my head tilted of its own accord. My body was fluent in the language his incubus spoke. When he nuzzled my neck, chills shot up my spine. He wanted to bite me but was hesitant. One of his arms snaked around my waist. The other traveled up my stomach, over my breasts and then on to my neck.

"We've gone through so much in just a short period of time. Coming into our powers while finding out we have bounties on our heads because of said powers…and that's on top of getting all our memories from our past lives back. My head is still spinning and I can't wrap my mind around it all. I also thought it was impossible for there to be a full moon two nights in a row," I said.

The sexual energy wafting off of him was palpable. "It is impossible, but this is Salix Pointe." He placed both hands on my waist as he nuzzled my neck.

"Strange things are always abound in this place, and now we know why. Your father said there are fairies here and all sorts of other creatures afoot. How did we not know this before?" I shivered then leaned into his hold when he placed a gentle kiss against the most sensitive part of my neck. Every pressure point and erogenous zone I owned ignited in a fiery blaze.

"Who is *we*?" he asked with a tone that told me I was the only one late to the party.

"You knew?"

"I'm half angel and half demon, Elisa. Of course I knew."

I tugged at some of his hair which had fallen over my shoulder to hang over my left breast. The sheer, thin robe I had on did very little to hide my womanly goodies. I also knew by the intense heat emanating from his body that he was stark naked. I was beyond hot and bothered.

Still, I couldn't get over the fact that there were other-worldly beings in Salix Pointe.

"Were you not going to tell me?" I asked.

"No. I figure after your memories and powers were back in full force, you'd pick up on it on your own."

"What did Michael tell you guys in the kitchen?" I then inquired, abruptly changing the subject.

Dafari stiffened and pull away from his physical seduction at the moment. "That is something I cannot discuss."

I turned to face him head on. "Can't or won't?"

His red eyes glowed in the dark as he studied me. I took the time to run my gaze up and down the specimen that he was. His demon form had only scared me when I didn't know who I was. Now that I did remember, I couldn't be afraid if I wanted to. Every muscle in his body had been sculpted and defined by *thee* God herself.

I ran my hands up his chest and over his shoulders then down his back and up again. There was no shame in my game as I grabbed ahold of him, in all his blessed, thick, and hardened glory, and stroked slowly. His breathing deepened and intensified. Hair grew longer as he bulked, but not for battle. He needed a sexual healing…

I thought back to a time, many lifetimes ago, when he had taught me things, had shown me sides of sexual intimacy, that no self-respecting woman of that time period would even admit to. While other wives complained about bedtime and their men doing nothing to ensure their pleasure—more than half didn't even think a woman was supposed to enjoy sex— I could not relate.

"Won't," he finally answered then smirked.

His fangs were elongated to pleasure-bite proportions. He wanted to bite, feed, fuck, and possibly fight. His grin widened, fangs dropped further. He was reading my mind, sly devil he was. Because I was so enamored and in love with him, in incubus form, he could sometimes break down the blocks I'd put in my mind without even trying.

"Just like the old days," I whispered. "You have my permission…"

He snatched me to him. Used his chin to knock my head to the side then sank his teeth so far into my neck, a scream ripped from my throat right as a violent orgasm rocked me. I knew what he needed and was willing to give it to him. He was half incubus, and a sexual healing took on a literal meaning for him.

There were things coming for us, and yes, Salix Pointe was very much in trouble. There were so many unanswered questions and things Tasmin and I still had no closure to. However, all of it would still be there tomorrow. I needed time to heal and time to think. I had my memories and powers back, but something still felt off.

Those things could wait for a few more days. Just as much as Dafari needed me, I needed him. His bite had the power to not only heal me physically, but mentally as well. We'd done it many times in the past when the stressors of the world got to be too much.

I had no idea what was in store for us next, but I hoped that whatever was coming—whoever was coming— understood they could come in peace or leave in pieces.

DAFARI

ELISA WAS GONE before I woke up. While I was aware that she had intended to leave earlier than usual, I was more than a bit surprised that she had not aroused me before she departed, especially since we had gotten back to our routine. Although the pressing issues of Salix Pointe troubled us greatly, Elisa and I still took some time out of our busy schedules to rediscover our love for each other. As in the past, so sure were we of our union, we decided to obtain a marriage license. While neither of us ventured away from Salix Pointe often, in this case, we had no choice.

In order to procure that piece of paper, we found it necessary to visit the Glynn County Probate Court located in Brunswick, Georgia, a town very similar to Salix Pointe in appearance. We both took the morning off, traveling via the Saint Simons Sound Car Ferry from Salix Pointe to Jekyll Island. From there we took the short drive to the probate court, obtaining the license within several minutes. Elisa even had time to peruse several shops before heading back. We were in Salix Pointe before the afternoon rush. While we had the license, and lived as if we were married in every sense of the word, I, for one, could not wait until we took our vows and made it official.

Despite it being Christmas Eve, Elisa had to work. I, on the other hand, decided to take the day off in order to prepare my home for one of my wife's favorite holidays. In Christmases past, even during their enslavement, Elisa and Tasmin, were up all night cooking an enormous feast, while Octavian and I had the inestimable task of decorating. This year, we would have adorned the place with the traditional Christmas fare earlier; however, recent events prevented us from being in any kind of festive mood. Tasmin and Elisa had still planned on a family affair, inviting Jewel and Silas, Rufus, even the Widows, their recent forced alliance, and subsequent teamwork in battle, causing them to release the animosity they harbored toward their fellow coven members.

Although daylight had yet to appear, I had a long day ahead of me and a multitude of errands to run, but first, I needed to see my beloved Elisa. Despite the events of the previous weeks, Salix Pointe's residents didn't let all the death and destruction stop them from enjoying the season. As I drove along Main Street, I took note of the trees decorated with Christmas lights. Storefronts boasted large wreaths on doors, while windows displayed various combinations of garland, flashing lights, and snow spray. A poinsettia, which symbolized good cheer and success, was placed outside each shop. Right now, Salix Pointe needed all the goodness it could acquire, and more, in spades. I paused for a moment as I drove past Doc Benu's clinic, a substantial makeshift memorial placed in front of the building. The good doctor was beloved by many, and while Salix Pointe's residents believed he was deceased, we knew otherwise.

I pulled in front of the still-dark café, figuring that Elisa was in the rear of the shop.

"You left without saying goodbye," I said after locating her, stepping out of a shadow in the large pantry.

She gasped, almost dropping a jar of cinnamon sticks she was holding. Turning to face me, mild annoyance laced her beautiful features. "Dafari Battle, you just about scared the life out of me," she chastised. "Why couldn't you use your key or knock on the door like a normal person?"

I tilted my head to the side. "And spoil surprising you? What fun would that be? Besides, I am *far* from normal."

"What are you doing here so early? You usually get here as soon as I open."

"You left our bed without so much as a word. Did I do something wrong?"

She looked at me, a smirk crossing her luscious lips. "Not at all. You were sleeping so peacefully, and I didn't want to disturb you."

"While I appreciate your concern for my well-being, my love, you should have awakened me. I've once again grown accustomed to waking up with you beside me, your head on my chest, and my hand on your..." I stopped speaking, closed the gap between us, placing a hand on her full, round derriere.

"Dafari, stop it," she said with a giggle, yet not removing my hand, the strong scent of honeysuckle wafting from her. "You know how busy the Christmas Eve rush is, and I'm going to be swamped today. Tasmin will be here in a while to help, but I need to get started now. I still have coffee to brew, pastries to make, and orders to pack. Although he more than deserves it, I wish I hadn't given Rufus the day off. His help has been invaluable."

"I'm aware. That little man has surprised all of us, in more ways than one. Octavian and I had long suspected there was something...special about him. Thanks to Nazila's description, we now know that he was the fairy man who helped save her mother and guarded them from harm while we were battling Eve. I gather he has yet to make mention of anything."

"No, he hasn't, and neither will I unless I have to. I'm just grateful he's on our side."

"As am I. Do you know what I'm even more grateful for?" I backed her up against a wall.

She bit her bottom lip, taking a deep breath before speaking. "What's that?"

"You. Having my wife back means the world to me." I lowered my head, brushing my lips to hers. "I heard what you told Eve when she had...possessed me. You said, 'Get out of

my husband'. I can't wait for you to officially be my wife…
again." I kissed her forehead, her cheeks, finally settling on her
neck. I felt her pulse racing, her body reacting to my touch.

"And I can't wait for you to be my husband…again," she
replied on a breathy whisper. "All I know is I refused to lose
you to anyone or anything, especially to the likes of Eve,
archdemon or not. Thing is I still I don't know how I was
able to reach you when she had an incredible hold on you, I
just hoped I could."

"Let me fill in that blank for you. After you invaded my
mind the first time and I summarily ousted you, I made a
vow to myself that I would never completely shut you out
again. I left a small window open for you. That's why you
were able break Eve's hold over me."

"I'm glad you did."

"Elisa, it was your love that saved me, you do realize that
don't you?"

"No, that was Tasmin," she countered.

"I beg to differ. Tasmin couldn't have healed my body
had you not *freed* my mind, my soul, my heart."

"Well, when you put it that way," she began, her arms
wrapping around my neck, "I'd do it again in a heartbeat."
She then pulled me into a passionate kiss.

Once we broke our embrace, I replied, "I would do the
same for you, without question."

"I wonder if you'd do something else for me." Her puppy
dog eyes told me that Elisa was about to work me. Like
Tasmin, she had her own methods of getting her way.

"What do you need, my sweet?"

She gently pushed me away, a playful smirk on her face.
"Since you've distracted me and I'm now behind schedule,
would you be a dear and help me set up?"

I knew better than to refuse her.

ELISA HAD FINISHED baking a fresh batch of pastries, with another on the way, had started brewing coffee, and had begun to box up orders of cakes, pies, cookies, and other assorted delicacies to be picked up by customers. I busied myself taking chairs off tables, setting out napkin dispensers, coffee stirrers, and various sweeteners. Once those tasks were done, I placed a small poinsettia on each table. Finally, I turned on the Christmas tree and lights. I breathed in deeply, the scents of apple, cinnamon, chocolate, and peppermint permeating the air as Elisa started preparing seasonal beverages.

"Dafari, can you unlock the door then help me with these orders?"

I turned the sign in the window to 'Open', unlocked the front door, then I joined Elisa behind the counter. She handed me an apron and a pair of disposable food prep gloves. I noticed she had set my white chocolate mocha, almond filled croissant, and chocolate chip cookies to the side. My woman always took care of me.

"Thank you," I said then kissed her on the cheek before she headed to the back.

On a normal day, I would have been Elisa's first customer. It had gotten to the point that everyone in town was aware of, and respected, that fact. Everyone save Adour-Nuru Citlali Daystar, one of Salix Pointe's legal eagles and law partner of Portia Achebe. He had become a proverbial thorn in my side since the mayor's Halloween-themed jubilee. The way he was leering at Elisa that night confirmed my suspicions that he was trouble. I also sensed a very potent...otherworldly aura, more powerful than my own, surrounding him. It unnerved me. To my chagrin, this morning he was the first customer to darken the café's doorstep. He seemed more than a little nonplus to see me, despite my very distinctive Mercedes Benz S-class sedan parked out front.

"Doctor Battle," he started after an awkward pause. "I saw your car but assumed you were at your office."

I could have been wrong, but I detected a sense of disappointment, most likely because Elisa was not the one behind the counter.

"One should never assume," I remarked.

Daystar gave me a once-over. "That's a new look for you." The smirk on his face irked the shit out of me. I'm sure that was his intent.

I stared at him hard for a few seconds before replying. "When *my* lady requests my assistance, I will not refuse her, despite the unflattering attire." I gave him the same self-satisfied smirk he gave me.

"Adour-Nuru, good morning," I heard Elisa say from behind me.

I turned around to see she had a fresh pan of apple tarts in her hands. She set the pan down on the counter then began carefully picking each one up with tongs, placing them inside the pastry counter.

"Elisa. How are you this morning?"

"I'm doing well. Busy, but that's to be expected considering. What can I get for you?"

He looked at the menu thoughtfully before answering. "I'm ordering for myself and Portia. She'll have a large hot caramel apple cider with whipped cream, caramel drizzle, and a cinnamon stick, and a white chocolate Christmas cookie with rainbow sprinkles. For myself, I'll have a cranberry scone and a large peppermint hot chocolate with whipped cream, chocolate drizzle, and a candy cane. You know how I like it."

I bristled at the way he said that.

"Dafari…" Elisa knew me too well. "Coming right up," she said to Daystar.

He watched Elisa attentively as she prepared his order. I didn't like it, nor did I appreciate the disrespect, especially in my presence. Elisa picked up on my thoughts. Damn me for keeping a window to my mind open to her.

"Dafari, stop it. You don't see me getting all bent out of shape when others look at you like they want to jump your bones. Besides, I only have eyes for you." There was mirth in the tone of her mental message.

"Yes, but it's not you I'm worried about. It's clear that Adour-Nuru had designs on you, despite us being together."

"Designs?" I heard her giggles inside my head. *"Now you sound like Octavian."*

"Well, I am my brother's brother, after all. Just promise me that you won't put yourself in any situation where you would be alone with him."

"Seriously?"

"Deadly serious." I knew I sounded like a jealous significant other, and, I admit, I was, but the ne'er-do-well vibes coming from Daystar gave me more than enough reason for concern. *"Please, do this for me."*

She gave me a side-long glance when Daystar wasn't looking. *"Fine. If you're being so adamant about it, you must have a good reason."*

After finishing his order, Elisa packaged Daystar's items then walked over to the cash register. Once she had rung up everything, and he paid, she said, "Happy holidays, Adour-Nuru."

"Same to you, Elisa." He paused before saying, "And you as well, Doctor Battle."

"Likewise, Attorney Daystar," was all I could muster.

Once he left, I could tell Elisa was about to question me regarding my reaction to the flirtatious barrister. As luck would have it, Tasmin walked through the door.

"Sister," I started, not giving her a chance to speak. "So wonderful to see you this morning." I quickly took off my gloves and apron, dropping the gloves in the trash and the apron on the counter. Grabbing Elisa by her waist, I pulled her into a heartfelt, impassioned kiss. "I'll be off, my sweet. The house will be ready for you tonight. Don't be late."

Both women remained silent as I bolted for the door. On the way to my car, I heard a pair of familiar voices.

"Mommy, I like that doll," I heard Nazila say.

"Baby, you know we can't afford it."

Nazila and her mother Tinashe were standing in front of Salix Pointe Toys and Curios. When I walked up to them, I saw the doll Nazila was referring to; a beautiful three-feet tall doll with a mocha complexion, short curly hair, big brown eyes, full lips, and a Kente cloth outfit. It was housed in a glass doll case with a large red bow. The shop was high end, so I knew it was expensive.

"Good morning, ladies."

While her mother appeared a bit apprehensive, which was understandable considering all she and her daughter had endured recently, Nazila held no such fear, as she ran up to me, motioning for me to bend down to her level. The small child hugged me tightly.

"Hi, Doctor Battle." Her exuberance was infectious.

"Good morning, Doctor Battle. Doing some last-minute shopping?" her mother asked.

"Among other things."

She relaxed a bit, becoming more talkative. "I'm headed to the café. I wanted to thank Elisa and Tasmin personally for the decorated tree and the gifts for me and Nazila. I really appreciate it."

"They enjoyed doing that for you two, believe me."

I watched as Nazila placed her hands on the toy shop's window, gazing longingly at the doll. Her enthusiasm reminded me of Zafer, Safiya, and Attalah around the holidays.

"I have to pick up something inside," I said to Tinashe. "Before you go to the café, do you mind waiting for me?"

At first, she had a confused look on her face, but quickly softened. "Not at all," she said, a warm smile appearing. "It is a bit cold, so we'll be sitting in my car."

I nodded in acknowledgement, then walked inside the store. It took no more than a few minutes for me to pick up what I needed. Tinashe climbed out of her car when she saw me.

"This is for Nazila," I said, handing her a large gift bag.

When she looked inside, tears immediately filled her eyes. "Thank you so much, Doctor Battle."

"No thanks are necessary. And it's Dafari. You two had quite an ordeal, and no child should have to experience what she did. I hope she enjoys it. Happy holidays to you both."

"Same to you, Doctor...Dafari." Tinashe placed the doll in the trunk of her car before fetching Nazila from the front seat and taking her to Elisa's shop.

The streets were filling up as the natives of Salix Pointe had begun to mill about, heading to eateries and doing last-minute shopping. The mad rush was on for the townsfolk, and me, as well. My next stop was to see Rufus. I had come to realize that while he was a jack of many trades, he was also a master of them all. I just couldn't figure out why I never picked up on his magick earlier like I did with the other locals. That was a mystery for another time.

When I eventually reached Rufus' home, which was on the outskirts of town, he was sitting in a rocking chair on his front porch, despite the biting cold, with another long-time citizen, David Hershel, whose family had been around for as long as the Ossoff's. Not only was he owner of one of the town's oldest construction companies, he also owned and ran the local theatre and was quite the thespian in his own right. When I got out of my car and walked up to the cozy, southern cottage-style home, I heard the raucous laughter of the two men conscientiously studying a chess board laid out on a table between them. Along with the chess board sat a large Thermos and two mugs with a steaming liquid. I assumed it was coffee, being that Rufus was an aficionado.

Next to Herschel's mug sat a bottle of his favorite libation, Devil's Benevolence bourbon. Despite the early morning hour, Herschel felt it was never too early to partake in spirits. "It's five in the afternoon somewhere!" I would frequently hear him say. He wasn't wrong.

"Good morning, Rufus, Mr. Herschel," I said, diverting their attention from their game.

"Well, good morning to ya, Dayfari," Rufus cheerfully exclaimed.

"How many times have I told you to call me David, son? I get you young'uns bein' respectful and all, but let's shuck the formality, okay?" said the man who reminded me of a thinner, louder Santa Claus. It amused me that he called me son, thinking I was younger than him. If only he knew.

I nodded. "David it is, but only if you call me Dafari."

"Deal," he concurred.

"I ain't never seen you in these parts," Rufus said. "Somethin' wrong?"

"No, no," I said speaking with my hands as I stepped onto the porch. "As a matter of fact, everything is going well." I took a deep breath before continuing. "The thing is, Rufus, I truly hate to bother you on your day off, and Christmas Eve at that, but I have desperate need of your many services. Since you're here, David, yours as well. Things have been extremely… busy for all of us lately, and I have not had time to prepare my home to Elisa's liking for the holidays. I'm planning something special for her tonight, but with all the errands I have to run, I don't have time to get a tree, decorate—"

"Somethin' special, huh?" Rufus winked at me. I wasn't sure how much he knew, but my gut told me that he was aware of all I had planned. If that was indeed the case, the little man's insight was actually becoming scary. Regardless, I laid out detailed instructions for the two men.

"Say no more! Me and ole David here gotcha covered. Decoratin' is one of my speshialities," he said, overemphasizing the word 'specialties'. "We'll get yo' place in tip-top shape before Elise gets off work."

"And I'll grab the missus on the way so she can bring some flowers and plants." David was referring to his wife, Opal, who owned the local flower shop.

"Splendid. Thank you, gentlemen. I can pay you now, if you'd like." I removed my wallet from the inside pocket of my full-length wool coat.

"No worries, Dayfari. We can settle up once the job is done, 'kay?"

"As you wish, Rufus. Here is my spare house key," I said, handing it to the wizened little man. Neither he nor the Herschels would have a problem entering my home, as the wards only affected evil entities. Knowing that Rufus was himself a magickal being and had been friends with the Herschels for many years, he, of all people, would have known if they were harbingers of ill will. "You have no idea how much I appreciate you both."

"Oh, I think we do," he replied, chuckling loudly. "We'll get right on it."

Rufus began packing up the chess set, while David grabbed the Thermos, mugs, and bourbon, carrying them into the house.

Rufus looked at me saying, "Why you still standin' here, Dayfari? I thought you said you had errands to run. Skeedaddle!"

"Yes sir," I said, walking down the steps, a slight grin on my face. He amused me so.

"WHERE HAVE YOU been, Dafari?" Octavian questioned as he stood in front of Taylor's Tailor Shop & Haberdashery, a perturbed look on his face. "You were supposed to be here thirty minutes ago. Good thing for you I was able to push the appointment back. You're welcome."

"My humblest of apologies, little brother," I responded, feigning remorse. "I encountered several minor interruptions which, in turn, caused me run behind. Best laid plans and all."

"Well, your plans may never come to fruition if we don't get this done now." He opened the door to the shop, ushering me in.

"Ah, Doctor Battle, good morning and happy holidays to you," said the shop owner, Isiah Taylor, a seventh-generation tailor, and member of one of Salix Pointe's founding families.

The tall, lanky man with milk chocolate-hued skin, blue-gray eyes, bald head, moustache and goatee had left the island for several years in order to study at The Fashion Institute of Technology in New York City. His efforts earned him two Bachelor of Fine Arts degrees; one in Fashion Design, the other in Advertising and Digital Design. A seasoned world traveler who sought to bring the family business into the digital age, Isiah created the family's website, which garnered a client base from all over the United States, and even some international ones, based on his reputation as a fashion innovator. My own father, who prided himself on his impeccable sense of style, had patronized the shop on several occasions since arriving in town. I was very fortunate that Isiah was still able to see me, despite my lateness.

"Good morning, Isiah. Please excuse my tardiness. As you know, this is very unlike me."

"No need to apologize, as unforeseen events can happen. Your suits are ready, but I wanted you both to try them on just to make sure the final alterations are correct. Afterwards, I'll steam them for you, and you can be on your way."

"Thank you," I replied.

Isiah set Octavian and me up in fitting rooms. We quickly changed, then stepped out in order for him to view the finished products. My custom-made suit was made of the softest wool, and consisted of a black single-breasted tuxedo jacket with silk satin peak lapels; single button, two flapless welt pockets; and a linen and silk pocket square. The straight-cut trousers boasted no turned-up hems and a thin black silk band along the external seams from waistband to hem. The look was completed with a white silk, collarless, hidden-button dress shirt.

Octavian's suit, on the other hand, was of the finest cashmere. The dark gray tapered trousers complemented the single-breasted, two-button suit jacket, also with a linen and silk pocket square. A black silk dress shirt and black background tie with a white polka dot design and lattice structure finished off his attire. Even I had to admit that my little brother looked quite nice. We were both more than pleased.

After Octavian and I had changed and had given our suits back to him, I said, "Isiah, you've outdone yourself. As many suits as I've purchased from you, I think this is the best one yet."

"I thank you for the high praise," he replied as he was placing our freshly-steamed suits in garment bags. "I couldn't very well disappointment one of my best customers. While I get business from all over, it's my local clientele I cherish the most, so thank *you*, Doctor Battle, and happy holidays."

"Happy holidays to you, Isiah."

I paid the man, including a hefty tip, then Octavian and I made our way back home. Much to my displeasure, the first thing I saw when I drove up was Father standing outside my front door. I parked in the garage, walking back to the front of the house.

"What are you doing here?" I queried.

"Hello, Son. Hello, nephew. Can't a father visit his son, especially on such a special day?"

Octavian and I looked at each other. "Can you go inside and check on the progress? I need to have a brief discussion with my father."

He nodded, waking up to the front door. "Happy holidays, Uncle. I would say behave yourself, but I am wholly aware that would be too much to expect of you."

"How thou dost woundeth me, oh nephew of mine," he replied, putting the back of one hand against his forehead, feigning hurt. Then he grinned at him. "I'm going to behave as much as my company will allow me, but you know the kind of company I keep."

Octavian sighed, shaking his head and walking into the house.

"Still banned, I see," Father spoke.

"With good reason. You did something, although I'm still unsure what, to Elisa and Tasmin, *and*, to add insult to injury, you flung Octavian and me out a window. If that doesn't warrant banishment, I don't know what does."

"So, I guess that means I'm not invited to your and my daughter-in-law's never-ending nuptials? How many times does this make?"

"How did you…? Never mind. The answer is no."

"What a shame," my father said, walking slowly back and forth. "I would have loved to have walked my soon-to-be-once-again-daughter-in-law down the aisle. I'd be a much better stand-in for the father of the bride than Michael, considering, don't you think? Then again, I'm sure he's also unwelcomed."

Sometimes it baffled my mind at the extent of Father's cruelty. Bringing up the fact that Michael was responsible for Elisa's father death, albeit not directly, was still immensely callous and heartless. I'm glad he said it in my presence and not hers.

"If that's the only reason you showed up, you're not going to get your way, so you can go."

"There is talk that Eve has not returned back to Hell, and this chatter comes from very reliable sources."

"Then where is she?" I asked, trying not to sound panicked. Eve possessed and almost killed me. Jewel and Martha also suffered greatly at her hands. Our group barely survived her assault. The likes of Eve could *not* be allowed to wander this plane unfettered.

"No one knows for sure, but I'm on it. She'll be gunning for me, and I need to stay ten steps ahead of her."

This was a rare occasion where father seemed…ruffled. While Eve would most assuredly have it in for all of us, father's betrayal would indeed put him in her crosshairs. While this was the latest unavoidable crisis, it would keep for a day or two. I could not, no would not, ruin the holiday, our first holiday together in decades, for Elisa, and the others, for that matter. I would advise them all after tomorrow.

"I appreciate you stopping by with this information, Father, but I really must be going. Once the holiday is over, the rest of us will also check with our sources."

"While I understand you wanting to…shelter the others during this most wonderful time of the year, I hope it won't be too late. Enjoy your nuptials, my son." He disappeared into a shadow.

When I opened the door to my home, the scent of honeysuckle flowers bombarded me. With its fruity and warm aroma, tinged with hints of honey and ripe citrus, the fragrance was unmistakable. As I walked further inside, I also detected the faint whiff of roses and baby's breath flowers. The sounds of boisterous chuckles were coming from the living room. When I walked in, Octavian, Rufus, and the Herschels were having a good laugh.

"Heyyy, Dayfari," Rufus exuberantly shouted once they noticed me. "We was just yuckin' it up with Octovian here."

"Yes, we were sharing with your charming brother the latest gossip surrounding the mayor and his tiresome wife," Opal chimed in.

The relationship between the Herschel and Lovett clans was acrimonious from the start. The feud escalated to epic proportions when the much-loved troupers wrote, directed, and starred in a play spoofing the current mayor and his wife, portraying them in a less-than flattering, yet exceedingly accurate, light. The play was a smashing success with the residents of Salix Pointe, as well as those from the surrounding islands. Ephraim and Ilene, however, were none too happy.

Ephraim made it his mission to destroy David and Opal, even going so far as to attempt to ruin both their businesses. Considering what I know now, I would have been surprised that he was not successful, being that he is a formidable Cajun warlock. However, knowing that the Herschels also have a powerful, magickal friend of their own explained the mayor's epic failure.

"Word has it that the mayor and that pale-faced hussy of his haven't been seen in days. Now we all know those two like to be the center of attention, especially around the holidays," Hershel said, cleaning up stray wood pieces. "If they're gone, good riddance to bad rubbish, and bless their mother—"

"David," his wife said, cutting him off while she swept up stray flower petals, leaves, and branches. "You know I don't like all that cussin'."

"Yes, ma'am. Bless their little non-existence hearts. You both would do well to learn from me. Happy wife, happy life," David said then cackled.

"You're an extremely wise man, sir," Octavian complimented.

I surveilled the room. A large, decorated Virginia Juniper tree sat in front of the bay windows. It brimmed with flashing, multi-colored lights; bows, balls, garland, and tinsel icicle strands in shades of red, green, and gold; and a Black angel adorning the top. Poinsettias were placed strategically around the room, as was the Norway Spruce that surrounded the fireplace and windows. The entire scene was a sight straight out of a Christmas movie.

In the middle of the room sat a tall arch, bedecked with various shades of honeysuckle flowers, baby's breath, and white roses. David did a remarkable job of creating it in such a short amount of time, as did Opal with the floral arrangement.

She walked over to Octavian and me, the bottom half of a box in hand. "Here are the bouquets, boutonnières, and wreath for Elisa's hair," she said, handing me the box.

Elisa's bridal bouquet was a created from the same assorted honeysuckle flowers and baby's breath contained in the arch, while Tasmin's bridesmaid bouquet was made entirely of red roses. A red rose, white rose, and sprigs of baby's breath comprised Octavian and my boutonnières, while the hair wreath was a combination of red and white roses.

At the time, I hadn't noticed that Rufus had left the room. When he returned, he had placed a plate containing a large, round three-tier cake on the coffee table. The sweet aroma of the caramel cake, Elisa's favorite, filled the room. Two extremely life-like figurines that resembled Elisa and me sat atop it. No doubt they were created by magick.

"You three have truly done an amazing job. I am eternally in your debt," I said. "And since I always pay my debts, how much do I owe you?"

Rufus and David looked at each other then laughed. Octavian and I shared befuddled glances, the cause of their laughter unknown to us.

"Did I say something to amuse you all?" I asked.

"We ain't laughin' at cha, Dayfari. We laughin' at the sitchiation."

"And why is this situation so amusing, pray tell?" questioned Octavian, raising an eyebrow.

Opal stepped forward. "Seein' as the menfolk have no couth, I'll speak for the three of us. While we don't know all the particulars of what transpired, what we *do* know is that you and yours had a hand in getting rid of whatever it was that attempted to uproot our town, and for that *we* are eternally grateful. This one is on us, no charge, and happy holidays."

"Happy holidays to you all," Octavian and I said in unison as they all walked toward the door.

Utter shock shrouding our faces. How much did they *really* know?

The sound of Rufus' voice shook both of us out of our bewilderment. "I'ma go get cleaned up and I'll be back in two shakes of a lamb's tail! Y'all best to go get ready ya selves, ya heard?" With that, the magickal man was gone.

Octavian had a way of reading my mind. "I am just as perplexed as you are, Brother, but, for now, figuring out what they know, and how much, will have to wait. Right now, you need to change, because Elisa and Tasmin will be here sooner rather than later."

Octavian was right. Tonight, my only concern was making Elisa the happiest woman on earth.

TASMIN

"GIRL, HE RAN out of there like he got caught with his hand in the cookie jar. I didn't even have a chance to say, 'Hi'." I couldn't help but laugh at Dafari's expense, remembering how he rushed out of the café this morning.

Elisa and I were on our way to Dafari's home after she had followed me to Aunt Noreen's house so I could pick up some clothes and toiletries, and to allow me to drop off my vehicle. I had planned to stay over for Dafari's big surprise, and to help Elisa cook Christmas dinner. Although I could cook, it wasn't one of my favorite things to do. My cousin, on the other hand, lived to be in the kitchen, which was why holidays were always a big to-do for her. I knew we'd be up all night.

"That's because he knew he was going to hear my mouth. When Adour-Nuru was there, Dafari was in my head. You should have heard him, 'It's not you I'm worried about. It's clear that Adour-Nuru had designs on you, despite us being together," she said, her voice lowering a few octaves imitating Dafari.

"Designs? He sounds like Octavian," I said then laughed again.

"That's what I said!" Elisa became quiet for moment before saying, "But then he asked me to never be alone with Adour-Nuru. At first I thought it was just him being jealous, which I'm sure was part of it, but there was more to it; there was a sense of foreboding."

I glanced at her while she was driving, a look of concern on her face. "Cousin, you're probably going to disagree, but I'm with Dafari on this one."

"Et tu, Tasmin?"

"Now hear me out," I started, holding my hands up. "While my bro may be overly protective at times, in this case, I don't think he's wrong. Adour-Nuru gave me a, for lack of a better word, hinky vibe, and now that we have our full powers back, that gut feeling is stronger than ever. Although I can't put my finger on it, there's something about him that you need to stay clear of. I'm just sayin'."

Elisa sighed deeply as she pressed the button on the garage door opener then drove her car into the space. "I've known both of you long enough to actually listen when either of you has one of your 'feelings'," she said, making air quotes. "Besides, I already told Dafari I'd do as he asked."

"Smart move, my dear cousin."

I looked at my watch, noticing how late we were. Elisa and I had been busy all day fulfilling orders. She even took some last-minute orders, which prolonged our day significantly.

I had been texting back and forth with Dafari, with me checking on the progress of the decorating, and him checking to see how much longer we would be at the café. About an hour before Elisa and I had finished cleaning, Dafari texted saying everything was ready. After we had gotten out of the car, Elisa popped the trunk. She had baked a batch of Christmas cookies, several assorted pies, a peach cobbler, and some croissants, for the house. We took the boxes out and walked to the door leading to the mud room. Just as we reached it, the door opened.

"Ladies, you're home." Octavian grabbed a box from me and one from Elisa. "Little sissy, please tell me—"

"Yes, Octavian, your apple pie is in one of those boxes," she said then giggled.

His eyes lit up instantly. While my guy didn't need to eat, being immortal and all, he did *like* to eat. One of the things he liked most was dessert, especially Elisa's apple pie. I knew he couldn't wait to heat up a slice and add a huge scoop of vanilla ice cream on top.

"Thank you, Sissy, from the bottom of my extremely grateful heart," he said, as he placed the boxes on the kitchen island then bowed to her.

After Elisa and I sat our boxes down, I said, "You're such as suck up."

"Ah, my dear poppet," he replied, scooping me up in his arm, "that is one of the many reasons why you love me." He leaned down, brushing his lips to mine.

"Is it?" I loved teasing him.

"But of course," he retorted playfully.

"Hey, where's Dafari?" Elisa asked. "And why do I smell flowers?"

"He's upstairs, but shall return forthwith," Octavian replied. "In response to your other question, follow me."

He grabbed my hand then Elisa's, leading us from the kitchen to the living room. Elisa gasped as we stopped in our tracks.

"Oh, my gosh," she began, excitement in her voice. "This place looks incredible." I watched as her eyes panned around the large space then settled on the large arch sitting smack dab in the middle of the room. She walked over to it. "Octavian, what's this?"

"That, my love," said Dafari, as he stepped out of a shadow, "is where we'll stand as we say our vows…tonight."

Elisa started to speak, but was dumbstruck, totally enthralled by the man who came to stand in front of her. I had to admit, Dafari looked good in his black tux. Clearly, Elisa thought so too.

Finally, she found her voice. "You look…amazing. But you know you didn't have to do all this. I still have to cook Christmas dinner, and that's going to take all night as it is. I would have been just as happy—"

Dafari put a finger to her lips. "Elisa, I promise you, you will have all the time you need to prepare your holiday feast. This won't take long at all. It'll just be you, me, the two people we love the most," he said, looking at me and Octavian, "and Rufus."

Elisa giggled. "Let me guess; he'll be officiating."

"The man clearly has many skills," Octavian said.

"That he does," Dafari concurred. "In the meantime, I need you to go get changed before he gets here."

"Dafari—" Elisa began to protest.

"Do this for me and you have my word that we'll keep this short and sweet, just like you are." He gently kissed her forehead.

Elisa looked at him, crossing her arms in front of her, a smirk on her face. "You're lucky you're such a charmer."

His eyes glowed golden. "I only live to charm you, my sweet. Everything is ready for you in our room. Now go."

Once we made it to Elisa and Dafari's room, we saw two garment bags and two shoe boxes lying on the bed, which Octavian and I had dropped off prior to my arriving at the café to help Elisa. A box with some flowers was sitting on the dresser.

"I can't believe you were able to keep this from me," Elisa said, picking up the garment bag with her name on a tag.

"Kept what from you?"

She turned to face me. "Tasmin, stop," she said then chuckled.

"I don't know what you're talking about." I chuckled along with her.

She pulled the dress out of the bag. "This is breathtaking," she said of the lace and crepe sheath wedding dress. The white dress, overlaid with a sheer black lace and beaded bodice, a lingerie-inspired lace strap at the back, and black lace surrounding the sweeping train made for a classy, yet sultry, gown.

"Your man has great taste," I said, taking my plum-colored charmeuse bridesmaid dress out of the bag. With a front illusion keyhole, crisscross spaghetti straps, and envelope skirt with pockets, it was simple yet elegant.

Elisa had taken off her work clothes and had begun to pull on her dress. "He always had great taste. Funny, even now he still knows how to surprise me. I would have been just as happy remarrying him at the café," she said giggling.

"Now you and I both know Dafari never would have gone for that," I countered, sharing her mirth. "Think about it this way, after the haphazard way you were awakened, and after all you've been through recently, you need this. Enjoy it for all it's worth."

I changed into my dress then helped Elisa with hers, zipping it up and fastening the clasp. Looking at the way the skirt hugged Elisa's curves, it was no wonder Dafari chose it for her. Sitting her in the chair in front of the dresser's mirror, I styled her hair, fashioning it into a neat bun. When I finished, I placed the wreath atop her head, just as she had finished touching up her makeup.

"Just like old times," I said, laying my hands on her shoulders.

She reached her hands back, resting them on top of mine. "No matter when or where in time we are, I can always count on you, Cousin."

"Back at you," I said.

Elisa put on her black satin platform shoes with crystal-encrusted heel caps in floral clusters, while I slipped on my block heel plum sandals. Picking up both bouquets, I ushered her toward the door. Once we reached the top of the stairs, I handed her the honeysuckle floral arrangement. I couldn't help but notice how stunning she looked, and, I may have been mistaken, but I could have sworn she was glowing.

"Ready?" I asked.

"To marry that man downstairs? Always," she responded with a smile.

I walked a few feet ahead of her, stopping at the bottom of the stairs. Octavian was waiting for me. He reached out to take my hand then kissed me on the cheek. "Poppet, you look delectable."

I appraised Octavian, appreciating how good he made his suit look. "You clean up nicely yourself."

I walked toward the living room, while Octavian waited by the stairs. When Elisa joined him, he held out his arm for her. "You are absolutely radiant, Sissy."

"Thank you, dear brother," Elisa said as she looped her arm through his.

When I came upon the entrance to the living area, I saw Dafari standing underneath the flower-laden arch in the middle of the room. Rufus was standing next to him. Dressed in a tailored black, pin-striped suit; crisp white dress shirt; black tie with thin, diagonal white strips; and spit-shine black, lace-up loafers, Rufus looked very much like a wedding officiant. The man's vast array of talents never ceased to amaze me. I stood diagonal to Dafari, just as Elisa and Octavian reached the entryway. Dafari and Elisa locked eyes, as they shared an amorous glance. Once they reached us, Elisa took her place next to Dafari, while Octavian stood opposite me.

"Before we get started, Elsie and Tasmania, I must say you two look finer than the hair on a long-haired guinea pig," Rufus said emphatically.

Octavian snickered, and Dafari smirked slightly.

"Thank you?" we both said in unison. I'd have to look up long-haired guinea pigs later, just to satisfy my own curiosity.

"Well now," Rufus said, taking his position in front of Dafari and Elisa. "Dayfari told me ta keep it short and sweet, so let's just get ta it, shall we? We here today ta unite, or should I say *reunite*, Elsie Hunte and Dayfari Battle."

"What exactly *does he know?"* Elisa thought.

"Apparently at lot," Octavian replied. *"But that's a conversation for us all to ponder at another time."*

"Elsie, whatcha got to say to Dayfari?"

Elisa turned to face Dafari, taking his hands in hers. "To all my Ancestors who wish me well, I call on you to honor my marriage. Guide me on this journey so that I may be the best wife I can be. To my husband, I will love, honor, and cherish you beyond parameters. While I am terrified of losing you once more, I will spend every day with you like I will never see you again. You send me, and while I'm not sure exactly where, I am enjoying getting there with you."

"Dayfari, your turn."

Still holding her hands, he looked deeply into her eyes before saying, "Elisa, you are my heart and soul, the part that makes me a better man, you make me whole. While I am not perfect, I will strive daily to be my best self with and for you. I will love, support, and protect you, with my very life, if need be, because without you, my life is incomplete. I vow today, and everyday going forward, to be the husband you so rightly deserve. We are bonded by a love that transcends time, and I promise you, nothing, and no one, will come between us."

While their words weren't exactly the same, much of what they had said to each other came from their previous vows. No matter how many times I heard them, they were still beautiful and heartfelt.

"Lovely, just lovey," Rufus said. "Y'all gotcha rangs?"

Dafari, Octavian, and I looked from one to the other. In our haste to get everything else ready, we forgot to pick up the rings. Then again, almost getting killed by an ancient evil archdemon could make anyone forgetful.

"Looky here," Rufus said, getting our attention. "Cards on the table, we all know what this is. If y'all will allow me, I can give y'all something better than any ol' rang from a jewelry store. May I?"

He waited for acknowledgement before placing Elisa and Dafari's left hands in one of his. He reached into one of his jacket pockets, pulling out a silver-colored powder.

Sprinkling the dust over Dafari and Elisa's ring fingers he said, "I bind Dayfari and Elsie in matrimony. May they marriage be as long-lastin' and unbreakable as this permanent bond."

As he recited those words, a bright, golden glow appeared, encircling the base of their ring fingers. When the illumination dimmed, the gold color remained in what looked to be a tattoo of sorts. In my eyes it was sheer genius. A tattoo, as opposed to an actual ring, made sense since Elisa wasn't much of a jewelry person, and since baking was her life's work, with frequent hand washing, wearing a ring would be impractical. The expressions on Dafari and Elisa's faces showed how pleased they were.

"I love it. Thank you so much, Rufus," Elisa voiced.

"Yes, I agree with my wife. Thank you."

"She ain't ya wife yet," Rufus declared.

We all shared confused glances.

"Not until ya kiss the bride, man!"

Without delay, Dafari grabbed Elisa in his arms, kissing her like it was the first time they'd ever been married. I was thrilled for them. After our most recent battle, this ceremony was exactly what they needed.

Octavian walked over to me, linking the fingers of one hand with mine. "I cannot wait for the day when you become my wife once again," he whispered in my ear.

Truth be told, I couldn't wait either. Before my awakening, I had already fallen for Octavian. Since getting my memories back, I remembered how deep my love for him ran, and what it was like to be married to him. I missed that. I gently squeezed his hand, letting him know I felt the same.

After Dafari had released Elisa from his embrace, he reached inside his inner tuxedo pocket, pulling out a piece of paper.

"Elisa, this is for you," he said, handing it to her.

She took it then keenly scanned the paper. When she finished, she gazed up at him. "Dafari, this says that everything you own is now ours, jointly."

"Yes, the money, this house, and all the other assets. Once you sign on the dotted line, it becomes official. Should anything happen to me, I know you will not be left unprotected."

I knew my cousin. While she never married Dafari for what he had, as she was fiercely independent and made her own way, after what I had been told, I was well aware of how much she had struggled to make ends meet after Dafari took the rap for Octavian and landed himself in Hell for seventy-seven years. It was definitely in her best interest to do what he requested. Giving Dafari a knowing look, she walked over to the coffee table, picked up a pen, signing without reservation. She walked back over to us, handing the paper to Rufus.

"There's a space for a notary's signature and stamp. Will you do the honors?"

"Gladly. Once I take care of this and ya marriage license, y'all will be good ta go," he replied. Once he did his part, he said, "Dayfari, Elsie, y'all are all set. Congratulations! On that note, I'ma git ta goin'. I'll see ya tomorra with my sweet tater pie. Save me a piece a that wedding cake, ya heard?"

Once he departed, we broke out a bottle of Dafari's best champagne, along with the caramel cake he baked. Elisa was ecstatic and vowed to add it to the menu at the café. Once our toast had wrapped up, we changed clothes, preparing for a long night of Christmas cooking.

Before Elisa got to work in the kitchen, she sauntered over to her once-again husband, putting her arms around him, saying, "I'm sorry we won't get to have a real wedding night, but I promise I'll make it up to you." She pulled him down by his collar, her lips meeting his.

Dafari returned her kiss in earnest. "I'm going to hold you to that, Wife."

"I feel bad because you planned such a wonderful evening."

"No need, my love, we have the rest of our lives for you to make it up to me."

I watched the two of them as they shared a few brief moments of bliss, an event that was seven years in the making. With everything that was happening around us, and clues hinting to some new deadly threat on the horizon, I hoped that we would all live long enough to experience some prolonged happiness.

TASMIN

NONE OF US got much sleep as we were up all night, and into the early morning hours, cooking the holiday feast, but after what we had experienced over the past few weeks, spending quality time with my cousin, the love of my life, and my once and future brother-in-law was what we needed to wash away the uneasiness we all felt, at least temporarily. We decided to catch a few hours' sleep prior to the arrival of our guests. It was mid-afternoon by the time I was up and dressed.

"Man, I did not intend to sleep this late," Elisa said in between yawns. She took a seat at the kitchen island.

"I'm actually surprised you're still not sleeping," I said, a smirk on my face. "Here, drink this." I slid a hot cup of coffee in front of her.

She took a whiff of the steaming brew then sipped it slowly. "Why do you say that?"

I sat on the chair next to her, placing my hand on her shoulder. "You and Dafari got to consummate your marriage after all, I see...or should I say heard?"

"Wh-what?" Elisa almost choked on her coffee. "You heard us? Oh, my gosh, I'm so sorry." There was a blush to her dark cheeks.

I chuckled, amused at her embarrassment. "Don't be sorry. Octavian and I are guests in *your* home. You and Dafari are entitled to express your love for each other however you see fit, especially on your wedding night...no matter how loud you are."

She laughed with me then became quiet for a moment, as if in silent contemplation. "My home. This really is *my* home. Dafari made sure of it."

"That he did, Cousin. And as the mistress of the manor," I said, getting up from my chair, "I suggest we start getting things ready before your guests arrive."

"HOW IS YOUR mother faring?" Dafari asked. He set down a plate at each place setting on the dining room table, while I laid out the silverware.

"She's recuperating...slowly. One day she appears to be fine, the next she can barely get out of bed. It's like her body is trying to fight off some waxing and waning illness. I've tried everything I could think of medically and magickally, but the result is still the same."

"Perhaps, Sister, it's taking your mother longer to get back on her feet because her assailant was an archdemon, an *original* archdemon. That's bound to put severe physical, and mental, stress on anyone. However, to ease your mind, I will also look into why it's taking Jewel so long to recover."

I had just enough time to thank him before we heard the doorbell ring. Octavian ran to answer it. When he returned, he was accompanied by the Widows. Cara Lee and Mary

Ann, and even Martha, seemed to have fully regained their strength.

"Ladies, make yourselves at home," Octavian said, taking their coats then rushing back to the kitchen to help Elisa.

After we exchanged greetings, Dafari spoke. "I'm pleased to see you're all doing well."

"Thank you, Dafari," Martha replied. "And thank you for your hospitality while we were recovering, especially me. Without it, and Tasmin's healing abilities, I don't think I would have made it. Your aunt would be proud," she said, looking at me.

I didn't know what to say. Although we had more or less buried the hatchet, I was still in some ways conflicted. Sooner rather than later I knew I'd have to fully reconcile the fact that Martha abetted Michael in killing Aunt Noreen with us having to work together as a coven. Luckily, I didn't have to say anything because Rufus came strutting into the dining room carrying two sweet potato pies.

"Hey e'rybody!" he said cheerfully. "Where y'all want me ta put these pies?"

I quickly took them from him, placing the pies on the dessert table. Even through the plastic wrap, I could smell the savory blend of sweet potatoes, cinnamon, nutmeg, and vanilla. I couldn't wait to get a slice. My parents were the last to arrive. My mom looked well. Dad and I had worked in tandem to make sure she was convalescing properly. Even Octavian helped, which aided in the creation of a truce between him and my dad. It appeared our care did her some good because she had gotten her appetite back and the color had returned to her cheeks. While I was pleased with her progress, considering her up and down course, I feared she'd relapse. Last night had been the first time since returning to Aunt Noreen's after the battle that I had slept elsewhere.

I felt a twinge of guilt leaving Daddy to attend to my mom by himself.

After I had taken their coats and hung them in the mud room, I asked, "Mommy, how are you feeling?"

"Actually, this is best I've felt since getting injured. Tasmin, you, your father, and Octavian have done a wonderful job of nursing me back to health," she answered. "Thank you."

"Of course, Mommy. I'm just glad you're better." I meant what I said. Despite all the mistakes she and my dad had made, I still loved them and wouldn't know what I'd do if anything happened to them.

Elisa, with Octavian following behind, joined us in the dining room. "Now that everyone is here, before we eat, I just want to welcome you all into Dafari's...I mean our home." She reached out a hand for him. He walked over to her, but instead of taking her hand, he embraced her, his arm encircling her waist. "We didn't want to just spring this on everyone, but we wanted to share some good news. Dafari and I got married last night."

Assorted congratulations were given, with my dad extending his well-wishes first to Dafari then Elisa, whom he pulled to the side. I couldn't hear what he was saying to her, but from the look on her face, and the fact that she allowed him to hug her, maybe she was finally softening to her uncle.

"Now that we've gotten that out the way, before we partake of the sumptuous spread my wife has prepared, Martha, will you do the honors?"

She stepped forward. "Everyone, please join hands." We did as she asked. "First off, I would like to give all praises and thanks to our Ancestors, who have watched over and protected us. Bless all the hands that have prepared the food we are about to eat, and lastly, I ask that you give us the strength to bond as a unit, trust one another, and grow together as a coven, friends…and family."

I heard what she said, especially the part about trusting one another, and I guess we'd all get there…eventually. Elisa, Octavian, Dafari, and I brought out the food, placing it on the table. Once we took our seats, with Dafari and Elisa sitting at the head, Rufus was given the privilege of carving the turkey.

"Ole Rufus is honored to be carvin' this here bird," he said while slicing the large fowl. "I really appreciate y'all invitin' me, 'specially since I ain't got no family here in Salix Pointe."

Elisa spoke up. "It's our pleasure, Rufus. Here, you are among family."

After Rufus dished out the bird, everyone filled their plates with the other fixins; collard greens, buttered corn, macaroni and cheese, candied yams, potato salad, homemade stuffing, black eyes peas and rice, and cranberry sauce. While I had usually spent the holidays with my parents when we lived in Brooklyn, we never had a meal as voluminous as this. The only other time I had feasts like this was when I was visiting Aunt Noreen.

The gathering was going well until I glanced at Martha, who was sitting between my mom and Cara Lee. Her face was flushed.

"Oh my," she began.

"Martha, is something wrong?" my mom asked, placing her hand on Martha's shoulder.

"All of sudden I'm not feeling very well."

I stood up, walking around the table to where Martha sat. Cara Lee pushed her chair back to allow me to kneel in front of Martha. In addition to being flushed, she was also pale.

"Martha, can you tell me what you're feeling? Are you in any pain?" I asked.

"No, no pain. It's…I-I don't know. I just feel strange. I…excuse me."

She covered her mouth, abruptly jumping up from the table and running toward the bathroom. Cara Lee and Mary Ann swiftly followed. I started to go after them to check on Martha, but my mom stopped me.

"Tasmin, hold on. I'm sure they'll come get you if the need arises."

"Yes but—"

"Tazzy, I agree with your mother. I get your need to help, but no one knows Martha better than her sisters. Just give them a minute."

My dad was right. Our differences notwithstanding, I needed to help Martha. I was a doctor after all. I was about go against my parents' advice when I heard footfalls coming our way. Martha walked slowly into the room, her sisters on either side of her. Her color still wasn't back, and she appeared frail, nothing like the woman I went into battle with.

"How are you feeling now, Martha?" I asked.

"I'm tired," she replied weakly.

"We told you this outing would be too much too soon," Mary Ann stated.

"Yes, we warned you that you needed to take things slowly, especially since you haven't been out of the house since we returned home," Cara Lee added.

"Perhaps you two are right. I'm sorry, everyone, but I need to go home."

"We understand, Martha. Please do feel better," Dafari said.

"Before you go, let me at least make you some to-go plates," Elisa said, standing.

"That won't be necessary—" Martha began.

"Nonsense," Elisa cut in. "There are plenty of leftovers. Besides, this way you three will have enough for at least a couple of days."

"Sister, that would be nice, don't you think?" Mary Ann asked.

Although she was hesitant, Martha eventually acquiesced. "Thank you, Elisa. We are truly grateful."

Elisa packed two plates for each of them along with a pie and several cookies. While the sisters put on their coats, Dafari and Octavian carried the food out to their car.

"Martha, if it's okay, I'll stop by tomorrow to check on you," I said as she was walking out the door.

"I would like that. Thank you, Tasmin."

"I'll see you tomorrow then, and you're welcome."

Once they left, the obvious topic of conversation was Martha's rapid deterioration. I thought about my mom and Martha's recurring and remitting courses, wondering how extensive Eve's damage truly was. The atmosphere of the gathering had definitely changed. Despite that, Rufus, being the jovial character that he was, had a way of lightening the mood.

"I know things done gone a little sideways, but Martha gon' be a'ight, mark my words. She a tough ole gal, I tell ya."

"You know what, Rufus, you're right," I replied. "We'll make sure of it."

"We sho' will, Tasmania. In da meantime, I'm gon' cut y'all some of that sweet tater pie. That'll cheer ya up."

While Rufus was cutting slices for each of us, Elisa brought out two carafes, one containing coffee, the other hot water for tea, along with assorted dessert teas and some mugs. Rufus set out a dessert plate with a nice-sized piece of pie in front of each one of us.

"Go 'head, eat up!"

I took a bite and had to admit that it was one of the best sweet potato pies I had ever tasted. An overwhelming sense of calmness came me.

Elisa ate a forkful, a smile crossing her face. "Rufus, you really put your foot in this."

"While it's quite tasty, I most certainly hope not," Octavian exclaimed, causing us to laugh loudly.

"That just means it taste real good, Octovian, das all."

We were still having a good laugh at Octavian's expense when my mom started vigorously clearing her throat.

"You okay, Jewel?" my dad asked her.

She coughed a few times. "Ye-yes, Silas, I'm okay." She cleared her throat again then drank some water. "Rufus, what's in this pie?"

"The usual pie stuff, sweet taters, eggs, 'vaprated milk, nutmeg, and my two special ingredaments, 'Gascar 'Nilla and West Indian cinnamon. Why, you 'lergic to sumin'?"

"No, I was just wondering, that's all," she replied, clearing her throat again. "I think something went down the wrong way. I'll be fine." She took another swig of her water.

Oh, 'cause nobody done ever had a bad reaction ta none a my pies 'cept..." his voice trailed off. "Yeah, ne'mind. Prob'ly went down da wrong way, like you said."

I looked from my mom to Rufus. That verbal exchange between them was odd, and it caused my empathic powers to fire on all cylinders. One or both of them was hiding something. Who had a bad reaction to Rufus' pie, and why was my mom having one now? At the moment I had no clue as to what was going on, but I was determined to find out.

OCTAVIAN

STANDING IN A clearing, just behind the veil where Salix Pointe and a world unknown to humans met, I watched as the moon danced atop a small, placid lake. It wasn't unusual for the sun and the moon to share the sky at the same time in such a place. It had taken me a while to set this up, and I needed everything to go off without a hitch, but I wasn't sure it would. I'd been summoned here days before, but as opposed to outright answering, I made plans for me and Tasmin.

After celebrating Christmas and my brother's wedding, my heart was full. I felt as if things that had been lost to my brother and me were finally back where they belonged, and by they, I meant Tasmin and Elisa. Still, I felt void in some ways. There the four of us were, celebrating reawakened love and redetermined commitment, but I couldn't bring myself to tell the other three that ghosts of our children had been haunting me since the battle.

It was odd, in a sense, the way the dreams kept coming to me. I didn't know what to make of them. After sending Eve and her minions running back to whatever hell they'd escaped from, lots of things had seemed off to me. I couldn't shake the feeling that while we'd won this battle, the war was just getting started.

Dafari remarrying Elisa had been beautiful, and I was happy for my brother and Sissy. Still, something in my gut wouldn't allow me to enjoy the moment fully. It could have been my mind was still trying to wrap around the fact that Uncle had let on he was playing Eve the moment he closed the gap between us and whispered in my ear.

"Don't let them see your eyes," he'd whispered, which told me that he had been planning to betray Eve all along.

His actions made it hard to trust him while still being grateful to have him on our side. At least for the moment. With Uncle, one never knew, yet, this would make twice now he'd come in and tilted the fight in our favor. What were we supposed to make of that?

"He's up to something," Dafari had snarled when he and I discussed it late night, after Christmas dinner.

When I came down the stairs, he was pacing his home office. Brother was trying with all his might to forget the night of the battle, especially after renewing his vows, but we knew this small space of peace we'd carved out wouldn't last long.

"We've been saying that since the moment he showed up here," I replied, nonplussed.

Brother nodded as he took a swig of the twenty-five-year-old Scotch he'd poured for us. "It's annoying the crap out of me that we can't pinpoint what exactly that something is." He frowned then pointed at me curiously with the same hand that was wrapped around his crystal tumbler. "What if us thinking he's after the girls is a smoke screen?" he asked.

I was standing next to the big bay window, after the ladies put us out the dining room when we tried to help clean. I turned to face him. "What do you mean?"

"What if we're thinking he's after them, when it's really us he's vying to get close to for some reason?"

My brows furrowed and I ran a hand over my kinky coils then scratched my jaw. "What in bloody hell could he possibly want with us?"

"Who knows when it comes to my father, but with everything else we have going on, being worried about his actions in the back of our minds can't be a bad thing. Sure, he's helped us twice now, but we shouldn't let those actions lull us to sleep. He is the Gray-Walker of all Gray-Walkers."

"Speaking of Gray-Walkers," I cut in, "think Uncle Demon Daddy will tell us where Doc Benu is?"

"I do plan to ask, but don't hold your breath."

That had been seven days ago. Now I stood, hoping I'd put in enough favors to be granted this one wish. I hadn't asked permission beforehand, and as far as they knew, I had no innocent blood on my hands and my heart was pure.

The landscape was lush with green grass and rolling hills. To the left of me, cherry blossom trees lined a pathway that led to a small gazebo. There were vines of white roses decorating the pillars on either side of the entryway. Pinkish-white leaves from the cherry blossom trees had fallen to the ground and made the walkway even more appealing and beautiful.

If I looked further into the distance, I saw centuries old Rhododendron, which wasn't a tree at all really. It was a shrub, but here, on this land, they had grown into trees that had the most beautiful clusters of showy pink and white blooms. The large green leaves gave a spectacular backdrop to the bell-shaped flowers. If I looked closer, I could see the almost invisible mist of rain that fell steadily upon them.

Japanese maple trees, which sat adjacent to the Rhododendron, glistened with different colors of russet, greens, and crimson. There was also a Methuselah tree and while the earth had been blessed with one of the same name in the west, this one was over seven thousand years old. It's brown trunk and branches bore no leaves. It's thick, barren limbs looked like a number of different wildly displayed arms.

Cypress trees and mighty Sequoias of all ages, shapes, and sizes made up a small grove to the right. Lining each side of the grove, they stood like regal centaurs, standing guard over the lone tree that sat at the end of the grove; the Boabob tree.

The tree of life, for those of us knew where the real Garden of Eden resided, used to bear fruit, but times had changed.

I gazed up at the blue skies. No sun was out today and that suited me fine. I hadn't been in the most jovial of moods anyway. This place tended to pick up on the person's, or being's, vibes and aura. It had read me fairly well. My mood, just like the weather, was a bit dark and gloomy, but not completely unwarranted. It was hard to remain truly at peace and happy having to always look over my shoulder for danger, those real and imagined. I supposed I had a bit of what the humans called PTSD. I knew my brother was on the same wave I was.

The way he checked and then triple checked on Elisa, and Tasmin for that matter, was not lost on me. I was no better. I'd shown up to Elisa's coffee shop, feigning hunger or needing a coffee refill more times than was normal for me. She picked on that just as Tasmin had noticed I'd been by the bookstore to buy random books that I wouldn't be interested in otherwise. It got so bad I'd picked up a book about some kind of weekend affair. The genre wasn't normally my cuppa, but to keep an eye on Tasmin, I'd read the Bible—not the true pages, but the ones the humans thought was a true accounting of events.

"You summoned me here," I said aloud. "Granted me permission to walk this land and to use it, this one time, why?"

Lightning lit up the sky, dancing across the pale blue horizon in violently bright flashes. A rumble of thunder shook the ground, causing me to have to brace myself against one of the trees.

"What do you want?" I yelled, the crack in my voice betraying me.

I'd gone to Him in prayer, asking for a little mercy or at least some reprieve. Yes, I'd become that desperate in my need to keep my remaining family safe. I didn't know how to admit to my wife—I knew Tasmin blanched at the idea of me calling her my wife, but for me, she would always be my wife— that I was terrified of what was to come. I was also miffed about why Tasmin balked at the idea of being my wife in this lifetime.

It didn't make a whole lot of sense to me. The only thing that had separated us was death and her loss of memory. Now that she had all of her magick and recollections back, why wouldn't the woman I loved more than anything still want to be my wife? That question had thrown a monkey wrench in all my plans. It was something that I had wanted to ask her for weeks now, but with us fighting for our lives, it took a backseat.

Had I done something to make her not want to be one with me again? Had my anger frightened her that badly? Didn't she know I would move Heaven, Earth, and Hell for her? I loved her past the parameters mere man put in place. I didn't need a judge or an officiant to announce us man and wife once more. I didn't get it, and it was bothering me.

Dafari had refused to even let on to Elisa that he was in pain, the kind of pain that a man felt when he knew his whole family had been decimated by his choices… the kind of pain that a man felt when he dreamed of his children nightly but could not commune with them. He, too, was handling Sissy with kid gloves.

I also found it odd that my brother didn't remember much of his time when in his hellish prison. Anytime I mentioned it, he acted as if he had trouble remembering anything beyond being sentenced there. Perhaps he had found some kind of way to wipe his memories clean of it? That was something to think about at another time. Now, all I could think about was the way he let his guard down when the two of us were alone. I'd never seen him so broken with fear before. It was alarming. My brother had always been the tough, strong, and protective one.

I was able to have a normal childhood because he was the one who, while I annoyed the piss out of him, always took the blame for my mishaps. He was the one to take most of my punishments when our powers merged, and our mother and my father couldn't figure out who'd done what. I didn't know how to take seeing him so unable to function around his fears and grief. Dafari was the tough one. He was the fighter, and that wasn't to say I was not either of those things. They just didn't come as naturally to me as they did to him. It took a great act of violence against those I loved in order for me to, for a lack of better words, lose the plot.

"He won't be coming. You know that," came a smooth, feminine but robust voice.

I knew who she was even though I couldn't see her. She sounded like the one who had created her. Her voice was soft yet authoritative. Comforting, but held a no-nonsense candor.

"Then why summon me here?" I asked, my guard, while still up, not as heavily fortified.

"He didn't. I did."

Now, her voice was in surround sound, all around me and nowhere at once. Even though I turned this way and that, trying to get a pinpoint on her location.

"What for? Our family isn't known for positive family gatherings," I drawled sarcastically.

Her chuckle was airy and light. "True indeed. Sometimes, I think being banished here was for the best."

I glanced around at the peaceful and serene landscape before me. "Considering where you could have ended up, this is a paradise."

"Indeed, it is, Nephew. Heard you and your brother ran into a bit of trouble with Eve."

With downturned lips, I nodded once. "You could say that."

The sound of a babbling brook drew my attention. The water was so clear and clean that I could see all the small aquatic life roaming about beneath it.

"I could also say for you and Dafari to make sure there are no cracks in your brotherly foundation. A battle with Eve can, and will, bring up all kinds of old trauma, hurts, and pains. Your wives, Tasmin and Elisa, while powerful, will need reinforcements. Trouble is on the horizon and none of you are safe."

"Tell me something I don't know, dear old aunty."

"Make room for one more and…expect the unexpected."

"Bloody hell, must you sound like Uncle Azazel with the riddles," I almost snarled through clenched teeth.

"It's the way of our kind, love." Aunty chuckled, something I hadn't heard in eons.

"I'm sorry we haven't seen much of you—"

"There is no need to apologize, Nephew. I am, after all, the black sheep."

"Don't let uncle hear you say that. He'd probably fight you for that title."

She outright cackled this time. "Yes, my brother does like his enemy of the state title."

"And he wears it proudly."

"Has he been of help to you and Dafari?"

"With his own agenda attached," I spat.

"As is his way."

I was about to ask a question then stopped. Did I want to know what I was about to ask? My anger said I didn't care. My heart…said yes.

"I'd like to tell you your mother is fine, but she is not," Aunty told me, as if she had been reading my mind. "I was," she confessed. "I feel the longing for your mother's presence and love. I also see how conflicted you are about that."

I slapped the lone tear that rolled down my cheek away. What in bloody hell was I crying for? She had caused this rift between us. Her actions alone did this. She didn't have to go along with the plan. And still, I was worried for her, worried about her.

"Yes. Yes, she did. You act as if she had a choice. When He gives an order, it must be carried out."

"Okay, but she, my own mother, also wishes death upon the woman I love! She gladly went along with His orders because of it."

My words had come out in fits and bursts. I hated this plane, hated that it made it so I had no choice but to be open, honest, and up front.

"So did Michael."

"Yes, but Father has always been a hard arse. He is a General."

"So…is your mother."

This time, Aunty's voice had deepened and taken on a tone that told me she was either offended or taken aback. More than likely both.

"I'm sorry," I told her, remembering her plight and how she ended up banished to this realm. "I didn't mean to come off like a—"

"I get it," she snapped and kept going, "but you don't have much time here. Summon your wife so that I may bless your reunion." She took a deep, resounding breath then said, "Octavian, son of Michael, you have been granted access to this realm. I, Lilith, Daughter of the Dusk and the Dawn, flesh of my mother's womb, honor your request to have your nuptials blessed by the blood of the One, True Son."

As she spoke, a small rip appeared through the atmosphere. Tasmin cautiously stepped through the thin veil, eyes wide with awe as she did so. I was pleased to see she had donned the lavender-colored thin, silk sleek gown I'd lain out for her. I'd gone the ways of what humans used to call The Silk Road to get the most precious fabric of silk I could find. The gown covered her ankles and pooled around her tiny, bare feet. The only time I could see them was when she moved to walk around. Her toes were painted with a beautiful shimmering lavender color that reflected off the sunlight.

Her locs were down and curtained her face, which was in its natural state. Only gloss adorned her lips. Small pearls in her ears called attention to her beautiful features. My woman hadn't aged at all.

The skies brightened, rain let up, and birds started to chirp. The hypnotic sounds of the waterfall became clearer and sweet, floral smells wafted through the air.

I smiled when she gasped. Her soul was also pure, and she had no innocent blood on her hands. This plane was probably giving her a natural high she wasn't used to. Everywhere her feet touched, the earth blossomed. Beautiful flowers, native to the most exclusive places in the world, sprouted as she walked toward me. I held out my hands to her. Dressed in only silk drawstring pants, my chest was bare save for the tattoos that decorated my right pec and sleeved my right arm. I was in my truest human form, but my wings unfurled at the sight of her.

She gave a sharp intake of breath when she took my out-stretched hands. "You have tattoos?"

"In my Father's house, I have many things. However, these are protection sigils. They can only be seen in this realm. Otherwise, they're hidden for my protection. As a full-blooded arch, the sigils are burned into our flesh upon birth."

My love frowned. "That sounds painful as heck. Why in God's name would they do that to an infant?"

Thunder rumbled the earth, and I pulled her close to steady her balance. She glared around, bracelet glowing. Always on alert, ready to defend us at the drop of a dime.

I had to chuckle. "You probably don't want to call His name here," I told her. "Also, remember, I'm not human, Poppet. What would hurt one of our children was just a pinch to me."

My eyes glowed white as I talked to her. I could tell by the way she studied my pupils as we spoke. I could never quite get over the way Tasmin gazed upon me. Any time she did, it was as if she was staring into my very soul, assessing me, trying to determine the ways in which she could reach me.

"I'm here, love," I assured her. "All of me. No guards. No walls. Just…my love for you. My desire… My…need for you and only you."

Her eyes shone with an unnatural sheen. I didn't know if tears were threatening to fall or if her magick was on overdrive by being on this plane. Her palms were warm, almost hot to the touch. She was nervous. Her energy was shooting up my arms like jolts of electricity.

"Why don't you want to be called my wife, love? It bothers me. Makes me think that perhaps you…don't want to be with me anymore?"

"I love you, Octavian Jerrod," she whispered. "Nothing changes that. Not time. Not death. I want to be with you, as your wife. While I am concerned about you and your recent, let's just call them changes, I know you won't hurt me, or anyone else you care about, for that matter. I'm worried for you because you can't totally control your anger yet, although I know it would never be directed toward me. But… I have this nagging, gut feeling that we should be official, even in this time and space. I know that in the grand scheme of things, our love doesn't need validation by human forces, and still, I want it on record that I, Tasmin Pettiford, am the wife of Octavian Jerrod, son of Michael—House of the Most High." Tasmin chuckled. I bit the corner of my bottom lip and grinned like a whole fool. "Okay, so I know that last part won't be on the official marriage certificate, but it's what I want."

I anxiously scooped her up around my waist then laid a kiss on her that sent my own head spinning. She kissed me back, just as eager, even greedier. I felt all my good sense and blood rush south like it was a raging river in the Amazon. The good thing about being dispelled to Earth was that I could feel all those human emotions that had been forbidden before now. Well, in some ways, for some angels and demons, the old rule still stood, and consequences would be instantly fatal. There would no longer be tribunals or any proceedings.

I knew when my aunt left the clearing because I couldn't feel her watching me. She left her blessings behind though. I had to chuckle when a light whiff of vanilla tickled my senses. Carrying on this way in front of any other celestial being while not being married wouldn't have gone over well.

"I don't know how to take you chuckling while we're kissing," Tasmin said softly as her warm brown eyes took in my black ones. She had pulled back from the kiss and was playfully glaring down at me.

"I was thinking about being on this level of Heaven and having my way with you," I muttered against her soft, plush lips.

I got a kick out of watching her eyes widen. "Level of…" Tasmin's mouth fell open as she gawked around. "This is… Heaven?" she then asked on a whisper.

I nodded while nibbling on her lips. I couldn't get enough of her. I'd denied myself her feminine wiles for so long…I wouldn't be able to contain myself much longer. I felt my body bulk. She turned me on just that much. The fleeting remembrance that she was a virgin skittered through my mind, but it didn't bother me. Her parent's spiritual chastity belt wouldn't stop me, had no effect whatsoever. I had more thoughts about them being so obsessed with their daughter's sex life, but it would be for another time.

Right now, I couldn't keep my mouth off her. As she talked a mile a minute about not being able to comprehend being in Heaven, I was busy licking, kissing, sucking her neck.

"I—oh my," she moaned softly when my tongue dipped into the valley between her breasts— "you mean to tell me I didn't have to die to experience this?"

I stopped tasting her long enough to say, "No. We're on the Seventh Level of Heaven. In the Garden of Eden to be exact."

She inhaled hard then gasped when my tongue traced up her neck to her chin then back to her lips. I'd done that on purpose, knowing she was about to ask me another question that I, quite frankly, didn't care to answer at the moment. I wanted her. Needed to be inside of her like I needed to breathe.

The winds whipped around us as birds flew overhead. A rainbow decorated the blue skies as I gently took her to the grass.

She gazed up at me with wanting eyes, a wanton expression on her face. Her locs splayed out around her head, looking like exotic strands. "Are you trying to get Him to smite us?" she asked, jokingly, her hands lovingly rubbing up and down the back of my neck and over my head.

"If that's what I have to take in order to be inside you, so be it."

I didn't give her time to respond, I took her mouth again, feverishly searching out her tongue. I was famished for her, long overdue to show her how much my body craved hers. Ripping the front of her gown as we kissed, I cupped her small breasts. My hands covered them with ease, but the feel of her pebbled nipples in my palms drove me a little more insane. I thought I couldn't get any harder, but the little cooing sounds she made sent me over the edge. It was as if the sound connected to my nerve receptors and sent me into overdrive.

"This flimsy gown be damned," I snapped, sitting back on my haunches, and completely removing the expensive fabric from her body.

I was set to be stunned. I hadn't seen or had her this way in so long that I was sure I was going to go mad. My wings fluttered of their own volition. She was so willing, ready, and—I inhaled—wet. Tiny trails of stretch marks decorated her round hips while her legs were toned, and her lithe body shivered in anticipation. To know she wanted me just as much as I wanted her gave me a renewed sense of purpose. She had very minimal hair covering her womanly parts, and I traced my hands from her belly button down to the creases of her inner thighs.

She hissed, bit her bottom lip, then tried to rub her thighs together. "No," I said evenly. "Let me see you, Poppet. All of you. It's been a while, yes?"

She giggled then nodded while trying to grab for me. I needed strength to be able to keep my composure lest I embarrass myself by pre-ejaculation. When I stood, my silk bottoms came off without fanfare. I was anxious. I took in the way she studied my body and didn't feel an ounce of shame about the rim rod stiffness of my manhood, especially not when her eyes widened at the sight of it.

I smirked cockily. She was remembering. I took my time exploring my wife's body, from her fingertips to her toes, I tried to put every part of her body in my mouth. Her breasts fit so perfectly in my hands that when I massaged them, I wondered if I was hurting her. However, judging by the way she was crooning my name, I put that thought to rest. After lavishing both her berried nipples, I let my tongue trail down to the gates of Heaven.

My mouth and tongue found her clitoris just as I chuckled at the thought and lightning violently ripped through the skies. I sucked her core bud into my mouth while I let my tongue firmly play against it. I paid close attention to her whole vagina, spreading her lips to lave my tongue through her folds.

I didn't pull back when she screamed, "Octavian..." as my mouth found its way back to her hardened bud. I still didn't let up as I slipped two fingers smoothly inside her wetness. I wanted to speak in different tongues just by how good she felt enclosed around my fingers.

"You feel...like Heaven, my love. Missed me, did you?" I teased her, fingers yet exploring, the glow of my white eyes on hers.

"Don't be a tease, Octavian," she whimpered.

I lost track of time pleasing her, and I was happy that she had been caught off guard by the whole thing. I didn't want her to try to compete with me when it came to this part, by trying to return the same favors. My pleasure was coming from pleasing her, and I needed to be uninterrupted.

"Time doesn't determine how long love lasts," came over the land as I slid my body against hers, placing myself between Tasmin's legs. My aunt's voice enveloped us. Tasmin jerked in my embrace. I assured her all was well and that while my aunt's voice was here, she wasn't. "When two souls are connected, human or supernatural, not even death can keep them apart. As your bodies are joined by an act as old as time and one as sacred as prayers of old, I bless this reunion high and low. Let no man nor entity try to put asunder what the gods have destined to be forever. And now, before the

Orishas, the Most High, and the Ancestors, may the circles of your lives begin again."

I eased into Tasmin, taking my time because she felt so damn good that I almost slobbered. She was so hot and wet and snug… She moaned loudly when my right hand gripped her thigh for dear life.

"Good…heavens," I growled like a wild animal.

In some ways, I felt like one.

"Hmmmm…" she crooned on a long, soulful moan. "You-will-have to explain all this to me…whe-when we get back… ooohhhh my…."

I was set to be madder than a hatter. Still, I composed myself as I felt her vaginal walls breathe around me then suck me deeper inside her.

I grit my teeth as I fought to keep eye contact with her. She tried to move against me. I quickly released her thigh then took hold of her hips. "Please…wait, my love. I must say my vows to you first… I must give you my part of our recipe for love."

She gasped then slapped a hand over her mouth. I grunted, moved against her, and we both groaned long, hard, and guttural.

"You, you…you remember that?" she asked when she was finally able to breathe.

I nodded. "Will never forget it," I told her.

Way back when…all those many lives ago, before we jumped the broom, we gave recipes for love.

I said as evenly as I could, "To you, my love, I offer mustard seeds, to represent the faith I have in you and in our love; allspice, because you have all the spice I could possibly ever need; and thyme, to represent my vow to love you forever."

I could tell she wanted to laugh, just like she did on our original wedding day. She'd told me that was corniest, sweetest, most heartfelt thing she'd ever heard. However, today, with me deep inside her, she could barely breathe.

"My beloved, I give you my recipe for love. Just for you, for us, I have gathered herbs from Africa, our Motherland. For you, I have given Grains of Paradise, to represent the haven I will create for you to come home to each day; Jasmine, for the sweet spirit that will fill our lives; and, cayenne, for the spice that will fill our nights."

As her words wrapped around me like a lover's embrace, I stopped holding back. I moved against Tasmin, in and out of her at a steady pace. The scratching, her legs wrapping around me tighter…the kissing…the touching, the panting… the way she sometimes cried out my name…All of it made me love her harder. Deeper. Longer…By the time we reached our climaxes, I was delirious.

I didn't know what the future held for us. The uncertainty of things along with all the unanswered questions hanging overhead told me that we were in for the fight of our lives, and still, none of it mattered in this moment. I'd gotten my wife back, and for now, that's all I cared about.

OCTAVIAN

NEW YEAR'S DAY...

W E WERE AT my brother's home, celebrating the new year, the champagne flowing freely. I was in a good place and so was the rest of the family. Tasmin and Elisa were having a spirited chinwag on how to merge the coffee shop and bookstore together, while Dafari and I were going over the blueprints for the bookstore. The ladies had gotten this crazy idea that they could combine the two, but they had seemingly forgotten that Doc Benu's clinic sat between them.

However, like always, my brother and I would do anything we could to help them bring their ideas to fruition. He and I had been going over the blueprints for just as long as the ladies had been conversing about their plans.

"You know, we should probably get Rufus to help us with this," Elisa told Tasmin.

She nodded then took a sip of her champagne. "Also, Mr. Herschel since he does own a construction company..."

We were going on about life as if we hadn't a care in the world. I understood the method to our madness, because it was madness. We had decided to hold on to any sense of normalcy we could. Which brought me back around to my life before Salix Pointe. I hadn't been back home or responded to the Uni's emails asking when I planned to return. It would have to be something I took care of sooner rather than later. Until then, though, my undivided attention would be on my family while we tried to figure out all the madness.

Dafari studied the two women as they continued to discuss merging businesses while he and I moved to stand in the doorway. "Elisa is a First Order Elemental, meaning she can control all the elements while also being telepathic. Not to mention she is a necromancer; something that, according to Silas, has only been passed down to the males of their family. Tasmin is an empath, can heal herself and others, she dream walks, and she possesses the power of telekinesis."

"They are also descendants of the Nephilim; offspring of fallen angels, and the Sybils, a group of women from the ancient world who were said to possess the powers of divination," I said, repeating the information we'd learned earlier then told him of overhearing the ladies making plans to commune with their Aunt Noreen, Mama Nall and Elisa's parents.

He nodded as if it was something he had already known then said, "Doc Benu is thought to be dead, but we know he's only missing."

"Which means the vision Silas saw, or whomever he spoke to from the other side, picked up on the doc's violent assault. On top of that, we still don't know how Afolabi and Aziza are related to Elisa and Tamin either."

Dafari grunted. "Those two have been scarce since the outright attack on the bookstore. Eve isn't in Hell..."

"Rufus is a fairy..."

"And you and I have always known otherworldly beings were in Salix Pointe."

I nodded. "Yes, but we were so focused on the women that we never gave it much attention."

My brother turned a curious glance to me. "You don't find it odd that they came back with even more powers than they had before?"

I shook my head then folded my arms across my chest. "Odd? No, dear brother. However, I do find it intriguing. They're quite literally the baddest women walking planet Earth."

"And each time they're reborn, it is us whom they're fated to love."

Both he and I let that sink in. They were all things we would have to face head on, sooner rather than later. With the new year came cold, but sunny weather. The curtains in my brother's living area were pulled back, allowing golden sunlight to illuminate the room. The faint smells of this morning's breakfast—bacon, eggs, pancakes, and grits for those of us who ate it— still lingered. Tasmin had her locs pulled back into a ponytail while Elisa's looked as if she simply threw a headband on and kept it moving. All of us were in casual wear of some sort, too drunk on love to really care about our attire at the moment.

Dafari and I were well into our discussion when I noticed someone walking up the drive to his home. I didn't readily pick up on who or what it could be, which gave me pause. Being that the feminine figure was dressed in all black with a hooded coat that looked more like a robe, I wasn't quite sure who it could have been.

Excusing myself, I trekked to the door, curious about our visitor's identity. I knew it couldn't have been Martha as Tasmin had forbade her from leaving her bed, even though the older woman swore she was better now. That also meant the conversation they were supposed to have was still on hold. I didn't think it was Jewel since Tasmin and I knew she was still a bit hurt from the battle. Tasmin had also put her foot down with her mother, telling her to either stay on bedrest or force Tasmin to take her to the nearest hospital to be admitted. My woman didn't play when it came to helping those she loved to heal. It could have been Nazila's mother, but the slim figure told me that wasn't the case.

I hastily rushed to open the door just as the person came up to the porch. I got ready to do my usual greeting but wasn't prepared to have my whole mind blown to bits when the person pushed the hood back on their coat. I didn't even notice Tasmin had come up behind me.

My eyes widened with something akin to horror, but probably more so shock when the young woman's face eased into a casual smile. She was tall, about five-nine, cinnamon hued, fit and toned with loose coils fanning her face and neck. She had a perfect set of white teeth which sat out in stark contrast to her black eyes. She looked every bit of her mother with faint traits of me thereabout.

In a British accent that rivaled my own, she said, "Hello, Daddy! Hello, Mommy!"

AZAZEL

AZAZEL WALKED ALONG Main Street, reveling in the early evening solitude. The thoroughfare was a virtual ghost town, with many of the townsfolk still at home, celebrating the new year. The only residents on the street were a young couple, gleefully embracing one another as they walked to a car. Once inside, the two fell into a lip lock, quickly fogging up the windows, enjoying each other for several minutes. Eventually, they drove off.

"Ah, young love...it won't last." He chuckled to himself before stopping in front of the Book Nook. Crossing his arms in front of his chest, he thought, *"This sleepy town, the gullible natives, so ripe for the picking. It's only a matter of time."*

He inhaled deeply, savoring the crisp, cold winter air. He looked up at the cloudless night sky, peering at the twinkling stars. He keened his eyes at what appeared to be a falling object. It seemed to pick up speed before crashing somewhere off in the distance.

His curiosity getting the better of him, Azazel followed the path of the projectile, stepping into the shadows to shorten his trip. He felt a twinge of nostalgia when he realized the object had landed near the caves where only a few short weeks ago he had found Octavian, wallowing in his own funk and self-pity. As he approached what he thought was a meteorite, he discovered that he was in for the shock of his life. That shock quickly turned to amusement.   Kneeling in front of him, dazed, confused, and stark naked, was his brother, Rafael, deep gashes on his back where his wings once were. As a Fallen, Azazel understood heavenly retribution all too well. Rafael must have committed something heinous, at least in His eyes, to be stripped of his wings. Tilting his head to the side, a broad grin crossed Azazel's face. Was he petty for relishing in his brother misfortune? Yes. Did he care. No.

His brother still disoriented, Azazel gazed down upon Rafael, a sanctimonious expression on his face, and said, "My, my, my Celestial, how the mighty have fallen."

CPSIA information can be obtained
at www.ICGtesting.com
Printed in the USA
BVHW091220160222
629249BV00002B/9